City of Stone
and Silence

DJANGO WEXLER

City of Stone and Silence

Book Two: The Wells of Sorcery Trilogy

TOR TEEN

A Tom Doherty Associates Book
New York

CITY OF STONE AND SILENCE

Copyright © 2019 by Django Wexler

Maps by Jennifer Hanover

A Tor Teen Book
Published by Tom Doherty Associates
120 Broadway
New York, NY 10271

www.tor-forge.com

Tor® is a registered trademark of Macmillan Publishing Group, LLC.

The Library of Congress Cataloging-in-Publication Data
is available upon request.

ISBN 978-0-7653-9727-0 (hardcover)
ISBN 978-0-7653-9728-7 (ebook)

Our books may be purchased in bulk for promotional, educational, or business use. Please contact your local bookseller or the Macmillan Corporate and Premium Sales Department at 1-800-221-7945, extension 5442, or by email at MacmillanSpecialMarkets@macmillan.com.

First Edition: January 2020

Printed in the United States of America

0 9 8 7 6 5 4 3 2 1

For Casey,
to whom I will hopefully be married
by the time this sees print

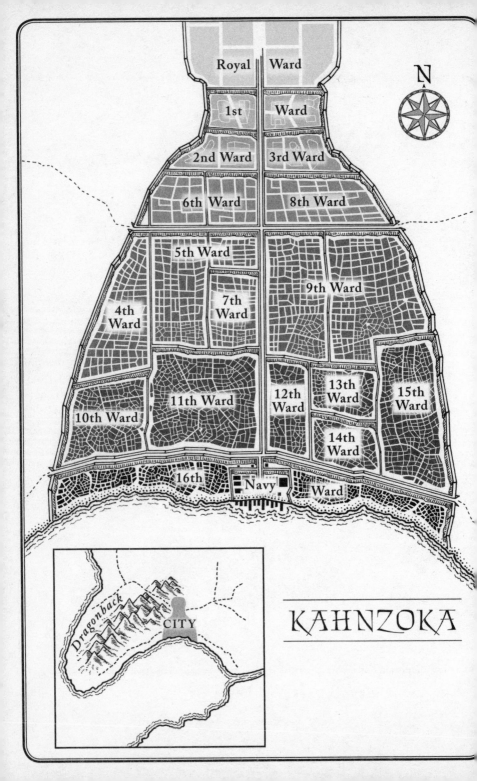

Royal Ward

1st Ward

Ward

2nd Ward

3rd Ward

6th Ward

8th Ward

5th Ward

7th Ward

9th Ward

4th Ward

13th Ward

12th Ward

15th Ward

11th Ward

10th Ward

14th Ward

16th

Navy

Ward

Dragonback

CITY

KAHNZOKA

N

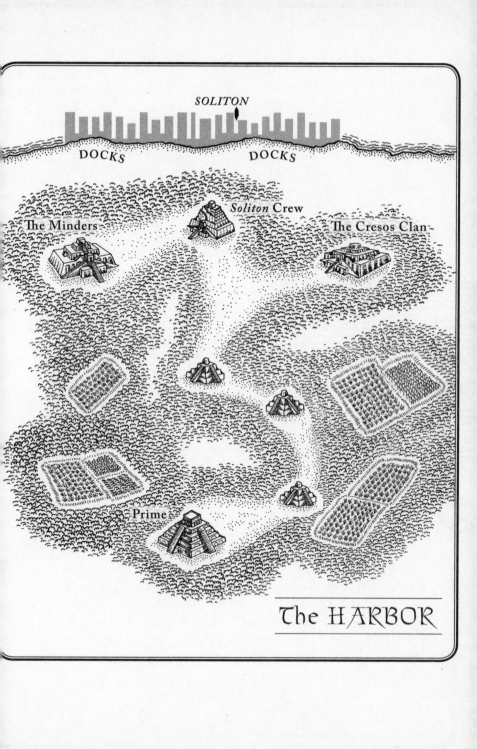

SOLITON

DOCKS   DOCKS

The Minders   *Soliton* Crew   The Cresos Clan

Prime

The HARBOR

The Nine Wells of Sorcery

Myrkai, the Well of Fire

Tartak, the Well of Force

Melos, the Well of Combat

Sahzim, the Well of Perception

Rhema, the Well of Speed

Xenos, the Well of Shadows

Ghul, the Well of Life, the Forbidden Well

Kindre, the Well of Mind

Eddica, the Well of Spirits, the Lost Well

City of Stone
and Silence

1

TORI

Nothing takes longer than a meal you're eager to be done with. There are no guests at the house this evening, which means that the long dining room is nearly empty, our small table set crosswise at one end with about a mile of empty floor mats beyond. On the far wall, the Blessed One smiles down at nothing from atop the house shrine, threads of smoke drifting up from the incense lit during the pre-meal prayer.

It's me, my tutor Ridatha, the house supplicator Narago, and the steward Ofalo at the table—not the most thrilling set of dinner companions ever assembled. Ridatha, at least, is interesting to talk to, with her endless font of stories and her rasping Jyashtani accent. Narago, needless to say, is a bore—*is there such a thing as a supplicator with a sense of humor?*—and his presence makes Ridatha stay quiet, lest she say something heretical.

That leaves Ofalo, who's nice enough, but has a tendency to forget I'm not eight years old anymore. You'd think he could manage to remember when we're talking about my fourteenth birthday—coming in less than a month, Blessed be praised—but in between the salad and the baked smallfin I have to dissuade him from hiring a troupe of *clowns*.

Honestly, does anyone like clowns?

"Well," Ofalo says, frowning—maybe he'd been looking forward to the clowns himself—"what sort of entertainment would you prefer, my lady? I believe there's a traveling menagerie that might be persuaded—"

Narago sniffs. "Only low people travel with such attractions.

Best not to risk having them in the house." He looks at me, posture perfect, his stark black-on-white robes stiff with starch. "Perhaps an excursion, my lady? I could arrange a private visit to Greatcliff Temple, and you could observe the theological debates."

Monks arguing over whether the Blessed One's left toenail is sacred in *itself* or only in *relation* to his divinity. Worse than clowns. At least you can throw things at clowns. I make a sort of *hmmm* face, because I can't very well tell a supplicator that I'd rather throw myself under a cart. I get an inspiration, and turn to Ridatha.

"Perhaps a drama?" I say. "We've just been studying the theater of the High Imperial period, haven't we?"

"Um," Ridatha says, startled at my enthusiasm. I admit my attention starts to wander when she talks about High Imperial dramatic trends, but she gamely plays along. "I'm sure something could be arranged. High Imperial might be a bit . . . formal, but—"

"I'm sure something more modern would be fine," I say blithely.

Ofalo scratches his nose. "Lady Amfala mentioned she hosted a troupe of players last week, and she said they were very fine. I'll make inquiries."

I heroically refrain from rolling my eyes. Any entertainment that withered old stick enjoys is guaranteed to be Upright and Moral and utterly bereft of anything interesting, but it's still got to be better than the monks. Besides, the only thing that really matters about my birthday is that Isoka will come to visit. Usually I don't know when to expect her, but she never misses a birthday.

Conversation moves on to the price of grain, what the rain has been doing to the garden, and the latest gossip from the Royal Ward. As always, I'm amazed at Ofalo's ability to keep up an inane conversation almost single-handedly, with an occasional assist from Ridatha or pious interjection from Narago. You'd think that he'd eventually have to acknowledge that important things were going on outside the high brick wall that surrounds the garden. Isoka pays him a lot of money to pretend that the rest of the world doesn't exist, and he's good at it.

Or maybe it's Ridatha's presence that makes things awkward. After all, it's her people that we're getting ready to go to war with.

The only interesting moment comes, oddly enough,
plicator's carping. His duties require him to return
Temple in the Royal Ward on certain holy days, and a
there has slowed to a crawl.

"I waited nearly an hour," Narago says, with a sniff. "In my ceremonial robe, which is stifling. And when we finally reached the
temple drive, it was blocked by a gang of miscreants trying to grab
everyone's attention."

"What did they want?" Ridatha says, as she methodically removes
bones from her fish.

"What the lower orders always want," Narago says. "To enjoy the
fruits of the Empire without having to pay their fair share or fight
to defend it."

"Maybe they just don't understand why defending the Empire
means people have to die on some island a thousand miles from
here." I mean to mutter this under my breath, but it comes out
louder than I intended, and Narago looks at me sharply.

"Defending the Empire," he says, "means defending the Empire's
interests, and the Emperor's honor."

"Small honor in being chained to an oar for twenty years," I say.

Narago reddens. "Perhaps you'd prefer the Jyashtani sailed into
Kahnzoka and put us all to the sword?"

"That is *enough*," Ofalo says. "These are not subjects for the ears
of an innocent child."

Narago harrumphs, but gives way. He glances at Ridatha suspiciously. "Perhaps some more study of the history of Jyashtani
aggression against the Empire is in order?"

"Of course, supplicator," the tutor says, lowering her head.

Wonderful. I manage to keep my sarcasm to myself, and the
rest of the talk is determinedly trivial. Eventually, finally, the fruit
course comes, and I'm released from this low-rent torture. I gobble
a handful of grapes, for form's sake, and get up as fast as my *kizen*
and decorum will allow.

"My lady," Ofalo says, "a pair of musicians arrived this morning
and asked for the honor of playing for you. Would you hear them?
They come well recommended."

"No, thank you," I tell him, with just the right inclination of my head to indicate apology-to-an-inferior. "I'm feeling poorly tonight. I think I'll go to bed early. But please, have these players perform for the staff, with my thanks."

Ofalo's dark eyes watch me thoughtfully, and he strokes his beard. I have to be careful, he's far from foolish. If I say I'm feeling poorly too often, I'll end up rushed off to the doctor and placed on a purgative diet or assigned calisthenics. Fortunately, it's been a while since I needed to make excuses, and Narago helps out with a distraction.

"Musicians," he sniffs. "Are we really to be imposed on by such vagabonds?"

"These are quite reputable," Ofalo says, a little irritated. "I am assured—"

I make it out into the corridor as they get into it, walking with the narrow, shuffling gait the *kizen* allows. I pass servants heading the other way, and smile at Irana, who's just a few years older than I am and always wears a fresh flower pinned in her hair. She gives me a bow in return, and a smile where the older maids won't see.

Back at my room, Pakala is waiting, and it takes me a few minutes to assure her I don't need a bath drawn or my hair combed or anything else for the evening. She departs, still sounding unconvinced, and slides the door closed behind her.

Alone. At last. I let out a breath.

My room is not the largest in the house, which still bothers Ofalo. When I was twelve, he offered to vacate the master's suite for my use, but I declined. I could use the space—Ridatha always tells me there's too much stuff in my room, and a cluttered space makes for a cluttered mind—but I can put up with a little junk in my brain in exchange for the other advantages. The master's suite is at the center of the house, letting directly onto the main courtyard and surrounded by servants' quarters, whereas my current room is at the far end of one of the wings, separated from the outer wall by only a tall hedge and a narrow strip of garden.

There's also a closet, tucked into one corner, and because of the shape of the servants' kitchen on the other side, it happens to be very narrow and deep. It's like a little tunnel that doesn't go anywhere, lined with wooden shelves holding my clothes, beautiful silk *kizen* and more casual embroidered robes. Squeeze past those, and there's a pile of spare bedding, folded mats and blankets. Squeeze behind *those*, I discovered, and there's a little nook at the very back, a soft, secret nest of threadbare blankets and pillows. It's a perfect place to keep things you don't want anyone to find.

I take off my *kizen*, unwinding the knot and the long sash at my waist, and fold it carefully for the maids to clean. Working my way back to the secret nest raises clouds of dust, and I rub my nose to stifle a sneeze. In among the ancient blankets, there's a chest, a battered old thing I'd rescued when Narzo the gardener was going to put it out for the dustmen. I flip the lid and pull out another set of clothes—rough trousers, a linen shirt, a leather jacket, a big lopsided cap.

I can't actually pass for a boy anymore, not up close, but I'm a lot less likely to draw attention like this than shuffling along in a silk *kizen*. I dress quickly, and take a few moments to pin my hair—which normally falls well below my waist—into a tight bun before pulling the cap over it.

I don't like lying to Ofalo. But he'd never let me out of the house without an escort, let alone allow me to visit the lower wards. Isoka pays him well to keep me safe, and I love her for it, but sometimes this place makes me want to scream. Not that I would ever tell *her* that, of course, after all she's done for me. So I lie, and I try not to get caught.

It's easier than it looks. For me, anyway. In the dark, quiet space at the back of the closet, I close my eyes and let my thoughts open. The house comes alive around me, full of bright, humming minds, and I can see every one.

I can't read thoughts.

It's not like *reading* at all, really. I don't have words for what it's like, because how can you explain that to someone? It's a little like seeing, a little like hearing, a little like tasting or smelling or feeling something press against your skin. And not like any of that at all.

It took me a long time to realize what I could do—what I *was*. I don't remember exactly when my power came to me, but it was before Isoka got us off the streets, when I was six or seven. (Later, I would learn this is unusually young for mage-bloods, who more frequently come into their abilities in their early teens.) At that age, I just accepted it as a fact of life, like the cold and the hunger. I could look at people and see what they were feeling, hear the pitch of their emotions, sharp, tangy anger or despair like a cold breath across the back of your neck. I could tell, sometimes, when someone was lying to me. I could feel Isoka's pain, and how much she loved me, the diamond-hard weight of her determination.

When her own abilities came, she made me promise never to tell anyone, ever, about what she could do, and I felt the barely restrained terror in her mind. Not long after, she brought me here, and told me I was going to live with Ofalo, the tutors, and the maids, and that she'd visit as often as she could. I cried, but I could feel how much she was hurting, too.

It wasn't until my tutors were hurrying me through my basic education, making up for lost time, that I learned to put a name to my power. *Kindre,* the Well of Mind, one of the Nine Wells of Sorcery. I read what I could about it, but there wasn't much to find. Kindre mage-bloods are so rare as to be practically legendary, with decades passing between each new user, and scholars are constantly speculating that it will become the next Lost Well. The stories about what it can do vary widely.

Whether my power makes me merely a talent or a full adept, I have no idea. As much as I can, I try to avoid it. Aside from the practical reasons—if the Immortals found out what I was, they'd drag me away to serve the Emperor—it just feels *wrong*. It's a violation, intruding into other people's most private spaces, like having the ability to see through everyone's clothes or read their diaries.

Unfortunately, sometimes I don't have many other options.

It's not like I'm trying to look *inside* anyone, not really. I just need to see where they are, and a little bit about what they're paying attention to, so I can get by them. It's not reading a diary, it's just noticing where the diary *is*.

I have a feeling Isoka would laugh at my little sophistries.

From the back of the closet, I can feel three servants chatting in the kitchen, a maid in the hall checking the lamps, a watchman in his covered booth on the roof. The last is of most concern to me, but his post faces the main entrance, not the back, and his mind already has the oily patina of drink.

I squeeze back past the folded mats and into my room. A large window overlooks the narrow strip of grass, between this side of the house and the wall, split by a gravel path leading to the rear gardens. It's real glass, smoked for privacy, and it hinges up and out. Checking one more time to make sure the watchman isn't looking this way, I climb up onto the sill, turn around, and carefully lower myself down, grass tickling my bare feet.

I keep my boots here, tucked behind a bush against the wall, so as not to tip anyone off with mud stains on the floor mats. They're big, stompy boots, hard leather with steel plates around the toe. I love these boots. Perversely, there's something *freeing* about them— wearing the soft shoes that accompany a *kizen*, I don't dare step off of the groomed paths, but in these boots I can go anywhere. I tie them up with mounting excitement, and use a long stick to push the window mostly shut.

That's the easy part. The hard part is the outer wall, nearly ten feet high and topped with a decorative iron railing. Fortunately, not far from my window there's an old willow tree, its bent branches hanging low to provide easy handholds. This wall faces the lane between my estate and Lady Amfala's, and the wall is more a notional defense than a real one. Still, it's a scramble, and I swing one leg over and take hold of the railing before dropping down.

What makes it tricky isn't the height, it's the watchers. The guard on our own roof is mostly for show, but there are other minds watching the house at night. Sometimes one, sometimes two or three, perched in a tree across the lane or crouching in a shadowy corner. Their focused attention stands out to my Kindre senses, strobing blue and peppermint.

They work for Isoka, I think. She doesn't trust Ofalo. I guess she doesn't trust anyone. I feel a little bad about fooling them, since they're only trying to protect me, but once again I don't have any other options. There are two of them tonight, and I watch their minds, timing my ascent for when their attention is elsewhere.

I must have made some unexpected noise, because I can feel one of them look back in my direction just as I cross the wall. I react automatically, reaching out to the distant watcher's mind. It's only a tiny push, honestly, a wash of fatigue and boredom. I feel the observer yawn, and their attention slips over me, like ice sliding across a hot griddle.

Yuck. Touching someone's mind like that is . . . *urgh.* Imagine sticking your hand in a fresh, steaming pile of horse turds in the street. I want to withdraw my senses as quickly as I can, but I don't dare stop watching the watchers, not until I'm clear of the house. Fortunately, the lane is empty, just a narrow dirt track with high walls on both sides, leading back to the rear garden gates. I slip out along it to the main road, a broader, winding thoroughfare slashed with wheel ruts. Two torches burn by the entrance to the main drive, but nothing marks this little back way, and I sneak off without anyone the wiser.

Once I'm away from the house, I let down my guard a little. It doesn't matter if someone sees me now, as long as they're not looking close. I live in the Second Ward, high on Kahnzoka's hill, with only the august heights of the First Ward separating us from the Imperial presence himself. The streets are curved and tree lined, with large circular stones engraved with family crests marking the entrances to the walled estates. Rich families mean servants, and while most of those servants live in the households of their masters, there are always day laborers and temporary replacements coming and going. Nothing unusual about a young woman in shabby clothes trudging home to the lower wards at the end of a long day.

Our street joins another, which leads, after several turns, to a gate. The ward walls, formidably high and broad enough for two men to walk abreast, are manned by the Ward Guard. I remember the Ward Guard with a hint of terror, from our days in the lower wards—brutal enforcers of order, who cared little about the people under their protection, always on the lookout for a chance to extort a few coins. Here in the Second Ward, things are different. If I were dressed as Lady Tori of the Gelmei estate, they would bow and scrape, but even as a poor laborer they're more polite. You never knew which maid might have the ear of her mistress, and plenty of families in the Second have enough pull to get a poor guard arrested.

Cabs gather at the gate. I find a two-seater heading for the Eleventh Ward, already occupied by an older woman with a long woolen shawl and a cheerful expression. She shoves over and I climb up beside her, passing a couple of copper bits to the cabbie with a nod of thanks. The horse snorts and starts moving, and we pass through the gate, gleaming spikes of the portcullis hanging threateningly overhead.

Then we're out, onto the broad thoroughfare of the military highway, joining a stream of carriages and pedestrians. I take a deep breath. My gardens smell of willow and fresh-cut grass, sharp and clean, but this is the real scent of Kahnzoka—dung, smoke, and the press of humanity. I give the old woman a grin, and she grins back.

2

ISOKA

Meroe rolls over, sending the sheet slithering to the floor, and mutters something unintelligible in her sleep.

I sit and watch her for a moment, her brow creased as though in deep thought, eyes shifting under closed lids. She's naked without the sheet, and I have to fight the urge to run my hands along her beautiful brown skin. I never get tired of looking at her body, so different from mine; soft and curved where I'm lean and hard, smooth and unblemished where I'm scarred and marked. Her face relaxes, brow uncreasing, and her breathing grows smooth and deep.

I wish *I* could rotting sleep.

Meroe spends her days doing useful things—managing our food supply, organizing guard shifts, going up to the deck to plot our course with her navigator's instruments. In the meantime, everyone calls *me* leader, even though all I do is nod and smile and drink. And fail to sleep.

My restlessness must be getting to Meroe, because she mumbles again and puts a hand over her eyes. I roll out of bed—an old mattress tossed on the floor of this chamber, high above the Garden—and pad around to her side. When I pull the sheet back over her, she relaxes again, and I slip out into the corridor.

The Garden complex is in better shape than the rest of *Soliton*, fewer rusted-out patches or mushrooms growing on the walls. It's like a ship-within-a-ship, a cylindrical section walled off from the rest of the vessel. A pair of big doors open onto the first level, the grassy plain where so many died to keep the rest of us safe from maddened crabs. Above that, a few more levels produce various kinds of food. Then there's the control room, where I killed the Scholar, where I've spent many frustrating hours since.

Higher up are more levels divided into smaller chambers, which is where we're living. I don't know exactly how many people survived the trek through the ship and the battle that followed—counting things had been the Scholar's job—but it's a lot fewer than were living at the Stern. A few hundred, none much older than I am, many as young as twelve or thirteen. What's left of *Soliton*'s crew.

I stop for a long piss, then make my way to the stairwell, winding up through switchback after switchback. *Soliton* is huge, bigger than a ship has any right to be, and it seems like it takes hours to reach the deck. Eventually, though, I find myself facing a door, improvised from rope and broken metal plate. At the moment it stands open, though a guard waits just inside, ready to slam it shut if the crabs return. I give her a nod, and she bows.

"Deepwalker," she murmurs, and it sounds like a prayer. I can feel my teeth grinding.

"Is anyone on the tower?" I ask her.

"Zarun," the guard says. "For about an hour now."

Too much to hope that I could be alone in the middle of the night. I suppose I've had worse company. I pause in the doorway for a moment, my breath steaming in the air. The Garden keeps itself heated, but out here it's getting *cold*.

Soliton's deck is cluttered with protrusions—small rectangular humps, mysterious snaking metal conduits, spires like tree trunks trailing cables. In a few places, such as the Captain's Tower near the Stern, these are the size of buildings. The tower rising above the Garden isn't nearly that big, just a couple of stories high, but it provides a good vantage point. There's a ladder set into the outside, and I make plenty of noise as I work my way up. Zarun isn't someone you want to catch by surprise. At least not accidentally.

Meroe keeps her equipment up here, a telescope and a few other mechanisms whose use I don't even faintly understand. To my surprise, Zarun has his eye to the telescope's lens when I reach the top.

"Anything worth looking at?" He's got it pointed almost straight up.

"The moon," he says, raising his head. His dark hair is cut short, framing a handsome face with the copper skin of a Jyashtani and startling blue eyes. "Want a turn?"

I glance up. The moon is near full, a slightly imperfect circle glowing in a diamond carpet of stars that is nothing like the smoky, sepia-toned city skies I'd grown up with. Staring gives me a faint sense of vertigo, as though I were going to fall up into that darkness and never stop.

"What's the use of looking at the moon?" I ask him.

Zarun shrugs. "No use. It satisfies my curiosity." He steps away from the telescope and leans against the waist-high railing that surrounds the top of the tower. "There's little enough else to do lately."

"Not enough scavenging expeditions to keep you busy?"

The crew had left almost everything behind at the Stern. *Soliton* was littered with goods, sacrifices loaded on board for generations, the greatest treasure hoard in the world. Our scavengers combed through it, ignoring the gold and jewels, bringing back cloth, wood, leather, books, anything useful.

"I've gone out plenty," he says. "But they don't need me. The last dozen teams haven't seen so much as a bent crawler."

"That doesn't mean the next one won't find a hammerhead."

"Let's hope." He grins.

"You're *that* bored?" My own battle with a hammerhead had left my leg nearly torn off, and that was before Meroe and I fell into the Deeps. It isn't an experience I look forward to repeating.

"Maybe not quite," Zarun says. "But we could use the meat."

"Fair."

The Garden provides grain, fruits, and vegetables in abundance, but it doesn't offer any farm animals. The crew are used to a lot of crab in their diets, and there's been grumbling since it ran out.

The crabs—a baroque variety of multi-legged, hard-shelled creatures—had always been a fact of life on *Soliton,* dangerous but valuable. Now they're gone, and nobody knows why. Some people say they're hiding, scared of us after the battle for the Garden, but I don't believe that. Meroe thinks they're going into hibernation as it gets colder.

A noise echoes across the ship, a gong-like sound followed by a long, metallic scraping. I look around, suspicious, and Zarun laughs.

"Iceberg," he says. "*Soliton* just plows them out of the way."

I give him a sour glare, which he ignores.

"If we keep heading this way much longer, it's going to be too cold to come up on deck," Zarun says. He looks up at the moon again, then over at me.

"If you're asking whether I've figured out where we're going, the answer's still no," I tell him. "We're well off any map I've ever heard of."

"You're the one who claimed to be able to talk to the ship."

"Apparently we're no longer on speaking terms," I mutter.

And that, unfortunately, is the crux of it. Since my confrontation with the Scholar, I've spent hours in the control room, trying everything I can think of. I can feel the Eddica energy flowing through the conduits, but when I try to reach it, the ship pushes me out again. UNAUTHORIZED/REJECTED, over and over.

Hagan hasn't said a word to me since that day. I'm worried about him, if you can worry about a ghost.

But what worries me more is that the hourglass is running out. Kuon Naga gave me a year to return with *Soliton* if I wanted to save Tori. There's still plenty of time to make it back to Kahnzoka if we turned around now—though the thought of another brush with the Vile Rot makes me shudder—but every day we're going full speed in the wrong direction, and the ship remains stubbornly beyond my control.

The crew is starting to worry. Before, when *Soliton* was going around and around its slow circuit, it didn't seem to matter where we went. Now, though, it seems to be *heading* somewhere, and no one is sure what will happen when it gets there.

"Well," Zarun says, after I'm silent for a few moments, "I'll leave you to your brooding."

I give a grunt of thanks, and take a moment to admire him as he swings nimbly over the rail. He may be a ruthless killer, but he's certainly easy on the eyes, and a good rut besides.

When I catch myself thinking that, I flush and look away. It's just a thought. I'm allowed to have thoughts. The trouble is . . .

The trouble is that this, what I have with Meroe, isn't like anything I've had before, and not just because she's a girl. Back in Kahnzoka, I'd take Hagan to bed, or a good-looking boy I met at Breda's, or one of Keyfa's prostitutes. It was always just a rut, with no pretensions, no promises. Simple.

With Meroe . . . I don't know. It's not like it's something we've *talked* about. But I'd rather bite my fingers off, one by one, than hurt her. So I'm working on it.

It would scare me, being so vulnerable to someone else's feelings, except that I don't seem to have any rotting choice in the matter.

Rot. Rot, rot, rot. I flop against the railing, metal cold against my skin, and stare down the Bow. Moonlight dapples the sea, and I can even see a few icebergs, drifting slowly past and bobbing in the wake of the great ship's passage. Farther ahead, there's only darkness, broken by—

—a glimmer of light.

The Council convenes on the tower the next morning.

These days, that means me, Meroe, Zarun, and Shiara. The journey up the length of the ship dissolved the packs and clades of the Stern, especially since so many of the pack leaders had died fighting to get us here. But old habits break hard, and Zarun and Shiara have a lot of accumulated respect.

Of the two, it's Shiara who makes me wary. Zarun, I understand. I can even see through his brash bluster, a little, to the more thoughtful man underneath. Shiara is a mystery to me, elegant and perfectly attired in a silk *kizen* like a noble lady of Khanzoka, wearing a slight smile with no humor in it at all. Alone of the old Council members, she isn't a fighter—her Well is Sahzim, Perception—but she has the loyalty of some of the crew's most experienced and dangerous hunters.

Not that she's caused trouble. On the contrary, she's been perfectly cooperative since our flight to the Garden. But I don't know what she wants from me, and that makes me worry.

Right now she's peering through the telescope pointing at the horizon. After a moment, she straightens, moving back with delicate, careful steps. Her cheeks are red under the powder she uses on her face. The sun is well up by now, but it does nothing to cut the chill, and we're shivering in the wind of *Soliton*'s passage.

"What is it?" she says.

She's looking at me. They're all looking at me. Even Meroe, who ought to know better. All I can do is scratch the back of my head and be a disappointment.

"I have no idea," I tell them. "Other than the obvious."

The obvious was that, far out ahead of *Soliton*, there's a faintly glowing hemisphere of soft gray light. Last night, I hadn't been able to gauge its size, and I'd thought it might be another ship. When morning came, though, it became obvious that the thing is much farther away—and much *bigger*—than I'd originally guessed.

"Is that Eddica energy?" Shiara says.

I give a slow nod. "I think so." I can feel it, a tickle on my mind, even at this distance.

"And we seem to be headed right for it." She raises one perfect eyebrow. "So it's reasonable to guess that it has something to do with *Soliton*."

"Reasonable," I parrot. "But I'm not sure what we can do about it."

"Make sure everyone's under cover, at least," Zarun says. "And that the doors are closed, in case the crabs go mad the way they did at the Rot."

"Take a look at this," Meroe says. She's wandered over to the telescope. "At the edge of the light. Either there's a *really* big iceberg, or that's land."

We take turns looking through the instrument. Sure enough, off to one side of the gray glow, pure white snow mounds up out of the surface of the sea in what looks very much like snow-covered hills. We look at each other for a moment, and Zarun says what everyone's thinking.

"Maybe this rotting ship has finally gotten where it's going."

That's the news that spreads through the crew, like fire over dry thatch. Wherever we've been heading, we're almost there—my best guess is we'll arrive by evening. Meroe and I do a tour of inspection, check the big doors on the first floor, the guards and food supplies. Hunters arm themselves and assemble in small groups, and the younger non-combatants are herded into rooms on the upper floor that'll be easy to defend. To my surprise, there's no panic, just an air of expectation.

"They're *excited*," I tell Meroe, as we leave another band of eager hunters behind.

"Shouldn't they be?" She's back in one of her long green dresses, with an asymmetrical silver band on her right arm. I'm wearing my Deepwalker armor, crafted to show off the blue marks on my skin. Meroe says it improves morale.

"My morale's not improved," I say. "Who rotting knows what that thing is?"

"Whatever it is, we'll deal with it."

"You have no way of knowing that."

She gives me a sly grin. "You worry too much."

"You don't worry enough." I can't help but smile back, put my arm around her shoulders, and give her a squeeze. She leans into me, and for a moment my morale *is* improved.

"Besides," she says, lowering her voice, "you're not making any progress on getting the ship back to Kahnzoka, are you? So any change has to be for the better."

I suppress the urge to say, *Unless we all die,* or something similarly cheerful. I can tell when I'm not being helpful.

We make our way back up to the tower that evening, once Meroe has assured herself everything is in readiness, while the gray wall draws ever closer. The door there is the only remaining opening to the Garden, and the guards are ready to slam and bar it at the first sign of a crab onslaught. I've given that duty to Thora and Jack, and they greet us cheerfully as we approach.

"Deepwalker!" Jack gives a low bow. "Clever Jack reports a strange phenomenon indeed. Behold!"

I barely have time to duck as she hurls a snowball at me. It shatters against the wall behind my head, melting rapidly in the heat of the Garden, and Jack cackles. Meroe looks delighted.

"It's really snowing?" she says.

Thora nods. "Just a little bit so far, but getting heavier. Here." She offers a pair of heavy blankets. "If you're still set on going out there."

"You can trust Jack and lovely Thora with the watch," Jack says. "You may be needed below."

"I should be on the tower." I'm not sure why I think this—some vague notion, maybe, that if strange Eddica powers are afoot I may be able to influence them. And, of course, I want to *see,* even if there's nothing I can do. I take the blankets from Thora and hand one to Meroe. "Thanks. If anything goes badly wrong—"

Thora nods. "I'll shut the door."

"After *I* rescue the two of you," Jack says gallantly.

Meroe and I go out onto the deck. Snow filters down, nearly invisible against a sky that's white with cloud from horizon to horizon. Meroe stands, arms spread, staring upward with wide eyes. A fat flake lands on her forehead, and she flinches, then giggles.

"I didn't think it would be so soft," she says. "It's beautiful."

"You've never seen snow before." I hadn't put that together until now.

"In Nimar it only snows up in the highest mountains," she says. "When I was a girl, my father told me about getting caught in a blizzard on a hunting trip, and I didn't believe him." She turns to me and cocks her head. "Does it snow in Kahnzoka?"

"Not much. A few times a year." I shrug, uncomfortably. Bone-deep memories rise from my years *before,* on the streets of the

Sixteenth Ward. Snow didn't mean beauty and wonder, it meant a real chance you'd freeze to death before morning. "In the city it just piles up and turns to brown slush."

Somehow, she gets what I'm thinking. There are times when I wonder if Meroe is a Kindre adept. She takes my hand, and our cold fingers lace together.

Climbing the tower is considerably harder in the chill, the cold metal sucking the warmth from our hands. We wrap ourselves in the cloaks when we get to the top, and I stick my hands in my armpits, trying to coax some life back into them. Meroe's precious instruments have already been moved safely inside the Garden, so the top of the tower is empty except for us. Meroe walks in a circle, trying to get her blood flowing, then delights at the crisp footprints she leaves in the fresh snow.

My attention is focused on what's ahead of us. *Soliton* is still headed directly for the gray light, and I've had to revise my estimate of the thing's size yet again. It has to be *huge*, a circular dome several miles in diameter and half a mile high. Not a ship at all, even a ship as big as *Soliton*, but more on the scale of a mountain. It dominates the view directly ahead of us, but to either side it's still possible to see a snowy landscape stretching way into the gray distance. The water is crowded with icebergs, and they scrape and crash against the great ship's hull, though they don't impede its progress.

I can feel the currents of Eddica energy, more powerful than anything I've encountered aboard *Soliton*. It has a strained, *hard* quality, as though the magic were as frozen as the rest of this country.

"Nearly there," Meroe says, joining me at the rail.

"Yeah."

A few minutes, at most, before *Soliton*'s Bow touches the light. And then Blessed only knows. I stare at the top of the dome, as it gradually eclipses the cloudy sky overhead. My hands have gone tight on the cold metal rail, and I pry them loose with an effort. After a moment, Meroe's fingers slip through mine again.

"Kiss me," she says. "Just in case."

The tip of *Soliton*'s Bow disappears into the solid wall of gray. I turn to Meroe hait Gevora Nimara, First Princess of Nimar, and kiss her as thoroughly as I know how, my body pressed close to hers as we slip into the unknown.

There's a moment of pressure, and then release, the feeling of vast energies suddenly relaxing their grip. Then a gust of warm air, cutting the chill like the breath of a hot stove. Meroe pulls away from me with a gasp, and I reluctantly open my eyes.

The snowy landscape is gone. The clouds are gone, the icebergs are gone. All the gray has changed to gleaming blue—the sun bright and hot in a perfectly clear sky, the water a brilliant cyan. Steam rises from *Soliton*'s deck as the new hot wind blows across the cold metal, the ship's coat of snow slumping rapidly into streams of clear water.

Ahead, there's a shore, a riot of green that's almost painful to look at after so long in the gray-on-gray world. Huge trees stretch skyward, trunks tangling into a dense forest canopy. To either side, rocky beaches curve outward as *Soliton* pulls into a vast bay, but directly ahead of us the forest is broken by a line of enormous structures. They look like walls made out of metal spiderweb, the tops taller than *Soliton*'s deck, arranged in a regular pattern—

I match Meroe's gasp when I realize what I'm looking at. The huge things are *docks*, rectangular cradles stretching from the shore into the sea, built for a ship the size of *Soliton*. Not just *built* for— the titanic berths are lined up one beside the other, and several of them are occupied by gray leviathans. Not twins to *Soliton*—the shapes are different—but at least siblings.

I look at Meroe. Her eyes are shining, joyous. Her mind must be whirling away already, fitting all this into her theories about *Soliton*, who built it and why. There's nothing she likes better than figuring things out. Looking back to the docks, I can't help but feel more apprehensive.

The whole structure is clearly not in good shape. *Soliton* itself is full of holes, pitted with rust, in spite of the strength of its metallic construction. However bad it is, though, the docks are worse.

Whole sections of the spiderweb-walls have collapsed, metal beams hundreds of feet long scattered in the surf like a child's toys. And the other ships look . . . broken, their decks canted and collapsing, their towers shattered piles of rust. Looking closer, I can see vegetation growing across them, not just *Soliton*'s ubiquitous mushrooms but whole trees sprouting through openings in the metal, vines winding around the railings.

The dock to which *Soliton* is heading is clear, at least, a long trough of deep water with spidery gantries on either side. I can feel the ship start to slow as it approaches, for the first time since I'd come aboard.

I can feel something else, as well. Energy—Eddica energy, as I thought—is flowing out of *Soliton* on a huge scale, an invisible torrent of power rushing over us and out into the dock. In return, something reaches back to us, and I feel a hint of *intention* in the lines of magic beneath my feet. It feels like when I first met Hagan's ghost, down in the Deeps, that same sense of converging power that drew me to the conduit chamber. The flow is so strong here that I don't *need* a conduit. Hardly daring to breathe, I bend down and press my hand against the deck, thinking hard.

Hagan? Are you there? I didn't realize, until that moment, how badly I wanted him to answer.

There's no reply, at first. But something notices. Not Hagan—a new presence, sweeping into the ship. I feel it reaching out for me and, hesitantly, I answer, extending my mental grip. We make fleeting contact—

—a face, inches from mine, skin dried and pebbled into leather; a shock of wispy white hair; protruding, yellowed teeth; but most of all a pair of dark, empty holes where its eyes should be—

I don't scream. I might have shouted.

Meroe takes me by the shoulders as I stagger against the rail. I blink rapidly, trying to focus on her.

"Isoka! Are you okay?"

"I—" I shake my head. "Yeah. Rot. I'm okay. I just saw something. . . ."

"They're moving!"

"Who's moving?" I blink again, and follow her pointing finger.

Up and down the length of *Soliton*'s enormous deck, the angels are stirring.

At some level, I'd always known the angels were—not *alive,* but capable of action. I'd fought one, after all—two, if you counted the rogue the crew called a dredwurm. When I'd first come aboard, I'd found them deeply unsettling, like sculptures out of a nightmare, animal parts thrown together in illogical ways and mixed with disturbing human touches, faces and hands that seemed to reach out imploringly.

But the dread had faded, over the weeks I'd been aboard. The angels stood along the edges of the deck, as still as if they were statues in fact, and after a while they became just another part of the landscape. Legend among the crew say they'll hunt down anyone who tries to leave the ship, or attack anyone who tries to get aboard if they were too old or not a mage-blood, but I'd never seen either.

Now, though. Now they're all moving together, a tide of misshapen, multi-legged forms sweeping up the length of the ship from Stern to Bow. Their heavy footfalls set the metal decks ringing, a constant rumble like endless thunder.

Meroe and I retreat inside, and Thora closes the door behind us, for all the good it will do. We'd held the Garden against a horde of crabs, but *angels* were another matter entirely; the things were absurdly strong and practically indestructible, their stone-like substance animated by Eddica power. Still, I shout orders as we hurry down the stairs—fighters with me, to the main doors, and non-combatants to stay in place and wait.

I'd hoped the doors would slow them down, but I should have known better. The same guiding intelligence that controls the angels commands the rest of *Soliton,* and the huge doors at the front of the Garden fold smoothly outward as the horde approaches. We wait on the grass of the Garden's first level, everyone who can hold a weapon or throw a bolt of flame. Zarun stands beside me, Jack and Thora, mute, deadly Aifin. The angels pause for a moment, and we wait.

One of them comes forward. It has five legs, three on one side and two on the other, giving it a strange, lopsided gait. Its crystal eye glows blue, high on what passes for a head, a lumpy protrusion equipped with three human-looking mouths complete with long, lolling tongues. A small forest of arms reach out, hands twitching and grasping blindly.

I step forward to meet it, not yet igniting my blades. It moves slowly—if it were any other creature, I would have said *carefully*—stepping lightly enough that it leaves only shallow footprints in the grassy ground. I stop a few feet away from it, and it comes forward another step. Its arms reach out for me, and it takes all the self-control I can muster not to summon my armor. The thin, sickly fingers tug at me, pushing. Up the hill. Deeper into the Garden. Toward the Bow.

I tense, and try to step forward, toward the line of angels. The hands tighten—not to the point of pain, but enough to stop me. I give another tug, and the thing holds me effortlessly in place. It's like pushing on a marble statue. When I step in the other direction, it lets me go.

Options. We could attack the angels, and they'll kill us all. No rotting question.

Or . . . what?

Other angels are moving forward, toward the rest of the fighters. Myrkai fires ignite, and spears are leveled. Time to decide.

"Stop!" I shout. "Everyone stop. I don't think they want to hurt us."

A second angel, this one shaped like an upside-down jellyfish on a trio of baby's legs, nudges a few of the crew in the front rank with its dangling tentacles. It pushes them, not violently, but insistently, toward the Bow.

"What in the hell do they want, then?" Zarun says.

I watch the angels spreading out, pushing, prodding. Gentle, but firm. "They want us out of here."

It's a guess, but it turns out to be a good one.

We have time to send runners upstairs, to where Meroe is waiting with the non-combatants. The angels follow our people up, some of the smaller ones making their way up the stairs while others descend from the deck. Our people gather whatever happens to be within reach—clothes, food, water, weapons, and tools. The angels form a cordon, forcing us forward and downward, and they don't seem inclined to let anyone slip past to grab something they forgot. When I find Meroe, she's carrying her telescope and several other instruments under one arm and a bundle of clothes in the other, constantly on the verge of dropping one or both. I take the clothes, and she gratefully hugs the delicate gadgets to her chest.

It turns out there's another door, on the far side of the Garden. It opens, smooth and silent, as the cordon of angels contracts, pushing the entire crew together into a single mass. At Meroe's suggestion, I take the lead, getting people to start walking ahead of the advancing line to keep anyone from getting crushed or trampled. No one has ever explored on this side of the Garden, but there's nothing here except a wide corridor, leading straight toward the ship's Bow.

We pass several hours this way, trudging awkwardly forward, arms full of whatever we managed to grab. Some of the younger crew are crying. When someone trips, the angels stop, waiting patiently for them to rise again. By the time we reach the Bow itself, the sun outside has slipped past the horizon, and the sky visible through the innumerable gaps in the ship's skin is purple fading to black.

The corridor stops at a broad, flat space. The angels stop, too, blocking the way back, but no longer pushing us forward. The crew mills around, voices rising. I push my way through, glaring at the angels.

"All right, we're rotting here," I tell them. "Now what?"

Blue crystal eyes stare back at me. Then, with a groan like a dying whale, the skin of the ship starts to open. A huge flap of bow folds down, turning itself into a ramp. It strikes the dock with a sharp *clang*, and the groan stops. I take a deep breath—the salt-and-rust smell of the ship is cut by something else, the earthy scent of trees and soil.

The angels shuffle forward. An arm comes down and pushes me, very gently.

Meroe catches my eye, her arms full of telescope. She gives me a brave smile. "I think we get off."

3

TORI

Kahnzoka rises out of the sea, as Isoka once put it, like the enormous corpse of some great fish washed ashore. That might not be *exactly* how I would describe it, but the broad shape of the city is something like a fish head, narrowest at the top and widest at the base. The peak, set on the crown of the hill, is the Royal Ward, with the palaces of the First Ward just below it. The Second and Third Wards sit side by side below that, across the military road from one another, and so on as the city approaches the harbor. The farther down the hill you go, the poorer the people are, and the more tightly they're packed within the constricting ward walls.

This doesn't mean all the lower wards are the same, though. There are shades to poverty. The Sixteenth Ward, where my sister and I lived before she fought her way out, is unique, a broad strip encompassing the entire shoreline, where all activity is focused on the docks. The constant comings and goings of ships and sailors mean the Ward Guard barely cares about anyone who isn't actually trying to burn the place down, and what order there is comes from criminal bosses and their enforcers, like my sister.

(She doesn't think I know about that. I'm glad to keep it that way if it makes her happy.)

The Eleventh Ward, where I'm going, is only one tier above the Sixteenth, but it's a very different sort of place. Where the Sixteenth is messy, the Eleventh is tidy. Families might be packed two or three to a tiny tenement room, but they maintain a scrupulously polite air as they squeeze into their tiny nooks and take turns at the communal water pump.

It's a different sort of people who live here, too. Instead of sailors and dockworkers, the Eleventh Ward and its sisters in the second tier are home to servants and small craftsmen. Every morning, great tides of people flow upward, weavers and potters and ivory-cutters and smith's boys and every other sort of artisan, all those too poor to own their own shops and businesses.

They have a strange pride, these people. They may be poor, but they can look down on the Sixteenth Ward and say, at least we're not thieves or streetwalkers like *them*. Isoka would find that infuriating, their need to stand on their tiny shred of higher ground. It's not that there isn't crime here, it just goes on behind closed doors, protection rackets and smuggling. You can walk down an alley at night without being robbed, or raped, or murdered.

Usually. I carry a long knife thrust crosswise through the back of my belt, although in truth my best defense is the fact that I'd feel the mind of anyone with bad intentions in time to run away.

The cab drops me off at the ward gate. Inside the Eleventh, there are no carriages—the streets are too narrow, and filled with a tide of humanity, regardless of the hour. I take a deep breath, adjust my cap, and plunge into the chaos. Just past the gate is the High Market, packed solid with people returning from their labors in the higher wards and doing their shopping before going home. I can only make progress with liberal use of my elbows, jabbing my way forward.

The sounds and smells of the market are enough to overcome even the babble and stink of the crowd. Vendors shout at the top of their lungs from small wooden stalls, simple repetitive chants overlapping like raucous birdsong. The calls are singsong nonsense, unless you know the patterns—*car car car* for carrots, a high two-tone whistle for pork, low barks for the fat dumplings they call dog-heads.

I home in on a woman making a trilling *riii riii*, and burst out of the crowd in front of a stall hung with ropes of dough. I manage to work a copper bit out of my pocket, and the woman tucks it into the bandanna tying back her hair. She tears off a length of dough, dunks it in a simmering pot of oil with a pair of wooden tongs, then swishes it through a bowl of honey before handing it over. It's almost too hot to touch, dripping and sticky. I've already had dinner, but I can't resist.

The next stall over is wider, serving noodles to customers crammed shoulder to shoulder on a narrow bench. As I devour the fried dough, I get snatches of conversation.

"—the Bonira boy, and Vana Kujan's son."

"Terrible, rotting terrible."

"—say it's a death sentence if you get sent to the oars—"

"—better to volunteer. Might get into the Legions—"

"—can find a set of papers. I know a guy—"

I finish the dough, licking honey off my fingers, and push back into the crowd. Heading south, I soon reach the bottom of the market, where it narrows into Orchard Street, high tenements rising on either side. Ordinarily, I would expect the press to ease beyond this point, but the street is just as crowded as the square, a mass of people pressed cheek by jowl. I can hear angry muttering.

"—rotscum, it shouldn't be allowed—"

"—His Imperial Majesty, Blessed preserve him, wouldn't stand for it if he knew—"

"—Mommy, I have to *pee*—"

I'm close to the edge of the street, where the wood-and-plaster façade of the nearest tenement rises beside me, patched and stained from years of abuse. I fit my fingers into the cracks and climb up a foot or two, just enough to get a view over the mass of heads. A couple of people around me laugh, and a young boy shouts encouragement.

Up ahead, where Orchard Street meets Fishmonger Row, wooden partitions block the road. Two dozen men in Ward Guard uniforms man the barricades. They split the incoming traffic in two: women, children, and the elderly one way, men the other, and each man has a conversation with a stern-faced sergeant and shows a paper.

I can't make out the documents from here, but I can guess. The talk of the city (though not of *my* house, as Ofalo's made clear) has been Jyashtani aggression down in the islands. His Imperial

Majesty, through his servant Kuon Naga, has proclaimed that the Empire must be ready to resist the infidels. That means finding soldiers for the Legions and, more importantly, oarsmen to bring the Imperial Navy up to strength. Since most people would rather stew in jail than row in the fleet—as the joke goes, the only difference is that you're less likely to drown in prison—that means a draft.

Any likely-looking young man has to produce papers to prove that his family has already contributed a son to the cause. I can see a dozen sullen boys whose documentation was apparently insufficiently convincing standing between two burly guardsmen. Some of them will probably be rescued by friends and family with better paperwork or more bribe money, but the rest will be shipped out to power the Emperor's war machine.

There are no draft checkpoints in the Second Ward, of course. If the families there send a son or daughter to the war, it would be as a mage-blood in the Legions, or at least as an officer. Watching the crowd here shuffle forward, like pigs in a butcher's pen, tears at something in my chest.

More immediately, the checkpoint presents a problem. In a pocket sewn into the inside of my shirt, I carry my identity papers, but showing them here is likely to cause trouble. They might not even believe me; young ladies of the Second Ward simply don't turn up at Eleventh Ward draft checkpoints. I definitely don't want someone sending for Ofalo to spring me from a prison cell.

On the whole, it seems easier to take the long way around. I hop down from the wall and start pushing through the crowd again, heading for the entrance to an alley between this building and its neighbor. It *looks* like a dead end, but there's a broken slat in the fence on the far side if you know where to look, and a quick climb will take me into the back lot of a building on Fishmonger Row. From there it's easy enough to cut the corner and get to Grandma's.

The crowd spits me out into the alley like a broken tooth. There's not much here, just a long stretch of dirt between two buildings, smelling heavily of piss and rotting trash. Halfway along there's a stack of wooden boxes, the ones that hold cheap jugs of rice wine, and beyond them an alcove with a back door into one of the buildings.

I let my power sweep the alley, carefully. Opening my senses with so many people crowded so close can be distinctly uncomfortable. But there's no one hiding in the darkened corners, so I jog past the stack of crates to the crooked fence at the rear. Just as I remember, one of the boards pops off, revealing some easy-to-climb slats. I'm about to scramble up—they're splintery with protruding nails, making me thankful for my big stompy boots—when I feel several people in the alley behind me, their minds glowing with ugly suspicion.

If you're going to move, move fast. Isoka drilled that into me, before she left me to be educated as a lady, and I never quite forgot. I don't have long enough to get myself over the fence, so I duck to the side of the alley, flattening myself in the doorway behind the crates. I'm pretty sure that gets me out of sight, and it's dark enough they probably didn't notice me.

Probably. My heart is suddenly beating fast, and I feel the hard shape of my knife in its hiding spot. *Probably* they're not looking for me, either. I hear rapid footsteps, and focus my attention. There are three people, one close and scared, two suspicious and bored, farther back toward the mouth of the alley. Peeking out, I can see a shadow darting toward me, and the light of a lamp further along. Before I have the chance to make out much else, the shadowy figure rounds the crates and slams into me shoulder first.

I stagger back into the doorway with an *oof*. For a moment, I think of the knife, but I don't feel any menace in the stranger's mind, just high, tinkling worry. He—it's a young man, probably not much older than me—presses himself against the boxes and puts a finger to his lips, his eyes frantically begging for silence.

At the end of the alley, two older men are reduced to black silhouettes by the lantern one of them carries. As they approach, I can hear them over the babble of the crowd.

"—sure he went this way?"

"I saw something moving. He's a quick little rotscum."

"Blessed above, it rotting stinks."

One of the pair raises his voice. "Hey! Get out here!"

The boy stares at me, eyes wide. He has a broad, honest face and unruly hair with a hint of curls. His clothes are odd, though—he has a worker's leather vest like mine, but I'd swear the shirt underneath is silk.

Still, it's obvious enough what's happening. He must not have his draft papers, and so the Ward Guard are after him. That's . . . not good. If they come after him, they'll find me, too.

"Listen, kid," one of the guards says. "If I have to come back there and get shit all over my boots, you might have a little bit of an accident on the way back to the cells, you understand? Just rotting come out already."

Moving slowly, the boy slides away from the crates, coming closer to me. I shuffle backward, keeping my distance, but he's just trying the door handle behind me. It's locked, of course. I see him spit a silent curse.

Footsteps echo down the alley, and the light is coming closer. There's no chance of us staying hidden once they round the crates.

Rot. If you're going to move, move quickly, right?

I push the boy into the doorway, shush him, then hand him my cap, letting my hair tumble down my back. He watches, open-mouthed, as I shrug off the vest and hand him that, too. This idea is sounding worse and worse the more I think about it, but there's no time to change now. I tug the first few buttons of my shirt open, then one more, fighting a blush. I may not be able to pass for a *boy* but I'm still not . . . generously shaped. Not much to be done.

I step out from behind the crates. My heart is beating harder *now* than when I thought someone was going to attack me. I hope they'll take the red in my cheeks for paint.

"There he—Hold on." The two Ward Guards come to a halt and raise the lantern. I resist the urge to flinch. "What're you doing here?"

"Looking for a little rotting privacy." I try to let the cultured accent I've spent the last few years perfecting slip away, putting on a Sixteenth District drawl. "Do you mind?"

The guard's lip twists skeptically. I wouldn't believe me, either. I've met streetwalkers at the hospital younger than I am, but . . .

"It's just that you're making my gentleman . . . nervous." I give them a raised eyebrow that I hope conveys weary amusement, but probably just looks like a facial spasm. Oh, rot. "And I wouldn't want him to catch cold."

"Did you see anyone run through here?" the other guard says.

"Nobody. It's a dead end." I nod to the fence.

"Rot." The guard looks at his partner. "You were supposed to keep your eye on him."

"How was I supposed to know he'd take off?" The other guard shakes his head as they both turn away. "Sergeant's not going to like it."

"We'll just tell him the records got mixed up . . ."

Their voices fade as they rejoin the crowd. I lean against the pile of crates for a moment, breathing hard, skin feeling very warm.

It worked. I can't believe that worked. I try to picture Ofalo's face, if he saw me, and nearly laugh out loud. *Who's an innocent child now?*

"Have they gone?" the boy says, in a whisper.

I spin to face him. I'd almost forgotten he was there. He's still clutching my cap and vest to his chest, and at the sight of me his cheeks go crimson, and he looks firmly at the ground. I hurriedly do up my shirt, then clear my throat.

"Can I have my things?"

"Oh! Of course." He hands the cap and vest over, and I work on fixing my hair back in place. "That was brilliant. Brave. Both. I never would have . . . I mean, you . . ."

"Thanks. I wanted to make sure they didn't think I was a boy."

"They might—I mean, you're not—" He seemed to be having some difficulty, and took a deep breath. "Obviously you're not a prostitute."

"I know."

"I just . . . I mean, *I* know. It was a bluff. I just wanted to be sure you didn't think I thought . . . right."

His accent confirms what I'd suspected from the quality of his shirt—he's not an Eleventh Ward resident, any more than I am. I don't know what he's doing here. Kosura says that upper-ward men sometimes come down looking for diversions, though somehow he doesn't look like the type to be slumming for brothel girls. Whoever he is, I decide, it's long past time I was gone.

"Thank you," he manages, eventually. "I didn't know how I was going to get out of that."

"Don't mention it," I tell him, feeling a little sour. It takes a moment of thought before I figure out why—if he's from the upper wards, he didn't *really* need my help. He could always pull out his papers, just like I could, and the worst he'd suffer was a family reprimand.

Oh well. At least the Ward Guard didn't take me in.

"Be more careful next time," I tell him. "Or get some draft papers."

"I'll try. I mean, I will."

I give him a polite nod and go to the fence, knocking aside the loose slat. I'm nearly to the top when he shouts after me.

"Um. Please. What's your name?"

I look back. I'm not sure why. Something about what I can feel from his mind, a pulse of blue-white sincerity that makes my skin tingle.

He is, I note belatedly, quite handsome.

"Tori," I call back, before dropping over the fence.

It's a common-enough name. He certainly won't be able to track me back to the Second Ward. So no harm done.

Right?

4

ISOKA

Of course Meroe takes charge immediately.

She's been organizing scavenging and defense since we got to the Garden, so when she gives orders, people listen. Pack leaders are designated and duties assigned. Establish a perimeter, light torches to push back the darkness, gather supplies and see what we have left. The younger teens are delegated to keep the rest of the children together and make sure no one strays.

In a quarter of an hour, we go from a confused crowd of several hundred frightened people, clustered on an alien shore, to something like an organized crew. Through it all, she never even raises her voice, just listens and thinks and speaks so *reasonably* that no one even argues.

Blessed above, I want to kiss her. Nothing is more attractive than *competence*.

But that would be a distraction, for both of us. Sooner or later, people are going to start asking what to do next, and they're going to ask *me*. So: options.

Get back on the ship—apparently not going to happen. Not long after the last of us leaves the ramp, it starts to rise again, metal folding and groaning back up into *Soliton*'s titanic Bow. The angels retreat, glowing blue eyes turning away, until only one remains: a dog-shaped thing, hulking and broad shouldered, with wild feathery growths along its flanks. It stands at the top of the ramp as it rises, and I get the distinct sense that it's watching me. Soon, though, the rising metal blocks even this straggler from sight. When the ramp stops with a *clang*, there's no more movement from the great ship,

which rises above us like a steel cliff. I can feel Eddica power pulsing through the air, energy flowing out of *Soliton* toward . . . something, but I can't reach it with my own feeble strength.

Not the ship, which leaves the land. The dock extends out into
the water from a rocky beach bordered by a strip of grass a dozen
yards wide. Beyond that is a wall of trees that looks almost solid in
the gloom, with barely a speck of starry sky visible through their
interlocking canopies. The air is alive with animal sounds, hoots and
chirps that could be birds, insects, or something stranger. Everything smells of salt and rust.

From the tower above *Soliton*, I'd seen structures rising up
through the trees, but it had been too dark to get more than a
glimpse. From ground level, I have no idea where they might be,
even if we wanted to go there.

So—the land isn't too welcoming, either. Which doesn't leave
much, does it?

Rot.

When the pace of Meroe's orders slows, I nudge her and call the
Council together, a little ways off from the others. Shiara, for once,
is less than her perfectly composed self—she must not have had time
to apply her makeup. Zarun seems to be more in his element, bark-
ing commands to his crew, then striding over to me all swagger and
confidence. It fades the moment the four of us are alone.

"What," he says through gritted teeth, "the rotting *hell* is
going on?"

"I don't know," I spit back, "any more than I knew last time."

"You can't—" Shiara begins.

"Talk to the ship?" I give an aggravated sigh. "Apparently not."

"So now rotting what?" Zarun says.

The others look at me. Again.

"For now we stay here," I say. "Hunker down and wait until
morning."

"That's not much of a plan," Shiara says.

"It's a rotting lot better than blundering around a forest in the
dark," I say. "When the sun comes up we'll be able to see what we're
walking into."

"Assuming the sun does come up," Zarun mutters. "We're inside some kind of dome, remember?"

"We can see the moon and the stars," Meroe says reasonably, "so I think we can assume we'll be able to see the sun as well." She glances at me. "I agree with Isoka that we should stay put until dawn. We'll have to move pretty soon after that, though, to find fresh water."

I nod. "For now, make sure nobody wanders off. I don't want anyone outside our cordon."

Zarun glances over his shoulder. "You think there's something dangerous out there?"

"I'm just going to assume everything is trying to kill us until we prove otherwise."

Shiara actually smiles, pale and vulnerable-looking without her face paint. "I can get behind that."

The pair of them turn away, heading back to join the others. I step closer to Meroe, who's staring off into the jungle.

"Hey." She blinks and looks at me, and I take her hand. "You okay?"

"I'm okay." Meroe takes a deep breath. "Just . . . trying to think."

"You're doing great."

She looks a little embarrassed. "Everyone knows what they need to do. I'm just reminding them."

I squeeze her hand, and she squeezes back, returning to her study of the forest. I follow her gaze.

"So what are you thinking?"

"You saw buildings, right? When we were coming in."

I nod. "Just shadows, really, but that's what it looked like."

"I'm wondering if there's people here." She looks back at the ship. "The Scholar said that *Soliton* empties itself out every twenty years or so. We figured that was because every so often it went close enough to the Rot that everybody died."

"If anyone survived, though, it looks like the angels force them off the ship here." I frown. "Why?"

"Why does *Soliton* do anything?" Meroe shrugs. "But if there's buildings, maybe someone's living here. They might be able to help us."

"Or try to kill us," I say. "Or the buildings are as old as the docks, and full of crabs."

"You're such an optimist."

"Just trying to keep you grounded."

I look up at *Soliton* again, a dark thought forming in my mind. While the ship showed no signs of activity, obviously it won't wait here *forever*. Unless it's changed its usual pattern, eventually it will return to its yearly cycle, gathering fresh sacrifices from around the Central Sea. If Meroe is right, and it won't return for twenty years afterward, then that would be the end of any chance of getting back to Kahnzoka before Kuon Naga's deadline. If the ship leaves and I'm not on it, my sister will be kidnapped and sold to a brothel, or worse. I imagine her wide, innocent eyes as Naga's thugs break down her door—

No. The thought makes my heart beat louder, echoing in my ears. *I won't let it happen.*

Something moves, up on the deck. An angel? For a moment, I think I see the dog-thing again, silhouetted against the starry sky. And then—did it *jump off*?

"Meroe—" I begin.

"Deepwalker!" someone shouts.

We both turn. A young man with a long spear skids to a halt, breathing hard.

"We caught an intruder!" he says. "He wants to talk to whoever's in charge."

Meroe and I exchange a look.

Aifin, the boy we'd once called the Moron, is waiting beside the stranger, a short sword in hand. He's motionless, but a faint golden light surrounds him. Aifin can't hear or speak, but he's an adept in Rhema, the Well of Speed, and fully capable of slashing the prisoner's throat between eyeblinks.

He and Meroe exchange a string of hand signs. I've learned a few for use in a fight, but the two of them have been slowly fleshing out a whole vocabulary. Aifin nods and takes a step back, though the golden light of his Well remains.

The stranger is on his knees. He's a man in his early twenties, with Imperial features. His hair is long, bound up in a tight queue that's coiled in a complicated knot on the back of his head. In combination with his clothes—a long, somewhat threadbare gray robe with voluminous sleeves and a white under-tunic—it makes him look like an actor in a historical drama, something about the Rockfire War.

Zarun and Shiara arrive, and the prisoner looks between us. His eyes are wide with fear.

"Aifin says he came in from the forest," Meroe whispers. "He didn't try to hide, and he's not armed."

"All right," Zarun says, looking down at the stranger. "So what are you doing here?"

"Please," the man says. "You're all in the gravest danger. I entreat you to listen to me."

Zarun narrows his eyes. "Did you all catch that?"

"More or less," I say. Among ourselves, *Soliton*'s crew speak a polyglot accumulation of Imperial and Jyashtani, with words borrowed from the icelings and other tongues in the mix. The stranger's Imperial is pure and formal, archaic to my ears. I'm not surprised Zarun finds it hard to follow. It takes a conscious effort to revert to my own tongue after so many weeks speaking pidgin. "Who are you? And what kind of danger?"

The prisoner turns to me. He looks a bit shocked by my appearance—I suppose my crab-shell armor and blue-marked skin seem strange by traditional Imperial standards. But he clears his throat and says, "My name is Guran Veldi. I happened to be near the docks when *Soliton* came in, so I got here expediently, but it won't be long before Prime's creatures detect your presence. Please." His eyes flick to Zarun. "Leave these infidels and come with me. I'm certain my lady will welcome you."

I have so many questions I'm honestly not sure what to ask first, but a warning is a warning. "Double-check the perimeter," I tell Zarun, "and be ready to take the reserve wherever we need it. Something bad may be coming."

"Right." Zarun glares at Veldi, and his lip curls. "'Infidel.' It's been a while since anyone called me that."

"Later," I tell him. To Veldi, I say, "Start with what these creatures are. Some kind of crab?"

"Nothing so crude," Veldi moans. "Please, we have to *go*. If they find us it will be too late."

"You may not have noticed, but there's quite a few people here," I snap. "It'll take time to get them moving, *if* we decide we can trust you."

"Bring only the Blessed's Children," he says. "The others can fend for themselves."

It takes me a moment to even parse that. "The Blessed's Children" is an old turn of phrase from a more pious time, a way to refer to the people of the Empire that emphasizes our devotion to the Blessed One. These days people tend to say "Imperials" instead, probably because loyalty to the Emperor and the government counts for more than theological commitment.

"If we go anywhere," I tell him, "we won't be leaving anyone behind." I look around and get nods from Shiara and Meroe.

"But—" Veldi begins.

He's interrupted by a shriek, and he immediately curls in on himself as though someone had kicked him in the gut.

"Too late," he says. "They've arrived."

"Deepwalker!" Zarun shouts. "People coming fast, a hell of a lot of them!"

Rot. "See what you can get out of him," I tell Shiara. Then to Meroe, "We may need to fall back. Get everyone ready."

"Fall back *where*?" she says.

"Still working on that!" I shout over my shoulder, jogging in the direction of the cries.

Up ahead, at the edge of the woods, I can see the flash and glow of magic. Myrkai fire spits into the trees, bolts blossoming into balls of flame on impact. The blue of Tartak force flickers through the underbrush, and then the brilliant green of Melos energy, with its characteristic hissing crackle. That has to be Zarun himself—there are precious few Melos users left among the crew.

I reach the scene to find a pack of a dozen crew retreating in the face of dozens of silent figures stumbling out of the woods. For a moment, I look at the newcomers with their shambling, drunken gait and wonder if they need help. That thought lasts until the closest of them grabs one of the crew, a young man, and bears him to the ground, twisting his arm the wrong way with an audible *crack*. He screams, and bolts of Tartak force batter his attacker, who hangs on to the shattered limb with grim determination.

Well. *Score one for paranoia.* I concentrate for a moment, letting energy from the Melos Well flow through me. Twin blades of brilliant green energy ignite at my wrists with a *snap–hiss*, sparks crawling over them and running up my arms. The air around my body hums, suffused by more Melos power, an intangible barrier ready to crackle to life. I charge, sprinting past the line of crew hurling bolts of fire. Heat from a stray blast washes over me, but I ignore it, trusting my armor. I reach the fallen crewman and bring a blade around in a horizontal sweep, slashing through his attacker's neck. The head flies off into the trees, and I instinctively take a step back to avoid the gushing arterial spray.

Only it doesn't come. There's no blood at all, in fact. Nor does the attacker fall. By the light of my blades, I can see that it's a desperately thin woman, her rib cage visible under dark, puckered skin, and—

Green light gleams on bones. Her *ribs* are visible, peeking through gaps in her flesh. And her body is still moving, dropping the poor boy's arm to head in my direction.

This isn't a woman at all. It's a walking corpse, and the loss of its head doesn't seem to slow it down. It lunges for me, long, splintery nails scraping against a flare of Melos armor. My body reacts automatically, spinning away and chopping the thing's arm off at the elbow. I take off its other arm when it reaches for me again, and give it a kick that connects with a *crunch* of breaking bone. Even then, it writhes on the ground, the headless, armless body trying to regain its feet.

Oh, Blessed. *Dead is dead.* Dead is dead is dead, and there's no such things as ghosts. *So* what in the Blessed's rotten entrails *is going on?*

The sentiment seems to be shared by the crew fighting around me, who are giving ground rapidly as more and more of the things shuffle out of the woods. Several corpses are ablaze now, stumbling about wreathed in Myrkai fire, still trying to reach their prey even as they burn. I can hear the panic in the voices of the defenders as they call to each other.

"They're just rotting puppets!" Zarun roars. He has a long Melos blade in one hand and a shield of green light in the other. One of the creatures lurches against him, a big man whose corpse shows signs of having been sewn back together. Zarun lets it throw itself against his shield, raising a shower of sparks, then cuts it in half at the waist with a single blow. "Tear them to bits if you have to!"

I force myself to focus and add my voice to his. "He's right! Dead or not, they won't hurt you with no arms or legs!"

When the next creature comes for me, a heavyset woman trailing long, tattered folds of skin, I'm ready. I sidestep its first rush, remove one arm, spin to cut off the other as it turns to face me, then cut off its head with a crossing slash of both blades. It's a showy combination, but effective, and it puts some heart into the crew. Fire splashes out with renewed vigor, and blue Tartak bonds hold back the burning creatures until they collapse. Zarun and I take the lead, cutting apart the stumbling bodies one after another.

For a moment, I think we're winning. But there are too many of them, the crowd emerging from the woods getting thicker. I can see the flare and crackle of fighting all along the perimeter now, but there's no time to worry about the rest of the crew, no time to do anything but slash, sidestep, slash again, cutting apart the bloodless creatures like I'm chopping firewood. But it's not going to work. They're getting around me, hands grasping and scratching, and all I can do is keep moving. Beyond the oncoming horde, I see the boy with the broken arm take off running back toward the camp. A girl, spraying a torrent of fire from her cupped hands onto one creature, doesn't see two more grabbing her from behind. She goes down, and her scream cuts off abruptly amid wet, gristly sounds.

Rotting *scumsuckers*. I spin away from the pack, bulling through the group that's built up around me, blades slashing wildly. Cold, rotten flesh parts easily, but fingers continue to tear at me, sparks spitting and popping from my armor. I'm nearly clear when one of them gets a hold on my wrist, jerking me backward with inhuman strength. I can hear the creature's flesh frying in the continuous discharge from my armor, a wild coruscation of green light and a vile stench, but it hangs on. Another of the things throws itself on my other arm, my blade punching through its chest even as it pulls me closer. Heat washes over me, building up under my armor, and I start to feel the first hints of panic. I stagger backward, brushing up against another straining corpse, and—

There you are.

The voice rings in my mind, carried on a wave of Eddica energy wafting out of the creatures that hold me. I can feel Eddica power everywhere, in fact, flowing out of *Soliton*, pulsing under the soil like blood through a vein, and curling up into these withered corpses. For a moment, a face hangs in the air, the same monstrosity I saw on the ship, with flyaway white hair and black holes for eyes. Skin cracks as its lips move, speaking to me.

You can hear me, can't you? Yes, of course you can.

The world beyond the voice dims to vague shadows. I try to focus.

It has been a long time since one of us arrived, the voice says.

Who are you? I ask.

They call me Prime. There's a note of humor in the voice, a barely suppressed chuckle. *I wondered why so many survived the passage. No doubt you protected them.*

Call off your monsters, I think at him, desperately. *Tell me what you want.*

Come to me, he counters. *Leave the others. You don't need them anymore.* His withered face contorts into a smile. *This is our place. I will teach you. You will never need anyone ever again.*

Go rut one of your rotting corpses, I tell him.

Very poetic, he says. *We'll see if you still think—*

The voice cuts off as a glowing green blade severs the arm of the creature holding me. I find myself on my knees, my armor flaring all over, so hot it feels like I've stepped into a bread oven. It's all I can do to gasp for breath as Zarun cuts down another creature and kicks a third away from me. I drop my armor and let my blades fade, and he takes my arm and pulls me to my feet. I'm drenched in sweat, and I can already feel the hot pain of powerburn running across my skin.

"Isoka!" he says. "We have to get out of here!"

No rotting kidding. I raise my head, and catch sight of waves of flame rippling out. I point, and Zarun nods. We head that way, ducking and dodging through the ranks of the dead. After a few moments, I ignite my blades again and keep Zarun clear as he hacks a path.

The crew have pulled back into a tight circle, the children in the center, an outer perimeter of Myrkai users directing continuous streams of flame into the darkness. Behind them, crew with spears and Tartak force shove the corpses back, keeping a narrow area clear inside a growing pile of burning bodies. I don't even have to wonder who got them into formation.

There's no way to alert them to open the circle and let us in, so I take a deep breath and raise my armor, wincing at the pain in already-burned skin. Zarun and I kick through a waist-high heap of charred and burning bodies, then sprint forward, and I pray the brilliant green flaring from our armor will keep the Tartak users in the crew from flinging us away. It works, thank the Blessed, and we skid to a halt on the other side of the wall of flames. Zarun drops his armor, steam rising from his body, and absently slaps at his shirt where a corner of it has caught fire.

"Isoka!" Meroe fights through the press. "Oh, gods—I thought—"

"I got a little toasted," I say. My voice is a rasp. "But I'll live. If any of us do."

"We have to get off the beach," she says. "The crew can't keep this up for long."

"The buildings inland," I say. "There might be something solid enough to defend."

"Maybe." She chews her lip. "If there's not, though—or if more of these things are in there—"

"Where's Veldi?"

The stranger, in his old-fashioned clothing, is quickly dragged to us. He looks as terrified as any of the children, fire reflected in his wide eyes, and his ridiculous braid-knot is badly singed. I have to ignite my blade under his nose to get his attention.

"How far to your lady? Where you wanted to take us?"

"A couple of hours' walk," he says. "But—"

"Too far." I point at the jungle. "I saw a building close by. Who lives there?"

"No one," he says, and then seems to understand. "It's empty. Most of the city is abandoned."

"But it's still standing?"

He nods vigorously. I glance at Meroe.

"Better than staying here," she says. "Give me a minute to get everyone moving."

The tricky part is making sure the retreat doesn't turn into a rout. If we split up and lose ourselves in the jungle, the corpses will pull us down one at a time.

Meroe gathers the strongest fighters—me, Zarun, Aifin, Thora, and Jack—and makes them the vanguard. The rest, especially the less powerful Myrkai and Tartak touched, form the perimeter that keep the corpses back. Everyone else just needs to run and keep together, which is going to be no small feat in the woods.

I shed my crab-shell plates and most of my clothes, keeping only a chest-wrap and trousers, trying to cool off. Angry red lines crisscross my skin already, running underneath the blue cross-hatching left over from the first time Meroe used her Ghul powers on me. Zarun spares a moment to raise an appreciative eyebrow, and I roll my eyes at him.

Meroe gives the signal, and the wall of fire parts. The dead surge forward, toppling the pile of burning bodies in their eagerness to get at us, and we charge to meet them. Aifin and I take the lead, me slashing the corpses apart with my blades, him working with a short sword in a blaze of golden Rhema speed. Beside us, Jack fights with a long spear and her Xenos Well, shadows boiling all around her, reaching out with webs of darkness to snare the monsters. Zarun and Thora, both Tartak adepts, concentrate on clearing the path, shoving corpses to either side.

Other crew move in behind us, widening the breach. Step by step, we pick up momentum, battering a small section of the horde aside. Meroe shouts herself hoarse, directing her packs to follow us, keeping the dead from re-forming their ring. Through the narrow gap, the mass of the crew floods, those in the lead carrying swords and spears to deal with any straggling monstrosities.

In less than a minute, we're through. The dead are thinning out in front of us, not because we've cut their numbers, but because we're leaving the great mass of them behind. I plunge into the forest, slashing underbrush out of my way, and jog forward by the light of my blades. Fortunately, beyond the verge, the vegetation thins at ground level, so we only need to weave between the canted trees and cut down any corpses that cross our path. Zarun runs on one side of me, slamming a dead woman out of the way with his shield and cutting her in half, while Thora and Jack take the other side, fighting together with practiced ease. Jack hoots in triumph as she slashes a creature apart, then dissolves into a swirl of shadow and re-forms nearby as three more try to dog-pile her. Aifin darts in, almost faster than my eye can follow, and cuts the trio to pieces.

Behind us, there are shouts, screams, and blasts of fire. I turn to look for Meroe, and spot her in the first rank, waving the others on. The fighters on the edges of the crowd try to keep everyone together, directing bolts of flame at the pursuing corpses. I see a girl stumble, sprawl, then lift into the air in a nimbus of blue as a Tartak user sets her back on her feet. Farther back, a young man runs the wrong way, heading to grab a screaming boy who's fallen behind. He blasts one corpse with flames to reach the boy, but the great mass of dead swarms over them before he can get clear, and they both vanish under a tide of desiccated flesh.

"There!" Zarun shouts, gesturing with a glowing Melos blade. A hundred yards ahead, stone walls thickly carpeted with vines rise out of the jungle.

I gulp a breath. "Jack! Take Aifin and find us a way in!"

"Aye-aye, fearless leader!" she crows. "Clever Jack will break the path." She taps Aifin and points—he can't hear, but he gets the idea. He speeds up even further, blurring into a fading trail of golden light, and Jack follows in a shifting mass of shadow.

There are few corpses ahead of us now, and we spread out to either side, keeping them from working around the main body of the crew. I catch Meroe's eye and point, hoping she understands. The wall of flame guarding our rear is ragged now, Myrkai users stumbling in exhaustion, and Zarun and I join them, slashing apart any creatures that get too close. We back up, step by step, half my attention on treacherous, root-strewn ground. Trip here, and the horde will drown you.

Time seems to blur. My skin is getting hot again; I drop my armor, letting the splintered nails of the corpses rake my skin, but even using my blades continuously for this long is draining. Zarun is breathing hard, exhaling a dragon's plume of hot steam. Meroe's voice cuts through the mêlée, cracked and ragged.

"Isoka! Fall back! We're inside!"

Music to my rotting ears. I cut the head off a one-armed woman in the tattered remnants of a *kizen* and turn my back on the others, sprinting toward the dimly visible outline of the building. I catch sight of Thora, gesturing to us in between slapping corpses away with bolts of Tartak force, and head in her direction. An ancient stone staircase leads up a steep slope to an archway. I have a vague sense of a much larger structure stretching out around me, but my eyes are fixed on the arch, and I skid through it just ahead of Zarun and Thora.

We're the last, except for the dead. They come boiling up the stairway behind us, climbing over one another in their eagerness to reach their prey. But Meroe has crew waiting, and the monsters have to press into a narrow space to try to crush into the doorway. Waves of fire slam out, turning dry, cracking flesh into boiling ash, incinerating dozens of the things at once. I laugh with giddy relief—fighting surrounded in the open is one thing, defending a narrow gap like this quite another. They can try all rotting day and they won't make it through.

What's more, they seem to know it. After that first rush, the dead pause. Then, as though they've suddenly lost interest, they turn away, stumbling back down the steps and into the forest. Within minutes, they've slipped into the shadows, and the only corpses in sight are those still burning.

We'd made it. *But not all of us.* Exhaustion and rage war in my chest. I push through the crowd of crew, looking for our hapless prisoner.

Veldi has a *lot* of questions to answer.

5

TORI

Once I knew the Ward Guards were on the watch for draft-dodgers, it was relatively easy to avoid their checkpoints. The closest thing the Eleventh Ward has to a main road is Orchard Street, which connects the High Market (centered on the gate to the military road) with the Low Market (centered on the gate to the Sixteenth Ward), running roughly north-south through the district like a spine. Move away from this artery, and the cross streets quickly splinter into a hundred interwoven lanes, impossible for most outsiders to understand.

I'd had a hard time navigating, the first time I came here. Now I move with confidence, ducking around sharp corners and taking the occasional shortcut through a ground-floor shop. The buildings closest to Orchard Street are the most respectable, offering lodging for those on the upper end of the Eleventh Ward's scale of poverty and shopping for people who don't want to brave the crush of the markets. Head west, as I am now, and the tenements are old and run-down, sagging façades patched with boards and flaking whitewash.

My destination is a large, dilapidated block of a building that stands on its own, as though even the surrounding architecture wanted to give it a wide berth. It's eight stories high, with a gray shingle roof that's missing so many slats the top floor has been abandoned to mold and damp. Stairways zigzag up all four sides of the building, each of them broken in places.

It was once a block of apartments, back when the Eleventh Ward wasn't quite so overbuilt and it was an easier walk from here to the gates. As it aged and the area became less fashionable, at some point the owners had simply cut their losses and walked away. Eventually the place will either collapse or burn down in one of the fires that periodically sweep over the city, and something new will be built in its place.

Until that time, though, Grandma Tadeka has moved in and made it her own.

A lantern burns beside the main entrance all night, and Hasaka, the doorman, gives me a friendly nod as I approach. He's a tall, powerfully built man, with a slight Jyashtani tint to his skin and dark hair to his shoulders, his arms banded with intricate, abstract tattoos. Grandma says he can pull a man's head off like a butcher with a chicken, but I've never seen him do it. Aside from watching the door, he spends most of his time taking care of his boyfriend, Jakibsa, who lives in the upper stories.

"Evening, Tori," he says, in his deep bass rumble. "Running late?"

"Just a bit." I check, for the tenth time, that I've buttoned my shirt back to modest levels. Even *thinking* about what I did back in the alley makes my cheeks burn. *Really, Tori, of all the unnecessary risks* . . . "There's draft checkpoints all up and down Orchard."

"Don't I know it," Hasaka says. "Rot Naga and his war. What good's some southern island to us anyway?"

"It may not come to war," I say. "The Emperor hasn't given the word yet."

"Sure. And maybe the Blessed One will come down from Heaven and blow the Jyashtani fleet away with a fart." He shakes his head, dourly.

"Stranger things have happened." I pause. "Well. Maybe not."

Hasaka grins broadly.

"Is she here?" I ask him.

"In her office," he says. "No catastrophes so far tonight. Not more than usual, anyway."

I nod my thanks and go inside. What had once been a narrow corridor leading to a set of claustrophobically small apartments had long since been gutted, wood-and-plaster walls ripped out to leave the concrete support pillars standing alone. Every available space is laid with bedding, sleeping mats in a hundred different styles, each with a patchwork of yellowing sheets and wadded-up rags for pillows. A narrow aisle leads under the central lightwell to a space at the back cordoned off from the rest of the floor by rag curtains.

A half-dozen older women move along the aisle, checking on the patients who occupy the beds. They smile at me as I pass, and I wave politely. I feel bad for not knowing them all by name, but for the most part my duties aren't out here on the floor, and Grandma has an extensive rota of assistants. It's become something of a badge of pride, locally, to work in the hospital one night a week.

Calling it a hospital, of course, is misleading. Hospitals are for the upper wards, with doctors, surgeons, and alchemists to mix scented unguents and potions. In the lower wards, doctors make house calls to those who can afford them, to stitch a cut or lance a boil, and in the face of disease the most they can offer is to rest and pray to the Blessed One.

They say Grandma Tadeka's husband died when she was a girl, for want of a few bits' worth of medicine, and that's why she keeps this place going. I'm not certain it's true—it's hard to imagine her as a girl, she seems as craggy and eternal as the stones underfoot—and I've never dared ask her. All I know is that for as long as anyone can remember, Grandma has maintained a sanctuary for the sick, hurt, or mad. The people of the Eleventh Ward love her for it, which, given her personality, is saying a lot.

The curtained-off section of the floor is her "office," a space with a writing desk and a few low cushions arranged around a stone hearth. She's scribbling away when I slip inside, licking the tip of one withered finger delicately to turn the page in a homemade "book" bound with twine. Her pen is an old-fashioned goose-quill, lying beside a pot of sludgy ink.

No one seems to know how old Grandma Tadeka actually is. Certainly she's been an old woman for as long as anyone remembers, and she seems set to go on as one indefinitely. Her hair is iron gray, with a curl that hints of southern blood, and her face is a leathery mass of wrinkles around a pair of diamond-hard blue eyes.

When she squints disapprovingly at the page in front of her, I half-expect it to burst into flame.

"Tori," she says, without looking up. "You're late."

I give an unobserved bow. "I'm sorry, Grandma." Grandma Tadeka refuses any other honorific. "I got held up at the draft checkpoint by the High Market."

Her pen skitters and pops across the cheap paper. "Thought you were smarter than that."

"There was a boy running from the Ward Guard," I say. "I . . . helped him."

Grandma snorts. "A pretty boy, I'd wager."

I flush again. "That's . . ."

"You're getting to that age. Kids start to think with what's between their legs instead of what's in their head. It's natural, but it doesn't make it less of a pain to watch." Grandma looks up, finally, wiping her quill on a rag and setting it aside. "Pretty girl like you needs to have a care."

"Yes, Grandma," I manage, still blushing furiously, because what else can I say to that?

"I suppose you're better equipped to deal with that than most, aren't you?"

I take a deep breath, but say nothing.

"Well." She gets up, the pops in her joints audible. Her robe is embroidered cloth, a pretty gift from some long-ago patient, now threadbare and patched at the knees and elbows. "If you're done flirting for the day, we have work to do."

The streets around Grandma's hospital are full of her friends and associates, built up over the course of a long career. Talk to a shop-keeper or stallholder anywhere in the neighborhood, and you'll hear a story about someone she helped—a son, a niece, an aunt, or a cousin. Braggi of Braggi's Salt Fish owes her more than most, and the nature of his business means he has a lot of cellar space he's happy to offer us.

He greets us out front, the shop dark and shuttered for the evening. A single lamp burns on the desk, and Braggi guides us to the heavily bolted door in the back corner. He's a big man, the only iceling I've ever met, with an inch or so of shockingly yellow hair. He speaks Imperial with a thick accent, and when he drinks he belts out mournful, rhythmic songs that nobody else understands.

The lamp illuminates a long staircase, descending into a windowless cellar smelling strongly of fish. Braggi hands the light to Grandma and stands aside, looking nervous.

"You'll be all right?" he says. "I don't know about these people."

"I've got Tori for a bodyguard," Grandma snaps. "She'll protect my virtue." She stomps down the stairs, light held high.

I give Braggi an apologetic bow. "She's running late."

"Don't make excuses for me, girl!" Grandma's voice drifts out of the dark. "I'm a cantankerous old ass!"

"That, too," I tell Braggi, who gives me a worried smile as I hurry down after her.

It's chilly in the cellar, and the walls are stacked high with casks. Three people are sitting against the far wall, a young man and woman huddled together under a blanket, and another woman slightly apart. The two women look similar enough to be sisters; the younger is in her late teens, the older at least twenty. Grandma looks all three over with a sour expression, the lamplight turning her face into a mask of shadows.

"You're her? Grandma Tadeka?" The young man gets to his feet. He's well dressed, handsome, maybe sixteen. "I'm honored to meet you. My name is—"

"No names. I don't want to know, not yet." Grandma glares at him. "How'd you know to come looking for me?"

"M—" He'd been about to start with a name, pauses at Grandma's expression, and nods at the older sister. "My fiancée's sister told me that you might be able to help us."

"And how did *you* find that out?" Grandma says.

"I met a man in a tavern." The older sister matches her gaze, and my estimation of her rises a notch; not many could. She remains huddled against the casks, wrapped in a wool blanket. "Paid him too much money."

"Don't suppose you caught his name," Grandma says sourly.

"I didn't want to know," the older sister says.

Grandma's lip quirks. She turns to me, and I take a deep breath.

Like I said, I don't like looking into people's minds. But it doesn't take much to see if someone's lying. Most people, at least, light up with yellow mistrust and acrid deceit, and I can't help but pick up on it. Right now, the older sister is radiating suspicion, a feeling like cloth brushed over the back of my neck, but I don't sense that she's being deceptive. I nod to Grandma, and she raises an eyebrow and turns back to the couple.

"Are you going to help us?" the younger sister says. She's prettier, with big, dark eyes and fine features.

"That depends, dearie," Grandma says, and I flinch, because Grandma only says "dearie" to people who've annoyed her.

"On what?"

"On whether you answer my questions." She looks across the three of them. "What are your Wells?"

All three seem taken aback. The younger sister and the boy look at each other, but it's the older sister who moves first, silently opening her palm. With a crackle, a dancing Myrkai flame appears, throwing Grandma's enormous shadow against the wall.

These three sought out Grandma for the same reason I did, the reason that first drove me to sneak out of the comfortable house up in the Second Ward and venture back into the lower districts I'd so recently escaped. While it's well-known that she runs a charity hospital and sanctuary for the mad, rumor insists there's more to it than that. Grandma Tadeka, they say, has a secret shelter for fugitive mage-bloods.

To be born as a mage-blood commoner in Kahnzoka is to face a set of awful fates. The luckiest, able-bodied men who rank as touched or talents, are sent to the Invincible Legions to serve the Emperor. In between assignments, they might be forced to stud for noble women wanting to strengthen their house bloodlines. The prospect of girls in the same situation is much worse, forced to bear noblemen's children until their bodies give out. Magical power runs in the blood, and the Empire's elite are loathe to see it wasted on the lowborn.

Those who qualify as adepts simply disappear. Ghul adepts are killed out of hand, of course, and the rest probably face a similar life as breeding stock. An elite few who join the ranks of the Immortals, the Emperor's personal guard, are responsible for hunting down other mage-bloods.

Most mage-bloods don't have the chance to conceal their powers. When they first come, they're hard to control, and the standing bounties offered by the Immortals for rogues ensure that there are always plenty of neighbors willing to turn them in. For those who survive and remain free long enough to master their abilities, life is still on a knife-edge, always one slip away from being dragged away by chain-veiled soldiers in black armor.

This is the life that Isoka saved me from, the risk that *she* takes on every day. Not just the ordinary threats of the gutter—starvation, disease, murder—but the prospect of spending the rest of our lives as prisoners, raped by strangers and bearing their children. And, in all probability, never seeing each other again.

Once I was old enough to understand that, to know the danger she courted to keep me safe, I could hardly bear it. I knew there were others, without someone like Isoka to protect them, hunted by Kuon Naga's Immortals, the Ward Guard, and the whole Empire. I went looking for a way to help them, and I found Grandma Tadeka. Since then, I've been assisting her as often as I can, and it soothes the pangs of my conscience.

And—at the back of my mind, in the moments before I fall asleep—a worm of a selfish thought: if the Immortals ever *do* come for Isoka, or for me, maybe we'll have somewhere to run.

Back in the basement, the younger sister grudgingly says, "I'm Myrkai, too, though I'm not as strong as she is."

"Mine is Rhema," the boy says, which perks my interest—I've never seen the Well of Speed in action. "I'm barely touched, just a sliver of power, but they were going to take me for the Legions anyway."

"And so you ran," Grandma says.

"We ran," the younger sister says. "M—my sister had been looking for a place for us to go. She finally spent everything we'd saved to get your name."

"That's a poor bargain," Grandma says. "My name's not worth that much."

"Is it true, then?" the older sister says. "Do you have somewhere we can hide?"

"Well." Grandma scratches her nose. "First I need to know I can trust you."

"We'll do whatever you ask," the boy volunteers, drawing an annoyed look from the younger sister.

"Nothing too difficult. Just swear by the Blessed One that if I find a place for you, you won't do anything to endanger me and mine." Grandma's smile is thin. "Easy enough, right?"

"I swear," the boy says.

"Repeat it," Grandma snaps.

"I swear by the Blessed One . . ."

All three of them stumble through the oath, and I concentrate, feeling the shades and vibrations of their minds. The boy is sincere, thick with lemon-bright fear. The older sister, too, means what she says, though she has more pulsing, deep blue determination. The younger, though . . .

Deceit. Hatred. Her mind is thick with brackish, foul odors. She mouths the words, and I can feel-hear-taste the lie.

Grandma turns to me, and I beckon her forward and whisper in her ear. She listens, blank-faced, then straightens.

"You and you can stay," she says, to the boy and the older sister. Glaring at the younger, she adds, "I'll ask you to leave, and not bother me again."

All of a sudden everyone is shouting at once. They're all on their feet, the older sister tugging at the younger's arm, the boy shouting in Grandma's face. I flinch away from the chaos, but Grandma holds her ground, unmoved.

"Why?" the boy manages to get in. "Why would you—"

"Because your girlfriend wants to sell us out. Maybe you, too, for all I know." Grandma shrugs. "I didn't get this old by hugging snakes."

"That's a lie!" the younger sister shouts.

"Meri . . ." The older sister is looking at her sibling with sorrowful eyes. "What did you do?"

"I didn't do anything!" She looks between her sister and Grandma. "I wasn't going to do anything! I just—" She shakes her head frantically. "You spent everything we had on this. How are we supposed to live, even if she does help us?"

"Meri," the boy says, but she shakes him off, advancing on Grandma. Her hands open, and fire blossoms.

I take a half-step forward, though what I'm going to do against an angry Myrkai user I have no idea. But Grandma just holds up a hand.

"Going to burn me?" she says. "Go ahead. I warn you, though, I plan to scream, and when I do I don't think much of your chances outside."

"You rotting horrible old *bitch*," the younger sister hisses. "I'm—"

"Meri, *don't*," the boy says.

After a dangerous moment, she closes her hands, flames disappearing with a hiss and a trail of black smoke. The girl shoots me a murderous look as she pushes past, stomping up the stairs.

"You two are welcome," Grandma says, as though nothing untoward had happened. "If you're still interested."

"I'm not leaving Meri," the boy says. He glances at the older sister, as though he expects her to agree at once. But she's looking down, toying with the end of her braid, and I don't need to peek into her mind to see what she's going to say.

"I'm staying," she mutters.

"But—"

"Meri made her choice." The older sister takes a deep breath. "Just like she always does."

The boy hesitates for a moment, then runs after his lover.

Grandma stands aside to let him go, then gives a slight bow to the older sister, who refuses to meet her gaze.

"Welcome to the sanctuary," she says.

The girl—she'd finally given her name as Giniva—had still looked half-stunned when Braggi had led her away. I made a mental note to visit her, though I wasn't looking forward to it. The anguish pouring off her mind had been practically palpable, like stumbling through a foul-tasting fog.

"I didn't think she'd stay," I say.

"There's history there," Grandma says. "There always is, with families. You can never tell."

"Her sister, Meri," I say. "You're not worried she's going to go to the guards now?"

"I expect she will," Grandma says. "But they've heard that song before, I dare say. And I have a few friends spread around."

"It still seems like a risk."

"What would you like me to do?" She gives me a sharp look. "Slit her throat?"

Isoka would have slit her throat. I push that thought down. Isoka lives in a different world, with different rules.

We're walking back to the hospital from Braggi's. The street is dark and webbed with shadows, lit only by lanterns hanging from a few late-night winesinks. At this hour, the Second Ward would be silent and empty except for patrolling night watchmen, but the Eleventh is never really deserted. Parties of drunken revelers stumble along, slurring their way through lewd songs, avoiding the dungmen with their covered carts. Streetwalkers wait at the intersections, cheap, gaudy robes hanging half-open, while discreet signs in a few windows indicate nighttime entertainment for the better-heeled.

Ofalo and Narago would be horrified by this place, but it doesn't feel dangerous. Partly, of course, that's because I'm with Grandma Tadeka. A drunkard lurches up to her, does a double take, then straightens up and gives a deep bow. Even the prostitutes incline their heads respectfully as she passes, and no wonder.

"Something's bothering you," Grandma says.

I look up at her. Sometimes I think Grandma has a touch of Kindre herself.

"Out with it," she orders. "I can't abide sulking."

"What I do." I glance around to make sure no one is close enough to overhear. "Touching their minds. It's not right. A person's thoughts should be their own."

Grandma is silent for a moment. "No, it's not right."

I bite my lip. "Then—"

"Would it be better if we'd taken that girl in, and she'd brought the Immortals down on us?"

"No." I shake my head. "Of course not."

"Or if I turned everyone away because I didn't know who to trust?"

"No."

"You want me to tell you you're a monster, because of what you can do?" She pauses for a moment, looking upward. "You know what they say about people like me."

That's the other secret, the one I didn't learn until long after I'd started working at the hospital. Grandma isn't just good with bandages, needle and thread. She's a ghulwitch.

Not a powerful one, of course. It's an open secret that the Immortals allow Ghul touched to operate in the city, providing minor healing and preventatives. But everyone knows that ghulwitches are unclean, unholy, which is reason enough for them to keep their abilities secret.

"I know," I tell her, feeling suddenly embarrassed. She's lived with this her whole life, however many decades that's been. "Sorry. I just—"

"Don't be sorry," she snaps, and starts walking again. I scurry to catch up. "Have I told you about the first time I saved someone's life?"

"I don't think so."

"It was my cousin. I wasn't much older than you, and he was about the same. My father and his brothers all lived together, so the boy was as close as a brother, and when he fell sick I stayed by his bed all the time. His guts swelled up, and he cried like a pig getting slaughtered. Worthless doctor my uncle brought in told us he was being tested by the Blessed One, said a few prayers." She pauses to spit in the road.

"Did you know . . . what you were?"

"By then I did. Can't explain what it's like, any more than I guess you can explain what you see when you're looking inside someone's head. But I could feel . . . anything alive, and what was happening. Just a little. I was a curious little thing. Used to practice on rats." She shakes her head. "Killed a lot of rats. But I touched my cousin and I could see what was wrong. Something had gotten tangled up in his guts, and he couldn't shit. That was all, just shit building up, but it was going to kill him."

"So you healed him?"

"I figured, what did he have to lose?" She shrugs. "Maybe I shouldn't have. I know a bit more now about what can go wrong. But I did it. Unknotted his guts and smoothed things along and saved his life." She glances at me. "Of course, when I did that, everything that had been festering came rushing out. Learned a lesson that day."

I wrinkle my nose. "What lesson?"

"You do what you can with what you have." Her grin is sharp as daggers. "Sometimes, you want to help someone, that means you get covered in shit." She rolls one shoulder with a *pop*. "Come on. Still plenty of work to do."

When I tell Kosura that story, she breaks down laughing, hiding her face behind a dirty bedsheet until she can get control of herself.

We're doing laundry, on the hospital's third floor. Keeping the sheets clean and mended is a never-ending battle, and we all pitch in whenever we have a few moments free. I'm worthless with a needle, so I pile the baskets of parti-colored bedding—stitched from rags, flecked with blood and who knows what else—into the great wooden tubs, then carry buckets of boiling water from the hearth in the corner. Grandma is a big believer in boiling water, which she says keeps disease from spreading. I suppose she would know.

Kosura, of course, stitches as tiny and neat as any professional seamstress, so she works on fixing rips and tears, saving what she can and putting aside what she can't to be cut into patches or torn up for bandages.

The thing about Kosura—

If I'm being honest, the thing about Kosura is that there is no thing about Kosura. She's from the Eleventh Ward, but she seems to have a natural grace that elevates her above the coarse manners of most people here. She's tiny, shorter than me with long, thick hair and lively eyes, and seems to contain enough energy for a person twice her size.

When I look at her, I feel like an imposter. She's not mage-born, has no Wells to draw on, no special reason to help. But she's here anyway, nearly every night. Her father is a merchant, successful as Eleventh Ward merchants go, but she spends her evenings sewing bedsheets and wiping up vomit and doing all the other awful things that go with running a hospital.

For all that, she's the closest thing I have to a real friend. She's a year older than me, though she's so innocent sometimes it makes her seem younger. Grandma trusts her, and she knows about the mage-blood sanctuary, though of course I haven't told her about my own power. As far as she knows, I'm here out of the kindness of my heart, just like she is.

"I'm sorry," she says, when she can keep a straight face again. "I can just see her saying that, you know?"

"It's a very Grandma story," I agree, stirring the cloth in the steaming tub. "I just have a hard time picturing her at our age."

Kosura grins. "Back in the time of the Blessed One, you mean? Before the Empire?"

"Right. Everyone had stupid haircuts and spent their time fighting duels and dying of unrequited love." History is not my favorite subject, and much of my understanding comes from popular dramas.

"I think the stupid haircuts were a little later, but otherwise that sounds basically accurate." Kosura leans forward over her stitching. "Speaking of unrequited love. I hear you had an adventure today."

I roll my eyes. I would trust Grandma to take any important secrets to her grave, but anything gossipy she passed on immediately. "It's not like that."

"You saved a boy from the Ward Guard! No doubt he's ever so grateful."

"He ought to be." I shrug, trying for nonchalance. "But I doubt I'll ever see him again."

"That's what makes it so perfectly tragic! Think of him, lying awake at night, pining for your half-remembered face glimpsed by moonlight."

"Maybe not my face." I flush, but only a little, and tell her the particulars of how I'd gotten rid of the Ward Guard. By the end, she's shaking with laughter, the half-mended sheet thrown over her head.

"You didn't," she forces out between gasps. "Come on."

"I couldn't think of anything else to do," I mutter, looking down into the tub.

"So you thought, hey, I'll take my shirt off, maybe that'll help?"

"I didn't take it *off*. And it worked, didn't it?"

"You should try that on Grandma the next time she doesn't like how you've folded the bedsheets."

She comes up for air, and I hurl a wet rag in her direction. She dodges, still giggling.

"Well," she says. "He'll *definitely* remember you, at least."

"Maybe." I poke at the sopping sheets with my stick. "I think—"

"Tori!" Hasaka, the doorman, appears in the laundry entrance, panting for breath. His face is white.

I drop the stick. "What's wrong?"

He hurries closer, lowering his voice. There's no one else in the laundry, but voices carry in the old building.

"It's old Sewagauri," he says. "He's gone off again. Ichi was trying to bring him his medicine, and he just snapped."

"Is Ichi all right?" I ask.

"A little singed, but he'll be fine. But we need your help before Sewa hurts someone."

I glance at Kosura, who makes a shooing gesture. "Go. I'll finish up here."

Hasaka shifts from foot to foot in anxiety. I drop the stick and follow him, out to the exterior stairs, hurrying down groaning, rickety steps to the first floor. From there we take another, internal staircase to the basement, an earth-walled cavern stuffed with sacks of rice and other essentials. Working by the faint light spilling from the stairs, Hasaka leads the way to the far corner, where a dirty, half-height door is mostly hidden behind several stacked barrels of lamp oil. It looks like nothing much, maybe a closet, sealed with a rusty iron padlock.

Hasaka unlocks this, and it slides open without the squeal you'd expect. Beyond the door, there's a stone-lined passage, broad and well-lit, ending in an iron staircase spiraling upward. We hurry over, crossing under the street outside the hospital, and I imagine the drunks wandering a few feet above our heads.

The staircase leads up into the central yard of another derelict tenement. From the outside, it looks abandoned, door boarded over and plaster crumbling. Inside, though, the courtyard is clean, with well-weeded beds of flowers and raked gravel paths. Windows looking into the lightwell reveal that the rooms are in good repair, too, with fresh floor mats and clean, whitewashed walls.

For the most part, the mage-bloods Grandma shelters hide in plain sight, as patients or assistants at the hospital—Hasaka is one of these, I know. People the government is actively searching for, though, need somewhere to lie low. For them, we've converted the first few stories of this building into a safe house, with several unobtrusive entrances.

A young woman with an old, ugly burn scar across the right half of her face is waiting by the door, wringing her hands, and she hurries over at the sight of us.

"He won't let anyone near him!" she wails. "Geraya tried talking to him and he set the curtains on fire."

"It's all right," Hasaka says. "Tori can always get him to calm down."

I swallow an acid taste and nod, trying to look reassuring. The woman looks me over uncertainly. Her right eye is incongruously bright in the melted ruin of its socket.

"Where is he?" I ask.

"Second floor," she says. "Come on, before he burns the place down."

The second floor is mostly apartments converted into single-room residences. Old Sewagauri's room is at the end of a hall, where a former parlor has been made into a common area with several apartments letting on to it. A small crowd of people are gathered at the junction, trying to peer around the corner. Many of them are my age or younger—one of the biggest groups that stay in the safe house are boys and girls who haven't learned to control their powers. Older teens and adults are mixed in, those lying low until the guards give up the hunt for them, and a few who, for whatever reason, can't take work at the hospital.

Old Sewagauri is one of the latter, obviously. I wave my hands to shoo some of the younger children out of the way, and Hasaka busies himself trying to drive the crowd back, without much success. Glancing around the corner, I see a lot of smoke and not much else, though deep in the heart of it there's a sullen red glow. Reaching out with my mind, I can sense Sewa, lost in a torrent of bitter, stinging fear and rage.

"Sewa?" I raise my voice. "It's Tori. Can you hear me?"

His fear flares, and his cracked voice calls back. "Go away! Leave me alone!"

"I just want to talk to you." I motion to Hasaka to keep the others away, and slip around the corner, creeping down the corridor. "Can we talk?"

"I don't know you! Where have you taken me?"

"You're safe. This is Grandma Tadeka's sanctuary. You remember Grandma?" I edge farther, putting my arm across my mouth and trying to breathe through the fabric.

"I . . . don't . . ." Grandma can be hard to forget, and I feel his mind waver. Then the fear returns. "What have you done with my friends? I want to see them!"

"Your friends aren't here right now." My throat is thick, for reasons that have nothing to do with the cloying smoke. "Sewa, please. I'm going to come over so we can talk, all right?"

"Don't." I hear a crackle of flames. "I'm warning you!"

The brass jangle of his mind gives me plenty of notice to throw myself flat. A wave of fire passes overhead, hot enough to frizzle my eyebrows. I hope Hasaka is keeping the kids back.

"I'm sorry," Sewa says. "I just . . . I want to see my friends."

I scramble forward, through the smoke, and reach the common room. Sewa is standing in a circle of scorched floor mats, small fires still smoldering around him. He's an old, wispy-haired man, still straight-backed and solid from years in the Legions. His eyes go wide when he sees me, and I can feel his mind fighting through confusion, trying to remember.

It's not his fault. The only ways out of the Invincible Legions are death or the end of a forty-year term of service, and those who reach the latter milestone are kept on at Legionary forts and away from civilians. Desertion is punishable by execution, of course, but even so Sewagauri is far from the only former soldier Grandma has taken in. For the most part they keep to themselves, happy never to venture outside the confines of the sanctuary. Sewa is like that, most of the time.

"You're safe," I tell him. "Just calm down, please. Everything will be fine. Grandma won't hurt you."

His hands, swathed in Myrkai fire, drop a few inches. "What about my friends?"

I try to keep my voice soothing, and fight back a cough. "They're fine. Everything's fine."

"I remember . . ." He blinks. "Mika. She—she's dead." His hands come back up, fire roaring. "What did you do?!"

This time, there's no room to dodge. Instead I *reach* for him, Kindre power snapping out and wrapping itself around his mind. If sensing his feelings is like a distant prickle on the skin or a whiff of a smell, this is plunging my arm into ice water and taking a long draught of something vile. I throw myself on his rage, smothering it, pressing his fear back into the dark crevices. He's tired, unaccustomed to drawing on his Well like this, and I bring that to the fore, filling him with the feeling of exhaustion.

Sewa blinks, and the fire fades away.

"I . . ." He looks at me, and there's still no recognition in his eyes. "I'm . . ."

"It's all right," I manage. "Go to sleep."

His eyes close, and he topples over.

That night, I have the dream again.

I wake up in my bed, arms and legs still aching. When I go out into the hall, the maids are waiting. Normally they would bow and go in to change the bedding, but now they just stand and stare at me, blank-eyed.

I stare back. Wave to them. Step closer. And then I see the strings. Impossibly thin wire, gleaming like fishing line, running from every joint on the bodies of these two women up into the air. When I step backward, they move toward me in lockstep. I raise my arms to ward them off, and find the other ends of the lines looped around my fingers.

My hands move of their own accord, and the maids step back and bow, going into the bedroom with eerie synchronicity. I run away, leaving them behind.

My tutor Ridatha is waiting for me at the breakfast table, a book open in front of her. She looks up, trapped in a web of glistening strings, and I trace the movement back to my crooked little finger.

"Is something wrong?" she says, and I speak the words with her, *for* her. I let my hands fall to my sides, and she slumps across the table, as inanimate as a doll.

I run to Ofalo's office, on the other side of the building. On the way, I pass other servants. Puppet guards, marionette footmen, gardeners going about their business, and I feel my fingers twitching to direct their every move. They call out to me, and I'm talking to myself.

Looking over my shoulder, I run into Ofalo in the hall. He bounces off me with a wooden clatter, his limbs swinging wildly as he bobs on his gossamer strands. I clench my fist, and he twists as though in pain, though his expression doesn't change.

"Lady Tori?" he says, and I can feel *my* lips moving. "What's wrong?"

There's a clatter by the front door, a carriage arriving. I race out onto the drive. The mannequins are getting cruder, less lifelike, unpainted toys with fixed expressions. Two of them bob around the carriage, opening the door.

Isoka gets out. Her Melos blades are ignited, brilliant green energy crackling and spitting as she moves. Very deliberately, she raises one of them above her head and brings it sideways in a decisive stroke. There's a *twang* like a piano string breaking, and threads cascade down all around her, their severed ends drifting in the breeze. I look down at my hands, and they're covered in blood.

"I'm here, Tori." I mean for Isoka to say it, but the words come out of my own mouth, and she only cocks her head.

"I should have known," she says, raising her blades. "I should have known you were a monster."

When I wake up, this time in reality, I can still feel the searing heat of her blade sliding into my chest. My heart hammers, and my shift is drenched in sweat. I don't scream, but only because I have a lot of practice.

The feeling of touching old Sewa's mind is still all over me, an oily taint I can't clean. The sun is low in the sky, which means I've only slept for a few hours, but I can tell closing my eyes again would be pointless.

I had to, I try to tell myself. *He could have hurt me badly.* I didn't think he *wanted* to, even in the depths of his fear, but he hadn't been in control of himself. *He could have burned half the building down, killed someone. I* had *to.*

Sometimes, you want to help someone, that means you get covered in shit. Grandma's voice makes me feel a little better, but only a little.

I get up and take a bath before breakfast. The water in the tub is chilly, but I don't want to wake the maids to heat it, and it still sluices away the sweat. I soak my hair, press it dry carefully, and go over it with a brush. Then I dress in a sky-blue *kizen* embroidered with purple plums, and pick a silver comb set with amethysts to match it.

None of the servants seem to notice anything's amiss, but Ofalo is more observant. After breakfast is cleared away, he leans toward me.

"Are you feeling unwell again, Lady Tori?"

I shake my head, a dull, throbbing pain behind my eyes.

"It's nothing," I tell him. "I didn't get enough sleep."

6

ISOKA

As it turns out, I don't get my chance to interrogate Veldi, our mysterious stranger, until the following morning.

There's too much that needs doing in the meantime. At Meroe's direction, teams fan out through the stone corridors of the ancient building. They find other entrances, one on each of the four sides, and we set guards on them. There are large central chambers on several levels, big enough to accommodate the crew several times over. We search one thoroughly and herd everyone inside. Another team finds a spring trickling into a rocky pool on the bottom level, and Meroe hurriedly orders every available skin and bottle filled.

The crew is a mass of confusion, friends and families separated in the chase, the crowd milling desperately as they seek familiar faces. Shiara takes charge there, sorting people out and restoring order. Most of those who were separated get reunited, but not all. We lost people in the mad dash, overrun and torn to pieces by the walking corpses.

A year ago, I wouldn't have cared. Even a month ago, I was ready to leave the crew behind, take Meroe and flee to the Garden on my own. She'd convinced me to try to help, instead. And now, somehow, they *expected* it from me, *relied* on me to keep them safe. And I hadn't done it.

It hurts. *Why does it hurt?*

I pause for a rest at some point. Just briefly, sitting down on a blanket some kind soul has spread across the stones, closing my eyes. When I open them, sunlight is slanting down into the chamber through high slit windows, and Meroe is sitting beside me, her head leaning on my shoulder. As I move, she yawns and stirs.

"Hey," I manage.

"Hey." She sits up and wipes gunk from her eyes. "I guess we're still alive."

"I guess so."

I kiss her, with only a brief hesitation due to the eyes all around us. It's not like we're keeping our relationship secret, but some habits die hard.

"If the sun's up," she says, "I want to go up to the roof. Maybe we can finally get a decent look at this place."

After confirming with the teams watching the doors that there had been no further attacks overnight, I follow Meroe up a four-sided spiral stair that runs around a shaft at the center of the building. With the fading of adrenaline, the pains of the night before are making themselves felt, and my legs are twinging by the time we get to the top. My arms have the bone-deep ache of powerburn, something I'm intimately familiar with. The crew's healer, Sister Cadua, is still caring for the injured, but I'll have to see if she salvaged any of her ointments.

The stairs end in a flat platform with a ladderlike arrangement of stones leading up through a square hole in the roof. I groan at the sight, and Meroe gives me a sympathetic look. She goes up first, and I follow, gritting my teeth. I'm breathing hard when we emerge into the glare of the sun, and I shade my eyes and look around.

At least all that climbing brought us a good view, far above the tops of the jungle trees. The building we've occupied stretches out below us, an immense stone ziggurat, pyramid-shaped but stair-stepped, built of huge stone blocks. Ramps run up the center of each side, leading to the four main entrances we'd discovered the night before, and bands of narrow slit windows ring the structure. Everything is carved from stone.

Ours isn't the only such building. Looking out over the jungle,

I can see more step-pyramids rising through the trees. Some are smaller than ours, others roughly on the same scale, while three in particular are truly enormous, towering half again the height of our viewing platform. In between, tall obelisks jut upward, tapered pillars of cut stone like enormous swords thrusting toward the sky. A few are intact, but most have lost at least part of their upper reaches, and some have toppled over entirely, barely visible through the jungle.

Turning, I look toward the sea. *Soliton* is still berthed in the gargantuan dock, along with the decaying hulks of the other ships. I can't see any activity among the angels on her deck, but there's a steady flow of Eddica energy still pouring out of the ship, invisible but strong enough that I can sense it easily from here.

"Look," Meroe says, tugging at my sleeve. "Over there. That looks like fields."

I follow her pointing finger. A large strip of land does seem to have been cleared of jungle, covered with a checkerboard of different colors. It's hard to tell from here, but I think I can see something moving, dark figures reduced to ants by the distance.

"Are those people?" I ask.

"I don't . . . think so." Meroe squints. "Should have brought my glass. But they're too big. Look, beside the trees. That thing must be the size of an ox."

She's right. Whatever the distant creatures are, they're not human. I'm not sure if that makes me more or less worried.

Toward the horizon, the sun gleams off a solid white mass. It takes me a moment to realize that I'm looking at *snow*. The misty dome we'd seen from *Soliton*'s deck is invisible from the inside, but the boundary line is still obvious. It's warm enough here that I'm considering shedding some of my leather armor, but somehow this whole jungle has been grafted into the middle of an icy wasteland.

"It has to be the same people," Meroe mutters.

"What people?"

"The people who built *Soliton*." She waves a hand excitedly. "Look at this place. A tropical forest, here in the far south. And those docks! Someone *made* all of this."

I nod slowly. It seems logical—well, not logical, but *plausible*—that people who could make a steel monstrosity the size of *Soliton* might be able to use magical power on a scale big enough to create a place like this. I've never heard of anything like it, but that doesn't mean much; I would have said *Soliton* itself was impossible before I'd seen it with my own eyes.

"It's all powered by Eddica," I tell her. "I can feel it. Power is running out from *Soliton* and into . . . something else, but there's smaller flows all through the place."

"That makes sense." She sighs. "As much sense as anything makes, anyway."

I pause. "Are you okay?"

"Fine." She leans against me. "Just don't . . . scare me like that. Last night, I thought . . ." She swallows. "Be careful."

"I'll do my best." We kiss again, more leisurely this time, although it reminds me how long it's been since I cleaned myself up. But there are more important things to worry about, for the moment. "Shall we see what our guest has to tell us?"

"I think so," Meroe says. "Though to be fair, we're the guests, aren't we?"

Back down in the belly of the ziggurat, the crew has started to explore. It looks like there's not much to find—just more big, empty rooms, striped with light from the narrow windows, any furnishings long since decayed. People spread out what blankets and cloth they have, though few had salvaged much in the rush to get off the ship. We have water, but food is going to be a problem pretty quickly. If those *are* fields out there, it might be worth an expedition to see what's growing in them.

First things first, though. Veldi, looking somewhat the worse for wear, sits on a blanket with Zarun standing behind him, backed up by a couple of armed crew. He looks up at me imploringly, tugging nervously at his braid-knot.

"I warned you that you were in danger!" he says. "I don't understand this suspicion. I'm only trying to help."

"Since I have no idea what in the Rot is going on here," I tell him, "you'll forgive me for being a little paranoid. I take it those monsters last night weren't friends of yours?"

He shudders. "Of course not. Those are Prime's creatures."

"Who is Prime?" I remember a withered face and dark eye sockets. "For that matter, who in the Rot are *you*?"

"Perhaps it would be better," Meroe says gently, "if you began at the beginning."

"Right. Yes." He straightens up a little and risks a smile in her direction. "We call this place the Harbor. Because the ship docks here, you see? It's . . . a city, I suppose, though somewhat overgrown now."

"Who's *we*?" I say.

"The Cresos clan." He gives a slight bow. "Servants to my lady Catoria."

"You arrived on *Soliton*?" Meroe says eagerly.

He nods. "Perhaps five years previously. At least, this is the fifth time the ship has returned. There are no seasons here, so time can be hard to judge."

Meroe frowns. "And the ship brings more people every time it comes back?"

"Not every time. Twice it has brought no one, and twice only a handful of souls. Yours is the first large group we've seen."

"The Rot," I mutter. "When the ship sails past the Vile Rot, the crabs and diseases kill everyone, unless they hide in the Garden."

"My lady believes that to be the case, yes," Veldi says. He seems to have relaxed a little, or at least forgotten Zarun looming ominously behind him. "I only followed her directions, so I know little of such matters."

"So—" I want to ask him if someone in his clan has an Eddica talent, but I think better of it. I don't want to tip our hand. Fortunately, Meroe fills the gap.

"Are you the only people here?"

"Unfortunately not," Veldi says. "We occupy one of the great ziggurats. Another is held by the Minder fanatics"—and here he *does* look at Zarun, with a disapproving twist to his lip—"and the third is Prime's territory."

"They were here when you arrived?" Meroe says.

"Prime has always been here, I think," Veldi says. "The Minders came with us on *Soliton*. They were our allies, until they betrayed us."

"So—"

Meroe's eyes are bright, eager to explore the mystery, but I hold up a hand to cut her off. "Where do you get food?"

"The angels bring us what we need," Veldi says. "They work the land, maintain this place."

"Can you get them to bring *us* something?"

"We cannot make them do anything," he says. "But we have more than enough in our stores." He bows again. "Please, let me return to my clan. I swear I will bring you a proper delegation and what food and supplies we can spare."

"Can you make it back there?" I ask him. "What about the corpses?"

"For the most part, they are only active at night," he says. "By day, the angels are about, and they destroy Prime's servants if they encounter them. But I thank you for your concern."

I purse my lips, and gesture to Meroe and Zarun. We step back a few paces.

"He's an odd one," I tell them. "The way he talks is . . . old-fashioned. But I don't get the sense he's lying."

"I don't see the harm in letting him go," Meroe says. "We *are* going to need food, and more besides. Bedding, clothes, medicine."

"He doesn't seem to care for Jyashtani," I say, looking at Zarun.

He shrugs. "He wouldn't be the first Imperial I've met to feel that way. As long as he doesn't try anything, we'll manage."

"All right. Tell him he can go, and we'll gladly accept his offer. Even if he just runs off, I suppose it can't hurt."

Meroe nods agreement. Zarun turns away to tell the prisoner the good news, leaving me and Meroe alone.

"Have you ever heard of a Cresos clan in the Empire?" she says.

"No, but I wouldn't have. Shiara knows more about court history, she might remember something." I glare at Veldi as Zarun helps him to his feet.

"You don't trust him?" Meroe says.

"That's not it. If *Soliton* comes back here every year, then . . ." I shake my head. "It has to leave soon. And I rotting *have* to be on it when it does, or else. . . ."

"I get it," Meroe says. "We'll find a way." Then her forehead creases, deep in thought.

Veldi departs on his own, jogging without fear into the jungle. He was serious about the monsters not being a problem during the day, apparently.

He claims he'll be back by evening. In the meantime, we keep everyone inside the ziggurat and guards on the doorways. Meroe and Shiara gather what food there is—scraps that happened to be in people's packs, or that they grabbed in haste when the angels came—and share it out as equitably as they can. It's a tribute to how much trust the crew has in Meroe after the Garden that those who have food give it up without a murmur.

Some of the fighters press me to let them go into the woods to hunt. If Veldi doesn't come through, tomorrow we'll have to risk it, but right now I don't want to split our strength when we have only his word for what's out there. One hungry day isn't going to kill anyone, I hope. I walk restlessly to the guard posts, checking up on things. It's something you learn as a ward boss—the value of being *seen,* even if you aren't really doing anything. Sometimes people treat leaders like fairy stories: if they can't see you with their own eyes, they don't believe you're real.

I wonder what's happened to the Sixteenth Ward. I've been gone long enough that they've probably appointed someone to fill my place. No one will question my disappearance much, I'm sure.

Except Tori. That thought gnaws at the back of my mind, and I pause by the northern entrance, which looks out to sea. *Soliton* is still there, docked beside her decayed sisters, looking for all the world like she's never going anywhere. But she is, and soon. I have to get back aboard.

"Deepwalker!" A trim young Jyashtani woman hurries up to me, offering a crisp salute. I recognize her, vaguely, as a fighter from one of Zarun's packs. "Someone's arrived."

"Veldi?" I ask her, turning away from the looming, silent ship.

"No, sir," she says. Her manner makes me wonder if she was a soldier before getting tossed onto *Soliton*. "It's a Jyashtani. Says his name is Harak. He's waiting just inside the south entrance."

"I'll talk to him," I say. "Find Zarun and tell him to meet me there. Meroe, too, if she's not busy."

"Yes, sir!" She salutes again, and takes off at a jog.

I thread my way through the ziggurat, passing through the big chamber most of the crew occupy. Now that it's clear the building is empty, a few have pitched their meager blankets in some of the other rooms in search of a little privacy. Back on *Soliton*, practically everything that hadn't been scavenged from tribute had come from the bodies of dead crabs—meat for food, shells for armor and construction, sinew for fiber. What hadn't come from crabs had been made from mushrooms. Learning to survive here in the jungle would be starting from scratch for the crew, unless the trees happened to hide enormous shelled monsters.

The ziggurat helped, sturdy and defensible in spite of its enormous age. And Veldi's people clearly manage, so if we have to stay here—

But I *can't* stay here. My hands tighten into fists. It's easy for the immediate problems to get in the way—back on *Soliton*, I'd let that happen, and my only excuse was that I'd had the better part of a year still to go. Now I have less time, probably *much* less, and I can't let myself get distracted again.

On the heels of these thoughts, I stride into the chamber just inside the southern doorway, where five crew with spears are waiting. "Well?" I bark, probably too loud, as they snap to attention. "Where is he?"

"Here I am," a deep voice says, and I turn.

The man—and it is emphatically a man—is a tall one, topping me by a head and a half, and broad to match. He wears the full, flowing trousers I associate with Jyashtani, gathered at the ankles with dark ribbons, plus leather sandals and little else. His torso looks like a doctor's anatomical diagram, with each muscle painstakingly picked out under dark, coppery skin. His hands are long-fingered and surprisingly delicate, but his arms are thick and fringed with short black hair. His head is shaved bald, gleaming like it's been oiled, but he's kept a thick black mustache, which droops down past the corners of his mouth.

I stop short, looking him over, and he clasps his hands Jyashtani-style and gives me a bow. It makes the muscles in his core shift in interesting ways, and I have an urge to feel them tighten under my fingers. Historically my preference in men has been lithe instead of bulky—like Zarun, for example—but I can't deny my eyes linger. The *scale* of him—

Focus, Isoka.

"Deepwalker," one of the guards says, sounding relieved.

"You said your name is Harak?" I ask the stranger, and he nods.

"I am. And you are Isoka Deepwalker." I'm able to follow his speech only with difficulty. In addition to a thick accent, he's speaking pure Jyashtani, and my knowledge of that language is limited. "I am here to welcome you to the place of the Divine Being."

"Okay," I tell him, mustering all the Jyashtani I can manage. "So who are you?"

"I am Harak," he repeats patiently. "Of the *gara-tseni*."

I grit my teeth. "I'm sorry, I don't understand."

"My order," he says. "Your people call us 'Minders.'" He mangles the Imperial word, but I recall Veldi saying something about "Minder fanatics." "Our *garash*, my *vettatol*, has sent me to bid you welcome, and to offer friendship to all those who would *gara tsen volta*—"

At that point I lose the thread entirely. Fortunately, there's a clatter of footsteps, and I look over my shoulder with a sigh of relief as Zarun arrives. Harak perks up as well, bowing deeper, and Zarun, looking surprised, matches his formal style. Harak rattles off a string of Jyashtani too fast for me to understand, and Zarun blinks.

"Can you understand him?" I ask.

"I think so. He sounds a little . . ." He cocks his head. "Pretentious?"

"Ask him what he wants."

Zarun nods and answers. After a short dialogue, he turns to me again.

"He says he's here to welcome us to the Harbor, the holy place of the Divine Being."

"I got that much. Something about 'garash' and an order?"

Zarun frowns. "You have monks in the Empire, yes? People who retreat from the world and devote themselves to religion?"

"We do. Less than we used to, I think." I remember something about a war between the monks and the Emperor, but I'm not sure if that's history or just a story. "Is that what he is?"

"More or less."

"My image of a monk is an old man with limbs like sticks and a long white beard." I nod at the avatar of masculine perfection in front of us. "Not *that*."

"There are many monastic orders in Jyashtan, and their traditions vary widely. His is called the *gara-tseni*, which is something like 'those who carefully watch,' or—"

"The Minders."

"Right," Zarun says. "*Garash* is the head of the order. He says anyone who wants to join them is welcome." He scratches the side of his head. "I think. He gets a little flowery there."

"Well." I pause for a moment, considering. "Tell him . . ."

I'm saved from having to continue that statement—since I have no rotting idea what to tell him—by the arrival of yet another out-of-breath messenger, this one a boy with a peach-fuzz beard.

"Deepwalker!" he says. "There's—"

"Let me guess," I say. "More visitors."

He gulps and nods. "Veldi's here, but there's a whole group with him. And they brought a bunch of stuff. They say there's food!"

That would at least be something to get excited about. I've been steadfastly ignoring the rumbles from my stomach since morning.

"Okay." I beckon to the leader of the door guards and nod at Harak. "Take him somewhere out of the way, politely, and tell him I'll be back as soon as I can. Zarun, stick with me, let's see what Veldi's friends have to say."

We follow the boy back through the central chambers. People are talking in small, excited groups, and I can almost see rumors winging their way through the air. If Veldi *hasn't* brought food after all, there's going to be a rotting riot.

"It looks good on you," Zarun says in my ear.

I frown at him. "What does?"

"Command."

"Please. You know I'm making this rot up as I go along."

"Of course. But you don't let it show." He gives me that brilliant smile, and I shake my head.

This time, our guards have already escorted the visitors to a small chamber inside the ziggurat. There are, as the messenger warned, quite a few of them. I count a dozen armed Imperials, including Veldi, all young men wearing old-fashioned swords, dark robes, and with their hair done up in the same strange, elaborate style. Four of them stand in a square around a young woman in a long, voluminous *kizen*, with a silk veil drawn in front of her face.

To one side of these dignitaries, there are another dozen people in less elaborate costumes. They're evenly split between dark-skinned southerners and pale, blond icelings dressed for labor in rough vests and trousers. Beside them is a pile of heavy canvas sacks, and barrels that seem to be mostly full of silver-skinned fish. Just the sight of it makes my mouth water.

Meroe and Shiara arrive only moments after we do. I'd badly like some time to consult with Meroe, actually, but that doesn't seem to be an option. As soon as they notice us, the Imperials stand and bow, and I respond automatically. The young woman steps forward, her four retainers following. Her bow is shallower, carefully precise.

"Isoka Deepwalker," one of the men says. "You represent the new arrivals?"

"In a manner of speaking," I say.

"My lady of Cresos, ruler of the Harbor, bids you welcome," he says. "She brings you these gifts as a token of her generosity."

"She has our thanks," I say.

The veiled figure beckons, and the man speaking leans closer so she can whisper. He straightens again and says, "My lady wishes to meet with you in private, if that is acceptable."

I glance at the others. "If what she has to say concerns our crew, then the whole Council should be there."

Another whisper.

"The southerner may attend," the man says. "But not the Jyashtani. My lady has suffered enough at the hands of his kind."

I go tense. Zarun's face is smooth, unreadable. I glare at the veiled woman.

"Give us a moment?" I ask, and step back with the others. "Any idea what's going on?"

"Imperials hate Jyashtani," Zarun says, with a shrug. "It's not exactly news."

"It was never a problem on *Soliton*," I say.

"*Soliton* is a ship full of dregs and outlaws," he says.

"They were on *Soliton*, too," Meroe says. "Something else is going on here."

"Their language is . . . odd," Shiara says. "But I'd guess they're noble-born."

"Why would Kuon Naga feed nobles to a rotting ghost ship?" I say.

"Because he had some he wanted to be quietly rid of?" Meroe says. "That's what my father did to me."

Rot. I hadn't thought of that. She doesn't seem upset, but I make a note to apologize later.

"I'm missing something," Shiara says quietly. "Cresos. It sounds familiar."

"I could tell them to go to the Rot," I say to Zarun. "I don't want to start off with them thinking they get to push us around."

"We need the food," he says. "Besides, I can hardly follow this formal talk anyway. I'll go see if I can get anything more out of Harak, and you find out what you can from Lady Cresos. Maybe if we compare notes we'll get somewhere."

I nod, feeling sour. Shiara, Meroe, and I return to the visitors, while Zarun heads back the way we came.

"Lady Cresos is more than welcome to meet with us," I say, "though we can't offer much in the way of hospitality. In the meantime, we would like to distribute your gifts among our crew as soon as possible."

"Of course," the man says. "Our servants will assist. Some of the Harbor's fruits will be unfamiliar."

The servants—all the non-Imperials—start picking up the sacks and barrels. I let them pass, then extend a hand, and the veiled woman follows us out. I note some sour looks among her attendants, but none of them speaks up.

We settle in another empty stone chamber—the ziggurat certainly doesn't lack for those—with a blanket spread on the floor. Lady Cresos sits, folding her legs beneath her in the nerve-deadening formal style. Shiara matches her neatly, and to my surprise, so does Meroe, with grace enough that you might have thought she was raised in the royal court. I suppose she was raised in *a* formal court, and probably had special training on dealing with Imperials.

I sit beside her, legs defiantly crossed, and wonder if I should fart and pick my nose to make the point. Lady Cresos inclines her head and reaches up to fold back her veil. When she straightens—

There's a blurred moment of confusion, and my heart skips a beat.

She doesn't look *that* much like Tori, really. She might be about the same age, thirteen or fourteen—has Tori's birthday passed? I've lost track of the date—with the same long, smooth black hair, curling down past her waist. She holds herself in much the same way, the careful manners inculcated by etiquette tutors, and a touch of powder enhances the pallor of her cheeks. Her eyes are different, wider and light brown.

Meroe is looking at me, concerned, and I grit my teeth. *Focus, Isoka. Tori is in Kahnzoka, Blessed knows how many miles away, and if I don't get out of here . . .*

"Thank you," Meroe says. "For the gifts. The angels didn't give us much time to gather supplies."

"They can be rude things, can't they?" the girl says, with the ghost of a smile. "It is nothing. They bring us more than we need, and I am pleased to share. You are the first newcomers in a long time."

"Lady Cresos—" I begin.

"You may call me Catoria, if you wish."

I pause, not sure of the etiquette, but eventually decide to take her at her word. "Catoria, then. My name is Isoka, and these are my fellow Council members Meroe and Shiara."

"An honor," Catoria says, with another slight bow.

"You said it's been a long time," Meroe says eagerly. "How long? And what happens when no one arrives?"

"Veldi said five years," I cut in. "What about *Soliton*? How long does it stay in the dock?"

Catoria holds up her hands, long sleeves brushing on the blanket. "I had a feeling you would be confused. Perhaps I should begin at the beginning?"

Meroe and I look at each other. I glance at Shiara, who has raised one painted eyebrow, as though to ask why I insist on making a fool of myself.

"Perhaps," I say, "that would be best."

7

TORI

"*Help!*" The boy sounds desperate. "Somebody help, *please.*"

His cry is nearly lost in the chaos. Grandma Tadeka's hospital, never empty, is now packed to the rafters. The longer-term patients have been moved upstairs, crowding two or three to a sleeping mat to make room for the flood of new arrivals. They started turning up just after dark, a blood-drenched, mud-spattered horde, stumbling in on their own or carried by friends, family, helpful strangers. There are five of us helping Grandma tonight, Kosura and I along with three older women, and while Grandma has sent out a call, extra assistance has been slow to arrive. So far, all we've been managing is to sort out the deluge.

The boy's voice nearly vanishes as I fight my way over to him, pushing through groups of men and women clustered around the injured. Kosura is trying to talk to a young man nursing a broken arm, while an older woman screams at her about her son needing immediate attention. One of the other assistants is pulling a man's twisted leg back into place—he lets out a piercing shriek and flails at her, which she ignores as she wraps the splint.

When I reach the boy, I find him standing over the prone body of a girl in her late teens, holding her limp hand in his. I don't see any injuries on her, but her robe is mud-stained, and she's unconscious. Her lips are flecked with blood.

"What happened?" I try to sound comforting, but I have to shout to make myself heard.

"One of the horses kicked her!" The boy, close to my age, is fighting back tears. "She was trying to get me out of the square, and the Ward Guard rode in. The horses—"

The girl coughs, weakly, spraying blood across the mud-tracked floor. I bend over to listen to her breathing, and it bubbles wetly. Something's badly broken inside her, and she's going to drown in her own fluids. There's certainly nothing *I* can do about it.

"Come on," I tell the boy. "Let's get her up."

Moving her can't be helpful, but there's no choice. I pull her off the floor, trying not to picture the jagged ends of broken ribs shifting and grinding. The boy gets under her other arm, sniffling, his tears cutting tracks through the grime on his face. Together, we walk toward the back of the room, where the curtains around Grandma's office have been extended to separate a whole section of the hospital floor.

"I'll take her from here," I say, when we reach the curtain. The boy seems too numb to question me. I take the girl's weight and stagger forward—she's bigger than I am, and her feet drag on the floor—pushing through the curtain.

Beyond, there are more sleeping mats, with more patients. All of these are considerably worse off than the people out on the main floor, and the air smells of blood and shit. Grandma Tadeka, her arms bloody to the elbows, works beside one heavily pregnant woman, while burly Hasaka carries a man's limp, bloodstained body to a mat in the corner with surprising gentleness. Giniva, the mage-blood girl whose sister I'd turned away from the sanctuary, is changing bandages, with the look of someone who's about to be sick but is determined to press on anyway.

I find the nearest empty mat and let the girl down as gently as I can. I check, and she's still breathing, though she seems weaker. As I straighten, I hear an infant's high, piercing wail, and turn to see Grandma calling Giniva over. She hands her a cloth-wrapped bundle that must be the baby.

"Take her upstairs," Grandma says, over the crying. "Find Menako, she'll know what to do."

Giniva nods, nervously, and hurries off. Grandma heads in my direction, wiping her gory hands on a rag.

"Is she going to be all right?" I can't help but ask.

"The baby will be fine. The mother won't. Too much blood." Grandma's tone is clipped, clinical, but I can hear the strain in her voice. If I dared to open my mind—which, right now, would be like inviting a hundred people to scream in my ears—I know I would feel her turmoil, in spite of her brave face.

As a ghulwitch, she can do more than any ordinary doctor. But her powers aren't unlimited, and the more she has to intervene the better the chance of something going wrong. On a day like this, she has to ration her strength, and I know she must already be nearing her limits. I can't imagine what I would do in her place, faced with so much pain, knowing that I could help some, but not all—

"Who's this?" she says, looking down at the girl.

I shake myself. It's been a long night. "I don't know. A boy brought her in, said a horse kicked her."

Grandma rips the girl's robe open, and I have to fight an automatic urge to look away, out of modesty. There's a mess of torn, bloody skin in the center of an enormous purple bruise. Grandma frowns, and lays her hand on the girl's forehead. I feel a faint prickling across my skin as she invokes her Ghul Well. This is forbidden magic, the stuff that created the Vile Rot and nearly ended the world, but it never seems like much when Grandma uses it. Often it has no visible effect at all.

"She's dying," Grandma says. "Broken ribs punctured the lung. She won't last an hour."

I sit back on my haunches, feeling the weight of exhaustion. Grandma looks down at the girl for a moment, then sighs and closes her eyes. A faint purple aura flickers around her hands. The girl stiffens, and draws in a sharp breath.

A few seconds, and it's done. The girl breathes out, without the awful wet sound. Grandma sits back, her shoulders slumping.

"Did what I could," she says. "The ribs will have to heal the rest of the way on their own. Tell her people to keep her in bed."

"I will." I bow my head. "Thank you."

"Don't thank me yet. We're not done." She gets back on her feet, a little wobbly, and gestures to Hasaka, who hurries over. "Take her out and give her a blanket and some water."

I tug the girl's torn robe so she's mostly covered. Hasaka comes back with a sheet, and we put it around her shoulders. Together, he and I lift her, and carry her back through the curtain. For obvious reasons, only those who know Grandma's secret—people from the mage-blood sanctuary, for the most part—can be allowed in the back.

The boy explodes into tears when I tell him the girl—his sister? I have no idea—will live, and we set her on a mat and give him Grandma's instructions. He nods, frantic and sniffling. I turn to go back to the front, to see who else needs help, but Hasaka takes me by the shoulder.

"Tori," he says quietly. "I've been in the back with Grandma since this started. Has anyone told you anything about what happened?"

"Just a little," I tell him. "There was a group stuck at the draft checkpoint near the High Market, and they started shouting at the guards, chanting, that kind of thing. The Ward Guard ordered them to disperse, and . . ." I shake my head. "Nobody seems to know how it started, but pretty soon people were throwing rocks, and the Ward Guard were laying out everyone in sight. When their cavalry showed up, they charged the crowd."

That's the story I've pieced together, anyway, from the two dozen people I've talked to. Wounded are still coming in, though the flood has slowed a little. The majority were hurt in the stampede that had followed the guard cavalry's charge, thrown against buildings or trampled underfoot.

It's becoming a depressingly familiar sight here at the hospital. Nearly every day sees someone injured by the guards at the checkpoints. The haul of recruits must not be meeting the quotas, because the enforcers have daily become more insistent.

"Again," Hasaka says with a sigh. "Rotting idiots in the guard. Don't they see where this is going to end? How long do they think they can keep pushing people?"

I give an uncomfortable shrug. "I'd better go see if they need help at the front."

Hasaka nods and trudges back behind the curtain, and I hurry to Kosura, who is setting yet another broken arm. Thankfully, the girl with the broken ribs is the last serious case of the evening, and we spend the rest of our time dealing with injuries that fall within my competence. At Grandma's direction I've learned to bandage, splint, and stitch, and a little bit about herbs and poultices. Kosura knows more than I do, as usual, and her inner reserve of kindness and patience seems limitless. By the time we close the doors, long after midnight, she still has a kind word for patients begging for extra blankets we don't have and liquor we won't give them, whereas my own attitude has turned distinctly snappish.

Hasaka arrives to lock up the main doors, speckled with blood as though he'd just come from an abattoir.

"Tori, Grandma wanted to see you before you leave," he says, as he passes. "Go talk to her so she can get some sleep, would you?" Hasaka considers himself the guardian of Grandma's health, though no one else—least of all Grandma—agrees with this.

I nod and head back to the curtained-off section. On the way, I pass Giniva, dressed in a fresh robe but her skin and hair are still smeared with gore. She's clutching her soiled clothes to her chest, looking at the ground. I give her a bow as she passes.

"Thank you for your help."

"What?" She looks up, and there's a moment before she recognizes me. "Oh. Yes. I thought . . . it was the least I could do."

"Go back and get some rest." It feels strange to be giving advice to this girl several years my senior, but she looks so lost.

"I will." She gives another halfhearted nod and wanders away.

Grandma is cleaned up and behind her desk, leaning back and staring at the cracked, cobwebbed ceiling. At first I think she's fallen asleep like that, but without looking down she says, "Did you see the new girl?"

"I did," I say. "She seems a little shaken."

"She'll be all right in the end." Grandma rolls her head, wringing a series of *cracks* from her neck that make me jump. "It would be a kindness if you would check up on her from time to time. When things are calm, anyway."

"I will," I say. Though when that will be I don't know. "Hasaka said you wanted to see me before I left?"

"I did." She sits up and looks at me. Her face is drawn, very pale, exhaustion kept in check only by her iron will. "Got something for you today. A letter."

"A letter? From who?"

"Don't know. Some street kid dropped it off." She produces an envelope, sealed with unmarked white wax, and pushes it across the desk. "Tori" is written on the outside in a neat hand. "I don't want to pry into your affairs. But if there's some kind of problem, just tell me, you understand? I have friends, we'll take care of it."

I nod, dumbly, as I pick up the letter. The paper is startlingly white. Expensive. It's the kind of thing I'd expect to see back home in the Second Ward, not here.

"That's all," Grandma says. "Go and get some sleep."

A few minutes later, I'm in the back of a cab, rattling up the military road toward the Second Ward. The passes and identification I carry are enough to make the Ward Guard at the gates snap to attention, and a coin or two encourages them not to ask questions. Normally I try to get home earlier than this, and the thought of my sleeping mat is already pulling at my eyelids.

I resist the urge to doze in the carriage, though, and turn my attention to the letter. When I break the wax seal, I find several folded pages inside, written in the same well-tutored hand.

> *Tori,*
>
> *I hope this letter doesn't cause you any alarm. Your secrets are in no danger, I promise. After our meeting, I asked around the neighborhood for anyone who matched your name and description, and from what I was told the best place to reach you is at Grandma Tadeka's hospital. I pray that the Blessed allows this to find you.*
>
> *We met in an alley behind the High Market, where you saved my honor—and very possibly my life—with an exceedingly brave deception. I admit that it has taken me some time to work*

up the courage to pen this. But, ultimately, I felt that if I let this chance meeting slip by, I would regret it for the rest of my life.

I must be honest with you. I am not a native of the Eleventh Ward, as I pretended to be. My name is Marka Garo, and my family resides in the First Ward. My father is an Imperial Minister of the Fourth Degree, and I am his oldest son and heir.

I break off reading for a moment, surprised. I'd guessed the boy that I'd rescued wasn't a commoner—he wasn't fooling anyone, really—but I hadn't thought he was a *Marka*. They're a noble family, and not an insignificant one, either. A Minister of the Fourth Degree is high up the Imperial bureaucracy, only one or two steps removed from the Emperor's inner circle.

Why had I given him my name?

I take a breath to calm my beating heart. All he knows is that I work at Grandma's, and anyone who lives near the hospital could tell him that.

I know that you are no commoner, either. Your breeding shines through, however you might try to hide it. Rest assured I will make no efforts to discover your identity. Hearing about you from the people of the Eleventh Ward, it is evident that you have been doing for years what I have only recently and hesitantly tried to put into practice—helping those who truly need assistance.

I must see you again. I have given you my name, and I am at your mercy. Choose a place and a time, whatever you need to feel safe, and I will be there. Please. You can leave a note for me with the proprietor of Walka's noodle shop, and I will receive it within a few days.

> *Your devoted admirer,*
> *Marka Garo*

I let the letter fall into my lap as the cab pulls in through the Second Ward gate.

Well. Rot.

* * *

"Oh, Blessed above!" Kosura's voice is a high-pitched squeal, and I frantically motion her to keep quiet.

We're on the second floor of the hospital, in the back, working at stripping and rolling up some old sleeping mats so the whole area can be cleaned. It's far enough from any patients or other assistants that I judged I could risk showing her the letter, after swearing her to secrecy on the direst oaths I could think of.

I had to show *someone*. Kosura seems like the best choice in a field of one—I don't want to trouble Grandma, and I can't trust anyone back at the Second Ward house.

"Would you be quiet?" I hiss.

"Sorry." She looks over the letter again. "It's just so . . ."

"I know!" I shake my head.

"If I didn't know any better, I'd think he was playing a prank on you. 'Your devoted admirer'?"

"Who *talks* like that? Writes. Whatever."

"Nobles, I suppose." She shakes her head.

"So what am I supposed to do?"

"Do?" Kosura looks at me sharply. "You're going to go meet him, of course."

"Why 'of course'? It seems like the dumb move to me."

"Because he's *obviously* madly in love with you. You can't just ignore someone when they're madly in love with you."

"Why not?"

She sniffs. "It's rude."

"Anyway." I feel a flush creeping into my cheeks. "He can't be madly in love with me. He only met me for a couple of minutes!"

"A couple of minutes where you saved his life."

"I didn't—"

"And you took off your shirt."

"I didn't take it *off*." I snatch the letter back from her, cheeks fully red now, and she dissolves into giggles. "Are you going to help me or not?"

"What did *you* think of *him*?"

"I told you, I only met him for a couple of minutes."

Kosura rolls her eyes. "Is he handsome?"

"I don't remember," I say, exasperated. "Maybe. I suppose."

"You liar." She grins. "You have to go and meet him."

"And say what?" I cross my arms. "I have no plans to fall madly in love with anyone, so if that's what he wants he's going to be disappointed."

"He *says* he wants to help people." Kosura's tone sobers. "Which is the same reason you and I are here, isn't it?"

I give a reluctant nod.

"And if he really is the heir to the Marka family, he might be able to." She cocks her head. "You know Grandma always says we can use more of everything."

That's true, now more than ever. In treating the victims of the riots, the hospital is running short of everything from bedclothes to bandages.

"If he's sneaking out like I am, I doubt he's going to be able to hand over a big purse," I say.

"You never know. It's worth the meeting, anyway." Kosura claps me on the shoulder. "Just set it up somewhere nice and public. You'll be fine."

I let out a long sigh and look down at the letter.

"I'm going to have to do this, aren't I?"

"Make sure to wear something slinky," Kosura says, then runs away, laughing, as I look for something to throw at her.

A few days later, I'm sitting at a low table in Takabo's dumpling shop, off the High Market.

I've been in Takabo's many times, but only on the bottom floor, where you order your dumplings from sweating men working behind the counter and eat them standing up, pulling them off the wooden skewers as soon as they're cool enough to stomach. The upper floor is more refined, with individual tables, and correspondingly more expensive. Since my only way of getting spending money involves selling things from home—which always carries the risk that Ofalo will notice and accuse someone of the theft—I've always stayed down below.

For today, though, this place has several advantages. It's above the draft checkpoints, so there's no danger of Garo running into trouble again before he even gets here. And while the second floor is higher class than the first, it's still a dumpling house, with no privacy screens or curtained-off nooks. Takabo and his staff are no strangers to altercations, and if Garo has anything ugly planned, I'll be able to summon help easily.

So I hope, anyway. If someone with the resources of the Marka family wanted to prepare a trap, I'm sure he could manage it. Whatever Kosura says, this meeting is a risk. The only reason I'm willing to chance it is that my Kindre power should warn me well in advance of any ill intentions. Right now, the restaurant is the usual mix of everyday emotion, happiness and sadness, pleasant food, liquor, and conversation.

I'm wearing a colorful linen robe, sleeves rolled up, less formal by far than a *kizen* but still more obviously feminine than my usual disguise. No point in trying to confuse Garo on *that* score, and the thought makes me blush again. I try to fight it, but I realize I'm nervous, in spite of the tranquility of the minds around me.

It's not just fear of some kind of trap. This whole situation isn't something I'm comfortable with. Kosura is practically the only person close to my age I know well—most of the hospital assistants are much older, and I've never let myself get close with many of the patients.

What if Kosura's right, and Garo *has* fallen in love with me? His note was certainly . . . intense. It's all well and good to sigh about, but what do I actually *do*?

My fingers beat a fast tattoo on the table. One of the servers comes over, clearing his throat, but I wave him off.

I'm still trying to think when Garo arrives, coming up the stairs and looking hesitantly around the room. He's wearing the same simple clothing as the last time I saw him, subtly too well-cut to actually belong to a member of the lower classes. His dark brown curls are a little more pronounced, and I wonder if he's put some effort into them. When he sees me, his eyes go wide for a moment, and he nearly crashes into a server with a tray full of dumplings.

"You came," he says.

"I said I would, didn't I?" I say, trying for confidence.

"I wasn't sure." I don't need Kindre to feel the relief pouring off him. "I wasn't even sure I'd written to the right place."

"Sit down, would you?" I glance at the surrounding diners. "We don't need to make a spectacle."

"Of course." He sits, with the unconscious grace of someone trained from childhood in formal etiquette. "You look . . . different. If I'd seen you like this I wouldn't have thought you were a boy—I mean, until you—that is, I—"

"Please stop." I can't help but smile a little. "Relax."

"All right." He takes a deep breath. "I'm sorry. It's just . . . you don't know how much I've been thinking about you."

"Thinking about me?" Now it's my turn to look flustered.

"You saved my life."

"Let's not be dramatic," I say, looking at the table. "Even if they'd taken you in, I'm sure your family would—"

"Nobody knows I'm here," he says. "Certainly not my father. He'd have me beaten black and blue if he found out."

"Well. I'm glad I saved you a beating, then."

"It's not just that. I—"

The server chooses that moment to reappear, getting down on her knees beside the low table to ask for our order. This appears to throw Garo completely off stride, so I intervene. I order two portions of each of my favorites: soup dumplings, crispy fish rolls, and the sort of fried pork dumplings that the street vendors charmingly refer to as "dead mice" for their vaguely rodent-like shape. Garo looks on as though I'm performing some great feat of scholarship, and leans forward over the table after the server leaves.

"Sorry," he says again. "This is all a little new to me."

"What is?"

He waves a hand. "You know. All of this."

"Restaurants?" I say it half-jokingly, but he gives an earnest nod.

"At home we'd be served in our chambers, or in the hall if we had guests." He looks around at the other patrons. "Do you know when we're supposed to pay? Is it before we eat, or after?"

"After." I stare at him for a moment. This is the point at which Isoka would say *rotting aristos,* especially if she thought I wasn't listening, but I'm more bemused than anything. Obviously, I didn't go out to restaurants with Ofalo, but . . . "What are you *doing* here?"

"It's a fair question, I suppose." He sighs. "What I *want* to be doing is the same thing as you. I think."

"What do you think that is?"

"Doing something for these people." He lowers his voice again. "That's why you're here, isn't it? You work at the hospital."

"I do," I say, cautiously.

"Back home everyone *talks* about helping the people. My friends do, anyway." He shakes his head. "A bunch of . . . of rich layabouts, sitting in silk robes eating off silver plates, wondering how they can *help.* Every so often they'd find some beggar who the servants had vetted to make sure he was clean and worthy, and make a great show of sending him off with a bag of gold. Then everyone would congratulate each other." Garo takes a deep breath. "I may be . . . inexperienced, but I know that isn't going to solve any problems."

I nod. We pause, for a moment, as a pair of servers lay the table with wooden plates covered in steaming dumplings. Garo looks intrigued, and grabs a soup dumpling immediately.

"You want to wait a little bit," I say, "or—"

He gives a squeak as he bites into it, and I sigh.

"Or you'll burn yourself." I pour him a cup of tea. "Here."

"Sorry," he mumbles. "Again."

"So," I say. "Why are you and your First Ward friends so worried about people down here?"

"I . . ." He looks worried. "For some of them it's . . . fashionable, I suppose. You know, the sort of thing people talk about at dinner."

"For the sake of argument, assume that I don't," I say, fighting back a grin.

"It's like . . . the Plight of the People." I can hear the capital letters. "The Moral Decay of Modern Society. And how it's our duty to Give Back, and to Lead by Example." He squares his jaw. "I used to laugh at all that, you know. When I was younger. But then I started reading about what actually happens down here! Families crammed into tenements, thick with fleas, nothing but rice and weak soup for dinner. . . ."

He trails off, and I realize my incredulousness must show in my expression.

"Of course," he says, looking down at the table. "You must think I'm ridiculous."

"I don't." Not entirely, anyway. I take a few moments to sort through my feelings.

What I want to say is, it's so much worse than you can imagine. Where I grew up, people killed one another over a half bowl of rice, or a place to sleep, because that rice or a bunk in the warm for a night could mean the difference between making it through another winter or not. Every spring, when the snow melted, we'd find street kids in the alleys, frozen as hard as icicles.

Where I grew up, my sister taught me to stay away from anyone who offered me food, because the kidcatchers would use scraps of bread to lure children off on their own. And if they caught you, that meant rape and sale to a slave brothel somewhere, or just a slit throat if they thought you weren't worth the trouble.

It meant waking up to find your sister's knife at your throat, and seeing the tears in her eyes, and knowing exactly what she was thinking. And half-wishing she'd do it, just to make an ending.

I can't say any of that to Garo, of course.

Cautiously, I open myself to his mind. There's a hint of the citrus taste of embarrassment, the twinkling shimmer of anxiety, even—unless I imagined it?—a hint of the rapid drum-hammer of attraction. But under and around all of that, drowning it out, is sincerity, a brassy trumpet note like a clarion call.

He's staring at me.

"All right," I say. "You wanted to help, and you were fed up. So you came here?"

He nods. "I thought . . . I don't know. I thought it would be simple, somehow. Everyone always talked about fixing our problems like it would be easy, if only the right people got together. I should have known better." He gives a bitter laugh. "I didn't even know where to begin. And then the guards started chasing me."

"Because you ran away from a draft checkpoint."

"I didn't know they wanted me to stop." He shifted uncomfortably. "Guards shouting at me is . . . another new experience. I ran into the alley, and you . . . distracted them."

"Okay." I don't want him to dwell on that part. "So what do you want with me now?"

"I want you to teach me." He puts his hands on the table. "I'm not too proud to admit I don't know what I'm doing. And you . . . when I asked about you, they said you've been coming here for years. You can't have been more than ten years old at the beginning!"

"Eleven," I say, which is rounding up just a fraction. For some reason I don't want him to think I'm *that* much younger than him.

"You were eleven years old and you were just *doing* what I'd only talked about for so long. Making a difference to actual people."

"I suppose."

"Will you let me be . . ." His brow wrinkles awkwardly, an oddly adorable expression. "Your apprentice, I guess?"

I snort a laugh. "*That* isn't something I ever thought someone would say to me."

"But you understand—"

"I understand." I peek at his mind again, guilty and fascinated, and feel that brassy sincerity. He really means it. "You know it's not going to be anything grand, right?"

"I understand that. Now I do, at any rate."

"Half of what I do is . . . laundry, cleaning, that sort of thing."

"I may not be very skilled at that," he says earnestly. "But I can learn, I swear it."

"Well." I scratch my cheek in a show of consideration. "I suppose I can ask Grandma if she has any use for you."

I'm unprepared when he reaches across the table and grabs my hands. I nearly leap backward, but he's already bowing his head in thanks, his eyes sparkling.

"You won't regret it," he says. His hands are warm, larger than mine, skin smooth and free of calluses. I hold still for a moment longer, then pull away. My cheeks are very warm.

"Let's hope not," I say. "Now. First lesson, apprentice."

"Yes?"

I grab a dumpling with my chopsticks and pop it into my mouth, and it practically explodes with warm, fatty flavor. "Eat your dumplings before they get cold."

8

ISOKA

"I was only twelve years old when my clan was destroyed," Catoria says. "Two of my wicked uncles had conspired against the Emperor's peace. My father, the youngest son, had nothing to do with it, but the Emperor ordered our family torn out root and branch. My mother took poison, as did my older sister. My father met with the Imperial Guard when they arrived, to beg for my life, and for that the Emperor's marshal rewarded him with a painful death in the dungeons. I expected to die myself. Instead I was imprisoned with two dozen of my relations, children and teenagers, mostly cousins from the lower branches of the family.

"Some of us thought we were going to be exiled, as an act of Imperial mercy. Others guessed the Emperor had devised an even more gruesome fate for us. I suppose both were correct, in a way. One foggy summer night, the Guard drove us in a sealed wagon down to the docks."

"And rowed you out to *Soliton*," I guess.

She inclines her head. "Indeed. You all shared that experience, so I don't need to explain the conditions aboard the ship. When we arrived, *Soliton* was empty of human life, though we found plenty of scraps and ruins. We huddled together in the lower decks, hiding from the crabs, only slowly learning to hunt. Few of us had any experience using our Wells in combat."

Aristos. I manage to keep the thought to myself. *They work so hard to keep mage-blood in their family lines, and then do rot-all with it.* It's hard to hold on to my scorn, though, seeing the sorrow on Catoria's face.

"I was the heir to the Cresos clan," she went on. "My uncle's families had been exterminated, and so I was the last survivor of the main line. My cousins defended me as best they could, and though some of them gave their lives, little by little we established ourselves. As *Soliton* passed through the Southern Kingdoms and the Waste, more sacrifices came aboard, and they agreed to serve the clan in exchange for our protection.

"Later that year, however, another large group came aboard somewhere in Jyashtan." Her voice went hard. "They called themselves the Minders, and at first they refused any offer of cooperation. There were even fights between us, though we kept apart. Other Jyashtani sacrifices joined them, and soon there were two growing communities.

"From Jyashtan, *Soliton*'s path took it north and east, into the lands of the icelings. More sacrifices came and they split between the two groups. But there was one among them, a girl named Silvoa. She . . ."

Catoria pauses, swallows. I can feel Meroe nearly bursting with unasked questions, but she manages to restrain herself.

"Silvoa brought us together. She came to me and to Gragant, the Minders' leader, and showed us the folly of our feud. She was . . . persuasive." Again, that very slight smile. "We agreed to work together, under her leadership, and we gained the upper hand over the crabs. Some of my family even started to talk about finding a way off *Soliton*, back to Kahnzoka, to revive the clan."

"Did you find a way past the angels?" I say, trying not to sound *too* interested.

Catoria shakes her head. "Silvoa had some ideas. But things changed before we could try any of them."

"Changed how?" Meroe says.

"Silvoa started hearing . . . voices." Catoria pauses for a moment, takes a deep breath. "I didn't believe her at first. We fought. It wasn't until later that she . . . convinced me. She said that *Soliton* itself was talking to her, and it wanted us—"

"To find the Garden," I say, grimly.

"Yes." Catoria gives a satisfied nod. "I suspected as much when

Veldi told me so many of you came ashore. You have someone who can hear the voice of the ship, too."

"We do," I say. Shiara catches my eye, silently urging caution, and I stop there.

"Then I imagine you know what happened. We and the Jyashtani fought our way forward to the Bow, and Silvoa led us into the Garden and closed the doors behind us. Sometime later the ship passed the Vile Rot, and we heard the crabs going mad outside."

It sounds like they'd had a considerably easier time of it than we did. Part of that was down to the Scholar trying to kill everyone in his mad bid to seize control, of course, but if we'd set out earlier, I wonder how many more might have been saved. Another thing I wouldn't have cared about, before.

"We arrived here, at the Harbor," Catoria says, "and the angels forced us off the ship. When we reconnoitered inland, we encountered Prime's monsters, and they began to harry us by night. Silvoa led us to shelter in one of the great ziggurats, and the angels began to deliver food from the fields. Eventually we explored the rest of the city and found the second empty ziggurat, along with the one inhabited by Prime. We pushed his creatures back, and for a while it seemed . . ."

She trails off, her face pinched. I notice one sleeve of her *kizen* is wrapped in her fist, fingers squeezed tight.

"Silvoa had a theory," she goes on eventually, when none of us break the silence. "In each of the great ziggurats there's a . . . she called it an *access point*. A room studded with metal bars and pipes. Silvoa said she could talk to the city there, the same as she could talk to *Soliton*."

I thought of the chamber where I'd fought the Scholar, deep within the Garden, full of the metal conduits that conducted Eddica power through the ship like blood through a body. There were other places I'd been able to feel the flow, but never so strongly as in that room.

Here, in the Harbor, I'd felt nothing of the kind. Only the vast current of energy from *Soliton* into the city was visible at all, and even that felt distant, obscured. Certainly my attempts to touch it with my own power had been fruitless. I'd wondered if the city functioned in the same way as the ship—it apparently had angels of its own—but . . .

"After visiting the two ziggurats we could access," Catoria says, "Silvoa thought that if she could only reach the third, the city would . . . recognize her. Accept her as its master. I don't fully understand what she wanted, but she insisted she had to go to Prime's fortress. I tried to convince her it was too dangerous." Catoria lets go of the twisted loop of silk and looks down at her hands.

"I begged her not to go, and in the end she agreed. She *agreed*." The girl pauses again. "But Gragant talked to her while I was asleep, and convinced her to try. He and some of his Minders went with her, and some of my men as well. Silvoa was certain that she could speak to Prime, negotiate with him." Catoria shakes her head. "Only Gragant returned. Silvoa and the rest died there, at the hands of Prime's creatures. Just as I'd said they would."

"Did he tell you what happened to them?" Meroe says. "Or who 'Prime' actually—"

"He claims he saw little," Catoria spits. "The guilt, I imagine, was too much for him. He betrayed me, and he betrayed Silvoa, whom he'd sworn to serve. I do not . . . wish to speak of him." She clears her throat. "The Minders left us soon afterward, taking up residence in the other great ziggurat. Since then, we've waited for *Soliton* to return. It's been five years. The first four times, no one disembarked. I suppose no one survived the passage of the Rot. But now you've come." Her smile widens, becoming a little more genuine. "Swear loyalty to the Cresos clan—to me—and you can join us."

"Well?" I ask Meroe. "How much of that do you believe?"

"That is . . . a good question," Meroe says.

We're standing against the wall of one of the large chambers, where most of the crew has settled. Shiara is helping supervise the distribution of the Cresos clan's gifts to the crew. In addition to the food, there are blankets and rolls of mottled, tightly woven cloth. I wonder if that comes from the angels, too.

Our crew gather around eagerly. Catoria's people open the sacks, distributing large, round fruit with hard rinds, which they demonstrate how to crack to get at the sweet, grape-sized seedpods. There are berries, also unfamiliar-looking but delicious, and some kind of yellow tuber. Cookfires are hastily kindled for these, along with the barrels of fish, and the smell drifting over to us is unbearably delicious.

Meroe is eating a stone fruit, a bit like a plum but with an apple's firm flesh, with the careful delicacy I would expect of a princess. I've already torn through a bowl of berries and one of the hard-shelled things, and I'm working on a second, wiggling the pods out of the shell and popping them into my mouth, then spitting out the small, hard seeds.

"Something doesn't add up," Meroe says. "Literally add up. Catoria said *Soliton* delivered them five years ago."

"Veldi said the same thing."

"But *Soliton* didn't come here five years ago. It was still sailing around the Central Sea. You and I weren't onboard yet, but plenty in the crew were."

I frown. "The Scholar said the oldest people in the crew had been there more than fifteen years."

"Right. And obviously *Soliton* didn't go past the Rot in all that time, and it certainly didn't stop here and throw everyone off."

"So Catoria's lying," I say.

"She doesn't *sound* like she's lying," Meroe says. "She sounds . . . I don't know." She looks away, uncertain.

"What?"

"Lonely." Meroe sighs. "Maybe I'm just seeing a little of myself there."

"She seems to have plenty of people around."

"They're retainers and servants. Believe me, it's not the same." Meroe shrugs. "Anyway, I don't think she's lying to us deliberately. But she may be confused."

"She says *Soliton* comes here every year," I mutter. "But obviously it can't be doing that, since we know people who've been on it for years."

Meroe's eyes widen. "Could there be more than one ship? You saw the docks."

"Blessed help us. One of the things is bad enough." I shake my head. "Kuon Naga seemed certain there was only one, and he would know, if anyone would."

"Then maybe Catoria is wrong about how long it's been," Meroe says. "Veldi says there's no seasons here, so maybe what she thinks is a year is . . ."

She trails off, and I can see why. "Twenty years? Someone would notice *that*. She says she was twelve when she was picked up, and she looks younger than me." If it really had been five years, that would make her my age. I had guessed her at closer to Tori's. "She's sure as Rot not *thirty*."

"She may be older than you think," Shiara says.

Shiara glides over, graceful as always. In one hand she holds three skewered, blackened fish, from which a fantastic smell is rising. She hands one to me, and I tear into it with my teeth. It's unseasoned and unevenly cooked, and still the best thing I've ever tasted. It's amazing how a couple of hard days without food change your perspective.

Meroe takes her fish and pulls it apart with her fingers, popping white slivers into her mouth. Shiara follows suit, which makes me feel like a barbarian, as usual. For now, though, I'm too absorbed to worry about it, sucking scraps of meat from the thin, flexible bones.

"What do you mean?" Meroe says, between bites.

Shiara pauses before answering. She'd remained silent through Catoria's story, which is typical of her. Of the old Council—Zarun's easy smile and casual violence, Karakoa's bluff honor, the Butcher's cruelty and pride—Shiara is the one I understand the least. Since we came to the Garden, she's worked with me and Meroe without complaint, but I still know almost nothing about her. From manners and appearance, at least, you'd think she was Imperial highborn, but something makes me doubt it.

"I remembered where I'd heard the name Cresos," Shiara says now. "I knew it sounded familiar."

"And?" I mumble, licking my lips. My fish is mostly bare, and I already want another.

"It was in a history book. The Cresos clan plotted treason against the Emperor, but they were discovered and exterminated."

"That matches what Catoria said . . ." I begin.

Meroe is quicker on the uptake, as always. "*When* were they exterminated?"

"In the reign of the current Emperor's revered grandfather, if I'm remembering correctly," Shiara says, with surprising calm. "At least eighty years ago."

"*Eighty* years?" I manage.

"Probably more like a hundred," Shiara says. "I don't have the exact dates, but I remember a little about the period. That was a dangerous time for the Emperor. He'd just lost a war against the Jyashtani, and the nobles were restless."

History has never been an interest of mine, so I focus on the matter at hand. "How can Catoria have gotten to the Harbor a hundred rotting years ago?" Something awful occurs to me. "Blessed's balls. Is she even rotting *human*?" If corpses could walk, then maybe—

"I thought so," Meroe mutters. "It's the only thing that makes sense. Some kind of sense, anyway—"

"Please enlighten us if you have any idea what's going on," I snap, then take a deep breath. "Sorry."

Meroe's shaky smile is reassuring. "Okay. I don't know how any of this is possible, but I'm just thinking aloud. If nobody's lying, and there aren't multiple ships, then somehow *time* has gone rotten."

Shiara raises one eyebrow. "That *would* explain things."

"Gone rotten how?" I say.

"What if it runs differently under the dome? One year passes in here, and twenty years pass outside. So for Catoria *Soliton* comes by every year, but outside—"

"And they think it's normal," I say, struggling to stay ahead of her, "because they only spent a year on the ship before it came here."

"Five years for them, a hundred years for us," Shiara says. "*Soliton* came and went four times, gathering sacrifices all the while. But none of those groups had an Eddica user so none of them could find the Garden. They must have all died at the Rot."

"I've never heard of any Well that could affect time," Meroe says, thoughtfully. "But the city is powered by Eddica energy, the same as *Soliton*, and obviously we don't know half of what that can do. So I can't—Isoka? Is something wrong?"

I'm already turning away, fighting a rush of acid from my stomach. Meroe calls after me, but her voice is dull through the roaring in my ears. Before I realize it, I'm running back toward the chamber where we'd left Catoria.

One of her men is on guard in the doorway, but she gestures him aside when I arrive. He gives me a suspicious look, but steps back, and Catoria herself gets up from her blanket to greet me.

"Lady Isoka," she says. Apparently I rate a "lady," somehow, which would have made me laugh under other circumstances. "Have you considered my offer? I hope our gifts—"

"*Soliton*," I growl, and she stops, taken aback.

"Yes?"

"How long does it stay?" I almost can't force myself to ask the question. "When it arrives, every year, how long before it leaves again?"

"It varies," Catoria says, nonplussed. "A week, at least."

My panic recedes a fraction. I have a little more time. But—

If Meroe and Shiara are right, and time runs differently in the Harbor, then the window I thought I had to rescue Tori is rapidly closing. One day inside equals twenty outside. In one week, five months will pass—even with *Soliton*'s speed, I would be hard-pressed to make it back to Kahnzoka in time after that. Two weeks, and Tori might be suffering Kuon Naga's imaginative torments before I even make it out of the harbor.

I'd known the sand was hissing away in the hourglass. I hadn't realized there was a *hole* in the rotting thing.

"Has anyone tried getting back on board?" I ask Catoria. "What about the other ships?"

She shakes her head. "A few of the Minders tried to board *Soliton*, the first time it returned. The angels kept them off, though they didn't harm anyone. And the other ships are wrecks. We explore them sometimes, to look for old treasures, but there's nothing else aboard but crabs." She cocks her head. "You want to go back, don't you?"

I nod, breathing raggedly.

"Silvoa thought it was possible," she says, voice turning hard. "But she was wrong. *Soliton* has stranded us here, Lady Isoka, and it means for us to stay. I suggest you come to terms with that."

I fight the urge to say something nasty, and turn away.

Later, I assemble the Council.

With the sun setting, Catoria and her entourage have departed. Meroe saw her off with appropriate diplomacy, promising an answer to her generous offer at a later time. Catoria, in turn, promises to deliver more food. Harak has also departed, apparently unafraid of traveling alone back to his order by twilight. *I wonder what his Well is.*

The four of us come together in the room where we interviewed Catoria, sitting on the same blanket. They're sitting, anyway. I'm too anxious for that, pacing back and forth while Meroe repeats what Catoria told us for Zarun's benefit, along with our later speculations.

"That fits with Harak's story, more or less," he says, when she's finished. "At least until the end. To hear Harak tell it, Gragant and Silvoa told Catoria what they were doing, and Catoria refused to allow any of her people to support them. He says that Gragant only escaped because Silvoa sacrificed herself, and Catoria turned on him afterward."

"I wish I could have met this Silvoa," Meroe says. "She sounds remarkable."

Zarun grunts. "In any event, Harak's offer is about the same as Catoria's. Anyone who wants to join their order is welcome." He looks sour. "So we can swear loyalty to a lost Imperial princess, or throw in with a bunch of fanatic monks."

"Did Gragant say how many people are with the Minders?" Meroe says.

Zarun shakes his head.

"Catoria didn't mention that, either," Meroe says. "It makes me wonder if the dozen or so she brought with her are most of her strength."

"You think?" Zarun perks up. "That puts us in a much better position. If we call her bluff—"

Shiara shakes her head. "I don't like it. The last thing we need is a fight with other humans, when there's Blessed-knows-what wandering out there at night."

"Easy for you to say," Zarun says, his expression turning dark again. "It sounds like the Cresos would welcome you Imperials with open arms. What about the rest of us?"

"Enough," I cut in. "We're not picking a side, and we're certainly not going anywhere that's only going to take half of us."

The three of them look at me, and my knuckles tighten. I take a deep breath.

"So what's the plan?" Zarun says. "We need food, and from the sound of it the angels only deliver to the three big ziggurats. This Lady Cresos isn't going to keep sending us gifts after we turn her down."

"We might be able to scavenge something from the jungle," Shiara says, "but not indefinitely."

"They deliver to the three big ziggurats," I say. "So we're going to take one of them."

"Catoria's?" Shiara says, dubiously. "I still don't think it's wise."

"If we take them by surprise, we can do it with a minimum of bloodshed," Zarun says. "Isolate the leaders. Hell, most of their servants will probably turn on them given half a chance."

Meroe looks at me, quietly, and I shake my head.

"The Minders, then?" Zarun scratches his chin. "That's harder. We don't know much—"

"Neither," I interrupt. "Shiara's right. We don't need to fight humans when there are monsters out there."

"You want to attack the third ziggurat," Meroe says. "Attack Prime."

"We know even less about him than about the other two," Shiara says.

"Not to mention Gragant and Silvoa tried that already, didn't they?" Zarun says.

"I think we have more fighters than they did," I say, trying to put confidence into my words. "Think about last night. Prime's monsters were all over us, but we cut our way through them pretty easily."

"We still lost people," Meroe says.

"I know. But we had a lot to defend." I stalk across the room, unable to stay still. "A smaller group, just fighters, would have an easier time. I don't think those corpses could stop us." I force a smile. "They're rotting sure not as frightening as blueshells and hammerheads."

"That's true," Zarun says slowly. I wonder if he's remembering the nightmare march to the Garden, cutting our way through an endless horde of maddened crabs, pack members dying all around us. It certainly haunts *my* nightmares.

"What about Prime?" Shiara says. "Do you have any idea who they are, or what they can do?"

"I've been thinking about that," I say, recalling blank, empty eye sockets and a cracked grin. "I got a . . . a message from him, while we were fighting. I *think* he's an Eddica adept, like me and Silvoa. He must have come here with *Soliton* in an earlier cycle."

"Can you raise the dead with Eddica?" Zarun says.

"Not raise them, exactly," I say. "But you can make inanimate objects move like living things. That's what the angels are, so it makes sense that you could make it work with corpses." I raise my hand. "And before you ask, I have no rotting idea how, so don't tell me to try it. It just seems like it ought to be possible."

"So he's just one man and an army of puppets?" Shiara says. "It's still mostly guesswork. We should move carefully. Send scouts—"

"*No.*" My voice is too loud, and I swallow hard. "If we wait too long, Catoria and the Minders are going to demand answers, and we'll end up fighting in three directions. We have to move *now*, before they get a handle on us."

"I'm in," Zarun says, with a lazy grin.

"I'm . . ." Shiara shakes her head. "I'm not sure. But . . ." She sighs. "The crew will follow you, Isoka. I just hope you know what you're doing."

I look at Meroe, and she stares back at me, biting her lip.

"Why don't you tell them?" Meroe says.

"Tell them what?" I don't know why I say that. She already knows everything, of course.

"About Tori."

We're in the corner of one of the empty chambers, made a little less stark with the addition of some blankets and a lantern. There's plenty of room to spread out, but for the most part the crew has stuck together, turning a few of the largest chambers into a communal barracks. This one is empty except for us, a stone space the size of a small house, and it feels echoing and vast. The sun has set, and the room is in shadow beyond the narrow circle of light cast by our lantern.

Meroe is sitting on the blanket, cross-legged. Her head turns to follow me as I continue to pace.

"Is it that obvious?" I ask her.

"Only because you already talked to me about it." She shrugs. "If there is something strange happening with the passage of time—"

"Catoria said we have at least a week until *Soliton* leaves. We've used two days of that already." I reach the wall, and resist the urge to slam my palm against the stone. "If I can get back on board before then, and head right back to Kahnzoka, I *should* get there before the deadline. Barely."

"And you think this attack on Prime is the best way?"

"It's the only lead I have. This Silvoa thought that an Eddica adept could get control of the city by using the access points in all three ziggurats, right? That's why she went to Prime in the first place. If I can get to that one, we might be able to talk the Cresos and the Minders into letting me use the other two. Or force them, if it comes to that. That might get me back onto *Soliton*."

"That's a lot of 'mights,' Isoka."

"I rotting *know*." I grit my teeth. "But what else am I supposed to do? I am *open* to rotting ideas here, but there's no time."

"I know." She holds up her hands for peace. "I'm not disagreeing with you."

"Sorry." I run one hand through my hair. It's getting longer than I like it, nearly to my shoulders. "I just . . . before we got here, I thought I'd have the rest of the year to figure this out. Now I have the rest of the rotting week, if I'm lucky."

"Sit," she says.

"What?"

"Just sit down, would you? Your pacing is making me seasick."

I let out a breath and flop gracelessly to the blanket beside her. "Better?"

"A little." She shifts sideways, sitting behind me, and twines her arms around my neck, head resting on my shoulder.

"I . . ." The warmth of her, pressed against my back, makes me shiver. "Rot. I *am* sorry."

"I understand," she says. "I just want to make sure you've thought this through."

"I have," I say. "I know it's asking a lot of the crew. But if we win, it'll work out best for everyone. We'll have food, and we won't have to worry about being attacked by monsters at night." I lean my cheek against hers. "Honestly, if not for the walking corpses, things wouldn't be so bad here."

"But you still want to leave?"

"You know I have to."

"What happens after you save Tori?"

I laugh. "I haven't dared think that far ahead. What about you? If *Soliton* could take you anywhere, where would you go?"

There's a long silence, long enough to make me realize I've said something wrong. After a few moments, her voice a little thick, Meroe says, "That might depend on . . . your plans."

Rot. Rot rot rot. Leave it to me to miss the point. Obviously, I still don't understand people.

"Meroe," I manage. "I didn't mean . . ."

"It's all right."

"It's not." I grit my teeth. "Look. I've spent my life with exactly one person who means a rotting thing to me." I bring my hand up and grip one of hers. "Now I have two, and I don't intend to leave either of you behind, wherever we go."

She squeezes my hand. There's another silence, of a much more comfortable kind.

"You're wrong, you know," she says, after a few moments. "It's not just me that you care about. Not anymore."

"That's your influence," I say. "You're a better person than I'll ever be."

Meroe holds me a little tighter, but says nothing.

The next morning, the fighters among the crew gather in one of the unused chambers. I stand in front of them, with Meroe, Zarun, and Shiara behind me, and try to look like I know what the Rot I'm doing. I explain to them what I told the others the night before, and I watch their faces. There's respect there, and skepticism, and fear, and excitement, and Blessed knows what else.

I know so few of them by name. I recognize people, from the nightmare march or afterward, in the Garden, but most of the pack leaders and others I came to know before the passage through the Rot are gone. A leader—if that's what I am—ought to know her people, and I resolve to start learning.

Zarun steps forward. "I think the Deepwalker has the right idea. If we're going to stay here—and it doesn't seem like *Soliton* has given us any choice—getting rid of the army of hell-spawn corpses seems like a good start."

A few in the crowd mutter in agreement. Shiara steps up beside him and says, "It's a risk, but if it pays off it will put us in a strong position to bargain with the Cresos and the Minders. I think it's our best chance."

More mutters and nods. These aren't soldiers, who march into the jaws of death for a king or because they'll be whipped if they refuse. *Soliton*'s crew are rebels, outcasts, discards. Deepwalker or not, I have to convince them.

Jack and Thora are the next to step forward. Jack turns to face the crowd, giving an elaborate bow.

"You all know Clever Jack is always up for a scrap," she says. "And this seems like a good one. That's all I need."

That brings a round of laughs. Thora puts an arm around Jack's shoulders, nearly pulling the smaller woman off her feet.

"For my part," Thora says, "I never figured on seeing home again. If we're going to be staying here, we'd better make this place our own." She looks at me. "And I owe the Deepwalker for bringing us to the Garden. We all do. If this is what she thinks is the right move, I'm with her."

One by one, the rest shout their approval. I stand up a little straighter, and can't help but smile.

9

TORI

The upper floors of the hospital are reserved for its permanent residents.

As usual, we're badly shorthanded. Grandma has called in every favor and friend to help deal with the fallout from the draft riots, but most of those assistants are needed downstairs, caring for the freshly hurt. It's been several days since the last disturbance, but the mats down there are still full of people with splinted limbs, mending under Grandma's watchful eye.

Meanwhile, the daily work of the hospital piles up. Some of it is simply going undone—it's past time, for example, to replace the light summer curtains on the windows with heavier winter drapes, but no one has time. Yet meals have to be prepared, chamber pots emptied, and linens cleaned regardless of how busy we get.

At the moment, Garo and I are delivering food. We turn on to the east corridor, one of us on either side of a big, wooden-wheeled serving cart rescued from a junk heap. The thing has a tendency to suddenly veer to the right at the worst possible moments, so I direct it carefully, while Garo pushes from behind. In spite of his slim frame, he's well-muscled.

We've been spending quite a lot of time together, in fact. Just as I'd seen in his mind, Garo was completely serious about becoming my "apprentice." It's ridiculous when you say it like that, both because he's a year older than me and because I don't really have anything to teach him other than the basics of life in the lower wards. But the basics are precisely what he needs, never having had to attend to them himself. It's quickly become apparent that, for all

Garo seems to consider us equals, his life at home is very different than mine.

The hateful cart bumps and jolts against my hands as we make the last turn. There's a wide landing, leading to one of the outdoor staircases, and then a hall of tiny rooms. A desk sits by the window, where it gets a little light during the day. Jakibsa, Hasaka's boyfriend, sits behind it, dressed in a long, loose black robe.

Garo sucks in his breath, and I realize I should have warned him. Jakibsa is a bit of a gruesome sight. His career in the Legions ended while fighting frontier barbarians, one of whom happened to be a Myrkai adept. Burned across most of his body, he'd been expected to die, and the Legions hadn't quite known what to do with him when he survived. He'd turned down their offer to live in one of their communities for retired soldiers and come here instead.

He has hair on only one side of his head, and wears it long, pulled over the burned part of his scalp and down across his face. It almost obscures the ruin the fire made of his flesh, angry red-and-white scars running down his cheek and neck, one ear entirely gone. He wears gloves, because his hands look much the same, with two of the fingers on his right fused together, and he walks with a cane.

Given all this, he's cheerier than he has any right to be. He's writing, as usual, when we come in, a nib pen held in a delicate, flickering blue aura dancing unsupported across the pages of a leather-bound journal. It pauses at the sound of the cart, and he inclines his head as we appear, a little stiffly.

"Evening, Tori," he says. "And who's this?"

"This is Garo," I tell him. "Garo, this is Jakibsa. He helps keep track of things up here."

Garo gives a grave bow. "It's an honor to meet you."

"Very polite, this one!" Jakibsa says approvingly. The pen zips to one side, blotting itself on a cloth, and settles down.

"Your control is very impressive," Garo says. "I don't know many Tartak users who could do that."

"Just a matter of practice," Jakibsa says, but I can tell he's pleased. He raises one arm, with obvious difficulty, and his gloved hand shakes. "The alternative isn't pleasant for me, so I learned."

"He writes satirical plays," I put in. "They're quite good."

"Now you're just flattering me," Jakibsa says. "Go on, the grumblers are waiting for their dinner."

We push the cart past him. Garo says, quietly, "He's very open with his power."

"He's not a part of the sanctuary, actually. He's got a medical discharge from the Legions, so he's fully legal."

Garo nods. "That must be useful for keeping up the front."

"It can be."

Grandma had agreed to let Garo in on the secret, and he'd readily sworn the oath as I watched his mind for falsehood. It was a little odd for me, actually—we'd accepted refugees to the mage-blood sanctuary, but he was the first new assistant to be brought into the fold since I arrived. I'm used to being the newest member of the circle.

I hadn't, of course, let him in on my *own* power. And for his part Garo hadn't volunteered anything about his abilities, though as a member of a noble family he's certainly a mage-blood.

We lapse into silence as we reach the first door. I can feel him *watching* me. It's . . . unnerving, if not entirely unpleasant. I try to ignore the sensation and knock.

This hallway's residents, the ones Jakibsa calls the grumblers, are mostly old men Grandma's taken in because they don't have anywhere else to go. There's a certain sameness about them—bent-backed, white-haired, with tired, rheumy eyes and liver-spotted skin. I deliver their meals and spend a few minutes with them, listening to their complaints and stories about how much better things used to be, and they pat my hand and tell me I'm a good girl. I try hard to keep my mind closed to their thoughts.

I have a hard time keeping their names straight, if I'm being honest. I feel guilty about that, but there are so many people in the hospital, with new ones arriving all the time.

I wonder if Garo can tell. He watches me with one ancient, a man who's so thin he looks like his bones would shatter like glass in a sharp breeze. I smile at him, and his face lights up.

"They like you," Garo says, after we close the door.

"I bring them their dinner," I say, feeling uncomfortable.

"It's not just that," he says, taking hold of the empty cart. "You care about them."

"I listen to them, at least." I shrug. "It's all they really want, someone to listen. It's easy."

"It's more than most people would do," Garo says. He cocks his head. "You never told me why you came here to begin with."

"About the same reason you did," I say, picking my words carefully. He doesn't know about my real origins, obviously. "I was . . . reminded how fortunate I am. It could have been me in these beds, easily. Or worse." So much worse, if not for Isoka.

Isoka hasn't come to see me lately. I'd expected that, since my birthday is in less than a week, and she always comes on my birthdays. Still, I miss her.

Garo thinks about that as we drop the cart off by the dumbwaiter and trudge back down the outside stairs to the first floor. He pauses on the landing, looking out over the tight-packed tenements of the Eleventh Ward, lit by a thousand lamps and torches.

"Do you think it's enough?" he says. "What you do here?"

"I warned you, apprentice." I flash him a smile. "That this wouldn't be grand or glamorous."

"I know." Garo sighs. "But no matter how much we do here, the basic problems won't go away. Commoner mage-bloods will still be taken away by the Immortals, people will still starve in the winter." He shakes his head. "The draft checkpoints are only getting worse."

"We do what we can with what we have," I tell him. Grandma's phrase. "That has to be enough."

His expression tells me he's not convinced. I clap him on the shoulder.

"Come on. Grandma's waiting."

On the first floor, we pass Kosura, tending to some of the victims from the latest round of "disturbances" at the draft stations. She sees Garo at my side and keeps her head down until he's past, then catches my eye and gives me an exaggerated gesture of approval. I roll my eyes at her.

Kosura's not even the worst of the bunch. All the older women who help Grandma Tadeka have decided that Garo and I make a cute couple, and I'm getting sick of their encouraging looks. For his part, Garo doesn't seem to notice, which has to be a polite fiction. No one can be *that* oblivious.

And it's not like I'd be . . . entirely opposed. In theory. But I don't even know if the admiration he professes for me translates into anything . . . romantic.

I try very hard not to read his mind, but there are times when I can't help but slip, and I'd swear there's *something* there. Using my powers feels like an intrusion under the best of circumstances, though, and checking on the feelings of a . . . whatever we are . . . seems like possibly the *worst* of circumstances. So I refrain. Mostly.

Grandma is waiting for us in her office. She looks tired, but she always looks tired recently. Between finding space and funds to accommodate everyone who comes to us, and using her own powers on the worst cases, I'm surprised she holds up.

"Tori," she says curtly. "Garo. Are you getting used to the work?"

"Yes, ma'am," Garo says, polite as always with her. "Tori is an excellent instructor."

"Of course she is," Grandma says. "Tori, can you get him up to the High Market without too much trouble?"

"It shouldn't be hard," I say. "We've been using the shortcut through Laundress Lane."

"Good. Then you can both go." She taps one finger on the desk. "There's a place called Nirata's, a restaurant. He's a friend, and he's got three people in the back he's hiding from the Ward Guard. Find them and bring them back here."

I get a sudden rush of anxiety. I know Grandma helps keep people from the authorities, but—"Hiding from the Ward Guard for what?"

She shakes her head. "What do you think? They're escaping the draft, just like everyone else."

"If we start sheltering draft-dodgers, this place is going to fill up fast," I say.

"Leave that to me," Grandma says. "Just go and collect them." She makes a shooing gesture with one hand and goes back to her ledgers.

"She puts a lot of trust in you," Garo observes, as we slip back out through the curtains.

"Not enough, sometimes." I sigh. "She's spreading herself too thin."

"You know she has to."

"*She* can't help everyone, either." I look at him, raise an eyebrow. "You're up for a trip to High Market, I take it?"

"If you're leading the way." He grins. "We wouldn't want a repeat of the last time."

"Probably not."

It's still only an hour or so after dark when we reach the market, having threaded the narrow, clothesline-choked alley at Laundress Lane and circumvented the draft checkpoints at the major intersections. In the market itself, there are more Ward Guard patrols than I would like—there have been ever since the draft riots started—but at least they're not actively harassing us. There are still plenty of people around, and the stalls are doing brisk business.

"We've got some time to kill," I announce, as we push through the crowd. "If we give it another hour, we'll have fewer Ward Guard to dodge once we pick up our refugees."

It's true, more or less. The fact that it gives me an hour to wander the market with Garo is entirely coincidental.

"Fair enough," Garo says. "So now what?"

"You haven't spent much time in the market, have you?"

He shakes his head, and I smile again.

"I'll show you around." When he looks a little dubious, I add, "If you're going to be working here, it's important information. You never know what's going to come in handy."

"Ahhh." His face clears. "Of course."

Of course. I give him a sidelong glance. I don't know that I've ever wanted so badly to read someone's feelings.

We begin our circuit, hardly able to hear one another over the babble of voices and the cries of the hawkers. I take him for fried honey-dough—obviously—and lemonade from old Kaga, who makes it sweet enough to hurt your teeth. From there we circle around to the rows of stalls selling pretty bits of jewelry. I have jewelry at home, of course, with real gold and silver and precious stones, but somehow it never looks as entrancing as the glitter of these paste-and-glass baubles in the half light of the lanterns. Garo is getting into the spirit of things, and by the time we reach the end of the row he's arguing excitedly whether the purple earrings are better or worse than the little china porpoise.

Either of us could buy out the whole stall in our other lives. Tonight, neither of us can afford a thing. We debate, and laugh, and keep moving.

There's a puppet theater on the east side of the market, the play just starting as we arrive. It's a court drama, the latest to come down the hill, re-staging the rumors and intrigues of the Imperial household in miniature in a way that combines entertainment and political gossip. The puppets are finely articulated figures, painted to resemble court fashion, controlled via dozens of individual strings by a hidden puppeteer. Garo is laughing immediately, but I find the things unsettling. *That dream* . . .

The crowd is engaged, though, partisans of various factions cheering whenever their heroes appear. By convention, the Emperor himself is never depicted in these shows, appearing as a booming voice from offstage, but everyone else is fair game: his uncles, siblings, and court functionaries like the Chief Eunuch all have their fans. Not keeping up with the gossip, I find myself a bit lost, but I have to appreciate the puppeteers' skill. The little marionettes look nearly alive.

"He's not as bad as all that," Garo says in my ear, as the crowd roars with laughter.

"Who?"

"Videka. The Emperor's uncle." He nods at one of the puppets, a fat old man with a shiny bald head.

"You know him?"

"We've met. He's a friend of my father's." Garo shrugs. "He can be a bit of an oaf, but he's against the war, and he has some good ideas about improving things for the people."

"So why won't the Emperor listen to him?"

"The Emperor only listens to the Council of State," Garo says, his expression darkening. "And the Council of State is packed with Kuon Naga's sycophants. My father says . . ." He catches my eye. "Sorry. It's not important."

The play ends, and amid the applause and the sound of coins landing in the puppeteers' open trunk I consider Garo in a new light. The figures of the Imperial court are larger than life for everyone in Kahnzoka, their exploits told and retold through gossip and rumor, which fascinate my neighbors in the Second Ward just as much as the crowds in the Eleventh. I've never met anyone who actually set foot in that rarified circle of power, who might know these shimmering creatures as actual human beings.

Part of me—the part that has carefully cultivated Grandma as a possible escape route, the part that the rest feels guilty about—is thinking that there must be some way to use him, something better than changing sheets.

"Is something wrong?" Garo says.

"Just thinking." From farther down the market, there's a crackle of sparks and a flash of green light. Garo blinks in surprise, and I grin. "Come on. This should be fun."

I grab his hand, before I can think about it, and pull him after me. I wouldn't have thought twice about doing the same to Kosura, but after a few steps my mind catches up with the situation. He's closed his fingers around mine—which means he must not object—

All of a sudden my heart is beating very fast. I'm trying to keep my palm from sweating by sheer force of will.

We come to a halt amidst the crowd in front of the pyromancer. She's standing on a box, a lithe young woman in a tight, gaudy costume slashed to show a barely acceptable amount of skin. Her movements are smooth and graceful, a kind of dance in place punctuated by dramatic upward gestures. When she raises her hands to the sky, blooms of fire expand outward, dissipating in clouds of colorful sparks.

Pyromancers have visited the house in the Second Ward a few times, though not quite so provocatively dressed. They're Myrkai Well users, touched or weak talents, who have trained themselves in the subtle control of their arts to make up for a lack of raw power. Like Jakibsa with his pen, they achieve a mastery beyond most mage-bloods, combined with a knowledge of flammable powders and potions to put on a show.

This one is good, but not as skilled as some of the others I've seen. Garo seems entranced, though, his breath catching as she blows a cloud of red sparks from her mouth and then gestures rapidly to surround it with a halo of hanging green fire. I wonder how much is the performance, and how much the costume, and the thought comes with a touch of unpleasant jealousy I've never felt before. I bite my lip, try to relax, and work harder than ever to keep my Kindre senses closed off.

He's still holding my hand. I squeeze his fingers, and he squeezes back, looking down at me. His handsome face is outlined in the flickering multi-colored light, eyes ablaze with reflections as though they were glowing from within. My heart gives a weak flip-flop, and my skin feels suddenly hot.

With that final flourish, the performance ends. The pyromancer bows low, but Garo is still looking at me. I clear my throat, inaudible in the tumult, and can't think of anything to say.

"It's getting late," he says, after a while. "We ought to find this restaurant."

Restaurant. Right. I give a jerky nod, and reluctantly release his hand. He smiles at me, and I watch him a moment longer before I turn away.

*   *   *

Nirata's is a simple eatery, one of dozens of similar places across the High Market and the rest of the Eleventh Ward. It occupies the ground floor of a large tenement building, with a main room full of cheap, splintery wooden tables. At the back, a curtained doorway leads into the kitchen, and a hole cut through the wall provides a counter. Customers get their food—usually bowls of rice topped with fish or chicken—and eat them standing up at the tables, in the midst of lively chatter.

It's unremarkable, but I find myself looking at it through Garo's eyes as we come in through the open doorway. There are so many unspoken rules. You can join a table that has fewer than four people, for example, but shouldn't try to crowd a fifth unless you know each other; meals you can't finish should be left in place for the other diners to pick over. No one ever *told* me these things, unless it was Isoka and I was too young to remember. You just . . . absorb things, through the air, until it feels like second nature.

No wonder Garo's efforts to fit in here were doomed. It makes me realize that I never would have been able to blend in, either, if I'd been the Second Ward girl I pretend to be.

The man behind the counter, in a sweat-stained robe with the sleeves tied up, catches my eye as we come in. There aren't many customers at this hour, just one trio of porters wolfing down their rice and a lonely old man picking through abandoned bowls. The proprietor waves us over, and I lead Garo through the curtained doorway. There's not much room—a cooking hearth, banked to a dull glow now, and a proper door leading to what must be a storeroom. Another door, which looks like it might lead to a back alley, is so dusty it seems like it hasn't been used in decades.

"You're Tori, aren't you?" the man says. He offers me a nervous bow. "Nirata Genza. You helped my son Toma when he got caught in the fighting."

I have no idea if I helped Toma specifically, but I bow anyway, accepting his thanks on behalf of Grandma and the hospital. "Grandma said you're giving some friends a place to hide."

He nods. "But you can't keep them here long. The Ward Guard

are searching storefronts, and Giba from the peanut stall says they're coming this way soon."

"We'll get them somewhere safe," I tell him, feeling a stab of guilt. Maybe tarrying for an hour in the market with Garo hadn't been *entirely* harmless. "Where are they?"

He glances out into the main room. The porters have left, and only the old man is still there.

"In here," he says, unlocking the storeroom with a key at his belt.

Inside, barrels and bushels are stacked high, one wall lined with shelves holding bottles of sauce and spices. Amidst the mess are three boys in their late teens, sitting cross-legged on the floor. They wear rough clothes, and from their disheveled state they've been hiding out for some time.

"Wik has to piss again," one of the boys says, as soon as the door opens.

"Again?" Genza says. "You're supposed to be *hiding*."

"I can't help it!" shrieks the youngest boy, presumably Wik.

"Well, get your things," Genza says. "This is Tori. She's going to take you somewhere safe."

"I thought this was supposed to be somewhere safe," the third boy says. He looks the oldest, and his eyes narrow suspiciously.

"Nowhere's safe forever," Genza says darkly. To me, he adds, "This is Gokto, Bel, and Wik. Try not to strangle them."

I raise my hands. "Just follow me, and everything will be fine."

"You?" The oldest, who Genza had called Gokto, glares at me. "She's just a little girl."

"She works for Grandma Tadeka," Genza says. "So you do what she says."

"Bel, I don't know about this," Gokto says.

"Tori," Garo hisses.

"I can handle this," I mutter. "Just keep an eye out."

"I *am* keeping an eye out," Garo says. "This looks bad."

Genza, with a squeak, runs back to the counter. A moment later I hear him say, "Yes, gentlemen? Can I help you?"

"It's 'Captain,'" a humorless voice answers. "And you can help me by letting my men search your premises."

I know that flat, arrogant tone. Ward Guard, for certain. I bring my eye to the slit in the curtain and swallow a yelp. There's a half dozen of them, the captain and a broad-shouldered sergeant backed up by four soldiers with swords and clubs.

"Now what?" Garo whispers.

"We just had a search this morning," Genza says, his voice taking on a wheedling tone. "Surely it isn't—"

"Don't lie to me, old man," the captain says. "And you can't afford my rates these days, so don't even ask about a payoff." The rest of the squad chuckles darkly. "Now open up the storeroom."

Genza glances in my direction. Garo's looking at me, too. So are the three boys.

Why is everyone looking at *me*?

"I can distract them for a few minutes," Garo says. "Can you get everybody out the back?"

I nod, grasping at this lifeline. Genza, hearing this, ducks back. "But—"

"What's going on back there?" the captain cuts in.

Garo's already moving. He grabs a colorful cloth napkin and ties it over his face, covering everything but his eyes. Then, as the captain starts toward the curtained doorway, Garo explodes out of it. He plants his knee in the Ward Guard's stomach, moving with easy grace, and brings an elbow down on the top of the man's skull as he collapses gasping to the floor. The other five stare at Garo for a moment, stupefied. Then they heft their clubs.

Garo raises his arms. Green energy shimmers into existence, encasing each of his forearms in a cracking, spitting field of power, as though he were wearing a set of translucent gauntlets. It has to be Melos energy, the Well of Combat, though it's a form of it I've never seen before. Certainly it seems to take the guards aback, and they shuffle away, looking at the sergeant uncertainly.

Unfortunately, the captain, writhing on the floor, chooses that moment to regain enough breath to shout.

"What are you waiting for?" he wheezes. "Get him!"

The soldiers step forward. Garo rushes them, intercepting a downward strike with one gauntlet. The solid wooden weapon shatters against the Melos energy in a spray of splinters, and Garo's fist lands in the man's midsection with a sound like a giant stomping its foot, a wave of power blasting the guard off his feet.

Okay. He's holding them off. Time to get out of here. I turn to Genza and the back door.

"Is that locked?"

He shakes his head frantically. "But—"

I yank at the door. The latch moves, reluctantly, but the door doesn't open. The three boys have piled out of the storeroom, distracted by the fight, but after a moment Bel notices what I'm up to and comes over to help. Between the two of us, the door swings inward an inch, scraping against its frame, then finally comes unstuck all at once and throws us to the ground. I roll over, gasping for breath.

Instead of an alley, there's the back side of a brick wall, roughly mortared.

"I was *saying,*" Genza moans, "they built over that alley *years* ago, there's no way out."

A cold hand grips my chest for a moment, and I force it away. *No time.* "Garo!"

"A little busy!" he shouts back.

I scramble to the curtain on hands and knees to see him facing off against a pair of soldiers, with the rest laid out on the floor in various states of distress. The remaining pair have split up to attack from both sides, forcing Garo to swing his gauntleted fists first one way and then another to drive them off.

Focused on this pair, he doesn't see the officer on the floor. The man has crawled to within arm's reach behind Garo, and he's drawn his sword. Even as I watch, he gets his legs under him, preparing a thrust.

"Behind you!" I shout. But one of the other soldiers has begun a feint, and Garo has already moved to block, off-balance. In that frozen instant, I can tell he won't move in time. The sword seems to crawl through the air, but I'm just as slow, one hand extended—

—and I lash out, Kindre power whipping around me, an invisible wind that sets my hair to whipping wildly. I feel the Ward

Guard captain's mind—his acid fear, his thumping humiliation, the copper tang of bloodlust, a hundred other emotions—and I reach for it. There's no time for subtlety, so my demand is simple.

Stop.

It slams into the delicate garden of his thoughts with all the force of a meteor strike. His eyes go very wide, and he freezes in place, sword still aimed at Garo's kidneys. A moment later, Garo spins, his boot slamming into the man's hand and sending the weapon skittering across the floor.

I reach out for the two remaining soldiers, flooding their minds with the same simple command. *Stop.* They freeze in turn, and Garo takes full advantage, his Melos gauntlets sending first one and then the other crashing to the ground. For a moment, things get quiet, broken by groans and the scramble of the lone customer frantically making a run for it.

"Tori—" Garo says, turning.

"Later," I tell him. "There'll be more patrols out in the street. Can you break through a brick wall?"

"Probably." Garo looks down at his gauntlets. "I've never tried."

"Try."

Bel, Wik, and Gokto scramble backward as Garo comes through the curtain, his green glow throwing weird shadows. Genza flinches as Garo's fist pistons into the bricks, raising a cloud of pulverized mortar. The third blow breaks through, making a hole the size of my head. Garo quickly widens it enough to squeeze into a dingy brick-lined hallway. At the far end there's another door, which I'm hoping leads out into the backstreets.

"Follow him," I tell the boys. I feel sick, my guts knotting as though I'd drunk a pint of cooking oil. The sensation of the captain's mind folding up under my power, giving way like wet paper—*Not now.* I turn to Genza. "You should get out of here, too."

He nods frantically. "I'll go out the front, tell them you threatened me and made a run for it. It might slow them down."

"Good. If you need help, come to Grandma's. We owe you."

He scrambles away. Garo has reached the other end of the hallway, splintering the locked door with another blow. Beyond, blessedly, I can see an alley. The three boys hover some distance behind him, reluctant to get too close, and I go through the hole and follow them. Genza shuts the door behind us.

"You'd better lead the way," Garo says, beckoning with a green-shrouded hand. "We're going to have to stick to the side streets."

"Right." I want to vomit, but there's no time. "Stay close," I tell the boys. "We'll get you to Grandma's."

"You saved my life," Garo mutters, as we start to run. "Again."

"Yeah." *I'm doing what I can with what I have.* I swallow bile. "I know."

10

ISOKA

I can't tell if Meroe is going to hit me or start crying. Possibly both at once. I hold up my hands and get ready to duck.

"I thought," I say, "we agreed on this plan."

Her eyes narrow, and the scales tip rapidly toward "hit me."

"*We* agreed it was the right thing for *us* to do," she says. "Not for you to run off and get into trouble by yourself."

"I'm not going to be *by myself*. I'm taking all our best fighters. Zarun, Thora, Jack, Aifin—"

"You know what I mean."

What she means is, not her. I'd made the mistake of thinking that went without saying.

"How many times have I saved your life, *Deepwalker*?" she says. We're in one of the smaller upper chambers of the ziggurat, which I've started thinking of as our bedroom. As yet, the only furnishing is a scratchy blanket made from the cloth Catoria's people brought us, which Meroe kicks aside as she stalks toward me.

"Too many to count," I say. "And obviously I'm grateful—"

"I don't need your rotting gratitude!" Meroe takes a deep breath, and suddenly she's blinking back tears again. "You don't understand."

"Obviously not."

Meroe swallows. "What happens when you get hurt, and I'm not there?"

"I—" I shake my head. "I'll be fine."

"Right. Just like when you fell into the Deeps, or when you fought the Butcher, or—"

"Someone needs to stay here and keep things running," I interrupt. "You're the one who's been holding this mess together ever since we marched to the Garden."

"And you'd like me to stay in a nice, safe padded room, is that it?" Meroe says.

"If anything goes wrong—not that I think that will happen—there's everyone who stays here to think of," I say. She stops, and I try a lopsided smile. "You're the one who told me that we can't just leave people behind."

Meroe's mouth works silently for a moment. "That's not fair," she mutters.

"Sorry."

For a moment we stand, facing each other. Meroe's breathing hard. Even in moments like this, she's so beautiful I can barely stand it.

"Don't—" She swallows again. "Don't think that you're keeping me safe."

"I—"

"If something happens . . ." She hesitates, then shakes her head. "If you don't come back, I'll have no choice but to accept Catoria's offer. I'll get everyone delivered to her protection. Then I'm coming after you, if I have to do it all by myself. Understand?"

"I . . . I don't think—"

"Don't rotting argue with me, Gelmei Isoka." She steps forward and kisses me, furiously, her breath hot against my skin. "Just . . . don't."

Then she tears herself away, turns her back, and stalks off.

I don't understand princesses. Or aristos. Or people.

But it's time to get to work.

Zarun and Thora have gathered the people we need. They ended up with a group of about two dozen, who report to the entrance chamber on the south side of the ziggurat as the sun begins to climb toward noon.

Some of them I know well: Zarun himself, of course, Thora

and Jack, Aifin. Others I'm familiar with in passing. A tall, blond Myrkai adept named Ylla who'd once served the Butcher, with half her head shaved and streaks of crimson dyed into the rest. An Imperial boy named Kotaga who looks about fourteen, bald as an egg. Vargora, who'd been a pack leader under Karakoa and was the only Melos user besides Zarun and myself. The Jyashtani girl who likes to salute military-style, who introduces herself as Safiya.

Most of them served in the hunting packs, and all of them went through the march to the Garden. They wait with bags slung over their shoulders, some with weapons, some not needing them. I've thought a little bit about what I was going to say, but in the moment all the platitudes I can dredge out of old dramas seem ridiculous.

"Prime is an Eddica user," I tell them instead. "Like me. It was his power that sent those monsters against us the night we arrived. They killed four of our crew." One fighter, caught and torn apart, and two of the younger children and a woman who'd gone to try to help them. "We're going to pay him back for that, and maybe find a way to secure our place here in the bargain. Any questions?"

Safiya raises her hand, and I nod at her.

"Do we know if he can do anything more with his power than send dead bodies after us?"

I shake my head. "Nobody knows very much about Eddica. So stay alert, would you?" I turn to Zarun. "Everything ready?"

"At your order, Deepwalker," he says, grinning.

"Then let's go."

Two guards pull our makeshift barricade aside, admitting brilliant sunlight. I blink for a moment, eyes adjusting, then start down the tunnel. The others follow.

The stairs down the side of the ziggurat seem to go on forever, but eventually we reach ground level. The forest isn't as impenetrable as I remember by the light of day. The trunks are well spaced, and a nearly solid canopy overhead keeps the underbrush down. Before we pass into the shadow of the leaves I sight on one of the obelisks, which I'd identified yesterday as being directly on the path to Prime's ziggurat. I hope there are enough clearings that I can keep us from going off course.

We make surprisingly quick and pleasant progress. In spite of the jungle, I never quite feel like I'm in the wilderness. The ground is too flat, evidence that long ago the hand of man had a role in shaping this place. I don't know if we're walking along old roads or across plazas, though. Not even cobblestones remain, just this gentle carpet of green, broken by the knobbled roots of the odd-looking trees.

The same strange noises I hear from the ziggurat are much in evidence, a continuous chorus of hoots, shrieks, and squawks. We even see a few animals, a pair of brightly colored birds that flap awkwardly away as soon as they spot us and a green reptilian *thing* that half-walks, half-slithers out of our path. In the distance, I spot a *face*, huge eyes staring at us, and I pause in alarm.

"What?" Zarun says, and follows my pointing finger. "Oh. That's a monkey. You don't have them in the Empire?"

"*That* is a monkey?" I've only seen drawings of monkeys in books. "I thought they were bigger."

"There's different kinds," he says. "That looks a bit like the fruit monkeys we have at home, but they don't have that white fur."

The monkey watches us suspiciously as we pass, and I return the favor. It looks almost spiderlike as it crawls through the tree branches.

As we continue onward—roughly south, I hope, away from the sea—the jungle thins. I get more glimpses of my guiding obelisk, which reassures me that we haven't wandered off track. Bits of worked stone start to appear, cracked and rounded by the passage of years, half-submerged in the soil like they're sinking into a swamp. In places the tree roots are tangled around them or splitting them apart, a centuries-long battle of rock against wood. Mostly they look like bits of flagstone, but here and there a fragment of carving remains, part of a face or something that might have been writing.

From the top of our sheltering ziggurat, Meroe and I had sketched out as much of the Harbor as we could see. The three great ziggurats form an equilateral triangle, with one side facing north toward the shore and our vantage point. Prime's ziggurat is the farthest inland, and our path crosses the center of the city. When we finally pass by my obelisk, it's in the middle of a vast plaza that hasn't yet surrendered to the encroaching vegetation. Some of its flagstones still sit flat and level, while young trees force their way up through the cracks and tip others on their sides. Something long and brown-furred darts away as we jog through and continue north, now keeping the obelisk to our backs.

"Catoria said that we didn't have to worry about Prime's monsters during the day," I tell the crew. The sun is at least a few hours from the horizon. "But that's only until we get close to Prime's ziggurat, and I don't know what 'close' means. From this point on, stay alert."

"Yes, sir," Safiya barks, practically vibrating with excitement. Zarun chuckles at her enthusiasm. The rest of the crew chorus their agreement, somewhat less eagerly. Bohtal, an uncharacteristically slim iceling boy whose skin is ghostly pale, comes to walk beside me at the head of the group. He's our only Sahzim user, better able to spot incoming threats than any of the rest of us. A faint yellow glow surrounds his head as we move on.

The jungle thickens, and my nerves start playing up. The corpse-things weren't very fast, but the trees offer them any number of places to hide in ambush. I don't know if they're smart enough for that. There's too rotting much I don't know, and for a wild moment I wonder if I should call a halt.

But we've spent most of the day getting this far, and I haven't got that many days left.

"Deepwalker," Bohtal says. "There's something off to our left. It's pacing us."

"One of Prime's creatures?" I pause, shading my eyes against the sun, trying to get a good look.

"I don't think so," he says. The yellow aura intensifies. "It looks more like an angel."

There. Something big, slinking through the trees, intermittently dappled with sunlight through the interlocking branches. It does look like an angel, long-bodied and multi-legged. I *think* it has the head of a dog, like the angel I saw the day we left *Soliton.* Whether it's actually the same one, I have no idea—each angel seems to be a unique nightmare, but I wouldn't swear there aren't several that look alike.

In any event, it isn't coming any closer. I clap Bohtal on the shoulder.

"We'll keep on," I say to the group. "Tell me if it comes this way." He nods.

Not long after, the great ziggurat comes into sight. It's about half again as tall as our shelter, though clearly following the same basic design, like a pile of giant steps or an enormous version of a child's block pyramid. Ramps run up all four sides, splitting to go around enormous open doorways, and continue on to the very top. The doorway directly ahead of us is surrounded by some kind of elaborate carving, and long ropes run down the sides of the ziggurat, supported by poles. The converging lines give the impression of a spider's web.

There's still no sign of any walking corpses. We slow as we get closer, picking our way through the last of the jungle. I frown, looking up, trying to place something about the ropes and decoration, but Bohtal with his enhanced vision gets it first and gasps.

"Bones," he says, taking a half-step back.

The "ropes" are strings of bones, long arm and leg bones bound one to the next. Each squat wooden post bears a single skull, fixed to look down at visitors approaching the ramp. They move slightly in the gentle breeze as we approach, with a faint, horrible clatter.

I'm not sure how many corpses you would need to build a display like that. A rotting lot, that's for certain.

The frieze around the doorway is no carved decoration, either. As we get closer, we can see that it consists of more bones, fixed to the stones in elaborate patterns. Skulls in the center of expanding circles of linked ribs, flowers built from hip bones, long, sinuous shapes formed from interlocking fingers.

I swallow and survey the crew. Even Zarun is looking a little grim.

"Well," I manage. "In case any of you worried this was a misunderstanding, and Prime wanted to make friends, consider yourself corrected."

There's a weak round of laughter. Aifin, who can't understand my meager joke, turns away from the bones and signs with his hands.

I haven't learned the full vocabulary he and Meroe worked out, but I know enough to work in a hunting pack, and he keeps it simple.

No enemies.

I nod agreement. "I thought we'd run into something sooner, too."

"Once we get inside, we have no idea of the layout," Zarun says. "It's a hell of a way to get ambushed."

"Yeah." I shake my head. "Everyone stay close. Zarun and I in front, Vargora in the rear." The three Melos users should be best able to defend themselves against a sudden attack. "Bohtal in the middle, and keep your ears open."

"As you say, fearless leader," Jack says with a grin. She doesn't seem at all discomfited by the bones. Nothing bothers Jack.

Thora cracks her knuckles. Those of the crew who carry weapons get them ready, and auras of various colors flicker throughout the party. I have a strange moment of homesickness—back in Kahnzoka, as a lone Melos adept, I'd been able to make myself ward boss. If I'd had a crew like *this* behind me, mage-blood fighters all, I could have ruled the city.

We climb up the ramp, flanked by slowly converging lines of bone. Ribs arc out over the edge of the doorway, like teeth around a gaping maw. Inside, there's only darkness, until several of our Myrkai users conjure flames, revealing a stone corridor like the one in our own shelter.

"Any idea how to find Prime?" Zarun says.

"Give me a minute."

I close my eyes, reaching out with Eddica. As usual, the whole Harbor is thick with flows of Eddica energy, including the massive amount of power still pouring out of *Soliton.* Closer to, though, I can sense energy moving within the ziggurat itself, a web of power converging somewhere in the interior. I pinpoint it in my mind and open my eyes.

"I think I know the way," I tell him. "Follow me."

The corridor leads to an intersection, and after another moment with my eyes shut we take the left turn. The Eddica flow leads me through a half-dozen more junctions—I really hope I'll be able to repeat the trick on the way out. We've also been trending upward, deeper and higher into the pyramid. After the last turn, I see light ahead, steady magical illumination spilling through an arched doorway.

I creep toward it, gesturing the others forward only slowly. Beyond the archway is a large, circular room. Several bright white lights shine down from the ceiling, and by their radiance I can see there's a balcony running along the far side of the chamber, about thirty feet up. Standing on it is a single human figure, so heavily backlit that it looks like a shapeless shadow.

"Someone's waiting for us," Zarun says.

Safiya sidles closer, kindling fire on her palm. "If that's Prime, sir, do you want me to try to take him out from here?"

I frown, and check the Eddica currents. There's a small thread linking the faceless thing to the greater flows, but not enough for it to be another Eddica adept. I shake my head.

"It's just a puppet," I mutter. "Prime apparently doesn't want to show himself."

Someone laughs, a warm, bass sound that echoes through the chamber. The voice that follows is nothing like the cracked whisper I heard when the corpse-thing grabbed me. It sounds like an actor declaiming, rich and thick as butter.

"My apologies," Prime says. "You don't live as long as I have by being incautious."

For a moment, we all freeze. Then I straighten up, square my shoulders, and walk out into the room.

Rot it. I never thought we'd get to Prime without a fight, and he obviously knows we're here. If he's going to come at us, I'd rather it be somewhere we have room to maneuver.

The rest of the crew follows. I crane my neck to look up at the shadowed figure, but I still can't see much.

"Welcome to my domain," Prime says. "I must say I'm a little surprised to have so many guests. It's been quite a while."

"We won't be staying long," I tell him.

"Oh, I imagine. Such anger." He gives that beautiful laugh again. "You'd think I'd done something to you."

"You attacked us," Zarun says, stepping up beside me. "Your corpses killed four of our people on the beach, and would have killed us all."

"Am I really to suffer this insect bleating at me?" Prime says, with an irritated sigh. "You, Eddicant, are welcome to stay. I am sure we have a great deal to learn from one another. The rest of these . . . people . . ." His tone turns contemptuous. "Well. I'm sure I can find a use for them as raw material."

Eddica swirls around us, and I hear the shuffling of many feet. My blades ignite with a *snap-hiss,* and my armor shimmers into being as I shout a warning.

"Here they come!"

There are three other doorways leading into the circular room, and corpses boil out of all of them, a dense crowd of the things scrambling over one another in a near-mindless attempt to reach us. Before they can even get clear of the doors, though, pillars of flame blossom in their midst. Safiya, Ylla, and the other Myrkai users in the crew stand shoulder to shoulder, orange-red auras blazing around their hands, lines of Myrkai power glowing across their exposed skin. The chamber is suddenly thick with the smell of burning flesh as the horde of corpses stumbles on, dozens of them crumbling into ash and bone, crushed and pulled apart by those coming on behind.

Some manage to get through the flames with only a light scorching. As we'd planned, though, Thora and the other Tartak users form the second line of defense, slamming the writhing bodies backward with bolts of concentrated force, magical energy flickering blue-white in the air around our little group. Thora herself is strong enough to break bones and crush skulls, but even some of the weaker talents can still fling the creatures backward into the flames.

The few that trickle through this gauntlet find the rest of us waiting for them. Honestly, there aren't enough to go around. Zarun and I confront them with Melos blades, and without darkness and panic on their side the shambling creatures are unthreatening opponents. Aifin, ablaze with golden light, flickers from place to place without seeming to occupy any space in between, and the corpse-things in his wake fall apart into neatly sliced sections. Jack, laughing, plays with the monsters, letting them close in around her before shifting into her own shadow and reappearing behind them, hamstringing them with a short blade.

It feels like only moments before the fight is over. Huge piles of burned corpses are heaped in front of each of the three doorways, with dismembered monsters scattered across the floor of the room. As far as I can tell, we haven't taken a scratch, our group still packed into a tight circle. I find a wild grin spreading across my face, and turn back to the figure on the balcony.

"We're still standing, *Prime*," I tell him. "You're going to have to do a lot better than that."

"I suppose I will," he says, urbane and unbothered. "Let me see what I have that might serve."

There's a new sound from the tunnels, the heavy scrape of claws against stone. I drop back into a fighting crouch, blades crossed in front of me, trying to watch everywhere at once. In spite of everything, I feel calm. *Whatever he has, we can handle it—*

Something jumps up on the mound of charred bodies. It looks like a cross between a lizard and a vulture, covered in colorful feathers, walking on two massive legs with short, crooked arms tipped with claws and a long reptilian tail. A narrow snout holds a jaw full of viciously curved fangs, and another claw like a sickle juts backward from each of its heels. I guess that its head would be about level with mine if we stood face-to-face.

The thing is as unmistakably dead as the rest of Prime's minions. Its hide is torn and decaying, with rotting muscles and polished white bone showing through the gaps, and huge clumps of feathers are missing or caked with dried blood. In spite of its state of disrepair, though, the thing moves fast, quick and graceful, head darting from side to side. It hops down from the corpse-pile and stalks toward us.

"Do you like it?" Prime says, genially. "I found it under the ice, out where the Harbor meets the rest of the world. It's amazing what you can turn up with a little digging."

In answer, Safiya hurls a bolt of flame at the lizard-thing. It side-steps, lithe as a snake, and the Myrkai blast explodes against the stone wall. A moment later, though, Thora spreads her hands and bonds of blue force close around the monster's limbs, locking it in place. A half-dozen more blasts of fire catch it head-on, blowing apart its rotting flesh and ancient bone, until there's nothing left but scattered, burning pieces.

"Now that's a shame," Prime chides us, with a sly chuckle. "Fortunately, there's more where that came from."

The wave of lizard-things emerges from the darkness of the three tunnels at a dead run, as fast as a charging horse but far more agile, dodging around one another in a chaotic maelstrom of feathers, claws, and rot. Bolts of flame whip out, but the monsters avoid them with preternatural grace, closing the distance in seconds. The Tartak users have more success, bludgeoning the things backward or—in Thora's case—ripping them in two, but they can only stop a few. I hurriedly reshape my left-hand blade into a shield as the onslaught rolls over us, and then I don't have time to spare for anything more than what's in front of me.

The lizard-things attack without subtlety or any regard for their own welfare, as one might expect of the dead. One of them comes directly at me, and keeps coming even as my blade carves a slice off its snout. I interpose my shield, and its jaws scrabble at the Melos energy, drawing coruscating sparks. It backs off, and I take the chance to lunge, spearing it through the throat. It's an instinctive move, striking for the vitals, and it's worse than useless here—the monster simply ignores me, its clawed hands tearing at my exposed arm and drawing more sparks from my armor, sending a wave of heat running across my skin.

I pull back, hurriedly, and give way a step. I'm aware of the others fighting around me, and out of the corner of my eye I catch sight of a shadow slithering across the stone floor. I attack again, this time with a sideways cut that severs one of the thing's hands at the wrist, then get my shield up as it tries to rake my stomach with its hind leg. My hand is starting to burn as green energy writhes between us, but I hold it in place long enough for Jack to materialize out of her shadow and take the thing out at the knee with a quick stroke. I sever its head as it falls, leaving the creature thrashing on the stones.

"Hey, pack leader," Jack calls, flicking shreds of rotten flesh from her blade. "Getting a little hot!"

Rot. I turn and give the battlefield a once-over. Several of the lizard-things are on fire or torn to shreds, and Zarun is finishing one off with a series of elegant cuts. But our tight group fragmented as the creatures bounded into us, and not everyone got out of the way in time. Ylla is standing over Kotaga, who rolls on the floor clutching a bloodied shoulder. Fire spurts aimlessly from the hands of a pigtailed girl lying spread-eagled on the stones, her stomach opened from navel to crotch and spilling crimson entrails. Beside her, an infuriated Safiya hammers firebolt after firebolt into the corpse of a monster already reduced to charred meat.

Blessed's rotting balls. My lips twist into a snarl. The remaining creatures have backed off, circling. *Prime, I'm going to carve you into tiny rotting bits—*

The ground shakes. First once, then again, dust puffing from between ancient stones. From the center tunnel, directly in front of us, something new emerges. It makes the lizard-things look like chickens; it's so tall it has to duck its head to get under the arch. When it straightens up, it rises above me, as high as a second-story window. It's shaped vaguely like its smaller cousins, but has no arms at all, only a massive set of jaws big enough to swallow me in a single bite. The feathers that run down its flanks are blood-red, with great rents torn through them to show gleaming ribs and muscle black with rot. Its tail, tipped with plumes, lashes back and forth like a cat with a cornered mouse.

"That's a rotting big beastie," Jack mutters.

"Deepwalker?" Zarun says, backing up.

Rot rot *rot*. He's looking at me. They're all looking at me. As usual.

I charge the thing.

It's not even the biggest monster I've ever fought. Maybe the tall-est, but the dredwurm was certainly bulkier. Of course, the dred-wurm would have killed us all if I hadn't managed to immobilize it with Eddica, and Prime already proved to me on the beach that won't work here. So we're going to have to do this the hard way.

It lumbers forward, head coming down for a bite. I dodge, feel-ing the wind of the thing's passage, the rotten meat stench of it. Then I'm past, shield shifted back into a blade, both weapons raised to carve a chunk out of the monster's chest.

I don't see the kick coming until it's too late. It's *fast*. If not for my Melos armor, the enormous talons would have carved me into four pieces. As it is, I feel myself screaming as bands of fire ignite around my body, excess power burning itself into my skin. I'm only vaguely aware that I'm airborne until I hit the ground, hard, too stunned to even turn the fall into a roll. As the crackling of green sparks fades around me, it's all I can do to breathe.

"Deepwalker!" Someone is shouting. Several someones. I raise my head, try to speak, but all that comes out is a dry croak.

With the mammoth creature's attack, the smaller ones have closed in again, working in perfect synchronicity. I see Zarun strug-gling between two of them at once, until Ylla blasts one aside with Myrkai fire; another jumps on her from behind, bearing her to the ground. Thora, Jack, and Safiya are running in my direction, but so is the enormous lizard-thing.

"Hey, ugly!" Jack shouts. "Over here!"

I don't know if it hears her, but it turns, coming after her with jaws wide open. Jack fades into a darting shadow, flickering behind the thing. Her sword slashes at its ankle, tearing dead flesh.

"I question your parentage and general morals!" Jack taunts. "And your past sexual companions have confided to me that their experi-ence was subpar!"

Thora skids to a halt beside me, with Safiya standing in front of us, fire blazing in her hands.

"Isoka," Thora says. "Can you get up?"

"Ngh," is about all I can manage. Rot. I try to sit up, lines of agony still hot across my skin. She helps me onto my hands and knees, panting. After a moment, I gasp out, ". . . get out of here. Everyone."

She nods, understanding. Thank the Blessed for Thora.

"Past instances in which I expressed affection for you were fraudulent!" Jack shouts.

The monster-lizard, apparently wearying of its efforts to squash the elusive Jack, turns around and heads for us. I try to muster the energy to summon my blades, but even the thought hurts too much. Thora springs to her feet, hands spread, and blue-white bands of Tartak force grab the beast like a choke chain. Somehow she holds it in place, in spite of the enormous bulk straining against her. I can see lines of smoke rising from her, as the power sears into her skin.

"Get Isoka back!" Thora shouts. "Now—"

One of the smaller lizards hits her from behind, a full-body tackle that sends both of them skidding across the stone floor in a heap. Jack screams, high and piercing. The monster-lizard, suddenly free of its bonds, surges forward. Safiya, standing between me and the creature, lets off a blast of fire that strikes it square in one eye, searing that whole side of its face, but it doesn't stop coming. Its foot comes down right on top of her, pinning her beneath those long talons with an ugly *crunch*. She's screaming, too, until its jaws descend a moment later. With a twist of its neck, the monster rips her in half. Blood paints the stone floor in a crimson slick.

The thing takes another step forward. A *careful* step, putting its foot down beside me, one long, curving talon setting its tip on my breastbone. The slight shift of weight, and it will spear through me like a knife through a rotten apple.

Hello again, Prime says, Eddica surging out of the creature to make a connection between us. The voice that echoes in my head is raspy and wet, as though emerging from the throat of a corpse. *Good of you to come all the way here. I hope you'll stay.*

Long enough to kill you, I spit back at him.

Such bravado. It will be interesting peeling that away from you. Will there be anything left afterward, I wonder?

If you're going to kill me, go ahead. I swallow hard, trying not to think of Tori, of Meroe, of *anything.* Terror gnaws at the pit of my stomach, held back only by the need not to give this rotsucker any satisfaction.

I'd rather not. It's rare that Soliton *brings one of us to the Harbor. An Eddicant. I've accomplished so much on my own. Can you imagine what I might do with a partner?*

A partner? My mind recoils. *You have to be joking.*

A junior partner, of course. I get a flash of a desiccated smirk. *You have a great deal to learn.*

Is that what you told Silvoa, before you killed her?

It's a shot in the dark, but at this point what do I rotting have to lose? And it seems to hit the mark, because I can feel confusion through the link, a sudden rage. Prime's voice is still under tight control, but there's genuine emotion underneath.

Silvoa was . . . difficult, Prime says. *She made it clear to me that she would be more useful dead than alive. You haven't demonstrated that, yet. For your sake, I recommend you reconsider your position.* The smirk again, blackened teeth showing behind lips like tanned leather. *Because you* do *have uses, even dead. Oh, yes—*

The connection cuts off abruptly, and the pressure on my chest vanishes. I open my eyes to see the huge lizard-thing staggering sideways, hammered by bolts of blue-white Tartak force strong enough to make even that monster give ground. Thora has risen to her knee, the wreckage of the smaller lizard strewn around her, thick crimson rivers staining her hunting leathers and pattering to the ground. One of the thing's claws has laid her cheek open to the bone, white peeking out under a gory hanging flap of skin.

Jack skids to a halt in front of her, shadow boiling around her feet. She grabs Thora's hand, trying to pull her up, but the other woman shakes her off.

"Go!" Thora says. Every word sprays blood across Jack. "Get out of here!"

"Go to the *Rot*," Jack screams. She pulls harder, but Thora is a big woman and Jack is skinny as a rake. "Get *up*!"

I feel someone grab me from behind, pulling me unceremoniously to my feet. Zarun.

"Time to go, Deepwalker," he says.

"Help . . ." I look around, past the slick of blood from Safiya's mutilated body. The rest of our fighters, those still on their feet, are falling back toward the door. The huge monster-lizard rights itself and struggles to stand. "Help Thora."

Zarun shakes his head. "I'm not leaving you behind."

"I . . . can walk." I gather my legs under me and push myself to my feet. It hurts, every motion stretching my powerburned skin, but I simply refuse to let the rising ocean of pain close over my face. *Help. Her.*

Zarun's eyebrows go up, but finally he nods and runs for Thora. Between him and Jack, they get her up, and half-carry her toward the door, leaving a trail of blood. I follow them, moving as fast as I dare, legs shaky underneath me. If I fall again, I know I'm not getting back up. Bodies are strewn across my path, mixed with rotting chunks of lizard. Ylla lies facedown in a vast pool of blood, her throat torn away.

Behind me, the monster has regained its feet. I expect it to come charging after us, but instead it ducks its head, one side bubbled and scarred from Safiya's final burst of fire. The few remaining smaller lizards cluster around it, watching us, but making no move.

He's letting us go. I look up at the balcony, but the faceless figure is already gone.

If not for Aifin's sense of direction, we'd never have found our way back to the entrance. The Jyashtani boy leads the way back out through the maze of corridors, until we emerge onto the face of the ziggurat. The sun is setting, painting the world golden as it descends toward the horizon.

At the base of the ramp, I call a halt. Most of the others collapse at once, but I stay on my feet, fearful that if I stop moving I won't be able to start again. The pain is subsiding, a little, but I'm no stranger to powerburn, and I know that it won't be long before the fever sets in.

Even so, I'm better off than some of the others. I do a quiet head count and come up with eleven.

"We didn't . . ." I cough, and close my eyes for a moment. "Leave anyone? Anyone who was . . ."

Zarun shakes his head. He seems intact, though from the way he's cradling one arm I suspect he's suffering from powerburn as well.

"Ylla's dead," he says dully. "Vargora, Emmie, Mokash . . ."

"I didn't see Safiya," someone says. "On the way out."

"Safiya—" My gorge rises. "Safiya's dead."

"Rotting Blessed," someone else mutters.

"Zarun," I say, taking a few steps away.

He comes over. Close up, his copper skin has faded to gray, and he looks nearly as dead on his feet as I feel.

"How many can walk?" I ask him.

"Aifin's all right," he says. "Bohtal. Kotaga. A couple of the others are torn up, but they'll manage." He lets out a breath. "Thora's going to die."

I look over at the big iceling woman. She's leaning against a tree, breathing shallowly, as Jack attempts to bind her wounds with strips of her own rapidly shrinking garments.

"It's a miracle she made it this far," Zarun says. "We can't carry her all the way back."

"She's *your* pack leader," I mutter.

"And a damned good one." He shakes his head. "But that's not going to keep her from bleeding out, or stop those punctures from festering even if she makes it through the night."

For some reason I remember Shiro—poor, stupid Shiro, who looked the wrong way and got a knife in the gut for his trouble. I'd killed him myself, a quick thrust to the heart. All the mercy I could offer, I'd told Hagan.

I swallow again. "I don't think *I* can make it back. We need help. I'm going to send Aifin to get a rescue party."

"A deaf-mute makes a strange choice of messenger," Zarun says.

"He's *fast*. And Meroe understands him. The rest of us will make for the obelisk."

"And Thora?"

"We carry her. As far as we can."

* * *

Aifin gives a curt nod when I hand-sign what I want him to do, and he takes off in a golden blur into the trees. The rest of us pick ourselves up and stagger on toward the obelisk, Zarun and Jack supporting the semi-conscious Thora between them. The raucous cries of animals accompany us on all sides, but now they sound more like jeers. The sun is going down, and the shadows between the trees grow long and twisted.

I'm sweating heavily by the time we're halfway to the obelisk, and not just from the walk. Fever and nausea are the next stages in powerburn. Sister Cadua, on *Soliton*, had used fungus-derived herbs to keep some of the symptoms away, but she was back at the ziggurat and in any case she'd had to leave her apothecary behind. I force myself to keep walking, step by weary step, when I want nothing more than to lie down among the cool ferns of the forest floor.

My mind feels numb. Eleven of us left. Counting Thora. Nine people had followed me, trusted me, depended on my word, and now they were dead. For nothing.

Dead, dead, dead. Dead is dead. That's what I'd always said, back in Kahnzoka, but it wasn't true. Here in the Harbor, the dead rose and tore you to pieces.

My dead. My fault.

Monkeys in the trees, staring at me.

Why are they always looking at me?

Tori's waiting for me, and I'm not going to make it. She'll be waiting for me when they break into her perfect house, her perfect little world, and drag her away. I wonder if she'll be smart enough to kill herself.

Dead. Tori, her fingers wrapped around a knife buried to the hilt in her breast, lying cold and still on her sleeping mat. Dead, dead, dead, everyone's dead and it's *my fault*—

"Isoka!" Zarun's voice.

I blink, and look up. The obelisk rises above us, a cracked and broken spire, relic of glories long gone. Aifin is standing by the base, with a crowd of people behind him carrying spears and torches.

"Oh." I swallow, suddenly desperately thirsty. "Good." Something in my brain seems to sizzle. "I'm going to. Pass out. Now."

I don't have any memory of hitting the ground. When I open my eyes, we're climbing the ramp up the side of a ziggurat. For a terrible moment I think we've gone the *wrong way*, that we're going back into Prime's labyrinth of monsters and corpses, but it's only our own smaller building. I'm lying on a makeshift stretcher, made from a blanket and a pair of sticks, with two crew bearing my weight. I raise my head as we pass under the archway.

"Deepwalker?" Sister Cadua bustles up to me, all business. "It's powerburn, I take it."

I give a weary nod. "What about the others?"

"Nothing I can't handle, although I wish we had more supplies." Her face falls slightly. "Except—"

"Thora," I say. "Is she alive?"

"For the moment. I'm not sure how. Jack won't leave her side."

"Take her upstairs, to my room."

Her lips press into a thin line. "As you say."

My bearers carry me up the sloping passages of the ziggurat, until they reach the chamber I've been sharing with Meroe. She's there, pacing back and forth, one hand playing nervously with the silver bangle on her arm. When she sees me, she rushes forward.

"Isoka!" Her face is several shades paler than normal. "Are you—"

"I'll be all right. Help me up."

She takes my hand, and I stumble out of the stretcher. I wave the two crew away with a mumbled thanks, then collapse into Meroe's arms.

"You're feverish," Meroe says, pressing her forehead against mine.

"Powerburn," I mutter. "It'll pass. Listen."

"You need to rest." We walk together to the blanket, reeling like a pair of drunks. "Here. Lie down."

"*Listen.*" I grab her sleeve. "They're bringing Thora up. She's . . . hurt badly."

"How badly?" Meroe says, then catches my gaze. "Oh."

"I can't . . . tell you to help her. I know that. But . . ."

"You don't have to tell me." Meroe takes a deep breath. "I'll try."

I lie down on the blanket, propped up against the wall. A few moments later, two crew maneuver Thora's limp body in, followed by Jack. The pair look at one another uncertainly, and one says, "We told her to stay behind, but—"

"It's all right," Meroe says, with a glance at me. "Thank you."

Jack is silent until they leave the room. Then she collapses to her knees, startling me. Her long, lanky frame folds up, shaking with silent sobs.

"Please." Her voice is tiny. "You have to help her. I'll do anything, I swear. I'll cook your food, kill your enemies, warm your bed. *Please*."

Meroe puts a hand on Jack's shoulder. "I don't have many enemies," she says. "And I don't need a bedwarmer. But I'll do what I can."

"Thank you," Jack mumbles. It feels vulgar, seeing her broken like this, without her witty persona, somehow more vulnerable than if she'd been naked. "Thank you. Thank you—"

"It may not work." Meroe settles herself beside Thora. "It may go . . . wrong."

Jack curls in on herself, rocking back and forth. Purple light engulfs Meroe, as she delicately lowers her hands to touch Thora's bloody skin.

Meroe is a ghulwitch, an adept of Ghul, the Well of Life. That fact would be enough to get her killed immediately in almost any nation in the world. The power to heal carries with it the power to kill, or worse to *change*. It was Ghul adepts who created the Vile Rot, that incomprehensible blight, source of monsters and sickness. A Ghul adept could give you a virulent plague to take back to your city, or seed your body with tumors to tear you apart from within.

Meroe isn't likely to do any of that, of course. But healing has its own risks. When she healed me, I was fortunate enough to come out of it with only blue marks on my skin. I still have nightmares about our packmate Berun, who'd bloated into a mountain of straining, writhing flesh and then exploded.

She can do it. I keep my eyes on her, as though the strength of my belief can be carried through my gaze. *She* can. She's been practicing with her abilities, after spending her life trying to hide them. *She can do it.*

For a long time, nothing seems to happen.

Thora coughs, blood bubbling across her lips. Jack whimpers, and draws herself into an even tighter ball.

Meroe pulls her hands back, and opens her eyes.

"Just kill me," Jack whispers. "If she's dead just rotting kill me, I can't take it I can't take it I can't—"

"She's not going to die," Meroe says. Her voice is shaky. "I didn't want to try to heal everything. The risk . . ." She glances at me. "But I stopped the bleeding, and . . . well. It's complicated." She lets out a deep breath. "It'll be a while before she's on her feet. But she'll live."

Jack is suddenly hugging Meroe, apparently without occupying any of the intervening positions, lifting her off her feet. I let my eyes close.

Eleven. I'd taken twenty, and come back with eleven. *Better than ten, thanks to Meroe. But still not good enough.*

Someone is calling my name, but I'm already asleep.

11

TORI

By the afternoon of my birthday, I know something is badly wrong.

People start congratulating me from the moment I wake up. My maids make extra bows as they lay out my most elaborate *kizen*, intricately dyed blue-green silk with delicate silver embroidery. The formal stays are complicated enough that I can't put it on by myself, so I stand stoically in my underthings while they putter around me, wrapping me in slick, cool fabric and arranging everything just so. They braid my hair, and accent it with gold and silver pins. Part of me wants to tear everything off and run to the trunk in the closet, dress in something that lets me *move*. But Isoka loves seeing me this way, and anything that makes her happy makes *me* happy.

After breakfast, with celebratory strips of fried honey-dough—I insisted, though the ones I get in the High Market are still better—Narago leads me through a series of prayers at our household shrine. The Blessed One looks down at me with an expression that's supposed to be enigmatic, but I always think just seems bored. In stilted, formal language I drone through my promises to abide by his teachings and my requests to be healthy and safe in the new year. Now that I'm fourteen—an adult, by ancient standards—there's a new set of prayers in which I ask for a kind husband and many strong children. I find myself thinking of Garo, and I hope that Narago can't see me blush.

I'm *not* madly in love with him, I swear. He's just . . . nice to look at, and unfailingly polite, and genuinely interested in what I have to tell him. And he seems to believe in doing good, even if his sheltered upbringing has given him a somewhat skewed idea how to go about it.

All right, I've been having some . . . inappropriate dreams. And perhaps spending more time in the closet than strictly necessary. (In addition to storing my lower wards clothes, my hidey-hole is a good place to masturbate if you don't want the maids walking in on you.)

If the Blessed One is watching my thoughts while I pray, I hope he forgives me.

Isoka usually turns up around midday, so I wait patiently through the morning audience. There are a dozen couriers waiting, sent by families of our acquaintance, bearing congratulations and small gifts. The household servants assemble, too, in order of rank, and wish me a prosperous year. Ofalo goes last, bowing his head to the floor in formal obeisance and telling me how honored he is to serve.

I wonder, if I'd been born to this life like Garo, if I'd take all of this seriously. As it is, I know the truth. The servants—even Ofalo—are here because Isoka pays them to be here. They do their jobs, but I don't fool myself that they *love* me. I remember too well how loyalty fractures when the money runs out.

Next comes the entertainment. I vaguely recall talking my way out of clowns and ending up with a theater troupe. They're really quite good, three men and three women taking turns acting, singing, and playing the three-string. Unfortunately, Narago has gotten his hands on their scripts, and so they present *A Series of Vignettes to Elucidate Correct Morals for Youth* instead of anything actually interesting. The actors give it their all, but smoldering glances between A Young Man and A Young Lady are about as intense as it gets. (And the Lady, of course, ignores the Young Man's Inappropriate Attentions in favor of the suit of A Gentleman, who courts her in the Proper Manner by first approaching her father for permission, taking her on exciting outings to the temple for extra prayers, and so on.)

I had hoped that Isoka would be there for the show, since then at least we'd be able to laugh about it later, in private. But there's no sign of her, even though I ask Ofalo to send someone down to the road to see if her carriage is on its way. So I suffer in silence, keeping my snide remarks to myself. When the players are finished, I applaud politely and accept their bows and congratulations.

The kitchen has laid a late lunch of—again at my insistence—dumplings and plum juice, Isoka's favorites. But she still hasn't arrived by the time we sit down. I keep glancing at the door, expecting someone to burst in and tell me her carriage has pulled up outside, but word never comes. I tear the dumplings from their skewers and try not to feel ill.

You can't pace properly in a *kizen*, but I give it my best shot. Ofalo hovers, offering various amusements—books, games, a trip to the market—and I ignore him. Finally, watching me wear a hole in the floor mats, he heaves a heavy sigh.

"Lady Tori," he says, his voice quiet so none of the other servants overhear. "You know Lady Isoka has a great many concerns."

He doesn't know the half of it. As far as Ofalo is aware, Isoka is some kind of rich merchant. I reach the wall and turn, slippers shuffling.

"I'm certain she has some pressing matter to attend to," he says. "She will be here by and by, or perhaps tomorrow."

"She never misses my birthday." I hate the way my voice sounds, weak and trembling. "She promised me she wouldn't."

"I know," Ofalo says. He sounds genuinely pained. "But the world sometimes conspires to make us break our promises, even to people we love."

He doesn't understand. How can he? He thinks I'm a spoiled little girl, angry that her sister has better things to do than come to her birthday party.

I'm not angry. I'm *terrified*.

There's no chance Isoka just has something better to do. If she's not here, it's because something has *happened*. Ofalo thinks she's stuck in a meeting or dealing with paperwork or something trivial, but he doesn't know the nature of Isoka's job. My sister would never admit it, but a great deal more can go wrong in a ward boss' life than a missing shipment of tea.

Isoka is a Melos adept, I tell myself. *She can take care of herself.* She's *probably* not bleeding out in some trash-strewn alley after a knife fight. It's more likely she'd decorate the alley with pieces of anyone who tried to stop her. But—

But there are still things that can go wrong. There are other mage-bloods in the underworld. There are ambushes, or poisons. And worst of all, there are the Immortals, and the Emperor's vengeance for the crime of being born an adept but not a noble.

By dinner, Ofalo has stopped pretending Isoka's arrival is imminent. There's a great feast, with more prayers by Narago, but my stomach is in a roil and I can barely touch the food. For once, when I tell Ofalo I don't feel well, he doesn't look doubtful.

"Go to bed, my lady," he tells me. "I'm sure we'll have something from Lady Isoka tomorrow. A note, at least."

I retire to the bedroom, let the maids undress me, and dismiss them for the evening. I don't, however, get in bed. Something has gone wrong, and tomorrow might be too late.

Garo is waiting for me in the High Market, in front of Kamura's, a noodle stall we both like. Of late I've been walking him to the hospital—just in order to make sure he doesn't fall afoul of the draft squads. The fact that it gives us a few minutes alone every evening is . . . a side benefit.

Today he's prodding his bowl suspiciously with his chopsticks. The top of the soup looks like a frothing, frozen sea, with limp tentacles a few inches long reaching out of it. In spite of the circumstances, I find myself grinning.

"You ordered the sea monster?" Kamura leaves it on the menu with no explanation.

"I was curious." He pokes one of the tentacles. "And I am not disappointed."

"It's egg white. I got him to show me how he makes it. Froth it up, pour it over boiling soup, garnish with squid. Sea monster."

"Remarkable." He grabs one of the tentacles, pops it free, and takes a bite, nodding approvingly. Then, looking over at me, he notices I haven't sat down. "Is something wrong?"

"Yes." There isn't time to beat around the bush. "Do you trust me?"

Garo blinks, sets down his chopsticks, and turns to face me. "Of course."

"If I tell you some things that you'll find . . . surprising. About me. Then what?"

"I don't know what you mean," he says. "But I've seen what you do here. I can't imagine anything you could tell me would be *that* bad."

"It's just . . ." I shake my head. "Will you help me? It might be dangerous."

"To the best of my ability," he says at once. "You saved my life, remember."

"I thought I told you to get over that," I say.

"I tried, but then you saved it again." He smiles. "What's wrong?"

"We need to get to the Sixteenth Ward," I tell him. "I'll fill you in on the way."

We trace a winding path through the alleys of the Eleventh Ward, working our way south, toward the Low Market, without taking the main streets. It's early enough that there are plenty of people about, and we don't attract any attention. Just a couple of young lovers, out for a stroll, right? *Maybe not.*

Garo's gained a lot of confidence in the time we've been working together. At least he no longer stares at everything, like he's just off a ship from distant lands. He's still a little too well dressed, but working at the hospital has gotten his outfits realistically dirty. I keep my Kindre senses open, on the lookout for draft patrols, but I can't help but pick up his emotions as well. He's worried, and . . . pleased, I think, to be able to help. Not afraid. Not suspicious. That's good.

"Okay," I tell him. "I have an older sister."

"Is that the big secret?"

"Not exactly." I shake my head. "When we met, you said you could tell that I wasn't a . . . a streetwalker, or even from the Eleventh

Ward. And it's mostly true. I live in the Second Ward, but I didn't start there. My sister Isoka and I grew up in the Sixteenth Ward, on the street."

"Fascinating." Garo strokes his chin. "My father always said that more commoners would rise higher, if they were given a chance. It was one of the views that kept him out of the Council of State. Your parents must be remarkable people."

"I never knew my parents," I tell him. "My mother was dead by the time I was old enough to walk, and Isoka never talked about her. She raised me herself."

"Even more remarkable."

You don't know the half of it. I'm walking a fine line here. I trust Garo, mostly, but I haven't told him I'm a mage-blood, and I'd rather not tell him about Isoka's powers, either. Not unless I have to. I feel guilty that I can't confide in him completely, but my harder self—the part that hasn't changed since the old days—balls up that guilt and tosses it aside. *Focus.*

"Isoka works for . . ." I hesitate again, then take the plunge. "A criminal organization. I'm not supposed to know about it. She's the boss of the Sixteenth Ward. That's how she's been able to afford to keep me away from . . . all of this."

"I see." He tilts his head. "Now *that* would make an interesting question for moral philosophers."

"I'm not interested in moral philosophy," I say. "Something's happened to her. She was supposed to come visit today."

"You don't think she's just busy?"

"Not today. It's my birthday." I color slightly; making a big deal over birthdays makes me feel like a child. "She always visits."

"Congratulations," he says, automatically. "So. You think something has gone wrong? That she's in trouble?"

"I'm sure of it."

"All right." He mulls that as we cross a busy side street, sidestepping a loitering sedan chair. "So how do we find her?"

I can feel trust pulsing off him, a smell like warm honey, and a rising tang of excitement. Something unknots in my chest, a tension I hadn't realized I'd been carrying. I'm not certain I can do this without him.

"I know her boss' name," I say. "But not where to find him. I figure we'll march into the first shady establishment we see and ask for an appointment."

"Not exactly subtle," Garo says, with a raised eyebrow.

"I don't have time for subtle," I tell him. "She might need our help."

"Fair enough," he says. "How do we find a shady establishment?"

"In the Sixteenth Ward?" I shrug. "Throw a rock."

The southern, downhill gate from the Eleventh Ward is directly across from one of the Sixteenth Ward's three northern gates, with a wide military road called the Cross-Harbor running between them perpendicular to the main military highway. The Sixteenth Ward is unusual for a number of reasons, but the most basic is its shape—unlike the other wards, which are rough rectangles, the Sixteenth is a strip, long and thin, stretching along the city's entire harborfront and inland perhaps a quarter of a mile. The ward wall that separates it from the rest of the city is higher and more heavily guarded than the rest, being an extension of Kahnzoka's outer defenses. Any attacker sailing into the bay, after fighting past the Imperial Navy and the forts on the headlands, would have to land at the docks and then immediately launch an assault against a fortification nearly as formidable as the landward walls.

In addition to its defensive function, the ward wall also serves to keep the untidiness of the Sixteenth's streets away from the rest of Kahnzoka. The city authorities long ago decided that a certain amount of criminal activity is impossible to separate from the normal business of the docks, and gave up trying to do more than keep a lid on things. The Sixteenth's Ward Guard barely patrols the streets, and never after dark. Bodies are hauled away to the paupers' cemetery with no fanfare, and other crimes only investigated if the victim has money for bribes. I'm not naïve enough to think there aren't criminal organizations in the upper wards, but here they work openly, their enforcers—like Isoka—more trusted than any representative of the government. The merchants who load and unload goods here pay protection money to be left in peace.

At least there aren't any draft patrols to worry about. With so many foreigners in residence—the Sixteenth is the only ward in which noncitizens are permitted to rent rooms or travel without a special pass—the pickings would be slim. I'm worried about trouble at the gate, but we pass through the Low Market—a rowdier, less organized place than the High, stinking of the fish that's the main commodity—and join a slow-moving queue. There are a dozen guards, but they only watch to make sure nobody tries to slip back the other way without documentation.

After the gate in the thin inner wall, we follow the crowd over the Cross-Harbor and through the second gate in the much larger seaward wall. Again, the guards aren't paying attention to anyone going this direction. The crowd is mostly men, many of them pushing wheelbarrows, porters and vendors returning from their days in the upper wards. A few, better dressed, cluster in small groups, talking and laughing. I assume these are patrons heading for the Sixteenth's bars and brothels, which are legendary.

The buildings on the other side of the wall are similar to those that crowd the Eleventh Ward, multi-story tenements with sloping slate roofs and external stairways, but everything is more dilapidated. Great cracks run through the plaster, and whitewash peels off the exterior in strips. Hardly any windows are glassed, and many are covered over with boards or bars. A half-dozen narrow lanes meander into the mess of twisty little streets in no particular pattern.

Garo stares around, until I grab his arm and pull him after me. "Stop looking like a tourist," I mutter.

"Sorry." He lowers his voice. "To be honest, this is more what I expected when I first went to visit the lower wards. Lots of . . ." He waves a hand vaguely at a nearby gutter, so full of waste it threatens to overflow its banks. "Filth."

"This is where I grew up." I shake my head. "It hasn't changed."

It's shocking how familiar everything is, actually. It's been years since I've visited the Sixteenth, and yet I can still look down an alley and see the hiding spots, where two buildings don't quite touch; the places where a skinny girl might squeeze into for the night to get out of the wind; the kitchen doors of restaurants, good for a few minutes warming your hands until the owners chased you away. It's still late summer, a warm night, but even so I shiver in memory of winters past.

Garo frowns. "I don't mean to pry . . ."

"You may as well," I say, leading him down a slender road, buildings packed tightly on either side. More fish smells issue forth from a doorway, while from another I hear the sound of drunken voices raised in song. Real estate this close to the gate is valuable enough that most of the bottom stories are occupied by businesses, and my eyes scan the signs.

"Why would you and your sister stay here?" Garo says, eyeing a pile of steaming fish guts someone has dumped in the street. Two lean dogs are already fighting over it.

"Where else were we supposed to go?"

"Up to the Eleventh Ward? You're Imperial citizens, aren't you?"

I give a hollow laugh. "Sure. Born and bred here in Kahnzoka. Though I couldn't tell you where our father came from."

"So why not?"

"You need a chit certifying you to get into the other wards, to prove you're a citizen."

He nods. "The Bureau of Migration provides them on request."

"Maybe if you live in the First Ward," I say. "Down here if you don't want your papers to get lost, you have to pay." I have a vivid memory of Isoka swearing up a streak about some petty extortion, pacing back and forth across our tiny room. "Pay the Bureau man who issues it, pay the Ward Guard who approves it, probably another Ward Guard on the other side."

"That's . . . not how things are supposed to work."

I shrug. "It's what happens. Besides, we could never afford to live in the Eleventh Ward. Up there if the Ward Guard find you sleeping on the street, they haul you away. Down here, you can usually find a place to lie down, at least." I wave my hand. "Away from the gates, half the buildings are empty."

"Ah." Garo looks vaguely horrified. I find myself taking a perverse pleasure in shocking him.

"Staying warm was harder. The winters . . ." I shiver again. "There were times when Isoka almost turned us over to the slave-brothels just to keep from freezing."

"There aren't slaves in—" At my expression, he stops and shakes his head. "Sorry. I'll try to be less of a hopeless aristocrat."

"It's all right. It's a good look for you." Before he can respond, I find the sign I'm looking for. "Okay. In here."

He blinks and looks up at the shop. "'Assorted Goods'?"

"It's a pawnshop." I take a deep breath. "Let me do the talking." Not that I'm an expert in talking to criminals, but neither is Garo, and I at least have my Kindre powers to help me.

"What do I do, then?"

"Loom protectively? And hopefully keep anyone from putting a knife in my back."

"I see." He rubs his arms, where the Melos gauntlets would appear. "Understood. Lead the way."

I push through a curtain of hanging rags into the shop. It's as dark and dirty as the pawnshops I remember from my childhood, with narrow aisles between dusty wooden shelves crammed with broken things. Anything remotely valuable is up front, where the proprietor can keep an eye on it, so the shelves by the door hold only junk: waterlogged books, broken dolls, soiled clothing, and blood-stained linens. There's a three-string with only one string remaining, and a lantern with shattered glass.

Toward the back of the shop, a low table sits in front of a small, banked hearth. An older man, long strings of hair teased out across a balding scalp, rests beside a strongbox and a few shelves of more intact items—clothes, knives, cookware, odd nautical tools. He looks up at us, and his mouth narrows.

"Buying or selling?" he says.

"Neither," I tell him. "I need to meet Borad Thul."

He barks a laugh, and his mind rings with honest surprise. I glare at him, and his expression hardens.

"You're *looking* for Thul?" His eyes flick to Garo. "I don't know what your business is, but trust me, you'd be better off elsewhere."

"My business is my business," I say. "I just need you to tell me where to find him. I can pay."

I put my hand in my pocket, where I have my meager savings in a small pouch. When I pull it out, I can feel the pawnbroker's derision.

"Thul doesn't like unexpected visitors," he says. "He prefers people to come running when he whistles, and not before. And trust me, you don't want him to call for you." He shakes his head. "Look, tell me your trouble. Might be we can work something out."

I take a deep breath and put my hand in my other pocket, producing a small object. It's a statue of the Blessed One, which normally adorns the shrine in my room. The little ornament is the size of my fist, and made of solid silver, with gold chasing and tiny diamonds set in the eyes.

I hesitate for a moment before offering it. Not because I'm sentimental about the thing—it was a gift from Narago, as part of the supplicator's campaign to make me more pious—but if it gets back to Ofalo that it's gone, things are going to the Rot. At best, he'll assume one of the staff stole it. At worst—

But Isoka needs me. No time for quibbling.

"Then I'd like to sell this," I tell the pawnbroker, offering the statue.

The level of greed that comes off his mind, a bilious, yellow-green fog, nearly makes me sick. It wars with the quivering high note of fear. He peers at the little thing, frowning.

"Where'd you steal that?" he says.

"Do you care?"

"Little girl"—I bristle, but he ignores me—"I care if it means some aristos' guards are going to break down my door looking for it. Plus a thing like that's hard to shift. If I melt it down for the metal, it's only going to be worth—"

"A visit with Borad Thul," I interrupt.

His expression sours. "You have to be joking."

"Do you want it or not?"

"I . . ." Greed and fear—fear of Thul, fear the whole thing might be a trap—war in his mind. For a moment I feel a hot wind of aggression as he considers simply taking the thing off me. But the fear grows, stronger and louder, and he shakes his head. "Get out of here," he says. "Go on. I don't need this kind of trouble."

I swallow hard. We can try to find another pawnshop, another of Thul's minions, or—

I lean closer to him, and lower my voice to a whisper, too soft for Garo to hear. "Let me tell you something."

His eyes narrow, and he leans forward, too. "Listen, girl—"

"You're going to take us to Thul," I whisper. *"Now."*

And I reach into his mind.

It feels vile, like sticking my hand in an open sewer. The pawnbroker's thoughts swirl furiously around me. I don't know what I'm doing, not really, but I reach out to the bilious cloud of greed and *pull*. It spreads, covering everything else, smothering the fear. I find a wellspring of suspicion, like deep black oil, and stomp down on it, pressing it out of sight.

My gut heaves, and I clamp down to keep from vomiting. The pawnbroker sits up, and blinks.

"And you'll give me the statue?" His mouth crooks in a grin.

I nod, too uncertain of my voice to speak.

"Well then," he drawls, all trace of wariness gone. "Let's go and talk to the boss, shall we?"

"What did you say to him?" Garo asks, as the pawnbroker—whose name turns out to be Nouya—locks up his shop and leads us outside.

"Sort of a . . . password," I say quietly. "I got it from Isoka, but she told me not to use it unless I really had to."

He nods thoughtfully. For the moment, I have my Kindre senses firmly shut down until my guts stop squirming, so I don't know if he's convinced. I'm too busy trying to justify what I just did to worry about it.

I touched Old Sewa's mind because he was going to hurt someone. And those guards back in the restaurant, when they were about to kill Garo. This is the same, isn't it? Isoka's in danger, and I need to help her.

Besides, it's not like Nouya will be harmed permanently. *I think. I hope.*

Even my excuses ring hollow. It's *wrong*, reaching inside someone and twisting their thoughts, violating their self. I try to imagine someone changing *me*, without my suspecting anything is wrong, and it makes me want to throw up all over again.

"Tori?" Garo says. "Are you all right?"

I look up at him, and for a moment I see only a marionette, wooden limbs and a painted face, strings coiling to lead back to my hand. . . .

Isoka needs me. I blink, and the vision passes.

"I'm all right," I say. "Just a little . . . nervous."

"That's understandable." He gives a tentative smile. "For what it's worth, you were impressive in there."

I risk a smile back. "Good to hear, because I'm making this up as I go along."

Nouya finishes locking up and beckons. "The boss will be up at the Black Flower by now. Can't promise you'll get to see him. I can get you in the door, but you're on your own from there."

"That's good enough," I tell him.

"And then you'll give me the statue?"

I nod. He grins, wide and guileless, and beckons again. I fall into step beside Garo, my heart hammering.

The hour is getting later, and the streets are abandoned by the standards of the Eleventh Ward, where things are so crowded it's never really quiet. Here, as we move away from the gate, it gets very dark and still. A few candles flicker, but always behind curtained windows, and people move about in big, boisterous groups with weapons to hand. In spite of my meddling, Nouya retains enough caution to move quickly and quietly, and we slip through the winding alleys without attracting attention.

"Just so I know what to expect," Garo says in a low voice, "do you have a plan?"

"Not really." I'm trying to keep my eyes on Nouya and simultaneously look in every direction at once. Each alley entrance seems to hide a dozen menacing shadows. "Find out if Thul knows anything, and go from there."

"What if he won't see us?"

"He'll see us." *Whether he wants to or not.* I've come this far, what's one more atrocity?

"All right. What then?"

"Find Isoka. Help her."

"What if—"

He cuts off as we round a corner and come into view of the Black Flower. Our path has curved around, west and north, until we've come up against the wall that marks the boundary of the Sixteenth Ward. The Flower is a huge, ramshackle building that leans against that wall for support like a drunk against a lamppost, slumping back and to one side as though it were moments from collapse. A broad first floor spreads out quite a ways along the wall to either side, while a narrower second story sits directly over the main entrance. Light spills out through an open doorway flanked by armed guards.

A large, muddy area to our right is devoted to carriages, which seems to be how most people arrive here. Groups of well-dressed men and women are conducted to the entrance by more armed servants, while grooms and footmen bustle about attending to their horses. Garo, looking around, suddenly frowns.

"That's Lord Mondara's crest." He squints. "And Lord Goruka. I *know* some of these people."

My heart goes cold for a moment. "Any of them likely to recognize you?"

"I doubt it," he says, as though he hadn't considered that possibility. "Not dressed like this."

"Try to keep your head down," I tell him. "We just need to see Thul and get out again."

"And then I get that statue," Nouya says, pathetically eager. I manage a nod.

He leads us right up to the front door. A man in a dark, fashionably cut robe bars our way, looking me and Garo over.

"Staff entrance," he says. "Around the side. You're late, but we're overbooked—"

"They're not working," Nouya says. "I'm Stashi Nouya. From Gleamon's group? They want to see Thul."

"They want to see Thul," the doorman responds, deadpan.

Nouya nods, happily.

"And who are *they*?" he says, turning to me.

"I'm Gelmei Tori," I tell him, emphasizing the family name. Sure enough, there's a flicker of recognition. "This is my man Garo."

"I see." The doorman sighs. "Wait here for a moment."

He disappears through the doors. Nouya grins at me. Garo eyes the guards.

"I don't like this," he says.

Tell me about it. The Black Flower looks like a cancerous growth on the ward wall, a poisonous blossom. *But Isoka needs me.*

The doorman returns, with a particularly large bouncer looming behind him. I tense, and I can feel Garo straighten up beside me.

"Master Thul says he's willing to see Miss Gelmei, in deference to her sister's long service," he says, sourly. "However."

He inclines his head, and the bruiser steps forward. Nouya barely has time to look surprised before a huge fist slams into his face. I hear his nose break with a *crunch,* and blood sprays everywhere. He staggers back a step and sinks to his knees, and the bouncer buries a heavy boot in his midsection. The pawnbroker collapses, curled up on himself and whimpering.

"Master Nouya, he is displeased by your lack of discretion," the doorman says. "You may consider your services to Master Thul at an end."

I look down at the gasping, wretching Nouya. *It's not like he'll be harmed permanently . . .*

"Come on," the doorman snaps at me. "Master Thul doesn't like to be kept waiting."

* * *

The interior of the Black Flower is nicer than the ramshackle façade, at least on the surface. We enter a great hall, done up Jyashtani-style with a stone floor, deep carpets, and flowing hangings along the walls. It looks like a picture of exotic luxury, but living in the Second Ward has taught me a little about what true luxury looks like. It doesn't take much effort to see the frayed edges here: carpets with threadbare spots, cheap dyed linen hangings instead of silk, gaudy plaster sculptures along the walls instead of real ones.

Most of the customers don't seem to care. The hall is full of people, the women in colorful *kizen*, the men in looser, blander styles, but all in cuts and fabrics speaking of wealth and status. They gather in small groups, talking and laughing, supplied with drink by circulating flunkies in black. Other employees speak with the customers in low voices, and then disappear through side doors.

"That's Min," Garo says, a note of surprise in his voice. "Garuka Minio." He indicates a tall girl in her late teens, elegant in an expertly tailored deep crimson *kizen*. "I know her from our family temple."

The girl is a head taller than me, and beautiful by any standard, perfect painted lips, powdered skin, and a woman's body. I try not to think about the contrast I make, in my laborer's trousers and with my hair pushed up. Garo's eyes follow her as we skirt the edge of the room.

"Don't let her see you," I mutter.

"I know." Garo looks at the floor. "I've known her since we were kids. What's she doing *here*?"

"At this place? My guess would be either rutting or losing her father's money." I risk a glance in the noblewoman's direction, and catch one of the handlers emerging from a side door with a young man and a girl, both in loose robes. Minio gives the pair a once-over, nods decisively, and follows them out of the hall. In spite of myself, I feel a stab of satisfaction. "Definitely rutting."

"She—" Garo's mouth snaps shut. "This is a brothel."

"Obviously," I say. "Though there's gambling, too, and probably narcotics. Where did you *think* we were going?"

"I just . . ." He looks down at me. "You shouldn't be here."

Oh, Blessed. *Now* he decides to get protective? "What exactly makes you say that?"

"Don't—" At my expression, he pauses. "You're too young."

I glance at the doorman, who's leading us the length of the hall. He's busy making small talk with the guests as we pass, not paying us any attention. I keep my voice low anyway.

"There are probably girls my age *working* here," I tell him. "If Isoka hadn't gotten us off the streets, *I* could have been working here by now. So please spare me your moralizing."

He blinks. "Sorry."

"Besides, you're not much older than me."

"That's . . ." He purses his lips. "I suppose not."

Blessed above. This is not an argument I want to have, and especially not now. I look over at him, trying to gauge his reaction, but he just looks thoughtful. Even if I was prepared to read his mind, this place is crowded enough that I don't want to risk opening my Kindre senses. So I swallow whatever I was going to say next and follow the doorman, and we finally break out of the crowd at the far end of the hall, where a wide stairway leads to the second floor.

Upstairs, another narrower hall is fronted by many doors. What's going on behind some of them is obvious from the muffled moans and cries, and I blush in spite of myself. At least, I note, Garo has the grace to do likewise. Other doors are quiet, but a strange, sweet smoke hangs around them in a haze.

At the end of the hall, a pair of double doors are carved with a stylized whale bearing a long, whorled horn, picked out in gold leaf. The doorman pushes them open a fraction of an inch, speaks quietly, and then beckons us forward.

"Master Thul is very busy," he says. "So don't waste his time."

He pushes the door open. Inside is a spare drawing room with a low table and cushions. The walls are lined with shelves bearing a row of clay pots, beautifully stained and ancient looking. In contrast with the hall downstairs, everything here has the quiet, understated solidity of truly expensive craftsmanship.

Sitting behind the table is a middle-aged man, powerfully built but running somewhat to fat. He has an Imperial cast to his features, but his hair is a startling blond, which speaks to an iceling ancestry. He wears a simple gray robe, and his dark eyes seem permanently narrowed in suspicion.

When I'd poked around to find out who Isoka worked for, years ago, I'd heard stories about Borad Thul. Few of them were complimentary. The child of a prostitute and an iceling sailor, he'd grown up in the Sixteenth Ward, just like we had. After doing a stint as a galley rower in the last war, he'd come back with a lot of money and taste for creative violence. His takeover of the lower wards—and in particular what had happened to the bosses of the incumbent organization—was the sort of thing people talked about in whispers.

"So you're the little sister," he says. At a nod from him, the doorman slips out. He glances at Garo. "Who's this supposed to be? A bodyguard?"

"Something like that," I say. "Thank you for seeing us."

"I was curious. Isoka doesn't like to talk about you, you know. Some of my men thought you might have died, or that she'd sold you for a whore."

"My sister takes care of me," I tell him, a little stiffly. "She was supposed to visit today, and she hasn't come. I think she might be in danger."

Thul gives a braying laugh. "So you charged to the rescue? You've got balls, little girl. I like that. Do you have the same stick up your ass your sister does?"

Garo bristles. I put a hand on his sleeve to restrain him. Thul notices, and laughs again.

"I would like to know where Isoka is now," I tell him. "And if you have any idea what might have happened to her."

"What happened is that she made the wrong enemies," Thul says, "and left me with a heap of trouble to clean up. If you see her, you can tell her I'm rotting pissed off."

"What do you mean, the wrong enemies?" My heart double-thumps, my guts squeezing. "What happened?"

"Best I can tell, she and her man Hagan were having themselves a rut in a little place on Bleak Street. Next thing anyone knows, someone's kicked down the door, Hagan's dead, and there's blood everywhere."

"What?" I take a half-step forward. "Have you tried to find her?"

"'Course I tried. You let someone take out one of your bosses, next thing you know they're coming for your scalp. But we asked around." He leans back. "People who live in the building said it was the *Immortals* who grabbed dear old Isoka."

The world seems to go slow and strange for a moment. My ears are ringing. "The . . . Immortals?"

"I'm guessing she got careless. Or else she pissed off rotting Kuon Naga. Either way, it's bad for business. And now I've got to find a new ward boss."

"Where did they take her?" I say. "The Immortals."

"Who rotting knows?" He shrugs. "Does it matter? Ward Guards are one thing, but I'm not stupid enough to go up against the throne. Or Naga, which amounts to the same thing."

"You can't just give up—"

"'Course I can." He narrows his eyes. "Your sister's dead, kid, or as good as. Get used to it. The Immortals play for keeps."

"Tori."

Now it's Garo restraining *me*. I've stepped toward Thul without realizing it. I want to reach out to him with Kindre, to twist his mind and *make* him eat his awful words, to admit that Isoka only needs to be rescued—

"She was a good ward boss," Thul says, his tone growing slightly more somber. "Had a temper, but she didn't pick fights or beat her bedwarmers or get stupid on smoke. So here's what I'm going to do for *you*, kid. One-time offer." He leans forward. "Walk out that door and never bother me again, and I'll forget about you, and about the trouble your sister caused in her unfortunate passing. Sounds square?"

"It sounds . . ." I take a deep breath. "Fine."

"Good. Get lost." He makes a dismissive gesture, then tilts his head appraisingly. "Though if you ever need work, you come to me. I'm sure we can figure something out."

I turn on my heel and stalk out of the room, Garo hurrying to keep up.

"We're leaving?" he says.

"We got what we need from him," I say. "We know where Isoka is."

"But—"

"Now," I say, with a great more confidence than I'm feeling, "we just need to figure out what to do about it."

12

ISOKA

The sun is setting, turning the clouds to blood and the ocean to liquid fire. The jungle cacophony has redoubled its efforts, a rising chorus of rhythmic animal sound, punctuated by flights of birds. I watch, exhausted, trying not to close my eyes.

When I close my eyes I see Safiya screaming as the king of the lizard-birds rips her in half. In my memory she's still screaming as it pulls her torso free, still screaming as she tumbles down its gullet in a spray of blood and a tangle of writhing guts. I don't think that's right—a person couldn't be *alive* through that, still shrieking in pain as—

"Isoka?" Meroe's voice.

My eyes snap open again, but I don't say anything.

I hear her padding across the stone. I'm sitting at the very top of the ziggurat on a flat stone roof that's featureless except for the hole leading down into the stairwell. There was a guard up here—Meroe's security is thorough as always—but I dismissed her. Now I sit on the edge, legs dangling over one colossal step, facing north toward the sea and the enormous shape of *Soliton* in its dock.

Still there. But not for long. *And still out of my reach.*

"There you are." Meroe pauses beside me, shading her eyes against the setting sun. "You didn't tell anyone where you were going."

"Sorry." I pull my blanket a little tighter around myself.

After a moment, Meroe sits down beside me. I don't look at her. I don't dare.

"Thora's doing well," she says. "She should be awake in the next day or two. It'll be a while before she's fit to fight, of course."

"That's good." I pause. "You've been practicing."

"A little," Meroe says. "I didn't want to be in a situation where I could save someone, and . . . hesitate."

"That's . . . good."

There's a long silence.

"Isoka," Meroe says, in the gentle tone of voice you might use to calm a frantic animal. "It isn't your fault."

"Don't be stupid." I hunch over in the blanket. "Of course it's my fault."

"The crew knew the risks. They volunteered."

"They volunteered to follow *me*. That makes it my fault. That's what being leader *means*."

Meroe lapses into silence for a while longer. I want her to go away and leave me alone. I also want, quite desperately, for her to put her arms around me. The remnants of the powerburn fever leave my skin pebbled and scratchy under the blanket.

"Venius Acuitus has a saying," she says, eventually. "'To command is to sacrifice.' My father likes to quote that, but I don't think he really understood it. He thinks it means that when you command, sacrifices are inevitable in the name of the greater good." She looks at me, sidelong. "I think Acuitus was talking about the burden of responsibility. To command *is* to sacrifice, not of others but of yourself."

"Is that supposed to make me feel better?"

"It's not supposed to do anything—"

"Because it's rotting *garbage*. They put me in charge to try to keep people alive. My 'burden' is I've done a rotting awful job at it."

"Back on *Soliton*, you saved us all," Meroe says gently.

"*You* saved us all. You got people to march, kept them fed, kept them going, kept them from killing each other. You and Shiara and Karakoa and even Zarun."

"You stopped the Scholar and got the doors closed."

"Right." I look down at my hands. "I can kill things. And I can talk to ghosts, apparently. Why in the Blessed's name did anyone think that would make me a good leader?"

"You know it's not that simple."

"I'm not sure it isn't." I shrug, still not looking up at her. "It doesn't matter anymore. I'm finished."

"That's not true." She leans closer. "The crew understands, Isoka. They—"

"It's not about them. It's about me. I'm done."

Meroe stops. "What's that supposed to mean?"

"I mean I'm *done* with this." My heart hammers, driving a dull, throbbing pain in my head. "I should never have started it. The crew can take Catoria's offer, go live with her or the monks or whoever will have them. I'm not making decisions for them anymore." I close my eyes, fighting the tears building behind them. "My sister's going to be dragged off to be tortured and there's nothing I can rotting do about it and I'm *done*."

"Ah." Meroe rises, then grabs my hand. "Stand up, would you?"

Reluctantly, I get to my feet. She turns me to face her, beautiful as ever, eyes full of a kind determination.

"Right," she says, gently.

Then she punches me in the face.

It's not an expert blow, but it has surprise and passion behind it. I take a stumbling step back, my cheek stinging, as Meroe shakes out her hand and examines her knuckles for a moment. When she looks up, all her calm is gone, replaced with a cold, quiet rage.

"You don't get to be *done*," she says. "You can't just abandon your responsibility. That's what responsibility *means*. It's not something you do because someone tells you to, or because you're in the mood. It's something you *feel* and can't let go."

"If I feel it, it's your rotting fault," I shoot back, spitting a gobbet of blood to the stones. "Do you know how much easier it was before—"

"Of course it was *easier*," she interrupts. "Nobody said doing the right thing would be *easy*."

"The right rotting thing for *who*? Not for Safiya. Not for everyone who died on the way to the Garden. Not for *Tori*."

"You do what you can with what you have," Meroe grates.

"And when that's not enough?"

"It has to be enough."

"Rot." My lips curl in a snarl. "Maybe the problem is I can't live up to *your* rotting standards. Maybe no one can."

"The problem," Meroe says, "is that I fell in love with a self-centered, self-pitying piece of *rotscum*."

"I—" Anger drains away, all at once, and a terrible guilt surges to take its place. "Meroe. I don't—"

But she's already leaving, dress whipping around her as she stalks away. I can't bring myself to call out as she clomps heavily down the stairs.

I sit back down, legs wobbling underneath me. Then, eyes still full of tears, I start to laugh.

The sun is long gone, and the sky is full of stars.

Go downstairs, something at the back of my mind tells me. *It's the fever, the guilt. Tell her that, tell her you're sorry.* She'll put her arms around me, and tell me she's sorry, too, and kiss me, because Meroe is a better person than I have any right to have near me.

But if I do that, then I'll have to figure out what comes next. Face the prospect that *Soliton* is going to leave, stranding me here, maybe for the rest of my life, while back in Kahnzoka, Tori will be at Kuon Naga's nonexistent mercy.

What rotting kind of life could I live, knowing that? Staying here with the crew, with Meroe, knowing that my failure had delivered my sister into the hands of a monster?

Fog has rolled in off the sea, swathing the forest in wisps of cloud. The moon, rising, glints across the top of the mist, like a cold ocean rising up over the treetops. It swirls unsettlingly, and as I watch, it parts to reveal a large, four-legged figure at the base of the ziggurat. It's an angel with a dog's head, the one I've glimpsed several times now, which followed us from *Soliton*. It stands on the steps at the bottom of the building, looking upward, and I swear it sees me. It makes a jerking motion with its head, over one shoulder. Then again, as though it wants me to follow.

Following it would be madness, of course. Prime's monsters could be out there, along with Blessed knows what else.

But it's better than going back inside and confronting the truth.

I stand up, leaving the blanket behind. I've got only a light tunic on, feet bare, but it's a warm night. The ramp on the side of the ziggurat doesn't come all the way up, so I step off the edge of the first tier, absorbing the ten-foot drop with a crouch and a flare of Melos armor. Then the next, and the next, heat rising along my bare legs, descending in an arc of spitting green sparks. When I reach the ramp, I start to jog, bare feet slapping against the stone. The angel keeps staring at me, unmoving, until I'm nearly to the bottom. Then it turns, and with a last look over its shoulder lopes into the misty darkness.

I go after it. It moves slowly enough that I can keep pace, far enough behind that I can barely make out its bulk through the fog. Swirls of mist open around me, and in every faint, moonlit shadow I expect to see a walking corpse or a lizard-bird waiting to claw my guts out. But nothing attacks me. Overhead, I hear the squeak and flap of bats on the hunt, and once the abrupt screech of something small dying suddenly amid the undergrowth.

I don't know which direction we're going, but we travel for some time. Eventually the forest stops at a neat line of trees, and the angel walks out into a plowed field. There are other angels here, inert and still, waiting for daylight to begin their appointed tasks again. Compared to *Soliton*'s guardians, who are all disturbing, fantastical shapes, the angels of the Harbor are utilitarian—great featureless bodies with four legs and two arms, looking like stone statues no one has carved in detail. They take no notice of us.

The dog-angel stops in the middle of the field, the blue glow from its crystal eye lighting up the ground. In the middle of the neatly plowed rows of earth, there's a pit, the sort of thing a real dog might dig to bury a bone. It's about as deep as I am tall, like a grave. I pause in front of it, skin sheathed in sweat after the long run, breathing hard and fighting a stitch in my side. The angel points its nose down into the pit, and waits.

"You want me to go down there?" I ask it. I'm not expecting a response, and I don't get one. Approaching the edge of the pit, I look down, and see something gleaming dully at the bottom. "Are you going to bury me alive?" I pause. "That's a joke, I think."

I climb down. What else am I supposed to do, at that point? Go home?

As I descend, the dog-angel lies on its belly and lets one foreleg hang into the pit beside me. It's just about long enough to reach the bottom, and it puts its heavy stonelike paw on a gleaming bit of metal. I kick away a few clods of dirt to reveal a long metallic tube buried in the soil, stretching into the walls of the pit as though this angel had excavated a hole around some kind of sewer pipe.

Maybe it *is* a sewer pipe. Or irrigation for the fields? My grasp of the principles of agriculture is pretty hazy. Or else—

Then I get it, and my skin pebbles into goose bumps. It's not a pipe for water, or for sewage. It's a *conduit*, carrying Eddica energy, like the ones I found in the control room on *Soliton*. I'd known there must be something like that here, judging by the flows of power I could feel, but not where. Bending over, I can see the rush of energy inside it, tiny motes of gray light tumbling through the metal in a current. They wash up and around the paw of the dog-angel, shimmering in the blue glow of its eye.

It lifts its paw, then touches the conduit again.

"Yeah," I say. "I get it."

I don't understand. But what else is new?

I put my hand on the conduit, and try to feel the Eddica flow through me. Then, all at once, there's another presence, and a voice in my head.

"It took you long enough."

"Hagan?" It comes out as a whisper.

His shape appears before my closed eyelids, outlined in gray Eddica-light. I fight the urge to sob at the sight of him. Not that I make a habit of that, but . . .

"Where have you *been*?" I say. "I haven't seen you since my fight with the Scholar. I thought—" I swallow and clear my throat. "I thought you were dead. Deader. Dead again. Whatever."

"I think—I think I nearly was." His shape wavers, as though it's made of fog and the wind has picked up. "I don't think I'm quite . . . whole, anymore. I don't remember everything. What the Scholar did . . . damaged me. It took a while for me to pull myself together, so to speak."

"I tried to help you," I tell him.

"I know." He shakes his head, leaving trails of gray light. "I nearly had it when the ship sailed into the Harbor."

"What happened?"

"I felt something reach out to *Soliton*. Take control of it. The city's system controls the ship's, it was designed that way. But I could feel some*one* coming with it, passing into *Soliton*'s system, rummaging around. Looking for something like me."

"Prime," I say, mouth dry. "It was Prime."

Ghost-Hagan nods. "He doesn't control the city's system, but he can ride it. And he's stronger than I am, much stronger. I pushed myself into this angel and ran. I don't know exactly how much I left behind."

"Left behind?"

"Parts of myself. My feelings, my memories. I crammed what was important into this thing." He shrugs. "I feel . . . incomplete. But it doesn't matter."

"Why did you wait until now to say something?" Unreasoning anger flares. He could have helped us against Prime—warned us, at least—

"I can't talk to the city's system, or else he'll notice me," Hagan says. "This is the only way I could figure out to talk to you, pig-gybacking directly on a conduit. Even here, I don't think we have long—"

"No, we don't," another voice says. A young woman, sharp and commanding. "So can we get on with it?"

Her ghost-image forms beside Hagan. It's indistinct, compared to his, blurred and constantly fraying and re-forming. She's about my age, with long pale hair and iceling features, tall and slender. Given Catoria's story, I can make a pretty good guess as to her identity.

"Silvoa, right?"

She grins, wide and infectious. Another blurry shiver runs across her image. "I see you're up to speed. That's helpful."

"More like a lucky guess," I say, shaking my head. "Are you . . ." I can't think of a tactful way to ask the question.

"Dead?" She gives a decisive nod. "As a doornail."

"Ah."

"Prime took me prisoner when Gragant and I tried to get into his ziggurat," Silvoa goes on, matter-of-factly. "When I wouldn't work with him, he tortured me to death."

"Um." Because how, exactly, do you respond to that? "Sorry. I mean. So . . ."

"Why am I still here?" she says. "He caught my spirit when I died, just like you did with Hagan. Except you seem to have given him free run of *Soliton*'s system, while Prime keeps the Harbor pretty well locked down."

"Why?"

"He likes to torture me from time to time," she says, waving a hand in a blurred gesture. "He's not very complicated, in some ways."

"She contacted me while I was following you to the ziggurat," Hagan says. "Told me where to look for the conduit. There's a network running under the entire city."

"And when he finds me, he'll close the loophole I used to get out," Silvoa says. "I have no idea how long it'll take to find another one, so let's not waste time. Isoka—It's Isoka, right?"

I nod, dumbly. Even without the added complication of being dead, Silvoa's rapid-fire style is a little overwhelming.

"Okay. You had the right idea, trying to get into Prime's lair."

"Catoria told me what you were trying to do. I thought we might have better luck." I swallow. "That was . . . stupid. I just—"

"Not stupid, but maybe a little premature. Catoria . . ." Silvoa's businesslike expression softens. "Is she all right?"

"She seemed fine," I say. "She talked a lot about you."

"I wish she wouldn't," Silvoa says. "I wish . . . well, a lot of things. Not relevant. The point is, I was right back then. If you can get to all three access points, the system will recognize you as an administrator. You can lock Prime out, shut off his power, use the angels against him."

"I thought I would be able to control *Soliton* after I got to the Garden, but—"

"This is different. Trust me. I know you have no reason to trust me, I'm sorry. But I'll help you."

"Even if you're right," I say, "I can't get into Prime's ziggurat. I'm not going to waste more lives with another attack."

"We're working on that," Hagan says.

"I have an idea," Silvoa says, nodding. "But you need to get to the other two accesses *first*. That way, when you reach the third one, you can shut Prime down on the spot."

"That makes . . . sense." Sort of. "But I don't know if the others—"

"He's on to us," Silvoa says. "Ice and rot. Isoka, Hagan will try to get in touch with you again. But—"

Her ghost-form freezes, mid-word, and then vanishes in a puff of Eddica energy. Hagan looks around frantically.

"I need to run," he says. "And so do you. Good luck."

I open my eyes.

I'm still at the bottom of the pit. The dog-angel is already moving, backing up from the edge, and I scramble up toward it, bare feet shifting in the dirt. The field is still dark and quiet, and the Harbor angels sit motionless, but other figures are rapidly approaching. Corpses, lurching toward us at surprising speed.

The dog-angel—Hagan—gives me a final nod, then turns and lopes off into the darkness. He leaves me alone at the center of a ring of monsters, which I suppose counts as a vote of confidence. I find myself grinning as I raise my hands, blades igniting with a *snap-hiss*. The first corpse-thing comes into range, and I take its head off with a single cut and send the flailing body into the pit with a well-placed kick.

The others pause, or at least I imagine they do. I spread my arms, blades cutting cracking trails through the darkness. The old rage sings in my veins, the old rush. No one else to get hurt, no one to get in the way.

Bring them on.

By the time I get back to our ziggurat, the eastern horizon is fading from black to gray. I jog up the ramp, clothes and skin spattered with mud and black blood from the corpses. The guard gapes at me, and I give him a manic grin, still high from the adrenaline of the fight. He hurries off ahead of me as I stroll down the corridor, stopping in the main chamber to borrow a rag and clean myself up.

Meroe arrives after I've managed to scrub off the worst of it. Her face is composed, but her eyes are puffy from crying, and just a look from her rips my heart in half. She stops in front of me, takes a deep breath, then looks around at the gathered crew, who are watching our every move.

"In here," I tell her, taking her arm and ducking back out through the corridor and into an empty storeroom. Some of Catoria's gifts are piled here, but no one is around, and a glance at the guard trailing Meroe keeps her at a safe distance.

"Isoka—"

"I'm sorry." The words spill out, without any conscious thought on my part. "I'm sorry, I'm so rotting sorry. You were right. You're always right."

"I'm not." Meroe takes a deep breath again. "I haven't been . . . I didn't think about how this must be for you. I got . . ."

"It's fine."

"It's *not*." She glares at me, tears forming in her eyes. "You don't get to make me the perfect one, Isoka."

"You're right." Her mouth curves upward, and I roll my eyes. "Sorry. You're wrong, too. But it *is* fine. At least, I don't know what will happen, but you and I . . ." I shake my head. "Next time, please punch me sooner?"

"I'll take that under consideration," she says. I can tell she's trying not to grin. "What *happened*? Are you all right?"

"Fine. Some of Prime's monsters turned up. Nothing I can't handle." My mind feels like it's fizzing. It won't last long—I'll crash hard, soon—but for now I'm flying. "Call everyone together, the pack leaders. I need to talk to them."

She nods, and half-turns. I grab her shoulder, turn her back toward me, and kiss her. After a startled moment, she melts into me, our bodies pressing together as though slipping back into the place they most belong. She holds me so hard I can barely breathe, hands sliding up and down my spine, sending warm shivers across my skin. For a moment there's nothing in the universe but her, the soft, dark, beautiful glory of her.

Fighting always leaves me wanting to rut, after, a deep, sweet ache. I consider, briefly—the bags of cloth in the corner look soft enough—

Meroe breaks the kiss, reluctantly. I let my arms fall away from her, and she takes a trembling step back, breathing hard.

"I'll . . . get everyone together." She gives me a shaky smile.

"After I talk to them," I murmur.

She raises one eyebrow. "And after you've had a bath."

Once again, the Council and the pack leaders gather in one of the smaller chambers.

I can feel the missing faces, like broken teeth in a punched-out grin. Shiara is with Catoria and her people, and Thora is still asleep upstairs. Jack is here, looking unusually disheveled and baggy-eyed, her short hair teased into unruly spikes. Zarun leans against the wall, a bruise blooming across his handsome face and a bandage wound around one arm.

Was Safiya here the first time? I can't remember. Guilt still tugs at me, but its pull isn't as strong as before, as crippling. *To command is to sacrifice.* I think Meroe and her father were both right. Their sacrifice *and* mine.

"I assume you've all heard what happened by now," I tell them. "I'm sorry if I've been . . . unavailable. I've been thinking."

"Thinking hard, it looks like," one of the pack leaders says from the back row.

I look down at myself—still barefoot, still smeared with dirt—and grin. The moment of tension dissolves into a round of laughter.

"People are dead because of me," I tell them. "I did what I thought was right, and now they're dead." I pause, because I'm not sure what to say next. *I'm sorry* doesn't seem adequate.

"That's what happens, on a hunt," Zarun says. "You make decisions. Sometimes people die."

There's a murmur of agreement from the others. And, I realize, they do understand. Zarun and the Council ran *Soliton* in the name of the Captain for years, and every pack leader faced the same choices on a smaller scale every time they went out into the dark. *You make decisions, and sometimes people die.*

I fight the urge to glance over my shoulder at Meroe. Instead, I look straight ahead, and push on.

"If anyone else wants to take a shot at this," I tell them, "now would be the time to say so."

One by one, everyone looks at Zarun. With Shiara gone, he's the last member of the old Council still here. He raises his eyebrows, then shrugs.

"You've got my advice, if you want it," he says. "But I'm still with you, Deepwalker."

"Clever Jack owes the Deepwalker and her partner her life, now," Jack says. Her old flair is returning, though her mask has not yet hardened, and I can still see pain in her eyes. "Speak and she will obey."

The rest of them agree, less volubly. A grunt, a nod. The pack leaders are not a group of men and women given to emotional displays.

"Just tell me one thing," Zarun says. "That's a dozen of our people

Prime has killed now. I assume you're not planning to let him get away with it?"

"Of course not. He needs to be dealt with." I take a deep breath. "But it's going to be more complicated than we thought. I think we're going to need help."

13

TORI

My bravado lasts almost until we get back to the gate to the Eleventh Ward.

I can feel it slipping away, the furious adrenaline that powered me through the interview with Thul, the determination I'd felt afterward. With every step, that energy drains from my body, replaced with a dread as black and thick as tar. By the time we reach the gate, I'm wobbling on my feet, and Garo has to help me through the short queue. I barely register the faces of the guards as we show them our documents.

Immortals. The word has loomed large in my nightmares since I was a little girl. Even before I knew the details, I understood what it meant. The Immortals had the power to tear my tiny family apart, to rip me and Isoka away from one another. Whatever other horrors they could inflict on us seemed almost immaterial, compared to that. In the Second Ward, they'd been an abstract fear, a vague worry about disaster, like the risk of a tsunami or a hurricane. Now, though, they're horrifyingly real.

I have no idea how long ago they'd come for Isoka. She could be dead—it's impossible for me to imagine that, death was too much like giving up, my sister would never do it. She could be trussed up in the back of a cart, headed out to some distant outpost of the Legions. She could be stalking back and forth in the darkest cell under the palace, beating herself bloody against the bars. She could be—

"Tori." Garo takes my arm. "Tori! Are you all right?"

I blink, looking up at him. "What?"

"You just about fell over." He casts around for a moment, spots an inn with lamps in the window in spite of the late hour. "Come on. Let's see if we can find you a place to rest."

I nod, feeling numb, and let him pull me toward the lit doorway. We're still close to the Low Market, and there are quite a few inns around, catering to merchants and fishermen. This one must be very cheap indeed, because it doesn't even have a common room, just a narrow counter where a pinch-faced woman hands out keys and sells clay jugs of liquor. Garo gets us one of each, and pulls me upstairs, where he struggles with the newfangled padlock on the door.

The room is barely big enough for two people to lie down side by side, but at least it's clean, a sleeping mat rolled up in one corner with a threadbare pillow sitting on top. Garo kicks the door shut behind us and guides me to a seat on the ground.

"I'm all right," I tell him. "Just . . . tired."

"You've had a shock," Garo says. He uncorks the little clay jug and holds it out to me. "Drink. Just one swallow."

The harsh scent of the stuff goes through my sinuses like a crossbow bolt, and I barely manage to take a pull. It burns my throat on the way down, too, but somehow turns warm as it hits my stomach, spreading out through my body like a cloud. Garo takes the bottle back, swallows a bit himself, and sets it aside.

"I'm sorry," I tell him. "I'm sorry I dragged you into my mess. You don't have to . . . do all this."

"You'd rather I abandoned you in the street?"

"I'd be fine," I insist.

"Maybe." He grabs the sleeping mat and unrolls it. "But you wouldn't have left me, would you?"

"That's different."

"Of course." He pats the mat. "Lie down. You need rest."

Lying down seems, suddenly, like an extremely good idea. I crawl across the room and roll awkwardly onto the mat, while Garo settles himself beside me, legs crossed.

But everything is still waiting for me when I close my eyes. Isoka in a dungeon, throwing herself at the bars like a caged animal. Isoka burning on a pyre. My sister, the one I owe *everything* to, dead, dead, dead, dying in a hundred ways, torn away from me.

Don't leave me behind. I remember a night, hungry and cold, watching her stare at a knife and not caring what she did, as long as she didn't go without me.

I feel Garo's hands on my shoulders, calm and warm, and realize I'm gasping for breath like I've just sprinted a mile. My eyes pop open, and he's looking down at me, hair falling around his face.

"It's all right," he says, very quietly. "It'll be all right."

It won't be. But it's nice to hear him say it. And then it strikes me how close he is, and how we're alone, a single room in a cheap inn. My skin pebbles to goose bumps, and my cheeks flush.

Idiot, something in my mind admonishes. *Isoka's captured, maybe gone forever, and you're thinking about . . . boys, is that it?* But some combination of alcohol and emotional backwash seems to be drowning that voice out. If Isoka's gone . . .

I won't think about it.

Garo is giving me a strange look.

"Garo?"

"Hmm?" he says.

"Do you want to kiss me?"

It pops out, before I can think about it. Which is good, because if I'd thought about it I never would have said it. Garo's jaw tightens, and he swallows hard. There's a long pause.

"Very much," he says, his voice tight.

"You can." My heart beats triple-time. "If you want to."

"Tori . . ." He runs a hand across my forehead, pushing my hair aside.

"It's all right."

"It's not." He lets out a deep breath. "Not like this." Garo smiles, a little sad. "Go to sleep."

When I open my eyes, they're crusted with dried tears, and it tastes as though something has died on my tongue.

Daylight is coming in through the tiny window, revealing the cracked plaster walls and fraying floor mats of the little room. I'm lying on my side, curled up on the sleeping mat, my joints stiff. It takes me a moment to raise my head and rub the crumbs from my eyes. Garo is at the other end of the room, sitting propped against the door, his head tipped backward, emitting faint snores.

Memory returns in bits and pieces, a little fuzzy. I feel acid churning in my stomach, but in the cooler light of day some calm has returned. I go over what Thul said, piece by piece, and try to think.

Then I look at Garo again. *Blessed above. Did I really ask him . . .* My blush returns with a vengeance. *Oh, Blessed One.* How am I supposed to talk to him *now?*

He gives a snort and wakes up, shaking his head. I sit up, pulling my knees close in front of me. Garo blinks and looks around.

"Tori." He lets out a breath. "How are you feeling?"

"Better." It's even true. "I'm sorry for falling apart like that."

"It's only to be expected." He yawns. "I'm not sure either of us has been getting enough sleep."

"Probably not."

"And—" I glance at the window, and swear, for the first time in quite a while. "Oh, *rot.*"

"I know. My father is going to be furious when I get back."

It's not a matter of furious. If Ofalo figures out I'm not there, he's going to send out *search parties.* And afterward there's no way I'll be able to get out again, not for *months* at least. The acid in my gut rises higher, and I clench my jaw, trying to force it back down.

"I've been thinking, though," Garo says. "About what we can do to help your sister. Father will know *something,* I'm sure of it. If I go home and throw myself on his mercy, he may be willing to help."

"I thought you said he'd be furious," I say, still trying to figure out how to deal with my own situation.

"Oh, he will. But I know how to handle him." He gives me a sidelong look. "Er. It might be better, actually, if I told him I was going out to meet a girl, not work at a hospital."

"I mean. You're doing both, aren't you?" I fight to ignore the rising blush. "It's not exactly a lie."

"Right." He yawns again. "What about your people?"

"I'll deal with them." Thank the Blessed he doesn't press for detail, because I don't have any. "I think we should go back to Grandma's first, though. She keeps track of the Immortals, she might know something."

"I suppose being a little bit later isn't going to make things worse."

Garo gets to his feet, stretches, and holds out a hand. I take it and let him pull me up. Then, for a moment, I don't let go.

"Thank you," I say quietly. "For helping me. And for . . . last night."

"It's . . ." He gives an embarrassed shrug, and squeezes my fingers. "I meant what I said. Just . . . think about it a little."

"I will."

There's a long moment of silence, awkward but warm. Finally, reluctantly, I let go.

Even after washing my face, I'm scarcely feeling my best. My hair is a mess, tucked up in a tangle under my cap, and my clothes feel stiff with yesterday's sweat. I move gingerly as we leave the inn.

In a way, this is an unfamiliar world. For years I've visited the Eleventh Ward only by night, and seeing the crowded streets in the daylight feels strange. The crowds are different, more purposeful, more hurried, less inclined to linger by a puppet show or a sweets stall. These are people heading to another day of making ends meet, or just beginning their long hours of labor. Men with pairs of buckets slung on a long pole walk the streets, dispensing wickedly strong tea into any proffered mug for a couple of bits. Garo secures a couple of cheap clay mugs and gets us some, and I sip the biting-hot stuff as we walk up toward the hospital.

I don't even know if Grandma will be there. She might be asleep—she must need to sleep, I know intellectually, but I have a hard time imagining her actually doing it. She certainly doesn't rest at night. But I need to talk to her now, before returning to the Second Ward, because I have no idea how long it'll be before I'll be able to get out again.

Unless, of course, I simply make *Ofalo leave me be.* The thought is chilling. Ofalo has been nothing but kind to me, even if he's been well paid for his services. Turning his mind against itself would be as wrong as knifing him in the back. *But it was just as wrong to twist Nouya, and I did that for Isoka's sake.* I look down at the cup of tea in my hands, and half-expect to see marionette strings trailing from my fingers like glittering spider-silk. Garo walks beside me in silence, leaving me to my thoughts. We've crossed half the Eleventh Ward and gotten within a few blocks of the hospital before I realize something's wrong.

I've never seen the building by day before. It's squat and ugly, all peeling whitewash and cracked plaster. A dozen chimneys poke out the top. I'm used to seeing their faint twists of gray smoke rising up against the clouds, lit by the glow of the city below. Now, though, a more substantial column is rising, black and thick. It's not wood in a hearth. The hospital is burning.

"Garo."

I tug him to a stop, and point wordlessly. He looks up, swears, and for a moment we both stand there stunned. Then, in silent unison, we toss our teacups to shatter in the street and start to run.

Fires always draw crowds, but there are more people gathered than I would expect, a knot of Eleventh Ward onlookers several layers deep. They're kept well back from the hospital by a line of Ward Guard, soldiers on the ground carrying hooded spears, with cavalry trotting behind the line. Garo and I come to a halt at the back of the crowd, and I rise onto tiptoe, trying to find the source of the flames. The building doesn't *seem* to be a blazing inferno.

"Can you see anything?"

Garo shakes his head. I look around, then turn away and pull him after me, heading for a butcher shop on the nearest corner. The front door is open, and the butcher—a woman named Karan who's worked with Grandma before—is gawking with the rest. I wave as I push past her into the shop, Garo in tow.

"Tori!" Karan turns. "Do you know anything? Is Grandma all right?"

"Trying to find out!" I call back at her. "Borrowing your roof!"

Karan's rooms are above her shop, a tangled mess of discarded clothes and soiled sheets. And, leaning against one wall, a ladder, which is just the right height to reach a trapdoor leading out onto the slate roof tiles. I know this because one night, a year ago, we used Karan's roof as a hiding place for a couple of scared mage-blood kids, and I sat with them and tried to calm their whimpering as Ward Guard patrols crisscrossed the district below.

I slam the ladder into place, and Garo, getting the idea, swarms up it, pushing open the trapdoor. I follow, blinking at the bright sunlight. The roof is sloped, and the slate tile uneven, so footing is tricky at best, but at least we can see over the heads of the crowd and the Ward Guard beyond.

There are a *lot* of Ward Guard. As a rule, they don't fight fires, leaving that to neighborhood fire brigades. The sour feeling in my stomach returns, stronger than ever, as I watch a whole squadron of cavalry troop past, with a company of spearmen on their heels. No one seems to be carrying buckets.

The smoke is billowing out of the main entrance, with trickles rising from a few of the first-floor windows. It can't be that bad inside, though, because Ward Guard are still moving in and out. I freeze as more of them emerge, followed by a line of men and women with their hands roped behind their backs. Many are bandaged, wearing stained hospital robes.

"Are they evacuating?" Garo says.

"It's not a fire," I mutter. "It's a raid."

My chest feels tight. Grandma has been raided before, though not in the time that I've been there. She talks about her friends in the Ward Guard, but there are times when they can't turn a blind eye to her activities. *She's always gotten through it. Unless they find the sanctuary* . . .

The smoke shifts, and I catch sight of a column of figures who are definitely *not* Ward Guard. They wear a uniform I've never seen in person, but recognize from a hundred hushed stories—dark leather armor, studded with blackened metal plates, their faces obscured by a hanging veil of chain mail. *Immortals*.

A moment later, they're gone, but I know what I saw. I turn to Garo.

"We have to get to the sanctuary."

"We're not going to get through that," he says, pointing down at the lines of Ward Guard. "And they may not find it. If we stay clear—"

"They'll find it. There are Immortals in there. That means they're not just looking for draft refugees."

His eyes go wide. "You're sure?"

"I saw them."

I will him not to argue, and Blessed be praised he doesn't. Instead he takes a deep breath, as though steeling himself, and lets it slowly whistle through his teeth. Then, with no trace of further hesitation, he says, "All right. How do we get there?"

Okay. I can admit, in the privacy of my own skull, that if I'm not falling in *love* with him, then . . . well. The thought distracts me from the madness of what we're about to do.

"Follow me," I tell him. "And stay quiet."

The sanctuary, housed in the hidden inner section of a decrepit tenement block, is not supposed to be accessed directly—that would, obviously, lead any watchers to conclude the block isn't as abandoned as it appears. But, because Grandma Tadeka is thorough in her contingency plans, there is a back door, carefully concealed against a day just like this one. It's outside the Ward Guard perimeter, and clear of most of the crowd, but there are still more people than normal on the streets. I lead Garo to the abandoned building and force myself not to look over my shoulder.

We move a loose slat from a boarded-up door and push our way in, padding through silent, cobwebbed hallways. Plaster has fallen from the walls in huge chunks, melting into gray slush, and mold grows over what's left in great blooms. The apartments visible through the open doorways are similarly ruined, floor mats black and rotting. I count doorways, muttering under my breath, and find an unremarkable door between two of the vacant suites. It opens into a closet, empty and full of dust. I reach out to the back and rap as loud as I can.

"Is there a secret knock?" Garo says, fascinated.

I shake my head. "There's supposed to be a sentry on watch. I hope they haven't run off, because it'll be locked from the other side." I raise my voice. "It's Tori! Please, I need to get inside to talk to Grandma."

A faint voice, a young girl's, comes back from the other side of the wood. "I'm not supposed to let anybody in."

I think hard. "Karuko? Is that you?"

"Yes." She sounds scared. "I don't know what's happening. Grandma's not here."

"Who's in charge?"

"Hasaka, I think," she says.

"How about if you let me in and take me straight to him?" I say. "That can't hurt, can it?"

I can feel her fear, seeping through the wood like black oil. For a moment I want to reach out and shove it down, steady her nerves with Kindre power, and then I recoil from the thought. *You can't just* twist *people!*

"Okay," Karuko says after a moment, a brassy note of courage peeking through. "Come quick."

The back of the closet swings open on noiseless hinges. Karuko, who is about twelve years old, blinks at us from behind round spectacles, her eyes big and owlish. I smile at her and climb through the narrow opening, Garo behind me.

"Where's Hasaka?" I ask her, as she shuts the secret door and locks it.

"In the storeroom, watching the tunnel," she says. "I should stay here and keep watch."

"I'll go right there," I promise her.

"Is Grandma okay?" Karuko says.

I nod, trying to look cheerful. *Blessed, I hope so.*

Most of the sanctuary's population seems to be out in the halls or in the common room. We pass dozens of children, and even a few of the old men have left their upstairs rooms to see what's happening. Old Sewa blinks at me from a seat on a staircase. *At least he's not trying to set me on fire this time.* The hospital must have had some warning, because I recognize some patients who normally live on the other side of the secret tunnel.

Questions are shouted at me from all directions. I can do nothing more than wave as I pass, jogging toward the storeroom, where the tunnel exit emerges. I hurry down into lantern-lit darkness. Most of the stores have been moved to the center of the room, creating a barricade of bags of rice and crates of dried meat. Hasaka sits on the dirt floor behind it, with Jakibsa and a dozen others.

"Tori!" he says, standing up as I enter. "And Garo. Oh, thank the Blessed. I was sure they'd got you."

He advances to hug me. When he pulls back, I tell him, "We were away. I saw the Ward Guard, and went up on Karan's roof to have a look."

"I had enough time to get a few people over to this side," he says. "Grandma stayed behind to try to talk to them, but they've arrested her, and Kosura, and everyone else who—"

"It's not just the Ward Guard," I blurt out. "The Immortals are here."

"*What?*" Hasaka hisses.

"I saw them from the roof, going into the hospital."

There's a chorus of alarmed swearing. Hasaka buries his head in his hands.

"Oh, Blessed's rotting balls," he moans. "We're all rotted."

"They might not find the tunnel," Jakibsa says. "If we stay quiet—"

"They'll find it eventually," I say. "We have to get *out* of here."

"And go where?" someone says.

I catch Hasaka's eye. "There's a backup. A safe house."

"*There?*" he says. "That place isn't a safe house. It's just a hole. There's no food, no beds—"

"Grandma told me to go there," I say, "if anything like this happened. She must have had a plan."

"I don't think she ever planned to get arrested by *Immortals*—"

Jakibsa puts one of his mutilated hands on his lover's arm. "Hasa," he says. "She's right. If they've sent the Immortals, they know we're here. Eventually they'll find us."

Garo nods agreement. Hasaka's lip twists for a moment, but then he gives a sigh.

"All right," he says. "We'll get everyone ready, and take as much food as we can. Maybe some of Grandma's friends can help us once the heat comes off." He turns to one of the waiting men. "Tano, go upstairs and start getting the kids together. Try not to panic anyone."

Tano, barely more than a kid himself, gives a nod and hurries upstairs.

"You'd better go with him," Hasaka says to me. "People will listen to you. See if you can organize something to help the old men move faster—stretchers or chairs."

"I can do that." Something to do will help keep my mind occupied. The fact that Grandma has been arrested—the polestar of my world, casually removed—still hasn't settled into my mind, churning as it is with thoughts of Isoka. "What about—"

My Kindre senses give me a flicker of warning. One moment the tunnel beyond the secret door seems empty. The next there are a dozen minds in there, burnished with determination and the copper tang of violent intent. I shout a warning—

And the door explodes from its hinges, shattering outward in a blast of wooden fragments. A figure in black armor rolls forward, chain veil jingling. Immediately behind it, an identical shape raises both hands and sprays bolts of flame.

Everything turns to chaos in an instant. Hasaka, Jakibsa, and I are standing behind the makeshift barricade, and we duck instinctively at the sound. Blasts of Myrkai flame hit the pile of sacks, detonating with a roar and spraying rice everywhere. The rest of Hasaka's people, spread out around the room, aren't as lucky. I see a boy barely older than me hit by a bolt that wraps his body in brilliant flames, and he stumbles shrieking toward his attacker. An older woman, leaning against the opposite wall, is blown backward by a blast and left in a tumbled heap.

After the initial volley, the Immortal who dove forward gestures sharply, and a wall of blue Tartak force springs up, sealing off the tunnel entrance. Hasaka jumps to his feet, fire swelling around his hands, and the other refugees do likewise. Bolts of flame fly back across the room, toward the dark-armored soldiers, but they slam into the blue energy and gutter and die. Immortals are piling into the room behind the shield of force, carrying swords and cross-bows.

More blue energy joins the fray, slamming into the shield with a shower of sparks and a sound like steel on glass. Behind me, Jakibsa grunts, his careful technique abandoned for brute force, tearing at the shield with Tartak power of his own. For a moment the blue curtain parts, and Hasaka triumphantly slams a bolt of fire through, wrapping one Immortal in a shimmering wreath of flame. It van-ishes an instant later, though, under the influence of another sol-dier's own Myrkai power, leaving the victim smoking but still on his feet.

"Out!" Hasaka barks. "Everybody out! Jak, get Tori!"

I shout an objection, but it's lost in the roar of the mêlée. The Immortals, clear of the confining tunnel, drop their shield of force and attack. Crossbow bolts, aimed by the preternaturally accurate senses of Sahzim talents, zip across the room. Jakibsa picks some of the bolts out of the air, but others find their targets. A girl goes down, clutching at the fletching emerging from her throat. Bolts of fire slam back and forth, bursting and burning.

An Immortal comes forward, sword in each hand, surrounded by a golden glow and moving so fast she *blurs*. She's coming right for me, and I don't have time to do more than throw up my arms. Then the world around me turns blue, and I'm yanked backward, crashing roughly against a sweating Jakibsa. Garo steps into the sword-wielding Immortal's path, Melos gauntlets shimmering green on his arms, blocking her strikes with a scream of metal against magic. He slams one gauntlet in her face, hard enough to send her tumbling backward in a jangle of chains, then crosses his arms as a flaming bolt explodes against him, Myrkai energy war-ring with Melos.

My Kindre senses are shut down in self-defense, blotting out the pain and death. Stumbling behind Jakibsa, I force them open, trying not to choke in the sudden tide of fear and rage from the fighters, mixed with agony and despair from the dying. I reach out to the Immortals, as I did to the Ward Guard in Nirata's restaurant, and flatten their thoughts.

Stop.

I'm prepared for revulsion, for the sick-making feeling of other people's minds cracking under the force of my will. What I'm not ready for is *nothing*. The wave of my Kindre power slides off an invisible barrier, dissipating harmlessly into the miasma of emotions. I try again, pushing as hard as I can, my skin growing feverishly hot as power floods through me. Something—someone—is *blocking* me, parrying my clumsy thrusts.

Of course they have a defense. Kindre users are rare, but I can't be the *only* one. The Emperor's personal killers could hardly be left vulnerable to such crude manipulation. Despair wells up, turning my legs to jelly, as Garo backpedals desperately in the face of a fresh assault and Hasaka barely ducks a bolt of flame. Jakibsa duels with one of the enemy Tartak users, force grinding against force, and eventually gets in an unguarded shot that lays the man senseless on the floor. It's only a small victory, and a moment later he's forced onto the defensive, blocking another volley of crossbow bolts.

We're all going to die. Blessed defend, rot and ruin, we're all going to rotting *die* here in the next few seconds—

The Tori who lives in the Second Ward would have fainted by now. Pampered and protected, shielded from blood and illness and danger, she would lie senseless and helpless, until someone cut her throat.

Thankfully, I'm more than that. I'm not Isoka—I don't have her steel, her fire—but I can pretend to be.

"*Back!*" My voice sounds like a screech. "Garo, Hasaka, everyone upstairs! Jak, push them back, just for a second!"

Jakibsa glances at me, sweat already pouring down his face, his ruined hands hanging at his sides as he fights a complex battle with only his mind. But I see him grit his teeth, and blue energy flares, slamming across the room in a solid wave. Broken bits of crate go flying, ricocheting off the shield erected by the Immortal Tartak adepts, then back off Jak's barrier. Eventually the two collide, and the scraps of wood are pulped between them. For just a moment, the room is split in half.

In that moment, we flee. Garo stumbles back toward me, and between us we haul the immobile Jakibsa up the stairs. The rest of the defenders follow, leaving the dead and dying behind them. Hasaka comes up last, dragging a sobbing young man by the collar.

The stairs up from the storeroom pass through a narrow doorway into the kitchens. I pull Jakibsa to one side, catching him as he collapses, his skin already welting into bright red lines. I've read about powerburn, the aftereffect of overexertion, though I've never seen it. From the heat still rising from my own skin, I may get to experience it firsthand.

Garo grabs a heavy table and shoves it forward, Melos power amplifying his blows to send the wooden barrier shuddering against the door. Two more defenders put another one in place behind it, just as the first starts to shiver and jump under assault from below.

"It won't hold them long," Garo says.

"We're not staying long," I pant. "Everyone out. We're going to the safe house." I turn to Hasaka, who is standing over Jakibsa, speaking quietly. "Can you carry him?"

He nods. "But not everyone is going to be able to run."

I know that, and my heart is already tearing.

In a panic, the sanctuary empties.

The children go first, in groups of a dozen accompanied by a leader. I wait by the back door, sending each group on its way and telling them where to go. Then the slower groups, the wounded, the old soldiers, splitting up to make their way through the city as best they can.

A few remain behind, Tartak users to hold the storeroom door, a handful of others to make a last stand. Old Sewa is with them, waiting at attention, Myrkai fire burning on his hands. No trace of confusion in his eyes now. Waves of pure force clash in the doorway, gradually reducing the thick tables to splinters. The Immortals are stronger, better trained, more coordinated. We can't hold for long.

Not to mention, there are other ways to get to us. *Even if they can't force the door, surely they're searching for a way around.* It might take them a few minutes to figure out which building houses the sanctuary, but—

Hasaka stumbles past, with Jakibsa on his back. "Come on," he tells me. "They're nearly through!"

"Where's Garo?" He'd gone back, to round up the last few stragglers.

Hasaka shakes his head. I wave him on, and he doesn't argue, staggering off into the street. A few onlookers have gathered, curious at this sudden exodus. But so far—

Our luck runs out. A squad of Ward Guard rounds the corner, uniformed and carrying spears. Their officer gestures, and they break into a run.

Still no Garo. My skin is already hot, but I reach out with Kindre again, sending a wave of power against their minds. I find fear there, suppressed under the discipline of camaraderie and orders, but still present, and I pull it out and bring it to full flower. A river of fear flows down the street, almost visible as a shimmer in the air.

The soldiers stop in their tracks, spears clattering to the ground. Then they run, consciousness submerging in the torrent of horror. The bystanders join them, my power terrifying and indiscriminate. I don't know how long they'll keep running, but for now the street is empty.

Almost. A lone solder remains, a woman, her eyes wide with terror, but apparently rooted to the spot. I give her another push, power crackling across my skin, leaving welts and burns. With a scream, she runs, but *forward*, directly toward me.

Panic, I realize, is unpredictable. She still has her spear, and she lowers it like a lance, aiming directly at me. I back up as far as I can, against the wall of the ruined building, then shift sideways at the last minute as she charges home. It's not fast enough, and I feel the tug as my sleeve tears. No pain, not yet, just a numb tingle in my arm and the feeling of warm blood running across my skin.

The spear embeds in the plaster, and the maddened Ward Guard can't get it loose. I try to slip sideways, and she abandons the weapon, reaching for me with her bare hands, her eyes wild. I grab her right arm, pushing it wide, but my other hand won't respond. Her fingers curl around my throat, and she pins me against the wall with a yell.

I'm calm. That's the strangest thing. I'm calm. I wonder if this is how Isoka feels, when she faces some criminal in a dark alley. Isoka has Melos blades, though, and armor, a supernatural powerhouse few can match. Whereas my power, clumsily applied, has *produced* this berserker, and I have no weapons but—

—a dagger, on the woman's hip.

I can't breathe.

I grab for the dagger with my good hand. It comes free of its sheath, and I nearly fumble it. The guard doesn't even notice, both hands around my throat now, squeezing hard. She's still screaming. I scream back, or try to, as I bring the knife up, slashing into her belly. She grunts at the first strike, but her grip doesn't slacken, so I stab her again and again, until the dagger gets stuck between her ribs.

I must pass out for a moment, because the next thing I know Garo is rolling the slack corpse off of me. I'm covered in blood, and I don't know how much of it is my own. My skin is boiling, and the world rolls and shudders around me.

"Tori!" His voice is distant. "Tori!"

My eyes close. I really would have liked to kiss him, I reflect, as I sink into darkness.

14

ISOKA

This time, there are only four of us leaving the ziggurat.

There's no question of Meroe staying behind, of course. We're going to talk to the Minders, and I want her at my side for that, just as I'd want Zarun with me in a fight. Besides, if I tried to make her stay, she'd probably just punch me again.

Zarun himself is coming, too, both to give us a little backup and for his knowledge of the Jyashtani language. And Jack accompanies us as far as the base of the ramp, then steps aside with an elaborate bow.

"Fare well, bold travelers," she says. "I hope to see you again 'ere I return."

"Good luck," I tell her. "Be careful."

"Clever Jack is always careful. And handsome. And clever." She grins. "I will find the Lady Shiara and inform her of your plans."

"Thank you," Meroe says.

Jack bows again, then turns and jogs off around the building. We strike out in the opposite direction, heading for the third of the great ziggurats, the one occupied by the Minder monks.

I find myself watching the woods with considerably more anxiety than on my first trip, even though it's early and we're not going anywhere near Prime's domain. His monsters don't *usually* move about in the day, but that doesn't mean never. He wants my power, and I don't intend to give him an easy shot at it.

Zarun, too, seems jumpy. He argued for bringing more fighters with us, but Meroe and I agreed that it wouldn't help. If the Minders attack us, a few more crew won't stop them, and we certainly don't want to attack *them*. And, as long as we're careful, he and I should be able to handle a few walking corpses.

Meroe, by contrast, looks around with the wide, fascinated eyes of a little girl, staring at every colored bird that breaks through the foliage. She laughs when we run across more monkeys—they have those in Nimar, apparently, but not the long-billed, bright green birds that Zarun says are similar to some he's seen from southern Jyashtan. Meroe has an eye for flowers, too, which she finds every-where—on the ground, growing from vines wrapped around trees, hanging from delicate tendrils in midair. I have to pull her onward before she starts investigating.

"So have you thought about what you're going to say to them?" Zarun says. "They seemed pretty emphatic about wanting us to join their order if we were going to make an alliance."

"I don't need an alliance," I tell him. "Just a one-time deal. They're threatened by Prime and his monsters, too."

"Maybe. Harak didn't seem too concerned."

I pause, looking sideways at him. "Can I ask an obvious ques-tion?"

Zarun smiles. "If you don't mind a condescending answer."

"Harak talked about the Divine Being," I say. "But I always thought the Jyashtani had a whole bunch of gods."

That was the general impression on the Kahnzoka docks, anyway—idols with the heads of animals. In the Empire, the wor-ship of gods is considered unbearably primitive, a practice of her-etics and barbarians who haven't yet accepted the teachings of the Blessed One. On *Soliton*, such matters were mostly not discussed. Zarun had never seemed like a particularly religious person, but you never know what someone does in private, and I was hoping not to offend him.

For that matter, it occurs to me, I have no idea what *Meroe* thinks on the subject of the divine, and whether there are gods of Nimar. Not being a particularly dedicated scholar of the Blessed One, it hadn't occurred to me to raise the subject. Back in Kahnzoka, I'd always stayed as far away from the supplicators as possible.

"It's . . . complicated." Zarun scratches the back of his head.

"Most Jyashtani worship the pantheon as a whole, and a few specific patrons in particular. But some priests talk about how all the gods are different aspects of one *overall* divinity, which presents different faces at different times. Frankly that's about when my head starts to hurt, especially since in the stories the gods are always fighting each other, which seems like it would be hard if they were all the same person."

"I don't know about the Minders specifically," Meroe says, "but the one god or many gods question has been debated in Jyashtani theology for centuries. They've fought wars over it."

"Of *course* you know Jyashtani theology," I deadpan.

She puts on a faux-haughty look. "A princess should be able to hold her own in *any* discussion." After I dissolve in giggles, while Zarun looks a bit lost, she says, "Honestly, it's mostly from history books. Different sects are always getting themselves declared heretics by the Grand Temple in Horimae for political reasons."

"If the Minders were a group that sought out mage-bloods, the Grand Temple wouldn't have liked that at all," Zarun says. "So maybe they packed them all off to *Soliton*."

Before long, we break out of the trees and into the open fields maintained by the Harbor's angels. They're a patchwork, some just harvested and plowed, others yellow or green with crops I don't recognize. The angels move among them, slow and meticulous, multiple limbs carefully sliding along each stalk.

We give them a wide berth, sticking to the fallow fields, and the angels pay us no attention whatsoever. Still, no one speaks until we've left them behind and crossed into another belt of jungle.

"I keep wondering what happened to them," Meroe says.

"Who?" Zarun says.

"The ancients." She gestures vaguely at the strange, artificial world around us. "The ones who built this place, built *Soliton*. They had so much *power*, but . . ." She spreads her hand. "Where did they go?"

"Maybe they wiped themselves out," Zarun offers. "Like the people of the Rot did."

Zarun doesn't know Meroe is a ghulwitch—at least, I think he doesn't. I give Meroe an awkward glance, and say, "This place isn't destroyed, though."

"If anything, it's preserved," Meroe says, nodding. "We *ought* to be buried under twenty feet of snow."

"Then maybe they left," Zarun says, clearly impatient with the topic. "Or maybe they just got bored and decided to walk into the sea. Does it matter?"

It might, I answer him, but silently. Zarun is visibly on edge as we come into sight of the great ziggurat, and not eager to contemplate ancient mysteries. I have the same impulse, but . . . *Understanding what the ancients did, where they've gone, may be the only way I get back to Tori.* I glance toward the sun, already near its zenith. *There's not much time left.*

The Minders' home looks the same as Prime's, so much so that my skin pebbles to goose bumps as we approach. Instead of bones, however, the monks have painted the stones of the ziggurat in bright colors, abstract patterns on the stair-stepped blocks that seem to shift and change as we come closer. A man and a woman, both in the same brown robes Harak had worn, stand watch at the base of the ramp. They straighten up at our approach.

"You want to do the honors?" I ask Zarun.

He makes a sour face, but nods. When he speaks in Jyashtani, I do my best to follow, though the pidgin I've learned aboard *Soliton* is inadequate to the task.

"Greetings!" he says. "We are *something* from the *something.*"

I glance at Meroe, pleadingly, and she leans close.

"He says we're the ambassadors of the newcomers," she says. Then, as Zarun continues, "He says Harak visited us, and now we'd like to speak to their leader."

The two guards look at one another, then make a deep bow. The woman speaks, rapid-fire, and Meroe translates, "She says we're welcome here, and Gragant will be happy to see us."

"That was easy." I feel tense, full of nervous energy. "So far, so good, right?"

* * *

The guards lead us inside, through a series of high-ceilinged halls, similar to the building we call home. The Minders have made it their own, however, laying down reed mats to soften the floors and stringing enormous tapestries over the stone walls. These hangings have no pictures, only long lines of text, written in a highly stylized hand with a calligraphy brush. I can't make heads or tails of it, but I assume it's religious.

There are more of them than I had guessed, at least a hundred spread throughout the rooms we pass through. In the first chamber, large groups are engaged in some kind of quiet, contemplative activity, either prayer or meditation or both, sitting in ranks with their heads bowed. The second room is given over to more energetic pursuits. The monks, stripped to loincloths—men and women both, I can't help but note—move in unison through complicated forms that seem half dance, half combat training. Beyond them, a pair are actually fighting, a young man and woman exchanging blows under the careful eye of an older trainer. The boy gets in a few punches solid enough to make me wince, but the girl gets her leg around his and sends him spinning to the floor, then immediately follows him down, her body laid across his and her elbow pressed against his throat. The referee barks something that sounds encouraging.

Our guide speaks, and Meroe raises her eyebrows.

"That's him," she says, nodding at the judge now offering the winded boy a hand up. "That's Gragant."

I realize that, somehow, I'd been expecting someone older, a white-bearded ancient like the monks in dramas back home. But, of course, Gragant had been put aboard *Soliton* and accepted by its angels not much more than five years ago—by his own personal time, at least—and so he doesn't look much more than twenty-five. He isn't as tall or broad as Harak, and his skin is darker, closer to Meroe's dark brown than Zarun's copper. But he has the same chiseled look, muscles toned to a fine definition I'm more used to seeing on heroic statues. He has the same blue eyes as Zarun, and a mop of dark, curly hair above a surprisingly open-looking face.

When he sees us, he sets the boy on his feet, pats him on the shoulder, and gives the girl a word of encouragement. Only then does he come over, accepting the deep bow of our guide with a wave. He speaks in Jyashtani, and then, to my relief, in a more understandable pidgin. It's not quite the same mix I'm used to from *Soliton*, but it's got enough Imperial in it that I can understand.

"You must be our new friends," he says. "Welcome to the Harbor. I am Gragant of the Minders." He gives a very slight bow.

"Thank you." I return the bow, to the same degree. "My name is Gelmei Isoka, sometimes called Deepwalker. These are members of our Council, Meroe hait Gevora Nimara and Zarun."

"Do you require water? Food?"

I shake my head. "Thank you, no."

"Straight to business, then." He smiles slightly. "I assume it's business that has brought you here. You don't seem like a seeker of truth. Though I would be delighted to be wrong." He spreads his hands. "The Divine Being is ever welcoming."

"Business, for now," I tell him.

"Though I would be interested in hearing more about your theology," Meroe pipes up, then adds, at a glance from me, "sometime later."

"Perhaps we should speak privately?" I say.

Gragant laughs. "I have no secrets from my people, I assure you. But if it would make you more comfortable, by all means. Follow me."

He leads us out of the training chamber and down a narrow hall, accepting a spare robe from an acolyte on the way. I watch him as he shrugs into it, unable to refrain from a little . . . aesthetic appreciation of the play of muscles in his broad back. But there's something about him that unnerves me—he's too *confident*, moving with the easy grace of someone absolutely sure of his place in the world. *Maybe that's what faith does for you.*

We end up in a small chamber with a high, Jyashtani-style table and simple wooden benches. Robed servants bring in jugs of water and clay mugs, then bow and withdraw. Gragant takes a seat, his posture achingly correct, and I settle myself uncomfortably on the too-hard surface. One thing I'll never understand about Jyashtani—what's wrong with a nice soft cushion on the floor?

"I've taken the liberty of summoning Harak," Gragant says. "I hope you don't mind. I often consult him before making decisions."

"Of course," I say.

Then, absurdly, I run out of words. This would be the point where I should start negotiating, which is what I actually *came* here for, but it seems ridiculous to just present my demands like I'm at the corner grocer. Why would he listen?

Fortunately, I brought Meroe, and she smoothly takes over. She says something in Jyashtani, fast enough that I can't follow it, and Gragant replies, sounding surprised. They share a laugh, and Meroe shifts back to pidgin.

"I'm curious," she says, "about the exercises you were overseeing back in the hall. I didn't know Jyashtani monks were so . . . martial."

Gragant laughs again, though I fancy there's a slight edge to his smile. "We are unusual in that respect, I must admit. Our faith instructs us that closeness to the Divine Being comes from perfection of the self, both the body and the spirit. The techniques we teach are for honing oneself to that ideal."

That explains all the rippling muscles around here. "Do you also use them for self-defense?" I ask, trying to make a contribution.

"If necessary," Gragant says. His tone is a teacher fondly correcting an errant pupil. "But that is not their purpose."

I feel myself bristling, and take a deep breath, striving for calm. This kind of self-confidence has always sat poorly with me. For a moment, I'm back with Kuon Naga, his spectacles aglow with lamplight, carefully peeling oranges with his long fingernails as he narrates how my sister will be kidnapped and raped if I refuse him. My throat goes tight, and I grip the edges of the table.

It's not the same, I tell myself. I fight the urge to get in Gragant's face, rattle his cage, unsettle him. *Focus, Isoka. Follow Meroe's lead.*

The awkward moment is broken by the arrival of Harak. I'd forgotten the sheer size of the man, a head taller than Gragant and equally well-muscled. Gragant gets to his feet to greet him, and I admit to a moment of surprise when they kiss, briefly but passionately. Zarun catches me staring, and shoots me an amused look.

"Welcome," Harak says, his pidgin more halting and awkward than Gragant's. "I hope you have come to join our community, as I offered."

"Not to join, I'm afraid," Meroe says. "But we were hoping to work with you. Isoka believes we can help each other."

"Oh?" Gragant says.

"You knew Silvoa," I say.

He nods. "I did indeed."

"She believed that if an Eddica adept were able to use the access points at all three great ziggurats, they could take control of the Harbor."

His eyes narrow. "I'm surprised you're aware of that."

"I spoke to Catoria about it." Silvoa's spirit had filled in the gaps, too, though I wasn't about to tell him that.

"Ah, Catoria." Sadness crosses Gragant's face. "She still hates me, I assume."

"She does."

He sighs. "I pray for the Divine Being to release her from her pain, but I fear she clings to it too closely. She's told you our sad little history, then."

"More or less. You must have believed Silvoa's theory, since you went with her to Prime's lair."

"I . . ." Gragant looks uncharacteristically uncertain. "At the time, I would have believed anything Silvoa believed. She was . . . unique. Her loss broke us all, I think."

Harak puts a huge hand on Gragant's shoulder, says a few words in Jyashtani. Gragant nods, and takes a deep breath.

"I assume," he says, "if you're asking me this, then there must be one among your people with the Eddica gift."

"There is," I say. "Me."

For a moment, everything is quiet. Harak looks between me and Gragant, his broad face suddenly unfriendly. Gragant himself has the expression of someone who has just solved a tricky puzzle.

"So," he says. "You want to use the access points and take control of the city. And then?"

"Destroy Prime, to begin with. I'm sure that would help all of us."

"Unless you set yourself up in his place," Gragant says. "You have to understand the danger here. Without the labor of the angels, we would all struggle to feed ourselves. If you were to damage the system, even by accident, it could mean disaster. And, at worst . . ." He shrugs. "You could starve us with a thought. Or simply send the angels to destroy us."

Meroe breaks in. "You were willing to help Silvoa try to do the same thing."

"I trusted Silvoa," Gragant snaps. "So far, I have no reason to extend the same trust to you. I ask you again—having achieved the power you seek, what would you do with it?"

"Leave," I say. "I would take *Soliton* and return to the world. Anyone who wanted to would be welcome to join me. You certainly don't have to worry about my setting myself up as a tyrant *here*."

Harak rumbles something in Jyashtani. Zarun, clearing his throat, translates, "He says that would be against the Divine Being's plan."

"Indeed," Gragant says. "We were delivered here to further pursue our own perfection. How else to explain this place but a miracle?"

"A miracle infested with walking corpses?" I raise my eyebrows. "Are monsters part of the divine plan?"

"That is a matter of some contention," Gragant says. "Some have said they are intended to prevent us from becoming too complacent, here in the Divine Being's chosen country. Others assert that they are a trial for us to overcome, to show we truly deserve paradise. Either way, though, they are a problem for those who have proven themselves worthy to attend to."

"Fine," I say. My patience is wearing thin. "How do I prove myself worthy?"

Another pause, and a look passes between the two men. Harak bends to Gragant's ear, and speaks quietly. Gragant shakes his head, then whispers something that makes Harak's face turn sour.

"It is not right," the big man says, in halting pigeon. "She is not . . . of us."

"Neither were you, once," Gragant says.

"I saw the truth," Harak says. "She sees nothing."

"The Divine Being may use many instruments," Gragant says. "Even unbelievers, should it suit the divine plan."

Harak falls silent, but doesn't look any happier.

"Well?" I prompt.

"I can offer you a chance to prove the righteousness of your cause," Gragant says. "If you best me in a trial, then we will know the Diving Being looks on you favorably."

I have to force myself not to grin.

"I don't like it," Meroe says. We're alone in the room now with Zarun, the two Minders having left to make preparations.

"Don't like it?" I got up from the awkward bench as soon as Gragant did, and now I find myself pacing the room, stretching my arms and trying to work the ongoing ache of powerburn from my muscles. "It's the best chance we're going to get. If I beat him, these mad monks will have to admit their god wants them to help us."

"We don't know what Gragant's Well is," Zarun says.

"I fought Ahdron in the ring," I say. "I fought the *Butcher*. You think he's likely to be worse?"

"I'm more worried about what happens if you kill him," Meroe says.

I wave dismissively. "He didn't say the fight was to the death."

"That doesn't mean much," Meroe says. "We don't know what we're getting into."

"It's worth the risk."

"Isoka . . ."

Catching her expression, I glance at Zarun. "Can you give us a moment?"

Amused, he retreats to the other side of the room. I pull Meroe to the wall and lower my voice. "What's wrong?"

"You're doing it again," she says. "Taking on all the risk."

"I don't have a choice. Time—"

"I know time is running out," Meroe says. "Zarun could fight Gragant, you know."

"I . . . I don't know if the Minders would accept that."

"Neither do I," Meroe says. "But it never even occurred to you, did it?"

"No," I admit. "I don't want to ask someone else to do my fighting for me."

"Sometimes you have to." Meroe runs her fingers through her hair and sighs. "You think I *want* to be the one who always says 'wait, stop, it's too risky'?"

"I'm taking responsibility for the crew," I say. "That's what you wanted."

"Charging headlong into every fight isn't the same thing as taking responsibility." Meroe sets her jaw. "Gods know I have selfish reasons to keep you intact, but have you thought about what this plan of yours means? If we need an Eddica adept to use the access points, what are we supposed to do if something happens to you?"

"That's—" I pause. "I hadn't thought about that."

Meroe smiles ruefully. "I know. Just . . ."

"Be careful?"

"Gods, I'm tired of saying it." Meroe leans forward, resting her forehead against mine. "You know you can rely on us, when you need to. Me, Zarun, the others."

"I know." I kiss her, quickly. "Next time, I promise you get to fight the crazy monk for me."

"I think our hosts are returning," Zarun says.

Meroe and I pull apart, and a moment later two robed monks enter. They bow, and one of them says, "If you are ready, we will escort you to the site of the trial."

"I'm as ready as I'm going to get," I say. "Lead the way."

Questions start to rise in my mind when, after passing through a maze of corridors, we leave the great ziggurat altogether. It's just past noon, and the sun beats down brutally on the western face of the stone building, though none of the monks seem uncomfortable.

"The trial is outside?" I ask our escort.

She nods. "It is not far. An hour's walk."

"An *hour*?" I look at Meroe, who shrugs and mouths, *Don't ask me.* Wherever we're going, then, it's well away from the ziggurat. And apparently we won't be going alone, either. A good thirty monks fall in behind us, loping across the forest floor in studied silence. I wonder if they're an honor guard, or watchmen to make sure I don't change my mind. Maybe both.

We walk almost due west, which surprises me as well. The Minders' great ziggurat is the westernmost of the three, so we're headed away from the center of the ancient city. The forest quickly gives way to more fields, then a rocky scrubland. The monks keep up a steady pace, though we're all sweating in the sun.

Then the light starts to change. At first I'm sure I'm imagining it. Shadows blur, as if the sun were obscured by thick clouds, though it still hangs over us as bright as ever. Ahead, the color of the sky changes, shifting from deep blue to a washed-out gray. And the Eddica currents, ever-present in the Harbor, are closer to the surface here. I can feel them under strain, creaking like the timbers of a house in a windstorm.

In the distance, something gleams bright. I can't quite wrap my mind around what I'm looking at, but Meroe gets it.

"It's the ice," she whispers, sounding awed.

I remember the Harbor, seen from the outside: a gray dome, carved out from a continent of ice and snow. Now we're approaching the same barrier, from the inside. The monks have brought us to the edge of the world.

Gragant and Harak are waiting only a few yards from the barrier. It's almost invisible up close, like fog, a translucent gray smear in the air. Just beyond it, the ground is covered in snow, only a few inches right at the border but deepening rapidly. Huge chunks of ice gleam in the sun, jutting out of the soft whiteness like bones poking up through soil. Farther off, great hills rise, then mountains, blued by distance.

For a moment, I find myself shocked into silence. It's both the scale of the ice—enough ice to bury Kahnzoka a hundred times over—and the corresponding scale of what the ancients have built. I'd thought that *Soliton* was a wonder, a ship faster than anything afloat and bigger than a mountain, metal-hulled and unstoppable. The Harbor, by contrast, seemed like a city—ancient and strange, obviously, but still something on a mortal scale. Now, for the first time, I realize that of the two, the Harbor is an incomparably more spectacular demonstration of power. To take *that* blasted arctic wasteland and turn it into a tropical jungle—well, it's no wonder that the Minders saw the hand of their god in it.

"Looks pretty rotting cold," Zarun says, and shivers.

"Deepwalker," Gragant says, coming over to us. "I'm sorry to leave your escort to others. As your opponent, there are certain rituals I needed to attend to."

"I understand," I say, though I'm not sure I do. "Is this always where you have your trials?"

He nods. "It is a reminder of what the Divine Being has given us. Where we would be, if not for divine favor."

"It's impressive." I try for nonchalance. "But it's a long way to walk for a fight. We could have done this in your training hall."

Gragant looks at me, perplexed. Then, unexpectedly, he throws back his head and laughs.

I look at Zarun, wondering if I'm missing some cultural context. He shrugs.

"I apologize," Gragant says, after a moment. "I hadn't considered things from your perspective. Of course."

"Of course what?" My eyes narrow. "Are we going to have our duel out on the ice?"

"We're going out on the ice," Gragant says. "But we're not going to *fight*. Trial by combat? We're not barbarians."

Harak is giving me a superior stare, and I can hear mutters and chuckles among the rest of the monks. I fight down an instinctive rush of embarrassment.

"So how am I supposed to prove myself against you in a trial?" I ask.

"Victory in battle is no proof of righteousness," Gragant says, serene. "The Divine Being demands the perfection of the self, the body and spirit. Demonstrating *that* will be our trial." He nods at the border.

"What?" I stare at him. "We just go over there, and . . ."

"Meditate," he says. "A perfected spirit can achieve calm, regardless of what storm rages around it."

"You have got to be rotting kidding me," I say.

"It is how we have resolved our differences since the beginning," Gragant says. "In the old country, we used closed rooms heated to boiling, but here the Divine Being has provided the perfect testing ground."

"So, what? Someone keeps watch to see which of us achieves inner peace first?" My spirits, perfected or not, were falling fast. A fight I could handle—if this was going to be some contest of idiot theology, Gragant could just declare himself the winner.

"Not exactly," he says. "Either of us may abandon the contest at any time, at which point the other will be declared the winner. Otherwise, the challenge ends at sundown. If we both endure that long, then we are clearly both in the Divine Being's favor."

Sundown. I glance at the sky. Even with the time spent walking out here, that's still another four or five hours. *Five hours of* that. Flurries of snow whip playfully across the ice, licking at the edge of the dome.

"And you've done this before?" Meroe says.

"Many times." I'm not sure if I'm imagining a hint of smugness in Gragant's poise.

"We just have to . . . sit there?" I say.

"You are welcome to do whatever you feel brings you closer to perfection and the divine," he says.

"Right." I take a deep breath. "Meroe, Zarun, can I speak to you a moment?"

We step away from the monks and put our heads together. Zarun is grinning, like this is all a joke, but Meroe looks worried.

"Okay," I mutter. "Ideas?"

"If you try to sit out there until sunset, you're going to die," Meroe says. "Nobody can do that."

"It's common among the monastic orders, supposedly," Zarun says. "There are always stories of monks spending days on mountaintops or under waterfalls. I never gave it much credit, myself, but . . ."

I glance at Gragant, with his perfect body and impassive expression.

"He certainly seems confident," I say.

"You can back out," Zarun says.

"And prove that his god hates me. Then we'll never get his help." I look at Meroe. "Come on. There must be something."

"You're allowed to use your Wells, aren't you?" she says, hesitantly. "Can they keep you warm?"

I'd been hoping for some brilliant diplomatic stratagem that would get me out of this, but that was probably too much to ask for. I look at the snow and shiver. "Maybe. My armor heats up my skin when something hits it, but I don't know if I could keep that up all day."

"Where's an iceling when you need one?" Zarun says.

"The icelings are supposed to make houses out of snow," Meroe says. "I read that, but I never quite knew what it meant." She shakes her head. "Maybe you *should* back out. We can find another way."

"We can't. Not soon enough." Meroe catches my eye, and I smile ruefully. "I know. But this time—"

"Are you ready?" Gragant says.

Meroe bites her lip, but nods. I turn away from them.

"As I'll ever rotting be," I mutter.

Gragant steps forward, with Harak just behind him. I square off opposite them, as though we're going to fight after all. He bows, and I match him. Outside the dome, snow swirls and flurries.

The monk reaches back and unties his robe, unwinding the cloth and folding it neatly. He hands it to Harak, leaving him in just a knotted loincloth. Then—

"You have got to be rotting *joking*," I say.

Gragant, naked and apparently without embarrassment—*not that he has much to be embarrassed about*, I think sourly—hands this last scrap of clothing to his second. He catches my look, and shrugs.

"It is traditional," he says, which apparently settles the matter.

Fine. Modesty isn't one of my virtues, and my clothes aren't heavy enough to make much of a difference. I wriggle out of my vest and trousers, kicking them in Meroe's direction, then unwind my chest wrap and step out of my underthings. Meroe and Zarun have both seen me naked—not that this stops Zarun from ogling appreciatively, of course—but I can feel the curious look of the monks. I ignore them, focusing on Gragant, whose gaze is appraising rather than prurient. I wonder what I look like to him—boyish, small-breasted, back and thighs crosshatched with old scars, still-healing welts from recent powerburn, and the weird, winding ribbon of blue marks that are the legacy of Meroe's first, desperate healing.

He gives me a nod of acknowledgement, and turns to face the boundary. I follow suit, my skin already turning to gooseflesh. Harak moves behind us and raises his hand.

"Begin!"

I step forward.

Oh, Blessed's rotting balls and all the Imperial mothers in a burning brothel, that's *cold*.

It hits like a hammer as the Eddica barrier parts in front of me. Wind slashes against my bare skin like a thousand-tailed whip, as though each fragment of snow is a razor-tipped missile. It shrieks like a dying man.

Beside me, Gragant stretches, calm and unhurried, muscles shifting under ice-rimed skin. He strides forward a few paces, to where the snow gets deep, and lowers himself into it, sitting cross-legged. Then he just closes his eyes, hands settled in his lap.

I don't know if he's using a Well, or if this monastic discipline is everything it's cracked up to be. Either way, he seems comfortable, which is the exact opposite of how I'm feeling. I thought I'd known cold, in the Kahnzoka winters, when wind and hunger were nipping at my heels. But this seems like another class of thing entirely, cutting into my flesh, worse than any powerburn.

Rot rot *rot*. Forget five hours, I'm not going to make it five *minutes*.

I activate my Melos armor, green energy shimmering faintly around me, but it doesn't help much. It's triggered by incoming threats, blows, or magic, and the rest of the time exists more as a potentiality than a barrier. It certainly does nothing to cut down on the wind, and only a faint shimmer of heat runs across my rapidly numbing body. I slam my fist against my chest, trying to get the armor to activate, but nothing happens.

Granted, armor that prevented you from touching *yourself* would be inconvenient, but this is a rotting awful time to experiment.

Igniting my blades provides a little bit of relief, at least for my hands. Green energy spits and crackles, each flake of snow that touches the Melos power puffing into steam, and my fingers and forearms feel a little warmth. Gritting my teeth, I lay one blade against my other arm, hoping to trigger my armor *that* way, but the blade itself shrinks away from touching my skin. Again, in the abstract, a useful quality, especially when monsters are tossing you head-over-arse. *But not right at the moment.*

My feet have already gone past pain and into deadened numbness. I remember the sailors in the Sixteenth Ward taverns who went on whaling voyages to the north, and how often they were missing digits or whole limbs. How long does that take? I'd never thought to ask.

The barrier shimmers behind me, seductive. All I need to do is take one step back, and the warmth of the Harbor will wash over me. It would be madness to do anything else, to spend one more second in this wasteland.

Gragant, sitting naked in the snow, is starting to *steam*.

Seeing that, seeing his serenity, just makes me angrier. Him and his Divine Being can *both* go to the Rot. There has to be a way to wipe the smug look off his face.

I raise a blade to my cheek. It brings a wash of warmth with it, but not enough. The problem is the wind, which tears away every scrap of heat. I need to get out of it.

The closest of the ice-covered hills is about twenty yards away. I start walking, kicking a path through the snow. It's surprisingly light and airy, scattering like fine-grained flour. Gragant doesn't even open his eyes to watch me, sitting now in a solid column of steam. I keep pushing as the snow comes up to my shins, then my thighs. My legs feel like solid, nerveless blocks of ice. If my toes fall off, I wonder if Meroe will be able to grow them back.

Getting in the lee of the hill at least cuts the driving wind. I start pushing at the snow, trying to clear an area big enough to stand in. There's an overhang of rock, and long icicles have cascaded over the side until they reach the ground, like an irregular row of columns. At first they're flush against the rock, but as I edge along the hillside the lip protrudes, and there's a darkened space visible through gaps in the ice.

A house made of snow. Meroe's phrase has been rolling around in my mind. I've seen that, too, now that I think of it—woodcuts of the savage icelings, invariably depicted alongside walruses and seals, living in hemispherical buildings made of blocks of ice. I'd always figured it was some explorer's fancy. *But . . .*

None of the gaps are wide enough to admit me, so I raise my blade and let it dig into one of the pillars. Magic zaps and crackles, the heat of the Melos energy melting easily through the thick ice. Another cut at the bottom, and a huge chunk falls away, raising a cloud of fine snow all around me. I wriggle through the resulting hole and into the void beyond.

Calling it a cave would be generous. Really it's just a lip of overhanging rock, with the ice pillars blocking off the open side, leaving a space just a little longer and wider than a coffin. But it's already infinitely better than being out in the wind—not warm, but not *quite* as skin-shredding. I huddle on the bare earth for a moment, trying to move my toes. I'm not sure I can.

When I unfold myself again, something crackles. Steam, rising from where I cut through, has settled on my skin and frozen into a fine layer of ice. Bits of the stuff cascade away as I move.

It gives me an idea. Blessed, I hope this works.

I carve a chunk off the fallen ice pillar, a circular section about the size of a cookpot, and haul it into the hollow with me. A little more work with the blades carves it out, creating a deep bowl. I fill this with chips of ice and handfuls of snow from outside, packing it down as hard as I can. Then I ignite my blades again, take a deep breath, and lower them into the slushy mixture.

Just keeping the weapons active, in the open air, doesn't take much power. This is different—I can feel Melos energy flowing out of me, and my hands and forearms heat up, a sensation which I positively welcome at the moment. More importantly, though, the mix of snow and ice rapidly slumps where the blades touch it. I push them down into my ice-bowl, which rapidly becomes full of slushy water as the smaller pieces melt.

I've never held my blades in water before, though I've seen rain spit and boil against them as if on a hot stove. Sure enough, after a few moments, the meltwater in the basin starts to bubble and froth. The steam that rises from it is tepid by any normal standard, but it feels balmy compared to the soul-killing chill outside. I lean over to inhale it, the first breath since I crossed the barrier without feeling knives in my lungs. I stir the water with my blades, until the whole bowl is frothing, then shift awkwardly on my bare arse and hold my numbed feet over the water. Sensation—burning, shooting pain—returns quickly.

Cold air is still gusting in through the gaps in the pillars. Once I'm temporarily thawed, I go to work filling in the holes with packed snow, returning to the bowl periodically to heat it to boiling and warm myself up. I prop the remnant of my cut pillar in the large gap I entered by, and keep packing snow around it until it makes a solid barrier.

With the wind hedged out, the next time I boil water, the cave rapidly becomes something close to actually *warm*. I wouldn't be able to keep my blades in the bowl for too long—not unless I want to char my hands off with powerburn—but the puffs of steam stay in my tight little enclosure, coating the walls, the floor, and my bare skin with damp condensation. The snow barrier collapses in a few

places, and I pack more in. It isn't long before, naked and surrounded by snow and ice, I'm feeling almost comfortable.

Favor of the Divine Being, ha!

I have no idea how much time has passed, not without knocking
a hole in my impromptu shelter and checking the progress of the
sun. But it can't be more than half an hour, and I doubt Gragant
will have given in so easily. I put my blades back in the water for
a few moments, generating a fresh cloud of steam, and settle in to
wait.

I nearly die, of course. Stupid, stupid, stupid Isoka.

The lassitude creeps up on me, slow and gentle, my eyelids feeling heavier by the moment. I don't remember nodding off, only waking up in a sudden panic, my heart hammering triple-time against
my ribs. I'm gasping for air, but what fills my lungs feels wet and
heavy, as though I'm drowning. My vision starts to go gray.

Fortunately, all I have to do is roll over and flail at the barrier
of ice and snow with a Melos blade. This opens a narrow gap, and
freezing air rushes in. It's bitterly cold—ice forms all over me, even
in my eyelashes—but I gulp it in greedily.

People die this way in the Sixteenth Ward, every winter, stuck
in basements or windowless rooms with a coal-burning stove, their
air going foul. Apparently, enough steam will give you the same effect. Stupid, stupid, stupid. And luckier than I have any right to be.

While I've got a hole cut in the barrier, I look for the sun, and
find it's made considerable progress to the horizon. I block it back
up, but only loosely, and boil more water. From that point on I fall
into a regular routine, melting snow for water, boiling it for heat,
then periodically opening a hole to refresh the air. I watch the shadows lengthen, the crags of ice fading from brilliant gold to black as
the pallid sun sinks toward the horizon. That golden spark slips
away, as though it were passing under the ice.

The hardest part is getting back to the dome. I stand up, sheathed
in sweat and condensation, and grit my teeth. A swipe of my blade
opens the shelter again, and the killing cold floods in. I start to

shiver immediately, my teeth chattering. As fast as I can, I wriggle through the gap, then slog through the snow back the way I came.

There's no sign of Gragant. I don't know if he gave up, or I stayed out longer than I had to.

The barrier looms ahead, and I tumble through it, feeling the faint tickle of Eddica energy passing across my skin. It's dark here, too, with the stars just emerging, and so warm I want to cry. I fall to my knees, shuddering, and Meroe and Zarun are suddenly beside me, throwing something thick and soft over my shoulders.

After a moment, Meroe pulls the edge of the blanket up and slips under it with me, pulling herself tight against me. She clutches me, desperately, and my shivering slowly subsides.

"You are completely *rotting* crazy, do you know that?" she whispers. "Gods and rot, Isoka. I was sure we were going to find you frozen solid."

"The thought . . . crossed . . . my mind." Speaking is hard, my throat raw from the cold.

"Why didn't you come *back*?"

"Didn't . . . want . . . to lose."

"Crazy." Meroe sounds resigned. "Completely rotting crazy."

"Deepwalker Isoka." Gragant. I kiss Meroe's cheek, then stand up, wobbling only a little, pulling the blanket around me like a cloak.

Gragant, I note, looks somewhat the worse for wear. I'm amazed he's upright—his arms and legs are tinged with blue, as though he were already half a corpse. I remember the agony as warmth brought back feeling into my feet; he must be in horrific pain, but he shows none of it on his face. Grudgingly, I have to admit that there may be something to monastic discipline after all.

"Sunset," I croak. "I made it, didn't I?"

"You did," Gragant says. "The Divine Being clearly holds you in favor."

Harak, looming behind Gragant, gives a disapproving grunt. "That was no proper contest," he says. "She knows nothing."

"I know what you promised me," I say.

"The Divine Being—" Harak begins.

Gragant cuts him off. "The Divine Being desires our perfection, using whatever gifts we have at our disposal. Isoka's technique may have been . . . unorthodox, but that only proves the breadth of the Divine Being's plan. She has done everything we asked of her."

"Then . . ." I take a deep breath. "The access point?"

Gragant nods. "I will take you there myself."

15

TORI

Isoka's Melos blades are ignited, brilliant green energy crackling and spitting. Very deliberately, she raises one of them above her head, and brings it sideways in a sharp stroke. There's a *twang* like a piano string breaking, and threads cascade down all around her, their severed ends drifting in the breeze.

I look at my hands, and they're covered in blood.

"I should have known," she says, raising her blades. "I should have known you were a monster."

"I'm sorry." It's all I can do to force the words out. "I'm so sorry."

When the searing heat of her blade slides into my chest, it's almost a relief.

I open my eyes. I should be in a panic, heart pounding, but I feel calm.

I'm on a musty pallet in a small room, empty except for a few broken bits of wood that look like part of a table. When I throw back the thin sheet, I find that my clothes are gone, replaced by a ragged linen shift of the sort we use for patients at the hospital. Bandages are wrapped around my left arm. I move it, experimentally; there's a throb of pain, but I can manage.

Isoka used to come home with wounds like that. I would bind them, washing the cuts and stitching them closed, with old rags for bandages. By the time she brought me to the Second Ward, her skin was a mass of scars, while mine was still unblemished. She'd wrapped herself around me, protected me, borne the blows and the wounds.

Until now. I close my eyes and remember the maddened guard's thrust, the curious not-pain of those first few instants. I would have a scar of my own—always assuming the wound didn't fester and kill me, of course. And my hands, which Isoka had tried so hard to keep clean, were stained crimson.

They had been for some time, if I was truly honest. Just because I'd kept the blood off my clothes didn't make me any less responsible— for the Ward Guards at Nirata's restaurant, for Nouya. For all my bleating about my power feeling wrong, I'd used it at the first real temptation.

Monster. Of course. Who would trust someone who could turn their own mind against them? *Not Garo. Not Isoka.* Even Grandma, herself marked as an outcast by her power, had only tolerated me as long as I was useful.

Tears threaten. I feel my hands curling into fists, fingernails digging painfully into the skin of my palms. *Now* my heart pounds, and my shoulders shake.

Let them be alive. Grandma. Kosura—Blessed, Kosura had been taken by the Immortals, and I'd barely spared her a thought. And Isoka, Isoka, *please. I don't care if she hates me forever, just let her still be alive, let me see her again.*

There's a rap at the door.

It takes me a moment to pull myself together. "Y . . . yes?"

"It's Garo." He sounds tired. "Can I come in?"

"Go ahead." I think about wrapping myself in the sheet, for modesty's sake, but it seems like too much effort.

The door slides open, and Garo enters. He's sporting a bandage of his own on one leg, and a spreading bruise across his cheek. His arms and hands are covered in strangely regular patterns of angry red welts. Dark circles under his eyes speak of lack of sleep.

In spite of all that, he smiles at me. "How are you feeling?"

"All right," I say.

"One of the hospital people stitched your arm and did the

bandage," he says. "She said it should heal clean, as long as you don't strain it."

I nod. "What about you?"

"Me?" He shrugs. "I'll be okay. Just tired."

"Your arms?"

He touches the welts. "Powerburn. It's not bad."

"How long have I been asleep?"

"Most of the day. It's past sundown now."

"I take it we got to the safe house."

He nods. "Most of us. We split up, and a few groups got tagged by the Ward Guard. Fortunately by then things were getting bad everywhere, and they didn't have the time to keep chasing us."

"What do you mean, bad?"

"You still need rest." Garo frowns. "I'm not sure—"

"Don't give me that, when you're about ready to fall over." I kick the sheet off and struggle to my feet. "What's happening?"

"Ah." Garo averts his gaze. "I'll get you some clothes, shall I? And then we can go downstairs and explain things."

I look down at myself—the shift isn't very long, and I'm only marginally decent. I swallow a comment and just nod, and he backs awkwardly out of the room, returning a few moments later with a simple brown robe. I put this on, folding it back where it doesn't fit, and join him outside.

We're on the upper floor of an old, boxy building. Garo leads me down a corridor flanked by dark, empty rooms. A stairway leads into a much larger open space on the first level. This place had been a warehouse, years ago, before it had been abandoned and Grandma had acquired it on the cheap. Since then it's served as her fallback, insurance in case the government ever really cracked down. I don't know if she ever expected to really have to use it.

Spread across the dusty, cobwebbed floor are a few hundred people, everyone who'd escaped from the hospital and the mage-blood sanctuary. There are no sleeping mats, so they've just stretched out on the ground, or spread out their coats if they're lucky enough to have them. It's mostly dark, with a couple of lamps burning on a table at one end of the room, and a pair of hospital assistants carrying lanterns as they work.

At the table Hasaka and Jakibsa are sitting, listening intently to a young woman. It takes me a moment to recognize Giniva, the girl who'd I judged worthy of entering the sanctuary the day I met Garo, what feels like a hundred years ago. Garo, seeing her, quickens his steps, and I follow.

"—tried to make a stand at the main intersections," she's saying. "But they got pushed back pretty quickly. A few guardhouses might still be holding, but other than that they've fallen back to the walls."

"Blessed help us," Hasaka says, shaking his head. His burly frame is hunched over the table, tattooed arms crossed

"Blessed help *them*," Jakibsa says, his eyes alight in the scarred ruin of his face.

"Tori's awake," Garo says. He holds out his hand to help me to the table. I settle on a spare cushion, and he sits beside me. "Good to see you made it back all right, Giniva."

The girl gives him a quick, awkward nod. Her eyes are on me, and I have trouble meeting them. I feel guilty—for denying her sister a place, and for ignoring her afterward. Helping her settle in the sanctuary was a part of my duties, which I'd brushed off in favor of pursuing . . . whatever it is I have with Garo. *She would have every right to hate me.* But there's no hate in her gaze, just wariness, as though she's worried that I might kick her out even now.

"Giniva volunteered to go out and see what was happening," Jakibsa explains.

"I've only been at the sanctuary a little while," she says, looking down at the table. "If they had lists of people they're looking for, I thought I might not be on them. And I . . . I wanted to be useful."

"It was very brave," Garo says. "Sorry to be late. Can you summarize?"

"It's—"

"It's chaos," Hasaka cuts in. "Riots."

"Only where the Ward Guard tried to make a stand," Jakibsa says. "Right, Giniva?"

Giniva gives another jerky nod. "There were lots of people on the streets, but most of them were peaceful. The Ward Guard tried to disperse the crowd, but from what I heard the fighting ended pretty quickly. Someone said they have orders to fall back."

"It's standard procedure," Hasaka says bitterly. "Kahnzoka was *designed* to prevent this kind of rising. That's why we have the ward walls. All the guards have to do is close the gates and wait for things to burn themselves out."

"Slow down," I say. "What exactly is going on? Why are people fighting?"

Everyone looks at me, and Hasaka scratches his stubbled cheek.

"Sorry," he says. "I forgot you've been out."

"It's Grandma," Jakibsa says. "She had—*has*—a lot of friends."

"And people in the Eleventh are angry about the draft," Garo says. "It all seems to have boiled over."

"And the Ward Guard have pulled out!" Jakibsa bangs his maimed hand on the table.

"For now," Hasaka says. "Mark my words, they're just waiting for daylight. If there's still a mob abroad by then, it'll be blood."

"You seem very certain of that," Garo comments.

"Used to be a guard," Hasaka mutters. "Ten years. Until . . . well." He glances at Jakibsa. "Grandma gave me a way out. But I've seen my share of ward risings, and it never ends well."

"So what do you suggest we do?" Garo says.

"Hide," Hasaka says promptly. "Thanks to all this chaos, we have a window, but it won't last. We can get in touch with Grandma's friends, see who's willing to take in some of our people. Split up, hunker down, and stay out of sight. Once the lockdown is lifted, maybe try to get out of the ward."

"Finding space for everyone is going to be a tall order," I say.

"I know," Hasaka says. "But we have to try. The children, at least."

"What about Grandma?" Jakibsa says. "And Kosura and the others?"

"You think I—" He cuts off, shaking his head. "There's nothing we can do."

"Why not?" Jakibsa says. "They're *right there*. They have to be."

"Right where?" I ask.

"Leftmark Road," Giniva says quietly. "I asked some people who watched the raid. They said the prisoners weren't taken to the regular guardhouses, but to a building on Leftmark Road, and now it's surrounded by guards."

"We can't be certain of that," Hasaka says. "Things have been confused. And even if it's true, what are we supposed to do about it? Attack them?"

"You fought the Immortals when they broke in to the sanctuary," I point out.

"Much rotting good it did." Hasaka looks on the verge of tears. "Gaf's dead. Vidge, Henka, Meiko—she was just a rotting kid, for Blessed's sake." He glances at me, then looks down at the table. "Blessed knows how many more, and we barely got away."

There's a moment of silence.

"What happened to Old Sewa?" I say.

"He went down fighting," Jakibsa says quietly. "Like the old days."

I take a deep breath, throat strangely thick.

"It doesn't have to be just us, though," Jakibsa goes on. "You said yourself that people are in the streets because they don't like what happened to Grandma. If we give them a chance to help *rescue* her, we'll have an army behind us! We might not even have to fight."

"And we might as well paint ourselves like an archery target," Hasaka says. "A mob's not an army, and when the Ward Guard come back we'd find that out quick. Chanting and throwing rocks is one thing, hard fighting with real troops is something else."

The pair of them glare at each other.

"I think we need to do both," I say. I wish my voice didn't sound so thin. "Prepare for the worst, obviously, and get as many children away as we can. But if we have a chance to help Grandma and the others, I think we should take it. We won't get another."

"Tori's right," Garo cuts in. "We have to try."

There's a strained, quiet moment. And then, somehow, Hasaka and Jakibsa—older and more experienced than either of us—are both nodding. It's something about Garo's tone, I think, simultaneously commanding and eminently reasonable, the voice of authority. Something you learn, I suppose, as a nobleman's son.

"I can try to get in touch with Grandma's contacts," Hasaka says. "Get the evacuation started."

"I'll manage things here," Jakibsa says. He looks ruefully at his maimed hands. "I might be a little conspicuous out on the street."

"Tori and I will handle that," Garo says, so authoritative I find myself nodding. "Though any volunteers to back us up would be welcome."

"I'll put the word out," Hasaka says. "But what exactly are you going to *do*?"

"People are angry and scared," Garo says. "They just need a little leadership to point them in the right direction."

"A little leadership?" I say.

Garo has the grace to look embarrassed. "It's true."

"You know this is crazy, right?"

We're standing by the main warehouse doors. Hasaka is talking to the other mage-bloods in small groups, looking for volunteers to help us, while Jakibsa tries to scrounge up some more durable clothing for me.

"What's crazy?" Garo says.

"You and me being any kind of leaders here," I say. "What in the Blessed's name do we know about being in charge of a . . . a *rebellion*?"

"Nothing," Garo says. "But neither does anyone else." He's far too cheerful for my taste. "They trust you, Tori. You were Grandma Tadeka's right hand."

"I was . . ." I stop. I can't tell him that Grandma only wanted me because my Kindre powers let her sniff out traitors. "That doesn't mean anything."

"They're scared and angry, like I said." Garo puts his hand on my shoulder. "They just need someone to point them in the right direction."

"Are we sure this is the right direction?" I have a powerful urge to lean on him, let him wrap himself around me, but I fight it. *Not now.* "What if we point the way, and people die?"

"Then it will be our fault. 'To command is to sacrifice.'" It sounds like a quote. "My father always says if you have confidence in yourself, you're halfway there."

"So we're going to . . . what? Go out and try to convince people to help us?"

He nods eagerly. "That, I can handle. I've studied this. The great speakers, rhetoric lessons—Blessed, half my education is about giving speeches. Just find me a crowd."

"I don't know." If confidence is the key, we're in trouble, because mine is draining rapidly.

"It will work, I swear on the Blessed." He glances sidelong at me. "You're thinking that your sister might be there, too."

"Yeah." I swallow. "Or at least information on where they took her."

His grin widens. "All the more reason to try."

"But—"

But that makes it worse. Leading people—innocent people, strangers who have nothing to do with me—into danger would be bad enough if I thought it would help them. But leading them just for something *personal* feels—

Monstrous? The word comes from a voice in my head. *Like twisting the mind of a poor pawnshop owner to make him help you, even if it gets him a beating? Like reaching into the souls of a squad of Ward Guard and driving them mad with fear?*

Puppet strings, wrapping around my fingers—

If it helps people. I swallow. *Grandma. Kosura. Isoka. If I can help them . . . save some of the others . . .*

My private agonizing is interrupted by Hasaka, who looks unhappy. Giniva is trailing quietly behind him, at the head of a half-dozen other people.

"These are your volunteers," Hasaka says. "I'm sorry there aren't more. Everyone's rattled, and going out on the streets . . . well." He shakes his head. "We all want to help Grandma. They just aren't sure they can do any good."

"I'm grateful for any assistance," Garo says.

"Giniva," Hasaka says, "are you sure you want to do this? You've been in plenty of danger already."

"Nobody is going to doubt your courage," Garo says.

Giniva looks down at the floor, but she nods. Her voice is soft. "Better than waiting here."

I examine the other volunteers. They all look like teenagers, some of the children who'd grown up under Grandma's protection. Every one of them is older than Garo and me, but they're looking at us with such deference it makes me uncomfortable. One of them, a gangly boy with a scruffy, fresh-sprouted beard, steps forward and clears his throat.

"We talked it over." He looks back at his companions and gets a round of encouraging nods. "Grandma needs our help. She put herself in danger for years for our sake. We can't sit around when the situation's reversed."

Garo smiles. The boy bows, and for a moment you'd have sworn Garo was the older one.

"What's your name?" Garo says.

"Vekata," the boy says. "My Well's Rhema. Only a talent, but I'll do what I can."

The others introduce themselves, Garo greeting them like a feudal overlord accepting a vassal's oath. For the first time since I woke up, I let my Kindre senses slip open. I have to fight not to close myself off at once, repelled by the huge cloud of fear and pain that fills the safe house. There's fear in Vekata and his companions, too, but it's shot through with red-gold determination. We should be able to rely on them.

Giniva is a surprise, though. A maelstrom of wild scents and spitting light hints at a storm of emotion she doesn't let show. There's determination there, too, but it feels like a thin skin hiding something darker. I give myself a shake as I pull my senses back in.

"We'd better move," Garo says. "This needs to be finished by the time the sun comes up."

Everyone nods. Hasaka opens the door to the deserted street, and we file out. I don't need any special powers to read the mix of fear and shame on *his* face, and I linger behind the others.

"We'll get them back," I tell him. "You keep the kids safe here."

He gives a jerky nod, and shuts the door behind me.

It's not hard to find the center of the crowd. Torches, lanterns, and bonfires are concentrated in the High Market, sending up a dull crimson glow bright enough to highlight the lowest clouds.

It's strange, though, passing through the streets and alleys I've walked so many times. The riot—rising, rebellion, whatever it is— feels like a weird inverse festival. There are the same crowds, press- ing close and forcing me to close down my Kindre senses, the same constant noise, the same jittery energy. But the voices are raised in anger rather than excitement, and people roam in tight packs, watching one another warily.

The story of the night is written in the debris still littering the road. I pass Kamura's noodle stall, half demolished, its timbers and boards pulled away to form a makeshift barricade. These barriers are everywhere, facing north toward the wall and the Ward Guard barracked there. People are milling around, not quite sure what to do next, still angry but without an obvious target. *This might actu- ally work.* If Garo can make them listen . . .

We push into the center of the market, where people are dens- est. All sorts are represented in the crowd, from laborers in rude vests to upper-ward servants still wearing their tailored uniforms, old men leaning on walking sticks, and young women in colorful robes. There are a *lot* of walking sticks around, I notice, along with empty sleeves and ugly scars. People Grandma helped.

In the center of the crowd, there's a small clear space. A dozen people are sitting in a circle, arguing furiously, with everyone else pressing as close as they can. I assume these are the leaders, or what passes for them. We manage to reach the edge of the council area by vigorous shoving. A ring of people at the front are holding the rest back, big, tough-looking men and women in leather vests and colorful bandannas. When Garo attempts to get through, several hands shove him backward, and Giniva has to catch him before he falls.

"I need to speak to whoever's in charge!" Garo shouts, though he has a hard time making himself heard above the clamor. "Please, let me pass."

"You and everyone else in the ward," one of the bouncers roars back. "Get rotted."

I push my way up beside him. "We have information."

"I don't—" the bouncer begins, but her companion leans close and points at me.

"Isn't that Tori?" he says. "From the hospital?"

I nod, vigorously. The bouncer detaches herself and talks to one of the people in the circle, and a moment later Garo and I are escorted through. I gesture desperately to Giniva, Vekata, and the others to wait.

A woman, in her thirties and hard-bitten from outdoor work, gives us a dismissive look as the bouncers return to holding back the crowd. Her companions in the circle don't even look up, continuing their frantic argument. The woman steps closer and half-whispers, half-shouts.

"Who are you supposed to be? A couple of kids?"

"My name is Garo," Garo says. "This is Tori."

"Grandma's Tori?" the woman says.

I nod again.

"Hmm." She frowns. "You probably don't remember me. I came in with—"

"Infected boil on your backside, right?" I force a grin. "I was the one who lanced it."

"Rotting *Blessed* that hurt." The woman gives me a friendly clap on the shoulder. "I'm Hotara. What are you doing here?"

"We need to talk to you. To everyone." I pull Garo forward. "We might have a chance to help Grandma, but we have to move quickly."

"Good luck getting this lot to move *anywhere*." Hotara waves at her fellow leaders. "The only thing they agree on is that they disagree on everything."

"Can you get them to quiet down?" Garo says. "Just a few moments will do."

Hotara gives me a questioning look, and I nod. She shrugs.

"I'll do what I can." Turning away from us, she takes a deep breath, and bellows at a volume I couldn't have achieved with a megaphone. "*Everyone shut your rotting mouths for a minute!*"

Astonishingly, people do, if only from sheer surprise. There's a moment of opportunity, and Garo takes it, raising one hand dramatically in front of him. He's smooth as anything, young, handsome, confident.

"Friends!" he begins. "People of the Blessed Empire! My brothers!"

Then he starts to speak, and I realize it's not going to work.

I'm not sure if the problem is that Garo didn't pay attention to his rhetoric tutors, or that he listened to them too closely. He certainly *sounds* good, lots of ringing phrases, good projection, with the stance of a dramatist on the stage. But what he's actually saying is—well, boring. He talks about the decline of the Imperial system, the rise of commercial interests, and the challenges posed by the increasing urbanization of labor. He tells the people of the Eleventh Ward, gathered in the middle of the night half in fear, half in fury, that what they ought to demand is tax reform and a reorganization of the civil service. It sounds like something he's practiced, and I'm sure it was very convincing to his First Ward friends, as they sat around his dining room trying to figure out how to save the world. Here, though, the muttering starts before he's gone through more than a paragraph, and by the time he mentions that the Immortals are holding people here in the ward—*I might have* started *with that*—nobody's listening. He's glancing around as he speaks, looking desperate. I want to hug him and slap him at the same time.

Blessed protect us from well-intentioned nobility. I may have spent the last few years in the Second Ward, but I remember being hungry and afraid.

We're not going to get another chance at this. By morning, the Ward Guard will have re-established control, and the prisoners will be moved somewhere more secure. Grandma, Kosura, and the others will be out of reach, along with any information about Isoka. I know what I have to do, but—

Monster. I take a deep breath. *What would a monster do?*

"Down with the Immortals!" I shout, as loud as I can. Garo, startled, stops speaking. "Down with the Immortals, down with the draft! Down with the Immortals, down with the draft!"

He blinks, swallows, and raises his voice with mine. "Down with the Immortals and down with the draft!"

I open my Kindre senses, and the tide of emotion floods in. Copper anger, caustic fear, bubbling excitement, all rushing back and forth across the market like waves in a bathtub, feeding on one another. Right now, fear is winning, a chain reaction that might send the mob flying apart. But I spread my will, rippling outward like a stone cast into the tub.

It's easier than I expected. Easier, even, than twisting the mind of a single individual. The currents of emotion run from person to person even without my help, and all I have to do is ride the wave, suppressing one feeling and strengthening another. I feel giddy, almost drunk, power flooding through me and spreading heat across my skin. Fear withers away, melting like fog in the sun, and I draw in righteous anger to take its place.

The chant spreads, gathering momentum, rolling downhill like a loose boulder.

"Down with the Immortals! Down with the draft!"

"Down with the Immortals! Down with the draft!"

"The Immortals are *here!*" Garo, whatever his faults as a speaker, can take a hint. "A nest of them, right in the Eleventh Ward! They have prisoners, innocent people from Grandma Tadeka's hospital!" His voice sounds hoarse, pained, dangerous. "Are we going to *leave them in chains?*"

"No!" The single word, chorused back from a thousand throats, is accompanied by a burst of emotion so powerful it nearly drowns me. I stagger, and desperately slam my Kindre senses closed. Garo grabs me before I hit the cobblestones, his arm around my shoulder, propping me up.

"Tori? Are you all right?" he says.

"Yes." I haul myself back to my feet. "You have to lead them. *Now*."

"I don't—I'm not sure I—"

"*Garo*."

"Right." He straightens up. "Lead." He pulls away from me, raises his hands again. "To Leftmark Road!"

The roar that answers is like the sound of the sea.

By the time the mob reaches Leftmark Road, it feels like half the city is with us.

It can't be, of course. It can't even be half of the Eleventh Ward. But the street is packed solid, the crowd spreading out into the alleys on either side. Packs of children follow across the roofs. There are torches everywhere, flaring and smoking, matched by more lights in the windows as we pass by. The chant never stops, like a heartbeat: "*Down* with the Immortals! *Down* with the draft!"

Garo and I have managed to secure a place in the front rank. Most of the other would-be leaders have been left behind, but Hotara is still with us, along with Vekata, Giniva, and the others from the sanctuary. Two of these are Tartak talents, and they've taken on the task of surreptitiously shoving people away to keep us from getting crushed.

It's not hard to tell which building is our target. The Immortals have seen the mob coming—how could they not?—and have opted not to hide. The place—an old factory—is set back from the street by the width of a gravel drive, and there's a line of Ward Guard soldiers stretching from the wall of one neighboring building to another, blocking off the main entrance. Behind them, a few paces back but still in plain view, a dozen Immortals in black armor and chain veils wait in stoic silence.

The Immortals have chosen their position with care. A multi-story tenement rises behind their hideout, and the buildings to either side are solid brick. There's no easy way in except across that driveway, under the eyes of the guards. *Unless*—I glance up at the roof, see two pairs of Ward Guard crossbowmen keeping watch, and shake my head.

Garo makes a similar assessment. "This is going to be ugly," he whispers in my ear.

"Ask for a parley," I tell him. "They have to know this won't go well if it comes to a fight. Tell them they can leave as long as they give up their prisoners."

He nods. "Are you sure you're all right?"

"Fine. Just a little . . . overwhelmed."

In truth, I feel an angry itch all along my back and shoulders. I wonder if it's the beginnings of powerburn. I've never done anything like that before—the memory of it still makes me giddy. I was *riding* the crowd, letting their emotion carry me along, but guiding it at the same time. I imagine being atop a champion racehorse, a solid mass of muscle and bone carrying you faster than you could ever hope to run, but still responding to the lightest touch on the reins.

The first rank of the mob comes to a halt, a dozen paces from the spear-wielding guards. Garo and I push forward, stepping out in front, with the others from the sanctuary close behind.

"Who's in charge here?" Garo barks.

The Ward Guard look at one another. There's a sergeant in the center of the line, but she's not ready to pretend she's in command, not with the Immortals standing in plain view. After a strained moment, three of the black-armored figures glide forward, chain veils jingling softly. They pass through the line of soldiers and face us.

One of them, a tall, broad-shouldered woman, squares off against Garo. Her voice is a rasp. "Explain to me why I shouldn't arrest you."

"You're welcome to try," Garo says, loud enough for the crowd to hear. "There are a few people who might object."

A wave of jeers washes over the Immortal. She shrugs. "Rabble."

"Then why wait?" Garo leans forward. "Let me make you an offer. Take your men and get out of here. Leave everything—all your prisoners—and we'll give you safe passage."

I almost reach out to the woman with Kindre, then hesitate. Back at the sanctuary, the Immortals had someone who could block my power, and I don't know if that extends to detecting it as well.

"I have an offer for *you*," the woman says, raising her voice to a grating shout. "All of you. Disperse and return to your homes. When order is restored—and it *will* be restored—only ringleaders will be arrested."

And then I feel it. Power like mine, licking out over the crowd in a wave of noxious fear. Someone in the line of black-armored figures is a Kindre user.

The Immortal officer cocks her head, waiting for the mob to come apart in terror. I reach out, operating by instinct, and throw my own will against the other mage-born. There's a moment of conflict, but while the Immortal's emotional push is elegantly crafted, I have more raw strength to draw on. The fear evaporates, shredding into fragments.

"I really suggest you take our offer," I say out loud.

The officer turns to regard me, and something in her stance registers surprise.

"It's you," she says. "The sister—"

What? I take a half step forward, just as everything goes to pieces.

"*Down* with the Immortals!" A stone, about the size of an apple, flies over the first row of the crowd and, more by luck than aim, slams into the officer's shoulder. "*Down* with the draft!" The chant is picked up again, louder and louder, and more objects start to rain over our heads.

The Immortal officer closes her fists, and blue bands of force reach out for people in the crowd, lifting them effortlessly into the air. A young boy screams and clutches at the Tartak power that binds his wrist. An older man unwisely urges his companions to hold him down, and a half-dozen people try; a moment later his arm breaks with a *crunch*, and he's screaming too. Another Immortal steps forward, flames leaping around him in what's intended to be an intimidating display. It doesn't work—a middle-aged woman pushes through the front rank of the crowd and swings a long-handled shovel into his stomach, hard enough to double him over.

"Wait—" Garo tries to say.

"*Down* with the Immortals!"

The crowd rushes forward.

They roll over the Immortal officer and her two companions and charge the Ward Guard, running straight at the wall of spears. The points waver in the face of this onslaught, but the soldiers don't even have time to break and run before the mob is on them. Men and women grab the weapons and tear them away, heedless of the steel points, ignoring cuts and blows. Some of the guards draw their swords, but only a few have a chance to use them before they're overwhelmed. The mob bludgeons them to the ground with whatever weapons are handy, with their bare hands, and crushes them under a thousand feet.

It's not natural, this rage. I watch the guard sergeant laid on her back, her screaming inaudible in the din, as two girls my age take turns smashing her head with rocks. I watch a man with a spear wound in his belly throw himself on a guard, bearing the soldier to the ground even as coils of intestine flop free. Garo and I stand among the small group of sanctuary mage-born, and the mob passes around us like a river splitting around a stone.

I did this. Like with Nouya. *I suppressed their fear, and gave them anger—*

The mob closes on the line of Immortals, and I squeeze my eyes shut. Even still, I can hear the roar of flames.

16

ISOKA

At the top of the stairway, the other monks turn back, leaving Meroe and I alone with Gragant. The blue tinge has faded from his skin, leaving him looking only a fraction paler than normal. I'm still fighting the occasional shiver, and Meroe stays close by my side, as though afraid I'm going to run off again.

"You're certain you're ready for this?" Gragant says to me.

I shrug. "Since I have no idea what's going to happen, there doesn't seem to be much point in waiting."

"Fair enough." He takes the lead, and we start down a winding circular stair, descending into the very center of the ziggurat. Gragant carries a lantern, which throws our shadows, huge and shifting, against the walls.

"I wanted to thank you," Meroe says.

"For what?" Gragant asks, not turning around.

"You didn't have to accept that Isoka had passed the trial." Meroe glances at me. "I heard what your people were saying. You could have declared her forfeit, and they would have backed you."

"My people might have," Gragant says. "The Divine Being would not." That hangs in the air for a half turn of the stairs. Then he goes on, in a softer tone. "I must admit that I am not devoid of personal feelings on the matter."

"What kind of feelings?" I ask.

"Silvoa was my friend. More than that. She taught me . . . many things. I would never have survived *Soliton* without her." He shakes his head. "And Catoria was my friend, once. Prime killed the one and twisted the other against me. Hate is counter to the divine will, but . . . he has a great deal to answer for."

I wonder if I should tell him that Silvoa is still—not *alive*, not really, but still *around*. Probably, I decide, it wouldn't make him feel any better.

"I agree," I say instead. "I'm going to see that he pays."

"The Divine Being does not sanction revenge," Gragant says, half to himself. "But the divine plan moves through strange orbits." He stops as we reach a landing, facing a single doorway. "Here. No one has entered this place since Silvoa died."

Five years ago, by the Harbor calendar. More like a hundred, as far as the world outside is concerned. Time rushes past, and I try in vain to grab for it. I wonder if it's already too late, if I'll return to the beach to find *Soliton* gone.

"Stay here," I tell Meroe.

"As usual," she mutters.

"I don't know what's going to happen," I say. "But Silvoa did this, didn't she?"

Gragant nods.

"I'll be fine." I touch Meroe's shoulder, and lean in to kiss her, then turn to the door.

The light from Gragant's lantern doesn't seem to reach past the threshold, leaving the room beyond in darkness. I step forward, and motes of faint gray ripple around me. I blink, and as my eyes adjust I can see the flows of Eddica energy, feel the power pulsing through the walls. The room looks similar to *Soliton*'s control chamber, the walls and floor made of interwoven, interlocking metal wires and conduits. They cross, merge, and divide in impossible profusion, but the energy flows toward a small dais at one end of the chamber, where a metal disc is linked to several of the largest pipes.

Something's different, though. I don't hear the whispers, the half voices of the dead that haunt *Soliton* and its angels. Here the Eddica energy feels . . . *pure,* maybe, refined. I cross the room and take the short step up onto the dais. The doorway behind me glows, a rectangle in the field of ghostly gray.

The flows coil around me, curious, almost *aware.* I reach out with my own power to touch them, and Eddica energy sparks across the gap between me and this—thing, machine, relic, whatever it is. For a moment I feel it thrashing at the back of my skull, and I suppress the reflex to shove it away.

Words write themselves across my mind, accompanied by a flat, dead-sounding voice.

access request received; home//melchior
result:
authorized/accepted

Well, says Prime, *look who's come calling.*

For one shattering moment, the pain is so great I nearly scream.

The flows that surround me, gray and calm, turn sharp and angry. They slash at my mind like vicious birds, biting and tearing. Prime has been waiting, deep in the Harbor system, coiled like a razor-toothed bear trap.

But he doesn't control it, not fully. If he did, he could have used the angels against us, not merely his reanimated corpses. I push my own power toward him, taking control, and the flows around me turn back. They ripple outward, thrashing against the stream of incoming energy, forging a narrow space of safety.

I don't know what I'm doing, here, in this strange domain. But I get the sense that Prime doesn't, either. He rakes my defenses, and I can feel his anger, his growing frustration. When he finally stops, I uncurl from my metaphorical crouch, and find his face hanging in front of me, built of flowing gray motes, eyes like dark holes in space.

Marvelous, he says. *You are truly an adept. I admit I had my doubts.*

So happy I didn't disappoint you, I answer.

On the contrary. He misses the sarcastic spin. *I have been nothing but impressed by your perseverance. When you join me, we will reach true greatness.*

I don't plan on joining you.

Not yet. His tone is insufferably smug. *But you will. You'll come to realize, as I have realized, what truly matters.* His phantom lips twist into a horrible smile. *That's why you've been brought here. Do you want to know the true history of this place?*

All I want is to get out *of here,* I snarl.

But the Harbor was made for you, he says, with a chuckle. *Quite literally. Our kind—the Eddicants—built it. A paradise that only we could rule, a base for our empire.*

I don't want to rule.

Of course you do, Prime says. *It's in our nature.*

Your nature. Not mine.

Oh? He lowers his voice. *Wherever you've found yourself, you've taken over, haven't you? Become a leader? Seized command?*

I— I stop, because, of course, he's right. First the Sixteenth Ward, then *Soliton*. But that was because I *had* to, not because I wanted to be some kind of tyrant.

You can't help *it,* he says, self-satisfied as a cat. *It's what you were born to do. It's what you—we—are* for. *Accept it, and you will understand yourself. You can have peace.*

I will have peace when I carve off your head, I tell him.

He laughs as I turn away, and the laughter lingers as I step off the dais and stalk out of the room.

"That's it?" Meroe says, as I emerge.

"It's done." *I hope.* "One down, two to go."

"Prime's presents the most obvious difficulties," Gragant says. "But getting Catoria to agree will not be easy. I regret that I cannot help you. Anything I do is likely to make her even more paranoid."

"We'll deal with Catoria," I assure him. *Somehow.*

We depart the Minders' ziggurat as soon as the sun rises.

Gragant comes to see us off, with the glowering Harak at his side. Meroe, Zarun, and I descend the ramp to the forest floor, our packs full of food from the monks' stores. I sight on the great obelisk in the center of the city, a needle of stone barely visible over the trees from this angle. The Cresos ziggurat is across the city, but still far from Prime's territory, so we're unlikely to run into trouble.

Even so, I feel a bit nervous watching Zarun run off on his own.

Someone needs to go back to the crew and give them an update, though, and he's promised to send a runner to meet us at Catoria's if there's any sign of *Soliton*'s imminent departure.

Or if it's gone already. All of this could be pointless. But I can still feel the great flow of Eddica power from the direction of the docks, and I *think* that means the ship is still in place. It's like it's *feeding* the city. *Maybe that's what the rotting thing is for.*

"There's an ugly thought," I mutter.

"What?" Meroe says.

We're well into our walk, the Minders' stronghold vanished into the trees behind us, nothing ahead but sun-dappled forest. After yesterday, I'm still glorying in air that doesn't feel like it's shredding my skin, and in spite of my worries I actually find my spirits lifting. I tell Meroe what I was thinking, about *Soliton* feeding the city.

"Prime said something, when I was in the access point," I tell her.

"He spoke to you again?"

I nod. "He still wants me to join him. He said this"—I wave vaguely at the forest—"was all created by Eddica adepts." I frown, trying to remember. "He called them 'Eddicants.' Like they were a separate race, almost."

"Hmm." Meroe's brow creases in concentration, an expression I find almost unbearably adorable. "I mean, obviously the system was created with Eddica power. And from what you've told me about the access points, it's designed to let someone with Eddica talent control it."

"I suppose. There's still too much we don't understand." I throw up my hands. "What's the *point* of all of it? Why build a giant dome at the end of the world, and then send huge ships to . . . what, collect sacrifices? Bring people here?" I feel like I'm on the edge of something I can't quite grasp. "Were the ancients just insane?"

"I doubt they were insane," Meroe says. "But that doesn't mean we can understand them. One thing about reading history: you come to appreciate that people at other times and places don't always think the way you do."

"I suppose." I shrug. "I always figured people were people."

"You'd be surprised what they can convince themselves of, if they try hard enough." She looks at me sidelong. "Do you know the story of Princess Vehnka?"

"I don't think so. Should I?"

"Not unless you've studied Nimari folklore. She lived a thousand years ago or more, before the time of your Blessed One. Our people were at war with a country called Gemori. Princess Vehnka was married off to a Gemori prince, in an effort to forge a peace. But after the wedding, she finds evidence in the palace that the Gemori are planning a sneak attack. So she goes on an epic adventure, evading her husband's guards, crossing the wild borderlands, encountering all kinds of dangerous beasts and unhelpful spirits. When she gets back to Nimar, she tells the king just in time about the Gemori treachery, and he goes out and wins a famous victory against their army. By the time he gets back, Vehnka has stabbed herself in the heart."

"What?" I miss a step, nearly stumbling over a tree branch. "Why?"

"Because she betrayed her husband," Meroe says. "Even if it saved her country, she knew she had damned herself by breaking that sacred bond."

"Rot *that*," I say. "I would have cut the guy's throat before leaving the palace, myself." I shake my head. "Did this actually happen?"

"Who knows? The point is that we tell the story for a reason."

I think about that, as we cross a stretch of open fields full of angels. There are so many of them, plain compared to the bizarre angels on *Soliton*, each with its several limbs working away as tirelessly as a watermill. One of them is weaving, creating the coarse fabric I've seen both the Cresos and the Minders use out of a pile of fibrous stuff it manipulates using specialized extremities.

Someone did *design this place for people to live here.* That's obvious enough. *It still doesn't tell us who, or why.*

After we cross into another stretch of forest, I call a halt beside a stream, dammed by a boulder into a wide pool. The day is hot enough to make me sweat, and it's a relief to sit in the shade.

Lunch is fruit and roasted vegetables, both of types I can't identify, and some crispy, salty stuff.

"I never thought I'd say this," I tell Meroe, "but I honestly miss crab meat."

"Meat in general," she says. "God, what I wouldn't do for a steak."

"Roast pork," I suggest. "Marinated and cooked slowly. The street stalls stuff it in a bun with spicy sauce."

"Fried *venu*." Meroe sighs longingly, then laughs as I give her a quizzical look. "You don't have *venu* in the Empire? They're like . . . big, stupid birds."

"Like chickens?"

"Much bigger than chickens. The size of a pony. And they can't fly."

"You're making that up."

"I swear I'm not! I visited a ranch once. You wouldn't *believe* the smell." She grins at me.

"When we get *Soliton* back to Kahnzoka, maybe we can start farming crabs."

I try to picture a farm full of blueshells and hammerheads and start laughing, and Meroe joins in.

"You," I say, wiping my eyes, "are a very strange princess."

"So I'm told." Meroe gets to her feet and starts taking off her silver bracelets, then unwrapping her dress.

I eye her suspiciously. "What are you doing?"

"Getting cleaned up." She gestures at the pool. "I don't know about you, but I haven't had a bath in days. I figured Catoria might appreciate the effort."

"Here?"

She undoes the last knot, and lets her dress fall away. As always, the sight of her makes my breath catch.

"Who's going to notice?" she says, still grinning. "The angels?"

She has a point. I watch, appreciatively, as she strips off her underthings and wades into the pool.

"Nice and warm," she says. "Come on, you'll feel better."

I glance at the sun, trying to ignore the hissing hourglass at the back of my mind. *Rot it.* I strip down and step into the water. It's as warm as Meroe promised, only a couple of feet deep, and the sandy streambed feels good on my weary feet.

Meroe is already sitting down, leaning back to put her head underwater and wet her hair. I try not to stare at her *too* obviously as I start cleaning myself up.

A paradise that only we could rule, Prime called this place. Without his monsters, he might be right. I rub wet sand across my skin, then lean back to wash it off, my thoughts wandering in odd directions. *If not for Tori, if not for Prime, would it be so wrong to stay here?*

Just thinking that feels . . . almost blasphemous, somehow. Ever since my powers came to me, I've been living my life for my little sister's sake, keeping her free of the river of blood and rot I had to wade in. Here, though, the river was gone. *No Immortals to hide from. No one has to starve or sell themselves for food, or fight to keep monsters from their door.*

If I *could* take control, destroy Prime and his madness . . .

Wherever you've found yourself, you've taken over, haven't you? His voice in my mind. *It's our nature.*

He doesn't know anything about me, what I've been through. *But he's not wrong, is he? Maybe he's right about your nature, too.*

Sudden weight on my shoulders, arms twining around me. For a panicked moment, I nearly activate my armor.

"You're thinking about Tori," Meroe says.

I nod, mutely.

"We'll get to her in time," she says. "This is going to work."

I nod again. Meroe hugs me tighter. Her wet skin shifts against mine, her breasts pressed against my back. I feel hot and cold at once.

I squirm around inside the circle of her arms, grab her at the waist, pull her close and kiss her. She gives an excited squeak and topples over with a splash, ending up on her back in the shallows, her wet hair a dark, gleaming halo around her. I crawl forward on hands and knees and bend down to kiss her more thoroughly. Time passes, imperceptibly.

Meroe pulls away for a moment, breathing hard, as I find her breast with one hand and the other slides up her smooth brown thigh.

"Here?" she says, raising an eyebrow.

"Who's going to notice?" I mutter, kissing her again. "The angels?"

There's still plenty of daylight left by the time we reach the Cresos ziggurat. I keep looking at Meroe—back in her dress, skin scrubbed to glowing, hair still damp—and shaking my head. *Strange princess, indeed.*

The third great ziggurat looks much like the others. Two vast cloths are draped on either side of the main ramp, painted with an Imperial clan symbol—Cresos, I assume, though I don't recognize it. There are two guards with spears at the base, one iceling and one southerner. They don't look particularly happy to see us. Fortunately, as we approach, I spot Shiara descending the ramp from above, and at her call the pair step aside.

"Isoka!" Whatever damage the exile from the ship did to Shiara's composure or her wardrobe has long since been repaired. She's in a long, elegant *kizen*, her face painted in the very image of the proper young Imperial lady. She manages to make good time down the ramp, even so. "We've been expecting you."

"I take it Jack made it here all right, then," I say.

She nods. "Though you may want to consider sending a more . . . conventional messenger next time."

Meroe snorts a laugh, and I grin. "I trust Jack to get through."

"I know. It's just . . ." She sighs. "Things are . . . more formal, here."

I look at the surrounding jungle. "It seems like an odd place for formality."

"Or maybe a good reason to cling to it," Meroe says. "Something familiar."

"Will Catoria see me?" I ask.

"She's agreed to give you an official audience," Shiara says. She sounds uncertain, which is unusual for her. "I'm . . . not sure how productive it will be."

"We'll find out." I feel energized. *We're getting there. One step after another.*

I picture the interior of the Cresos ziggurat as much like ours or the Minders', but instead of taking the corridors to the large room at ground level, Shiara directs us upward. Here, a warren of smaller chambers branches off the main hall. More guards wait at the intersections, wearing hanging shoulder tabards displaying the Cresos clan symbol. An Imperial warrior—a boy my age, really, but trying hard not to show it—is waiting for us, wearing blocky, old-fashioned armor and a red-painted helmet.

"The clan mistress will see you," he growls. His speech is beyond merely accented, phrased so archaically I can barely understand him. He turns on his heel and stalks away, without waiting to see if we follow.

"A hundred years," I say quietly, glancing at Meroe and Shiara. "Did people really use to talk like that all the time?"

"In the noble houses, at least," Shiara says.

The stone walls of the ziggurat are nothing like the wood-paneled corridors of an Imperial mansion, but the Cresos have done their limited best to decorate them as though they were. Precious objects stand on small pedestals at intervals, things they must have guarded since they were first exiled: a small porcelain statue of the Blessed, an even older-looking helmet and a sword sheathed in chipping leather, a comb picked out in mother-of-pearl. In between, someone has tried to re-create traditional Imperial wall paintings—the sort of thing I've only seen in stage sets—without very good results. *No artists among the clan Cresos exiles, I see.*

Two more warriors, an older man and a girl Tori's age, in patched and fading armor, wait outside the entrance to Catoria's audience chamber. A silk curtain is draped across the doorway, and our escort falls to his knees and edges through it, bowing deeply. I hear a murmured conversation inside, and he backs out, climbs to his feet with a clatter of armor, and gestures us forward.

"You will show proper respect," he says. "Especially you, Southerner. Lady Catoria is the sovereign of the Harbor."

I clench my teeth, but this isn't the place to make an issue of it. "Follow my lead," Shiara whispers.

That's mainly meant for me, it turns out. Meroe may be the only non-Imperial here, but I'm the one ignorant of courtly etiquette. I imitate the other two, walking through the curtain with my arms at my sides, my head down. Inside, the floor is covered with cloth matting, sewn into squares to resemble proper floor mats. People sit along both sides of the room on a row of cushions, women in colorful *kizen*, men in dark blue or brown robes with their hair in complicated braid-knots. At the far end, Catoria herself sits on a plump purple pillow, edged with pearls. Beside her is an older man, one of the oldest people I've seen in the Harbor, possibly past thirty. His heavy-lidded eyes look over the room with a proprietary air.

"Lady Catoria," Shiara says, after a deep bow. "Ladies and gentlemen of the Cresos court. I am honored to present my master, Lady Gelmei Isoka, called the Deepwalker, and her consort Meroe hait Gevora Nimara, First Princess of Nimar."

Consort? I glance at Meroe, who gives a grin and a tiny shrug. Shiara steps back beside me.

"Bow," she says. "And tell her you're honored to be here."

I do my best, bowing as low as Shiara did. "Lady Catoria. It's an honor."

Mutters run through the room, probably because I can't fake the formal court language. Meroe can, of course, and she steps forward to greet Catoria with all the dignity of a lifetime of diplomatic training. *I should have just sent her to do this, shouldn't I?*

"Lady Isoka," Catoria says. "It is good to see you again. After I heard of your battle against Prime, I feared the worst."

"Thank you, my lady," I say.

"I'm told," the older man beside her rumbles, "that this battle did not end well for you. Is that the case?"

"That's Cresos Toranaka," Shiara whispers. "Catoria's uncle."

And, judging by the looks he gets from the other courtiers, the person who is really in charge around here. My earlier enthusiasm starts to flag a little. Toranaka's is a face made for scowls.

"You have heard correctly, my lord," I say. "We destroyed many of Prime's creatures, but ultimately we were forced to withdraw, and some of my friends were killed."

"It is ever thus, when we attempt to confront Prime," Toranaka says to Catoria. "As I have often warned you."

"I don't plan to give up," I say. "Prime is a threat to all of us. We must all work together to defeat him."

"Indeed." Toranaka sneers. "And you, who have been here less than a week, have decided you are the one to lead this glorious battle?"

It is our nature. I try to blot out Prime's voice. "If someone else wants to lead it, I'm happy to let them. So long as we move quickly."

Toranaka looks dubious, but Catoria leans forward. "What do you propose?"

"My lady . . ." Toranaka says.

I speak quickly over him. *Probably an unforgivable breach of etiquette, but rot it.* "Your leader, Silvoa, knew that the key to defeating Prime is to take control of the Harbor's system and use it against him. I am an Eddica mage-blood, my lady. If you let me use the access point here, I will attempt to reach the one in Prime's stronghold." *Somehow.* "If I succeed, he can be destroyed with no risk to your own people."

There's a moment of shocked silence. I glance at Shiara, and her painted lips are tight, her eyes fixed on Catoria. The girl is looking down at me, almost doll-like in her formal attire, her expression unreadable.

Toranaka clears his throat. "*Lady* Isoka," he says, and from him it sounds like a slur. "Do you take us for complete fools?"

"Of course not—" I manage to get out, but he's rising to his feet.

"You *only* want use of the access point? How reasonable! You will destroy what is, at worst, an ongoing nuisance, and in return you merely want us to grant you total power over the Harbor and all its residents."

"Prime is more than a nuisance," I say. "He's killed my friends."

"We have not lost anyone to his creatures for more than a year."

"Because you stay cooped up in here, and don't dare venture out at night—"

"*In any event*," Toranaka grates. "If we grant you what you ask, and you attack, you may anger Prime and disturb our present balance. And if you succeed, what then?"

"If we act soon, *Soliton* could take anyone who wants to go back home," I snap.

"Is that your goal?" Toranaka sits back. "We of the Cresos are under sentence of death from the Emperor. This is our home now, and we cannot simply hand it over to an outsider."

I wonder if I should tell him that the Emperor who sentenced them is himself long dead, along with everyone else alive at the time. It might not matter as far as the sentence is concerned, of course. Emperors come and go, but the bureaucracy remembers.

"Lady Catoria, please." I bow my head. "Silvoa wanted this, didn't she?"

From Shiara's quick intake of breath, I sense this is the wrong thing to say. Catoria's eyes are hooded.

"Lord Toranaka is right," she says, after a pregnant pause. "Even if you were to succeed, Lady Isoka, how can we trust you?"

"But—"

She blinks, and for a moment there are tears in her eyes. "This audience is at an end."

"I should have warned you," Shiara says. "Catoria feels . . . very strongly about Silvoa."

"So did Gragant," I say. "That's what convinced him, in the end."

"It's different," Shiara says, quietly.

We're in an anteroom, furnished in the same quasi-Imperial style with hangings, cushions, and a low table. Two guardsmen wait outside, so we speak in low voices. Someone has gone to fetch Jack, who will be accompanying us home.

"Different how?" I say.

Meroe, who has been very quiet thus far, says, "They were lovers, weren't they?"

"I don't know," Shiara says. "But Catoria loved Silvoa, for a certainty. When Silvoa went with Gragant to confront Prime, over Catoria's objections, Catoria felt betrayed."

"But it was Prime who killed Silvoa," I say. "Surely Catoria wants him to pay for that?"

"I suspect she is unclear in her mind on the subject," Shiara says. "Which means she looks to Toranaka for guidance."

"Rotting great." My hands clench tight. "So what in the Blessed's name are we supposed to do now?"

I look at Meroe, my beautiful Meroe, who always has all the answers. Her forehead is creased in deep thought. When she notices us staring, she gives a rueful smile and shakes her head.

My fists clench tighter. Outside, I know, the sun is sliding toward the horizon. *How much longer does Tori have?*

17

TORI

"So how does it look?" Garo says.

They're cleaning the bodies out of the road.

Not even bodies, really. Pieces of bodies. Remnants of bodies. *Things* that used to be people, until they were hit with Myrkai fire, torn apart with Tartak force, cut down with Melos blades, or dissected by fighters with Rhema speed.

No wonder the Immortal captain had been so confident. Any normal mob would have broken under the onslaught of her adepts. Any mob still capable of fear.

I can see the cleaners, through a gap in the window curtain. Some of them are using *brooms*.

"Ward Guard cavalry has sortied a few times to keep the area around the gates clear," someone says. "But otherwise they're staying put. The ward wall is fully manned on the uphill side, and facing the military highway."

"But not facing the Sixteenth." Hasaka. His voice is ragged with exhaustion.

"They pulled out of there after midnight," Giniva says. "Back to the outer wall on one side and the military highway on the other. There have been a few messengers from the Sixteenth. Apparently riots broke out there about the same time they did here, but no one has really taken charge."

"Textbook tactics," Hasaka says. "Encircle the infection, wait while it burns itself out, then tighten the noose."

"Apparently," Garo says, "we're more virulent than they expected."

All the carnage hadn't helped the Immortals in the end. It might have made things worse. By the time the rioters reached them, the mob's blood was well up. Black-armored soldiers were torn apart, not by magical force, but with bare hands. Men battered their knuckles bloody against chain veils, turning the faces underneath into pulp. A group of young women, robes spattered crimson, beat a Melos adept with stones until she roasted in her own armor.

I did this. Puppet strings. *Monster.* I'm sitting here, in a clean robe, when I ought to be sodden with blood.

And for what?

Someone dumps a bucket of water on a bloodstain in the road below. I blink, aware that I've missed something. Everyone politely pretends not to notice. None of us have gotten any sleep, and now the sun is climbing up over the wall that encircles the Eleventh Ward like a noose.

"We need to break out," Garo says. "Get past the walls."

"Impossible," Hasaka says. "We'd be slaughtered if we tried an assault."

"Even if we could get past the cordon," someone else says, "what would it gain us?" The speaker is an older woman. *Hotara*, my mind supplies. One of the original leaders of the riots. "They'd still crush us in the end."

"We need to get out of the city!" A younger man I don't know. "If we can get through the outer defenses, we might—"

"Don't be stupid," Hasaka says. "In open country we're just a rabble. The Legions would cut us to pieces in a day."

"Then what?" the boy says, almost pleading. "Hide? Throw ourselves on the Emperor's mercy? What in the Rot did we do all this for?"

"Our best chance is to negotiate," Garo says. He sounds so confident. "Get the Emperor to declare a general amnesty, and press him for our demands."

"Down with the Immortals!" several people shout. "Down with the draft!"

Garo nods. "But right now we don't have anything to negotiate *with*. That's why we need to break into the upper districts. The government will let the Eleventh and the Sixteenth burn to the ground, just to make an example. If we can take the Fourth, or the Second, then we'll be threatening the property of people who actually matter. As far as the Emperor is concerned, I mean."

"That still doesn't tell us *how* we're going to get through the walls," Hasaka says. "Kahnzoka was designed for exactly this problem. If the Ward Guard use their siege engines on us, they could flatten all of the Eleventh Ward in a few hours."

"They haven't yet," Giniva says. "That means something."

"It means they're still hoping to salvage this," Garo says. "So we have a little time. If we can—"

"Garo," I say abruptly. "Can I speak to you for a moment?"

Everyone looks at me, and I realize I've been silent throughout the meeting. Hasaka clears his throat, nervously.

"Of course," Garo says. "Hasaka, Hotara, can you put the word around that we're looking for ideas?"

I stand up, and he takes my hand and leads me to an adjoining room. We're on the top floor of the former Immortal safe house, which was their barracks. The large common room overlooks the front entrance, and lets onto several smaller chambers, all laid with austere sleeping mats. As the lair of a squad of secret police, it's depressingly normal.

The cells, apparently, are down in the basement. I haven't dared to look yet.

"How are you doing?" Garo says, sliding the door closed behind us. "Did you manage to sleep at all?"

I shake my head, mutely. Every time I close my eyes, I see flames.

"You don't have to stay here," he says. "We can—"

"I'm staying." Of course I'm staying. This is my fault.

"All right." He leans against the wall, smiling. Even with the bags under his eyes, his hair rumpled and spiked with sweat, he looks like a hero. I wonder what would happen if I kissed him now. "What did you want to talk about?"

"I just . . ." I pause, toying with my braid for a moment. It's coming undone. "You're in there making decisions."

"Someone has to," Garo says. "Especially now. After last night . . ." He shakes his head. "Unless we do something, when they finally move in, it's going to be a bloodbath."

"So you're setting yourself as leader? You're comfortable with that?" I twist my braid around my hand and squeeze. "What if you get it wrong?"

"You think I don't worry about that?" he says softly. "If you're asking me whether I have all the answers, Tori, you know I don't." He shakes his head. "But nobody else does, either."

I watch him for a moment. He pushes away from the wall, comes over to me, puts his hand on my shoulder. I want to recoil, or to fold myself against him.

"You're half the reason they listen to me," he says. "Everyone knows Grandma trusted you, and Hasaka and the others from the hospital trust you, too. Without you I'd be an outsider."

"Is that supposed to make me feel better?"

"No. I'm saying I need your help." Garo takes a deep breath. "You're right. I don't know what I'm doing. But I'm not going to abandon people who've put their faith in me."

"I . . ."

I take a half-step forward, toward him, and he puts his arms around my shoulders and pulls me in. My head presses against his solid chest, and he's warm.

"I'll make sure you're safe," he whispers. "No matter what. Even if things go . . . wrong."

"That's not the point," I whisper back.

"I know. It's still true."

Eventually I pull away, wiping my eyes and sniffing. He's staring at me, and I wonder if *this* is the moment for a kiss, and I feel a strange lightness and a tingle in the soles of my feet. Then I think about the bodies outside, and come crashing back to earth. He turns away.

Garo goes back to the others, to planning the revolution. I slip downstairs. There are people I need to see.

The first floor of the building is open space, unfurnished and empty. A training hall, maybe, or an interrogation cell. Now it's been converted into an impromptu sickroom, laid out with those who were wounded in yesterday's fighting. Several assistants from the hospital arrived during the night and, along with a few volunteers, they're doing their best. That doesn't amount to much. No one has gone back to the hospital to see if any supplies survived the raid and the fire, so the caretakers are working with torn linen bandages, bowls of clean water, and little else.

At one end of the hall, a curtain has been raised, cutting off a small section of the room. I walk in that direction, stepping over people crusted black with horrible burns, or whose limbs were twisted by magical force. Men and women, young and old—once unleashed, the Immortals did not discriminate. The wounded moan, plead with the caretakers, beg for water.

It's almost a relief to push the curtain aside and step into another realm. There are twisted, broken bodies here, too, but they're mercifully still and quiet, lined up one beside the other and covered with white sheets. Off to one side of the line of corpses, there's a body laid out by itself, on a spare sleeping mat. It's surrounded by small offerings—flowers, white lilies for death. White cloths knotted to resemble a burial shroud, another traditional gift for the dead. Food, plain white buns, and a few bottles of liquor.

It's mostly appropriate. Grandma Tadeka certainly enjoyed a drink, though she never much cared for flowers.

Kosura sits in front of Grandma's body, resting on her knees, head bowed. Someone has cut her hair with a dagger, leaving a ragged-edged, boyish mess. I'd seen her briefly last night, wrapped in a torn sheet, spattered with blood. She's cleaned herself up since, but she still doesn't look like the friend I remember. Her face is mottled with bruises, one eye nearly swollen shut, but her expression is peaceful. Her lips move silently in prayer. I kneel awkwardly beside her.

"I thought she'd be all right," Kosura says, after a moment. "She survived so much, I thought for sure . . ."

"So did I," I say. Grandma's face is covered by a cloth, dressed in

a snow-white funeral *kizen,* her hands folded neatly. I wonder who
did that. "Are you—"

"At least I knew you were all right," Kosura says.

"How?"

"Because they kept asking about you," she says. "When they beat
me, they asked me where you might go, who your friends were. Every
time they did that, I knew they hadn't gotten to you. I can't . . . tell
you how much that meant."

I glance at her, trying to find some hint of sarcasm in her battered features. If it's there, I can't see it, and I feel guilty for looking. Kosura is a better person than I could ever be. I want to tell
her I'm sorry, but to say that out loud would expose its pathetic in-
adequacy.

I turn back to Grandma's body. It seems shrunken in death, too
small to contain the force of personality she'd wielded. Just a frail
old woman, now broken.

"What would she want us to do?" I say. "She would have hated . . .
all of this. She never wanted us to fight."

"Maybe." Kosura closes her good eye again. "Grandma would say
you do what you can with what you have. What *she* had was a hospital and a place for people to hide." She takes a deep breath. "Maybe
we have more than that."

"Maybe." *Or maybe we're all going to die.* I struggle to my feet,
knees twinging. "Is there anything you need?"

"No," Kosura says. She bows her head, returning to prayer. As I
go to leave the curtained morgue, she says, "Thank you, Tori."

Don't thank me. The bodies in the road outside are jeering. *Monster, monster, monster.*

One more visit to make.

The cells are empty now, but no one has scrubbed away the blood-
stains.

The basement under the Immortal safe house is divided into a
dozen separate chambers, with a large space at either end. They're
more like cages than cells, with floor-to-ceiling steel bars for walls

and no pretense of privacy. The place was overcrowded with prisoners from the hospital when we broke in, a dozen to a cage. They're free, now, joining the crowds in the streets or lying on mats upstairs. All the cells are empty, except for one.

The Immortal captain is naked, shackled hand and foot to the stone wall. This isn't for the sake of humiliation, or at least not *only* for humiliation. She's a Tartak adept, and Blessed only knows what other Wells she might be hiding. Even chained hand and foot, she's dangerous, and needs to be watched every moment. Clothes might conceal the telltale aura that means she's making a move.

Two young women with makeshift spears are on guard duty, one sitting outside the cell, the other well back. The first to watch the captain and make sure she isn't doing something subtle. The second to sound the alarm if the first gets torn to pieces. Hasaka suggested the arrangement, which makes me wonder what exactly he did in his stint in the Ward Guard.

Both girls stand up at the sight of me, though they don't bar my path. Garo's not wrong—people *do* respect me here, Blessed knows why. I take a breath to steady myself.

"I need to talk to her," I say. "Alone."

"It's dangerous," the guard says. "If you're in there with her, we won't be able to stop her from hurting you."

"I promise to scream," I tell her.

The pair look at each other, but neither seems to want to be the one to stop me. They open the cell door and I step inside. The Immortal captain raises her head at the sound of my footsteps.

She's a tall, handsome woman, probably in her forties, with dark hair cut as short as a man's and a surprisingly soft face under the sinister chain veil. There are scars on her arms, across her shoulders, the thin raised lines of cuts and the winding, shiny marks of repeated powerburn. Her breasts are heavy and sagging, and her belly bears stretch marks from pregnancy. Adepts breed, of course, for the benefit of the noble bloodlines. I wonder if she knows her children.

"You're Tori, aren't you," she says. Her voice is the harsh rasp I remember from outside. "The sister." She smiles. One of her teeth is missing. "You don't look much like your picture."

"You were looking for me," I say. "In the raid. Why?"

The captain barks a laugh. "Does it matter?"

"Tell me."

"Or what? You'll kill me?" She makes an effort to shrug, which only jingles her chains. "You'll have to do that sooner or later."

"We could . . . hurt you."

"You?" She laughs again.

"There are plenty of people who would welcome the opportunity."

"Then give it to them," she says. "I'm getting bored. But it won't get you anywhere."

I let my Kindre senses open, feel her mind. There's fear there, but less than I expected. Determination, contempt, hatred, rage. It's like looking into a sewer.

"Isoka," I say. "What have you done with her?"

"You'd like to know, wouldn't you?" The captain's grin widens. "Go rut yourself with a hot poker."

"Then you did have her."

The captain just shakes her head.

She knows. I can *feel* it, the satisfaction in her mind, the shape of the knowledge. I can't read it. But I *could* reach out, take hold of her with my power, and *squeeze*. Eventually, she would tell me of her own accord. She'd *want* to.

Monster, Isoka whispers, slashed puppet-string dangling. *Monster, monster, monster.*

I take a deep breath, and ask a different question.

Back upstairs, Garo and the others are still going around in circles. They pause as I enter the room, waiting politely as I retake my seat at the table. Hasaka is about to start telling everyone for the dozenth time how pointless an assault on the gates would be, but I interrupt him.

"I know how to get past the walls," I say. They go silent again, and I look at Garo. "That's what we need, isn't it? A way out of the lower wards, into the rest of the city?"

Garo nods cautiously. "You have an idea?"

"I think so." I force a smile. "We're going to go visit an old friend of ours."

18

ISOKA

"There's that look again," Meroe says.

I stop pacing and turn to her. "What look?"

"The look where you're thinking about something you ought to be telling me."

We're back home, inasmuch as "home" has any meaning anymore. Meroe, Jack, and I hurried to return to the crew's ziggurat before nightfall, with Shiara promising doubtfully to try and work on Catoria. Now I'm waiting for the light to finally bleed from the sky. *One more day gone.* That makes a week since we'd arrived. *Soliton* could leave any time.

"I'm just . . ." I shrug, trying not to show my tension. "If our guess about the time-shift is right, it's been more than half a year for Tori already. Anything could have happened."

"It's possible," Meroe says calmly. "But I have a strong suspicion Tori is more capable than you're giving her credit for."

I snort. "You've never even met her."

"I've listened to your stories," Meroe says, then smiles. "And she *is* your sister. She can't be that different."

"She is different," I say. "She's better. It's—" I shake my head. "It's hard to explain."

"Try." Meroe sits down on our sleeping mat, looks up at me. "Better than wearing a hole in the carpet."

She's trying to keep my mind off my nerves, Blessed save her. I take a deep breath.

"She's just . . . good," I say. "She *helps* people. She doesn't even think about it."

"So do you."

"That's a recent development," I grate. "Back in Kahnzoka, on the streets . . . it was an easy way to get killed. I'd watch Tori giving away our last crust of bread to some poor bastard in a gutter, or begging me to let an old man in out of the rain. I'd try to explain that, sometimes, people lied about what they wanted, especially to a pair of skinny little girls without anyone to care if they disappeared. But I hated myself for having to do it. She doesn't deserve to be kicked in the teeth by the world." I shrug again. "Once I could, I put her somewhere she wouldn't have to be."

"Was she grateful for that?"

"Of course she was grateful. You should have seen her, after a few months in that house. Clean, well-dressed, perfect. She was so happy." *Until I had to leave. Then she cried her eyes out.* I start pacing again, feeling Meroe's gaze on me. "What?"

"Nothing," she says, with one of her beautiful, unreadable smiles. "I'm looking forward to meeting her."

Blessed One willing. I take a deep breath. "It's probably dark enough by now."

"Probably." Meroe gets up. For a moment I think she's going to insist on coming with me, and my heart lurches, but she only crosses the room to kiss me, gently. "You'll be careful."

"Of course." I stare at her. There's something in her expression. "What's wrong?"

"Nothing." She kisses me again. "Just thinking about things."

"That sounds promising," I mutter.

She makes a face at me, and I laugh. *Strange princess.*

The guards let me out onto the roof of the ziggurat, beneath the wheeling stars.

It's another clear night. I can see the bulk of *Soliton*, still in its dock in the harbor, the flow of Eddica power unabated. The obelisks of the city are visible as knife-edged absences, outlined in flickering points of light.

I don't know if this is going to work. But it's the only thing I can think of.

I reach out, with Eddica, letting the strange ghost-gray power flow out of me. It merges with the streams that crisscross the Harbor, the network that underlies everything, and carries with it my message. Just one word: *Hagan*.

Prime will be aware of it—I'm sure of that, from our brief encounter in the access chamber. I just hope he won't know what it means.

It's the better part of an hour before I spot movement, down at the base of the ziggurat. I tense, expecting walking corpses, but eventually it's the dog-headed angel that emerges from the shadows. I breathe a sigh of relief and start jogging down the ramp toward it.

"I wasn't sure you'd be able to hear me," I say, slightly winded by the time I get to the base. The dog-angel shakes its head, silently, and lopes off into the forest.

I follow, staying alert, this time knowing what to expect. We travel a short distance, and then the angel stops at a shallow trench. It's not the deep pit it dug last time, and I look at it questioningly, but it puts one foot delicately in the hole. I lean over and see the dull gleam of a conduit at the bottom.

"—found one that runs closer to the surface," Hagan says, when I put my hand on it. His ghostly features materialize in front of the angel. "And Silvoa says it's deeper in the network, or something like that, and it'll take longer for Prime to find us."

"Not that much longer." Silvoa shimmers into existence beside Hagan, a slender iceling girl made entirely of gray light. "This is a low-level run, a few more branches from the primaries, but he's still going to catch on eventually." She cocks her head. "Good job not mentioning my name in your broadcast, though. I wasn't sure you'd catch on to that."

That the two of them came when I called—that they're *real*, and not figments of my imagination—fills me with a deep relief. On the other hand, Silvoa's brusque, patronizing manner can be almost immediately annoying. I take a deep breath.

"I won't waste time, then," I tell them. "I need help."

"With what?" Silvoa snaps. "How far have you gotten?"

"I talked Gragant into letting me use his access point."

"Well done." Silvoa peers at me. "I'm surprised he trusted you so easily."

"There may have been a naked snow meditation challenge involved," I mutter. Hagan raises an interested eyebrow, and Silvoa laughs out loud. "But Catoria and the Cresos turned me down flat." I glance in the direction of *Soliton*. "And I don't know how much time I have left. If time is really passing faster outside—"

"Time doesn't pass faster outside," Silvoa says. "What gave you that idea?"

I frown. *Could she not know?* It seems unlikely. Her post-mortal perspective has given her a lot of time to study the Harbor.

"We know the Cresos clan were exiled from the Empire around a hundred years ago," I say, cautiously. "But you and Catoria have only been here for five. So—"

"Oh, no question of *that*," Silvoa says. "But it's not that time passes at different rates, it's that there's not enough energy to run the Harbor."

Apparently I looked baffled, because she heaves a sigh.

"If it helps," Hagan says, "I'm lost, too."

"Look," Silvoa says. "Both *Soliton* and the Harbor are powered by Eddica energy. That's the energy of life and death. It's everywhere in the world where animals, especially humans, are living and dying. But you've seen what it's like outside the dome—not much life here. So the Harbor needs to get its energy from somewhere."

"It gets it from *Soliton*?" I think of the huge, steady flow of power I've been feeling from the ship. "So it's like a . . . a fishing trawler, that goes out and comes back with a big catch?"

"Something like that," Silvoa says. "Except there were supposed to be more ships—you've seen the wrecks. And *Soliton* doesn't work as well as it used to. So there's not enough energy."

"What happens when it runs out?" Hagan says.

"The Harbor shuts down. Everything sort of . . . stops." She gives a ghostly shrug. "From the outside, the dome becomes impenetrable until *Soliton* shows up again. From the inside, of course, nobody notices that years have gone by in the time it takes to snap your fingers."

"So," I say slowly, "*right now,* there's no difference between the inside and the outside?"

"Other than the temperature," Silvoa says, smirking a little.

"How do you know all this?" Hagan says.

"I've been locked inside the Harbor system for five years with nothing to do but occasionally get tortured by a lunatic," Silvoa says. "Obviously I'm going to poke around as much as I can. There's a lot of information in there if you know how to ask."

My mind is running along a different track. *There's no time difference* yet. That meant that a week here was *only* a week in the outside. *Which means only a week for Tori.*

In one sense, it doesn't matter. If *Soliton* leaves before I can get onboard, it won't return for twenty years, and Tori will still fall into Kuon Naga's hands. My deadline hasn't changed.

But I realize I still feel an enormous relief. The thought that six months had passed *already* has been weighing on my mind more than I realized. If I can get onboard the ship, turn it around and get back to Kahnzoka—

Tori will be waiting. It's easier to convince myself of that, now. *She* will *be. I just have to get there.*

"In any event," Silvoa is saying, "you're right that you don't have long if you want to take control of *Soliton.* When it finishes emptying its reserve into the Harbor, it'll leave to get more, and then you're stuck. Another couple of days at most."

"Right." I nod, but I'm grinning now, and it seems to confuse her. "That means we have to change Catoria's mind."

"That was never easy," Silvoa says. She smiles, too. "Stubborn girl."

"I have an idea." I look between the two of them. "But I'm going to need your help."

I never learned to ride a horse.

Meroe finds this odd—in Nimar, riding is as basic a skill as dressing yourself, especially for a princess. But in Kahnzoka, riding horses are the toys of the very rich, ill-suited to the cramped, cluttered streets. The horses I grew up with were draft animals, big, shaggy beasts bred to pull heavy loads. In the Sixteenth Ward, even these were rare, and mules and donkeys were more common, with a few ox-teams working at cargo winches on the docks.

Even if I had somehow found the time to learn to ride, however, I don't think it would have helped. I don't know what riding a horse is like, but I can't imagine it's very similar to riding an angel.

I sit on Hagan's back, trying to find something to hold on to. The angel doesn't have any fur, let alone reins, so I'm reduced to grabbing at its thick, stony neck. There's no rock or sway to its gait, each foot placed precisely and with effortless strength, leaving its back as flat and steady as a cobbled square. But around us, the landscape *blurs,* and my stomach lurches as Hagan shifts back and forth, smoothly avoiding the trees.

Why did I think this was a good idea?

I'd rushed back into the ziggurat to tell Meroe I'd be gone a while longer, and to consult Jack about what she'd seen in the Cresos stronghold. Armed with this information, Hagan and I set out, crossing the ground between our building and theirs at what turns out to be a blistering pace.

I can't communicate with Hagan like this, but I explained the plan before we set out. He veers to the left as soon as the Cresos ziggurat comes into view, circling around it through the jungle, away from the main entrance. The sheer size of the thing makes it hard to keep watch, especially at night. Away from the main ramps, there are no prying eyes.

Nor should there be, of course. The Cresos are on the lookout for Prime's monsters, or possibly a sneak attack from the Minders. Neither would assail an empty side of the step-pyramid, which would mean a long, exhausting climb up the man-sized blocks. For Hagan, however, the great steps of the ziggurat are an easy stride, and he ascends the building without even slowing down.

The way in at the very top of the pyramid is unguarded, just as Jack reported. Hagan skids to a halt on the flat platform, and I slide gratefully off his back, clutching my satchel under my arm. The entrance is blocked by a barred trapdoor, secure enough against Prime's creatures, but no match for a Melos blade. I saw through the bar in a few moments and haul the thing open, then drop down into darkness.

This is the most dangerous part, while I'm creeping around alone. Any wandering guard will, quite rightly, assume I'm up to no good and sound the alarm. I really don't want that to happen, and I also really don't want to have to kill anyone.

Fortunately, both Jack's tour and the information she got from Shiara indicate that the Cresos are stretched thin. Their non-Imperial servants sleep in barracks down below, and the Cresos nobility in the small chambers up above, with guards on the main entrances and outside a few of the rooms. Guest quarters, however, are on the next level up, and patrols are limited to an occasional check of the main stairway. I arrive during one of these, and flatten myself against the wall until the lantern-light below fades away. Then I pad down, moving as quietly as I can, and turn into the web of passages.

Finding Shiara's door is easy, since it's the only one showing a light beneath the curtain. I pause outside it, then rap my knuckles against the stone. It doesn't produce much sound, but the light flickers, as though someone has moved in front of it.

"Is someone there?" Shiara says, quietly.

"It's Isoka," I whisper back.

"Isoka?"

"Can I come in without you screaming?"

She doesn't answer, and I push the curtain aside. Shiara is standing on the other side of a sparsely furnished room, wearing a silk nightgown and looking perplexed. I move inside and out of view of the doorway, just in case.

"I take it," Shiara says, "you're not supposed to be here."

"I broke in through the roof," I tell her cheerfully. "You should tell our hosts it's a flaw in their security."

"Through the *roof*? How did—never mind." She shakes her head, long hair swaying. I've rarely seen Shiara with her hair unbound and face unpainted. She looks almost like an entirely different person—less poised, more human. "What are you doing here?"

"I need you to help me get to Catoria."

"Get to—" Her eyes narrow. "If you're planning to hurt her . . ."

I shake my head quickly. "Nothing like that, I swear it. I have something to show her, and it has to be alone. I don't want her uncle Toranaka interfering."

She lets out a breath. "I can see that. But what are you going to do when she screams for the guards?"

"I'll deal with that when we get to it." Actually, I have no plan for that, other than hoping like rot it doesn't happen. "Can you get me into her room?"

Shiara visibly composes herself for a moment. "Probably. But are you sure about this? If they find out you broke in, you'll never get them to trust you."

"Have you made any progress on that front?"

"Not much," she admits.

"We're out of time to try things the subtle way." *I'm* out of time. "So I'm going to roll the dice."

"Okay." She shakes her head, grimly. "Give me a moment."

She throws a more substantial robe over her nightgown and gestures for me to follow her. We creep back to the main staircase. Shiara moves with the catlike tread of someone with long practice keeping silent, which is a surprise. We wait through another patrol, a lonely lantern spiraling up the stairs and out of sight, before descending to the level below Shiara's quarters. She leads me through silent halls, and stops at a corner. I peek round and see a curtained doorway, with an Imperial man in archaic Cresos armor standing in front of it.

"Oh, good. Toshoda is on watch." Shiara apparently recognizes the guard. "He's not the brightest sort, and he's had eyes for me since I got here." She gestures to an empty doorway nearby. "Wait there until we go past. You'll have a quarter of an hour at most, though."

"Perfect." I find myself looking at Shiara with new respect. "Thank you."

"Thank me by not screwing this up," she says.

I nod. She steps out, strategically loosening her robe a bit to show more of the sheer garment underneath, and runs toward the door. I hear Toshoda bark a challenge.

"I saw something awful!" Shiara says, a touch of simper entering her voice. "One of those *monsters,* on the stairs!"

"Here?" Toshoda says. "Impossible."

"It was there!"

He goes with her, of course. If he'd been any guard of *mine* I would have reprimanded him for not asking questions like "what are you doing up in the middle of the night?" and "why didn't you sound the alarm?" but I got the impression that his duties in the Cresos stronghold were more ceremonial than real. I hide in the shadows of the doorway as the two of them hurry past, Toshoda carrying a lantern, Shiara walking closer to his side than strictly necessary. She knows her business, that's for certain.

When their footsteps fade, I creep out and pad to Catoria's room. There's no light leaking under the curtain, so I draw it carefully aside. Like the rest of the ziggurat, some effort has been made to make the chamber look like a proper Imperial bedroom, with a low table and a sleeping mat atop woven floor panels. Nothing can really disguise the fact that we're inside a giant stone step-pyramid and not an airy, wooden-walled manor, though. By the faint light from the hall, I make out Catoria's shape, a lump under the thin sheet.

I'm quiet, but apparently not quiet enough. When I'm halfway across the room, she sits up suddenly, long hair unbound and falling around her face. She's almost invisible in the shadow, only two pinpricks of reflected light showing her eyes. I hear her draw a breath.

"Who's there?" she says. But she says it quietly, which makes me think she's already guessed.

"Isoka," I say. "Please don't scream."

"Oh." Her voice is small. "Are you here to kill me?"

"Nothing like that, I swear by the Blessed One. I just want to talk."

"I was going to say that if you were here to kill me, I probably *would* scream, regardless." She shuffles the sheet aside. "Do you mind if I light the lamp?"

"Go ahead."

A fat spark of Myrkai fire jumps from Catoria's finger, and the lamp brightens, illuminating the room with a wan glow. Catoria gets to her feet and holds it up to see me better.

"So you're not here to kill me," Catoria says. "If you're willing to risk breaking in here, why not go straight to the access point? That's what you want, isn't it?"

"I considered it," I admit. "But I figured you would have people on watch, and I don't want to kill *anyone* if I can help it."

"I thought I had people on watch outside my room," Catoria says. "But I take your point. You took an awful risk, though, just to talk. I thought we went over things this afternoon."

"I would rather your uncle not be involved."

"My uncle doesn't make the decisions," Catoria says, steel in her voice. "I do. If you think that I will change my mind just because he's not here—"

"It's not that." I take a deep breath. "I have to show you something."

Catoria arches her eyebrows.

"I spoke with Gragant," I say, crossing the room to stand in front of her. "And Shiara. I know . . . how you feel about Silvoa."

"I very much doubt that," Catoria says. "Silvoa betrayed me, and she died. There's little else to say about it now."

"I don't think she betrayed you," I say. "And . . ."

"Don't tell me she isn't dead," Catoria says. Her voice is thick. "Prime sent us her *head*."

Rotting scumsucker. I grimace. "She's dead. But she . . . was . . . an Eddica adept, and so is Prime. Silvoa's . . . still here." I shake my head. "I know it sounds crazy."

"It *is* crazy," Catoria snaps. "Dead is dead. There's no such thing as ghosts."

"I said that, when I came aboard *Soliton*. But Eddica is the Well of Spirits, and I can't deny that it has power." I take a deep breath. "She wants to talk to you."

Catoria's expression hardens. "I believe I will scream after all."

"Please. Just . . . give me a moment." I dig in my pocket, and produce a jagged length of broken conduit.

Silvoa herself had promised me this would work. Eddica energy runs through the conduits, tying them to the Harbor system. That energy is . . . sticky, for lack of a better word. Break off a piece of conduit, and it remains part of the system, at least for a while, its connection slowly fading away. It should be enough.

Rot, I hope it's enough.

There's a shimmer in the air. Silvoa's translucent form materializes, wavering like fog in a strong breeze. It's blurrier than I would like, her face the vaguest smear of features. Her voice, when she speaks, comes as though from a great distance.

"Hurry, please," she says. "This takes a lot of effort, and Prime will find me soon." The figure glances around. "Catoria? Oh, spirits of the ice. You've grown."

Catoria blinks. She's looking at Silvoa, but her eyes are still narrowed. Eddica energy is harder to see for those who can't touch the Well, and I don't know if she can make out more than an outline. She gives no sign she's heard the projection's quiet words.

"She says you've grown," I fill in.

"So only you can hear her?" Catoria says. "Very convenient."

"You can see her, can't you?"

"I see *something*. You're an Eddica adept, too. I'm sure this is only a parlor trick for you."

Actually, this kind of parlor trick is well beyond my capabilities, but I can't convince her of that. I look at Silvoa, who pauses, thoughtfully.

"Tell her," she says, "that I remember what Gragant said to me, the first time we met."

I repeat this, and Catoria's brow furrows. "And?" she says.

I listen. "He said, 'Are you going to eat that?'"

Catoria's lips twitch in a half-smile. "We were fighting a blueshell. It had nearly gotten the better of us before he joined in, and once it was dead we were all lying around on the deck gasping for breath. And he . . ." She shakes her head. "He told you that."

"He didn't," I say, despairing. "Please. Ask something only Silvoa would know. We don't have much time."

"I . . ." Catoria turns away from me, hugging herself tightly, and she's quiet for a long moment. Without turning, she says, "When did she and I first kiss?"

Silvoa looks down at her. Even in her blurred form, I can see her pain. When she answers, it's barely audible.

"In this room," I say. "The night before she died. Just before she promised you she wouldn't go off on her own." I swallow. "She says she's sorry about that. So sorry. She thought—"

"I don't care what she thought," Catoria says, choking back a sob. "She promised me she would stay. That we would be together. And she *left* me."

"I did," Silvoa says. "I was certain Prime would listen to me. I was . . . not stupid. Hoping to talk instead of fight is never stupid. But maybe . . . not careful enough."

"You sound like Meroe," I say, with a slight smile.

"What is she saying?" Catoria says. "Is she—"

Without warning, Silvoa's projection doubles over as though she's been struck. There's a grating burst of white noise, and then another voice, much louder. Prime.

"*Dear* girl," he says. "You've been very naughty, I see. How unfortunate. You know what that means."

And Silvoa screams, high and piercing. Catoria can hear *this*, and she claps her hands over her ears. I drop the conduit, and the projection vanishes, but the sound seems to linger, echoing through the room.

"That was . . . her." Catoria stares at the twisted bit of metal on the floor, slowly lowering her hands.

"It was," I say.

"And he . . . has her." Her hands interlock, knuckles taut and white. "He's hurting her."

"She says that it's . . . not as bad as it seems. Now that she doesn't have a body."

"Now that . . ." Catoria blinks, eyes swimming in tears. "Oh, Blessed."

"We can help her," I say. "*You* can help her. If we take over the Harbor system, she'll be free."

There's a long silence.

Catoria looks up. Tears are running down her cheeks, but her eyes are fierce.

"What do you need?" she says.

19

TORI

The Black Flower is shut up tighter than the Imperial treasury.

Borad Thul's pleasure palace has been turned into a fortress. Every window has been boarded up, and the main doors are firmly closed and barred. The hordes of eager pleasure-seekers are gone, and no sound of music and merriment comes from inside. Lights burn in a few upper windows in the main building.

"Are you certain this is a good idea?" Hasaka says.

"Tori knows what she's doing," Garo says, with a glance at me. I try to hold a confident expression.

Tori hopes like Rot she knows what she's doing. The anger inside me flickers for a moment, threatened by fear. But I only have to think about the Immortal captain in irons, that defiant smile, to rekindle my rage.

"Do it," I snap.

Jakibsa, standing beside us in the street, raises his mangled hands like he's about to conduct a symphony. Blue light shimmers around the big doors. For a moment, wood and iron are pitted against raw magical force. Then the doors slam open, the bar shattering in a spray of splinters.

Behind it are a trio of guards with crossbows. Jakibsa snatches the weapons from their hands before they can fire. When the thugs go for their swords, Garo steps forward, igniting his Melos gauntlets. Their eerie light outlines the scene in flickering green.

"Who in the Rot are you?" one of the guards manages to croak.

"I'm here on behalf of the people of the Eleventh and Sixteenth,"

Garo says. "We'd like to talk to Borad Thul, please. Would you go and fetch him?"

Two guards look at the third, who nods and hurries back into the complex. One of the others follows. The last, standing in the ruined doorway, looks around at us and sneers.

"You're going to regret this," he says. "Thul doesn't forget an insult."

"Let's hope we get the chance to make it up to him," I say, with admirable calm.

It's not long before the flunky returns, frowning. "Master Thul will see you two," he says, pointing to me and Garo. "The rest of you will wait."

"That will serve," I say, before Garo can object. I glance at Hasaka. "If we don't come back, you know what to do."

He swallows and nods. Garo dismisses his Melos gauntlets, and the dark-suited guards escort us inside. The halls of the Black Flower are quiet now, no pretty young men or willowy girls hanging around looking elegant, and no customers to ogle them. The guards hustle us up the stairs, down the hall past darkened doorways, and across to Thul's office with the horned whale on the door.

Inside, Thul is waiting where I'd first seen him, iceling-blond hair shining in the lamplight. Unlike that first encounter, a pair of guards wait behind him, not the liveried thugs from downstairs but leather-armored mercenaries. They watch closely with carefully bored expressions. Thul himself affects nonchalance, but my Kindre senses are open and I can feel his unease.

"Miss Gelmei," he says. "Surprised to see you here."

I stare at him, this narrow-eyed, venal man, and try to contain my anger. Everything that has happened—the raid, Grandma's death, and Kosura's torture—is, in some sense, his fault. The only thing that keeps my rage at a slow burn instead of a white heat is the knowledge that, if fault is being assigned, a lot of it is mine. I piled the kindling in the stove. Thul just struck the match.

Still. I run the edge of my power across his unsuspecting mind, and he shivers as though from a draft. *You had better tell me what I want to know.*

Monster, goes the chant in the back of my head. *Monster, mon-ster, monster.* But it's getting easier to ignore.

I take a deep breath. "You seem to be lying low, Master Thul. Business not going so well?"

He shrugs. "Wise man takes shelter during a blizzard, Nan always said. Mobs don't make for good customers. And when the guards move back in, heads are apt to get broken. Better to stay quiet."

"Very wise. I can imagine this must be difficult for you."

"I've survived before. Will again." He frowns. "What I can't figure is why *you* would come back here." He glances at Garo and sneers. "Thought you lot had a revolution to run."

"We do," Garo says. "And we need your help."

"There are ways around the walls," I say. "I *know* there are. Tunnels, secret exits. For aristos who can't be bothered to get home from places like this before the gates shut. To move people between wards without the guards noticing. We want them."

I watch his mind. There's no guilt there. Suspicion, satisfaction. His sneer turns into a grin.

"Even if that were true," he drawls, "why in the Rot would I give you something like that? To put my head on a spike next to yours?" He barks a laugh. "Your sister understood how things work in the Sixteenth. We keep order, take our profits, and as long as the Guard get their cut nobody looks too closely. The wheel keeps turning, and we all get our share. But how long do you think they'd turn a blind eye if I helped a bunch of rebels?"

"If you don't help," I say, as calmly as I can, "those *rebels* might start to wonder which side you're on. There's no guards between the mob and your doors."

Rage rises in his mind, and his voice goes harsh. "Don't you rotting threaten me, you little whore." I feel an answering anger in Garo, and put a restraining hand on his shoulder. The two mercenaries tense, and Thul laughs again. "Oh, go ahead. Try it, noble boy. You know your girlfriend here is the scrapings of the gutter, don't you?"

"I know everything I need to know about her," Garo grates.

"As for your mob, they don't frighten me. I have friends in this district. Deep roots. People know this will pass, and when it does I'll still be here." He spreads his hands.

"Ordinarily, I think you'd probably be right," I say. My heart is pounding, but I affect disinterest. "But we took a prisoner after we stormed the Immortal safe house in the Eleventh Ward, and she had some interesting things to say."

I feel his emotions flare, crimson anger shading into ugly, yellow-green anxiety. *Gotcha.*

His expression remains dismissive. "So?"

"So she told me what prompted the raid on Grandma Tadeka's hospital." I lean forward. "It was a tip that *you* provided. A report of our conversation."

This is a lie, sort of. Without breaking her mind wide open, I couldn't extract that information from the stubborn Immortal captain. But I'd had a hunch, and when I'd questioned her about it the truth had been clear in her emotions. I have no idea why Kuon Naga and his Immortals are interested in me, but they came *looking*, and they did it after Thul passed along that I was trying to find out about Isoka's disappearance.

"They were offering good coin for information about you," Thul says. An edge of worry creeps into his voice. "I didn't know what they'd do."

"I'm sure you thought they were only going to protect me," I snarl.

"Business is business, girl. Your sister—"

"Shut *up* about my sister," I snap. "And I very much doubt the people of the Eleventh Ward will see it as *business*. I don't know how many friends you have, how many roots, but I'm willing to bet that Grandma Tadeka had more. If I bring our captive out to tell what she knows, this filthy place will be burning down around your ears before you can *rotting* blink."

I've gotten a little more heated than I intended. Garo is looking at me, mouth open, as though I'd grown horns. But Thul has leaned backward a degree, and as I watch a bead of sweat detaches from his hairline and runs down the side of his face. His head twitches, a suppressed instinct to glance over his shoulder at his hired muscle. I can see his next move in his mind, clear as day.

"You want to tell your thugs here to get rough," I say. "Before you do that, you should know that my friends outside are very clear on what needs to happen if we don't come out of here. It'll be spears and torches at your doorway by sundown."

"You . . ." Thul growls. "You little . . ."

"I suggest," Garo says, "that you watch your tongue."

The tunnel is narrow, and stinks of shit.

It's one thing to know, intellectually, that Kahnzoka boasts a large and intricate sewer system. A dozen small streams that once ran down the hillside have been captured, diverted into cisterns to provide drinking water, while their beds were hidden under bricks and earth. Waste washes down the hill in a disgusting tide, spewing into the ocean from hidden outflow pipes. The system is hundreds of years old, steadily patched, expanded, and repaired under a long succession of emperors, although I doubt any emperor ever devoted much personal attention to the problem.

Thul, or his predecessors, obviously had. Or, at least, to a related idea: if ancient rivers and human waste could pass unnoticed under the ward walls, why couldn't people?

Many of the secret ways he'd grudgingly surrendered had been cleaner than this one, since aristos returning home from a late night of rutting and smoke were hardly likely to want to trudge through a sewer. But this forgotten tunnel offers something none of the others do—not just a way to circumvent the wall, but passage into the gatehouse itself. The Ward Guard, it seems, aren't above illicit comforts.

I try to breathe shallowly, sticking close to Garo's back. I do my best not to think about what's coming.

We'd had a serious argument as to whether I should be here at all. I'm not a fighter. As far as he knows, I'm not even mageborn. This isn't like the march on the Immortal safe house, where we'd hoped to convince them to surrender. Garo and the others are going down into the tunnel, and when they come out, people are going to die.

With my help, though, it might be fewer people. So I ignored Garo's pleas to stay behind, and the twisting of my own stomach. I think about Isoka, and Grandma lying cold and dead, and the cuts on Kosura's body.

There are a dozen of us, moving in single file down a narrow, brick-walled corridor. No actual sewage runs through it, thankfully, but from the smell and nearby gurgles it can't be far away. This tunnel goes all the way from a fountain in the Eleventh Ward to an accessway in the Fifth, just across the road and through two sets of gates. We're only going half that way, underneath the gate on the Eleventh Ward side, then back up.

"I've found the ladder," Giniva reports.

She's in the lead, a tiny Myrkai flame kindled in one hand to light our way. Two others from the sanctuary are with us: Nari, a grim, skinny girl whose dark clothing matches her Xenos Well, and Vekata, the boy not much older than me who uses Rhema and swears he can fight. Then come Garo and I, followed by a small group of volunteers from Hotara's street fighters, men and women whose toughness she vouched for. We're all armed, even me, if only with a dagger.

At least I know I can kill someone with a dagger.

"If Thul hasn't screwed us, the grate at the top should be unlocked," Garo says. "It's supposed to lead into a storeroom. Get it open as quiet as you can."

Giniva nods, her flame bobbing, and then disappears. We can hear her footsteps on the rungs as she ascends.

"Got it," her voice drifts down. "Come on up."

One by one, we climb the ladder. It's just brackets set into the brick, rusted and rough under my hands. I follow Garo up, feeling cramped and helpless in the narrow vertical passage, and I'm breathing hard by the time I emerge into a long, narrow room. Shelves line one wall, stacked with gear—uniforms, crossbow bolts, lanterns, and jugs of fuel. There's barely room for all of us. The last of the volunteers, a big, heavily tattooed woman, swings the grate closed behind us.

"Main guard room is just outside," Garo whispers. "Normally five men. Maybe ten now. Giniva opens the door. I head to the stairs and keep any reinforcements from below bottled up. The rest of you deal with whoever's in there. Got it?"

Muttered assents. I wonder when Garo learned to speak so casually of "dealing with" people. Maybe it's another thing they train you in, being a noble.

"Ready," Giniva says.

"Go," Garo mouths.

Giniva pulls the door open. The guard room is lit by a large fireplace and several lanterns, and the light dazzles me for a moment. Garo plunges onward, Melos gauntlets already ignited, barreling into a surprised-looking Ward Guard. A slam and a crackle of power send him crashing against the wall, and then Garo's past, heading for the darker archway of the stairs leading down.

"Rebels!" a woman shouts. "We're under attack—"

The others charge. There are the expected ten Ward Guard in the room, unarmored and without their spears, but still wearing swords. Most of them are sitting around a big table, where a card game was in progress, while another pair are sitting by the fire. They all go for their weapons.

It's so *fast*. When the Immortals had attacked us at the sanctuary, the battle seemed to be over in an eyeblink, but I had chalked that up to my panic. Fights on stage and in books seemed to go on for ages, with plenty of time for the opposing parties to exchange dramatic lines. But here half the Ward Guard are down before they have a chance to even draw their swords, our people hacking at them as they tangle themselves in the benches or bump into the table, sending cards flying.

A few manage to back off, forming a circle near the hearth. Vekata and Nari move in on one side, Vekata glowing with golden light and moving faster than he has any right to, Nari cloaked in sticky shadows. The volunteers charge on the other side, and for a moment steel skitters against steel. The tattooed woman grabs a young guard's arm, breaks it with a twist, and cuts his throat with a dagger. The sergeant of the Ward Guards, the woman who'd called the alarm, delivers a cut to the arm of a young rebel that sends him reeling away in a spray of blood. Vekata slips behind her with Rhema-driven speed and buries his dagger in the small of her back. Nari screams as a young Ward Guard's wild swing slashes her hand, and she drops her blade. When he runs her through the stomach, he seems as surprised as she does. A moment later, a firebolt from Giniva sets the boy ablaze, and he's screaming, too.

Less than a hundred heartbeats, and it's over. Nari's on the ground, dying noisily, shadow energy evaporating around her in little puffs of darkness. The burning Ward Guard has gone still and silent, sheathed in flame, and the rest of them lie around the hearth in pools of blood. I'm trying very hard not to be sick.

"Winch room," Garo says, glancing over his shoulder. "Tori, take Momo and get the gate open. Everyone else with me!"

I can hear the clatter on the stairs already, weapons and armor. A Ward Guard with a crossbow appears at the next landing down and fires, the bolt glancing off Garo's Melos gauntlets in a shower of green sparks. She ducks out of the way as Giniva sends a firebolt back at her, and I hear raised voices.

Momo, the tattooed woman, falls in behind me as I take the other side of the stairway, up to the top of the guardhouse. This room is empty except for the winch, a contraption of rope and pulleys with a single big crank-handle on one side. I suspect Garo sent me up here in case the mechanism needed puzzling out, but all I have to do is point Momo at it. Muscles bunch and strain in her back as she goes to work, and I can hear the rattle of chains and counterweights through the walls.

There are windows here—arrowslits, really, but enough to get a decent view. The guardhouse is built into the wall itself, a tower just beside the gate. Looking south, toward the Eleventh Ward, I can see a crowd gathered in the squares of the High Market. They have spears, clubs, and torches, driving back the gathering darkness of early evening. The Ward Guard is spread out along the wall, armed with crossbows, but so far holding their fire. The mob can't get to them, after all.

As soon as Momo starts cranking, all that changes. The gates swing open, slowly at first, but with gathering momentum. A group of Ward Guard on the far side, caught flat-footed, struggles to block the archway, but they don't get a chance to set their spears before the crowd surges forward. I hear the twang of crossbows, and people fall, but not nearly enough. They don't need my encouragement, not anymore. The guards are pulled down, beaten to a pulp, trampled underfoot, and the mob surges past onto the highway.

I run across the room to the other windows, facing north. From here, I can see out onto the military highway that separates the Fifth and Eleventh Wards. Another wall rises on the other side, with a matching gate leading into the Fifth. A dull glow from beyond it indicates a mob has formed on that side, too—the people we sent through Thul's hidden tunnels have been working all day. More Ward Guard, arrayed to contain the threat, now find themselves assailed from both directions. They have better warning than their comrades at the Eleventh's wall, time to form up and make a line of spears. But they're badly outnumbered, and all their defenses are facing the wrong way—the walls were designed to contain insurrection from inside the wards, not repel an attack from the outside.

Run, I urge the soldiers, silently. *Just run. Take off your uniforms and lose yourselves in the crowd. Don't die for no reason.* The mob is hesitating, those in front not wanting to risk a charge onto that wall of spearpoints, but the pressure from behind is unstoppable. A bloodbath looms.

I open my Kindre senses, the world unfolding to me like a flower, minds full of powerful emotion all around. It washes over me: acrid fear; hot, sweaty rage; crimson pain; and the sick purple of a lust for violence. And duty, a sound like a distant skirl of drums, holding the terrified guards in place.

No. I reach out to them, still the drums, push that away. *No duty to die. Not here. Not now. Run.*

For a moment, the two sides are still, in balance. Then the first spear falls from a guardsman's nervous fingers. A sergeant shouts at him, inaudible in the din, but the young man pushes past, leaving his place in the line. Those on either side turn to watch him, and another spear hits the dirt. Then another, and another.

The Ward Guard crumbles, like a sugar cube soaked in water. The mob surges forward. My mind feels like I've rolled it in filth, but I find myself smiling.

Garo and I return to our impromptu headquarters at the Immortal safe house. Giniva stays behind, organizing a team to secure the gate. A couple of the volunteers carry Nari back with the rest of us. It's hopeless, unless there's another ghulwitch in the city with Grandma Tadeka's skill, but I don't have the heart to stop them. By the time we return, her faint moans have ceased, her dark tunic soaked with cooling blood.

I should care about that. She was one of ours, from the sanctuary. The people I'm supposed to be protecting. But I feel numb. There were bodies in the High Market, rioters cut down by crossbow bolts from the walls. No one seemed to be doing anything about them.

Back in the upper room of the safe house, someone has found a map of the city, started drawing lines in pencil. As the sun sets, reports start to trickle in from the other teams Garo sent out, and the picture they draw is one of brilliant success. Our people have taken the Ward Guard by surprise across nearly a dozen districts, opening gates and spreading the news of the rebellion. Some garrisons surrender outright, or even defect, turning on their officers and joining the mob. The fire of rebellion spreads across Kahnzoka, reaching out from the lower ward to move up the hill.

The guards, desperate, hold the line at the Third Ward. None of Thul's tunnels and secret doors go that high, and the walls are well-fortified. Garo gives orders to let them be, secure what we've won. The guards have abandoned the outer walls, now hopelessly outflanked, and he sends people to man them, in case the government tries to launch an assault from the countryside.

I sit beside him, nodding, while it all happens, excited people shouting at each other and sketching pencil lines on the map. They ask my opinion, and I defer to Garo. My thoughts have returned to the Immortal captain in the basement, and what she might know.

Where are you, Isoka? Does it even matter? If my hands were bloody before, they're positively steeped in crimson now. *What was I supposed to do?*

Not this.

Giniva returns, just after midnight. Garo is still at the table, deep shadows under his eyes, working by candlelight. He looks up as she comes in, and she wordlessly hands him a sealed envelope. In the flickering light, I catch the color of the wax: Imperial purple. Garo breaks it open with one finger, scans the contents, and smiles.

"It's from Kuon Naga," he says, as a hush falls across the room. "He wants to negotiate."

20

ISOKA

I'm walking toward Prime's bone-strewn ziggurat. Skulls grin down at me, and the ropes of bones clatter faintly in the afternoon breeze.

The last time I came here, I had the best fighters in the crew with me, and we failed. People died.

This time, I'm alone.

A dozen walking corpses wait in front of the entrance, a wall of desiccated flesh and blank, staring eyes. I ascend the staircase and stop in front of them, ready to ignite my blades.

"Isoka Deepwalker," one of them says, in Prime's rich, resonant tones, so different from the rasp he makes in my head. The corpse steps forward, its torn, dried lip twisting into a smile. "Are you here to kill me?"

"I'm here to take you up on your offer," I tell the thing. "If it still stands."

There's a moment of silence that I take for hesitation. Then Prime laughs.

"He'll know it's a trick," Meroe says.

"Probably." I inspect my boots, which have seen better days. There's a hole developing near my left toe. *I wonder if the angels make boots.*

It's nearly noon, and we're standing in the arched doorway of our own ziggurat. I'm checking my gear one last time.

"So," Meroe says, "how do you know he won't kill you immediately?"

"I don't, not for certain. But I have a hunch."

"This is not reassuring," Meroe says, pacing.

"You were there this morning when we went over this."

"I know!" She turns on her heel to face me. There's no anger on her face this time, just worry and pain. "I know. But . . ."

"Prime wants something from me," I say. "I have a guess what it might be. Even if I'm wrong, though, I think he'll keep me alive. You didn't hear him when he made his offer. He had to know how I feel, but he's . . ." I shake my head. "Desperate."

"Less sympathy for the guy who kills our friends with walking corpses, please," Meroe says.

"I don't have any sympathy." I lace my fraying boot tight. "I just feel like I understand."

I straighten up, and she comes over to face me. We look at each other for a few moments, in silence.

"You're leaving me again," she says.

"We talked about this, too," I say. "I'm not trying to protect you. I'm going to need you to pull my rotting hide out of the fire."

"I know." She closes her eyes. "But it always seems to work out this way."

"'To command is to sacrifice.' Someone told me that once."

"Smartass," Meroe says, and kisses me.

We press tight against one another, hearts beating side by side. I never want to stop, never want to leave that embrace. I kiss along the line of her jaw and into the hollow of her throat, tasting the faint tang of sweat.

"This is going to work," I say. "And when it's over, we'll get back on *Soliton,* and go keep Tori safe from Kuon Naga. And then . . ."

"And then?" Meroe murmurs.

"You know I have no rotting idea what happens then," I say. "But whatever it is, we do it together."

She squeezes me a little tighter.

"And," I whisper, "when we get *Soliton* sailing north again, we'll have some time to kill before we arrive."

Meroe giggles, and her hands slide somewhere inappropriate. "I might have some ideas there."

"Really?" I kiss her again. "*Such* a strange princess."

She laughs. When I pull away, there are tears in her eyes.

The corpses take hold of me, two to a side. More crowd around, forming a mass of stinking, rotting bodies. I hold my breath, waiting for the move that means that I was wrong, that Prime wants to kill me after all and this was a horrible mistake.

It doesn't come, at least not yet. The monsters drag me ungently, and I stumble trying to keep up. But they don't dig their fingers in to rip and tear. We walk arm in arm, like the world's worst dance troupe, up the steps and in the front door of the ziggurat. After a few turns, a ramp leads down, into the stony depths of the building.

It's all I can do not to sigh with relief when I see the cage. It's a crude thing, made from scrap metal awkwardly shaped into floor-to-ceiling bars in an otherwise unfurnished stone room. Inside the bars there's nothing but a wooden bucket in one corner. Stains on the stone around it hint that I'm not the first prisoner who's been kept here.

Two of the lizard-monsters wait on the outside of the bars, feathers ruffling as we enter, bones visible through gaps in their rotting, shrunken hide. One bar has been bent sideways enough to make a hole for me to enter, and I step through at the corpses' prodding. A lizard pads forward, grasps the metal in its teeth, and bends it straight. Up close, it looks like pieces of *Soliton,* rusted plates twisted into shape.

"Well?" I say aloud. "What now?"

"Now you explain what you're up to," Prime says, his sonorous, unreal voice coming from one of the corpses.

"I told you. You offered to partner with me. I'd like to take you up on it."

"Why should I believe you?"

"You're the one who said that our kind is driven to rule."

He snorts. "You'll lose that tone soon enough."

I shrug. The corpses turn, as one, and shuffle out of the room, leaving the two lizards behind as guards. Prime is taking no chances.

My Melos blades might be able to cut their way through the bars eventually—maybe, the ship-metal is rotting tough—but certainly not before these two monstrous jailers did something about it.

I eye them suspiciously. Prime can probably see and hear through them, just as he can speak through his walking corpses. I settle down in the corner farthest from the pair of them—thankfully not the one occupied by the bucket—and put my hand in my pocket. The bit of conduit I used in Catoria's chambers is still there, and I let words silently form in my mind.

Silvoa? Can you hear me?

Her face appears in front of me, the faintest ghostly sketch. She nods. I wait a moment, to see if my captors react, but either they can't see the Eddica-light or they don't care.

You must have made it inside Prime's stronghold, then, she says in my mind.

He tossed me in a cell.

More or less as planned. Her image glances around. *This is where he kept me.*

I thought it might be. I can't imagine he has many prisoners. I hesitate for a moment. *Are you . . . all right? Back in Catoria's room—*

It's not as bad as it sounds, she says briskly. *I ham it up a bit, honestly.*

It sounded like he was tearing your fingernails out.

He can make it painful for me, Silvoa admits. *But he can't do any permanent damage. I'm already dead, after all.*

And he won't notice you talking to me?

Not in here. This is his domain; it's where I'm supposed to be.

I nod, and settle back against the wall. There's not much to do now but wait. I watch the dead lizard-birds for a while, but they stand absolutely still, and that quickly gets boring. No one seems inclined to bring me food and water, which is fine with me for the moment, since I'm not eager to have to put the bucket to use.

So this is where he kept you? I ask Silvoa. *If you don't mind talking about it, I mean.*

I don't mind, she says. *The worst has already happened, after all.*

You seem remarkably cheerful in spite of that.

Well. I'm still around to be *cheerful. That's got to be worth something, right?*

I suppose. I manage a grin. Hagan isn't nearly so talkative. I have the strong feeling that I would have liked Silvoa, if we'd met before she died. *Why do you think he kept you around?*

At first I thought it was just because he was a vindictive, sadistic piece of rotscum, Silvoa says. *And I still think that's true, but there's more to it. I think he's lonely.*

Lonely? Prime? I shake my head. It's hard to think of the mysterious master of this place as experiencing anything so human. I realize that I picture him as one of his corpses, a desiccated puppet with dead-black eyes.

He talked to you about the Eddicants, right? she says. *How he thinks that only people like us, Eddica mage-bloods, have the right to be here? To exist?*

A little.

Imagine if you really believed that, but you're the only Eddicant you've ever met. And then, suddenly, there's another one.

I don't think I'd have responded by torturing her to death, I say.

He kept me here for quite a while. She shakes her ghostly head. *Tried to convince me of everything he claims. I think it was the fact that I didn't believe him that finally made him start hurting me. After I died, he couldn't bear to let me go.*

Or else he just wanted to keep torturing you, because he's sadistic rotscum.

That too, of course.

I draw in a long breath and let it out, slowly, trying to calm the beating of my heart. I can't get wound up yet. There's a long way to go.

What's it like? I ask Silvoa.

What?

Dying.

Oh. Her ghost-image smiles brightly. *It* really *hurts.*

*   *   *

We make a strange procession out of the Cresos pyramid, heading for the central obelisk and its plaza. It's just after dawn on the day I'm going to walk into Prime's lair.

A messenger, one of the Cresos clan's servants gifted with Rhema, has already made the dangerous nighttime journey to the Minders' ziggurat and back. As I hoped, Gragant was willing to listen, and his delegation should have set out at the same time we did. The Cresos know this, which makes them nervous, especially Lord Toranaka. Catoria, dressed in well-tailored traveling clothes, waits with more patience than I would have given her credit for, while he exhausts himself ranting.

"—and furthermore," he says, beginning to run out of steam, "this is exactly the kind of matter on which you need the considered advice of the elders of the clan."

"It seems like I require your advice on *all* matters, lately," Catoria says, making a show of inspecting her gloves. "I am seventeen, Uncle. Not a little girl any longer."

"And yet you rush into foolish meetings with our enemies!"

"I don't think the Minders are your enemies," I put in. "Especially not when there's walking corpses attacking both of you."

"If I was interested in your opinion, I would have asked for it," he says icily. He's wearing archaic wooden armor, like the guards last night, which makes him look blocky and heavyset. The helmet, face mask carved into a snarling demon, is under his arm. To Catoria, he says, "I thought that we had resolved this matter yesterday evening."

"Lady Gelmei presented me with some additional information," Catoria says. "I changed my mind."

"And are the rest of us going to be privy to this remarkable revelation?"

"No," Catoria snaps. "*I* am the heir to the Cresos, Uncle, not you. I rule here. Unless you wish to contest that?"

There's a strained moment, while a variety of emotions cross Toranaka's face. He glances at the rest of the clan, the Imperial mage-bloods and their servants standing ready, and I wonder if he'll try to make a play for their loyalty. Judging by the way people are looking at Catoria, I don't think much of his chances.

Maybe he sees it, too, because he just bows his head. Catoria nods, satisfied, and gestures imperiously. We depart—a column of Cresos nobility in their antique armor, followed by their servants from a hodgepodge of nations, haphazardly armed. And beside Catoria, of course, myself and Shiara, me in my *Soliton*-made leather armor, Shiara having traded her *kizen* for a lighter, sturdier robe. It could be a bad theatrical production, mixing costumes from various times and places and hoping the audience won't notice.

"He doesn't look happy," Shiara says, sliding in beside me as we set out. She nods at Toranaka. "Do you think he'll make trouble?"

"You'd know better than I would," I say. "But I'm more worried about Catoria and Gragant."

And Meroe, though I don't say that out loud. She is not going to be happy with this plan.

It takes longer than it should to reach the obelisk, since the Cresos in their armor aren't well-suited for maneuvering through the underbrush. Several of them, including Toranaka—to my secret delight—trip and have to be righted by their companions, like errant turtles. By the time we get there, the Minder contingent has already arrived, a dozen monks in brown robes. I recognize Gragant and the huge, brooding Harak.

"This could be an ambush," Toranaka says. "Be cautious, my lady."

"Tough to ambush someone when you have a quarter as many men as they do," I say. The Cresos party is considerably larger than the monks'.

Toranaka is about to say something cutting, but Catoria interrupts him. "Gragant is many things, but a liar is not one of them. He will not attack us if he has given his word."

"Did he not lie to you when he took Silvoa to Prime?" Toranaka says.

"No," Catoria says quietly. "Silvoa did that herself." She shakes her head. "Stay here, Uncle. Isoka, come with me."

"But—" Toranaka sputters.

Catoria is already moving across the courtyard, toward the obelisk. Seeing her advance, with only me for company, Gragant comes to meet us with just Harak at his side. He smiles when he recognizes me, but his expression becomes more solemn as he turns to Catoria.

"I admit that I was surprised to receive your message," he says. "It's been five years since you've wanted to talk to me."

"I was determined it was going to be the rest of my life." Catoria glances at me. "But it has been suggested to me that my anger is misplaced."

Gragant raises an eyebrow. Catoria takes a deep breath.

"Silvoa intended to confront Prime regardless. She lied to me about it, but that is on her account, not yours. As her friend, I . . . can't blame you for accompanying her."

"She was always impossible to stop once she'd made up her mind," Gragant says. He smiles, very slightly. "I've missed you, Catoria. You've grown."

Something passes between the two of them, wordlessly and too deep for me to understand. It lasts only a moment, and then Gragant turns to me.

"I take it Catoria allowed you to use her access point?"

"This morning," I say with a nod.

I had managed to catch only a few hours' sleep, which somehow made me feel even worse. This time, when I'd gone to the access point and let the tendrils of the Harbor's system wrap around my mind, I'd felt Prime's presence from the beginning. But he'd said nothing, only watched, as the system withdrew and made its announcement in its dead, flat voice.

access request received; home//balthazar
result:
authorized/accepted
Two down, one to go.

Gragant listens intently as I explain the plan that Catoria and I have worked out. Harak frowns, disapproving, but Gragant himself nods thoughtfully.

"It's an awful risk for you," he says. "With our combined strength, we might be able to simply overwhelm Prime's defenses."

"I'm not so certain," I say. "That ziggurat has to be packed full of traps and guards he hasn't shown us yet. Even if we won, it would cost too much." I hear, involuntarily, the screams of the crew I'd led to their deaths, Safiya's wet gurgle as the monster ripped her in two. "I can't accept that."

"Even still," Harak rumbles. "There will be a cost."

"Of course there will," Catoria says. "But it is a necessary one. We have avoided dealing with Prime for long enough."

"I think," Gragant says slowly, "that I agree. The Divine Being has set us a challenge, and we must meet it."

"If that is the case," Harak says, "then the Minders should act alone. The Divine Being's challenge is for *us*."

"Perhaps the challenge is not only the defeat of Prime," Gragant says.

Harak frowns, but doesn't answer.

It's hard to keep track of time in the cell, but it has to be getting close to evening when Prime comes to see me. I glare as a single human figure enters, the lizard-birds remaining motionless.

"You're late," I tell him. "The last time I was in a cell, things were a lot more interesting."

"I'm terribly sorry to disappoint you," Prime says, in his actor's baritone.

For a moment I wonder if he's finally come to see me in person, but it's clear immediately that this body is only another puppet. It's handsome, square-jawed with high cheekbones and slick, well-coiffed hair, but it looks more like a piece of sculpture than a genuine human face. It moves deliberately, under careful control, with none of the unconscious tics of a living person. When Prime isn't concentrating, it remains absolutely still, just like the corpse-monsters behind it.

"Are you ready to bargain?" I say.

"Bargain?" The dead face manages an ironic smile. "I'm not sure you're in much of a position to bargain."

"I think we're in the perfect position to come to an agreement. We both have something the other wants."

"That's a fascinating theory." He leans forward. "You're aware, of course, of what I can do to you whenever I choose."

"It won't get you what you want, any more than it did with Silvoa."

"You've been talking to my little wayward ghost, I see." The smile again, like something he'd rehearsed from a book. "What do you think you have that I want?"

"The ability to leave this building, obviously."

Prime's expression goes dead still, which I take for a good sign.

"You were already here when the Cresos and the Minders came ashore," I say. "I gather you'd been here for a while."

"A while," Prime agrees. He tries to sound nonchalant, but even the fake voice shows cracks.

"And you clearly want to use the access points. To take control of the Harbor system for yourself."

He gives a modest shrug.

"It follows, then, that it's not the presence of the other crews that's keeping you out. If you'd been able to take control, you would have done it before they arrived. Which also explains why you've only harassed them intermittently, without risking any of your little pets." I nod at the lizard-birds. "You *can't* get to those access points yourself, can you?"

Prime stares at me in stony silence. I lean back against the wall.

"Is it just that you're afraid?" I say. "Trapped in your own fortress?"

"Afraid?" He laughs, suddenly all confidence. "Is *that* what you think?"

"It fits the evidence."

"You have no idea who you're dealing with," he says. "What *class* of being you're dealing with. I am the *Prime Eddicant*. I was at death's door when *Soliton* brought me here. My power—the true power, the heart of being—has kept me alive ever since. Can you possibly understand that? The force of will necessary to transcend death for *centuries*?"

Centuries? I try not to let my reaction show. *Blessed's rotting balls. He's madder than I thought.*

"And now you think to . . . what, fool me?" He shakes his head. "Form an alliance, then stab me in the back? As though I would allow such a thing. Did you learn nothing from watching your friends torn to pieces?"

I learned quite a lot. "I wanted to destroy you. I tried to get the others to help me. Gragant and the Minders, Catoria and the Cresos."

"I know. I felt you use their access points."

"Gragant I defeated in a contest." Never mind what *sort* of contest. "But Catoria refused to grant me access, no matter how I pleaded with her."

He's smiling again. "So what you were not offered, you took."

"Yes." I lower my gaze. "I had to fight my way out again, of course."

I'm not usually a great liar. But this lie is what Prime wants to believe.

"You were right," I go on, as his smile widens. "I thought about it for a long time. I took over *Soliton*'s crew, just like I took over my ward in Kahnzoka. I didn't know what I was, then, but I do now. I want to help you."

"What about the others?" he says. "Your friends. Your lover."

"I have the access points. I don't need them anymore."

"Then grant me access," he says. There's no disguising the hunger in his voice. "I can show you how."

"And then you'll have no reason to keep me alive." I shake my head. "No, thanks."

"That leaves us at a bit of an impasse, doesn't it?"

I shrug. His face goes dead again for a while, its guiding intelligence elsewhere. When animation returns to it, his expression is thoughtful.

"Do you know how this place came to be?" he says. "The Harbor. Has Silvoa puzzled it out?"

"You told me it was built by Eddicants as somewhere they could rule."

"It was built by one man. The first Prime Eddicant. And the last, until me."

I shake my head, uncomprehending.

"The story is in the archives, if you know where to look," he says. "Millenia ago, this entire continent was as warm as the Harbor is now. There was a civilization here, developed to its fullest flower, and entirely based around the Eddica Well. Eddica is the first Well in more than name, you see. The other Wells were *created* with Eddica, down the centuries, to enable more people to access power. Vast quantities of energy were expended to drill holes in the fabric of the world.

"But the ancients didn't understand as much as they thought they did. With every new Well, Eddica weakened, got rarer. The world itself began to change, and their home grew colder. Eventually, the survivors left the frozen waste it had become and conquered the lands around the Central Sea. The locals had no Wells, and no way to oppose their new masters. But the ancients were few, and mongrelized their line with the lesser races. Soon they were gone, leaving only mage-bloods as a distant shadow of their legacy."

I watch him grow more animated in the course of this story, and I wonder how much of it he really found in the archives of the Harbor. It's not the maddest thing I've ever heard—at least, not given the existence of *Soliton* and the Harbor itself—but people claiming descent from ancient kings and heroes is the stuff of fairy tales and legends. I wish Meroe were here to quiz him about it.

I also realize that Silvoa was right. Mad or not, this is what Prime wants me for—someone to *listen* to him. For my purposes, it's all to the good, so I prod him onward.

"What does that have to do with the Harbor?" I give the words a doubting spin, and it works as intended. Prime draws himself up with a superior smile, leaning close to the bars.

"Not all the ancients abandoned their homeland. A few thought that the cold would be temporary. They used Eddica's power to put themselves in stasis, waking many centuries later. Their own people thought them mad.

"The sleepers woke, one by one, to find their country still frozen and their people gone. Some of them went mad in truth, or killed themselves. Others followed the path of their brethren and used their power to carve out short-lived kingdoms in the west. Only the last of them, the strongest, had the will to understand what needed to be done. He saw what his people had become, the petty tyrants, the endless wars, the hideous perversion that is the Vile Rot. The Prime Eddicant wanted to reverse it all, and re-create the ancients in all their glory."

"Ambitious," I mutter. Prime ignores me.

"He built the Harbor," he says. "Constructed armies of angels to maintain it and provide for the people who would live there. He created *Soliton* and the other great ships, and sent them out into the world to bring back mage-blood children. From them, he planned to purify the line of the ancients, the Eddicants, by carefully controlled breeding." Prime's eyes are locked on an invisible horizon. "By force of will, he would have reshaped this continent into a paradise."

"Let me guess," I interrupt. "They killed him."

"Of course they killed him," Prime says bitterly. "The lesser races could not understand his vision. They killed him, and then they killed each other. The angels maintained their vigil, and the great ships still sailed, though they grew ever more ragged. One by one, they failed, until only *Soliton* remained. It is life and death that provide the raw energy Eddica manipulates, and with the Harbor mostly empty and only *Soliton* to deliver power, the city began shifting into stasis to preserve itself, stuttering down the years at ever-shorter intervals." He smiles again. "Then *I* arrived. The Prime Eddicant's true heir."

"So what are you going to do, when you get control of the system?"

"Take the step the original Prime could not, of course." He looks at me, with the handsome, dead eyes of a statue. "His vision was grand, but too limited in scope. He wanted to re-create the ancients and ignore the rest of the world. But it was the passing of the heritage of the ancients to the rest of the world that must be reversed if the decay is to be repaired."

My mouth is dry. He spreads his arms, beatifically.

"Join me, and we will use *Soliton*'s power to do what must be done. We will destroy the lesser races. Each slaughter of the unworthy will release Eddica energy, and I will use that power to create new servants. My army will expand until the world is cleansed of the ancients' mistake, and only Eddicants remain. *I* will not be betrayed, because there will be no one left to betray me."

Oh, Blessed's breath and rotting ruin. I told the others Prime was mad, but I hadn't expected *this*. And the worst part is, it might actually work. Not the re-creation of an ancient race, but the rest: in my mind's eye, armies of walking corpses spread across the world like locusts, killing everyone they encounter, the very energy of those deaths fueling the creation of more monsters.

I become aware that Prime is staring at me. Waiting for me to respond. And what am I rotting supposed to say now? *Yes, that sounds great, sign me up for your transcendently insane program of universal genocide?*

Thankfully, at that moment, a shiver runs through the ziggurat. It's the faintest vibration, this deep inside, but Prime's head snaps around like a dog scenting prey.

"We will continue our discussion another time," he says, not looking at me. "I appear to have other matters to attend to."

He strides from the room, leaving me with the pair of lizard-birds. I put my hand on the conduit, and Silvoa's ghostly form takes shape beside me.

Is it time? I ask her.

Yes. She looks grave. *The attack has begun.*

21

TORI

It's been ages since I've visited the harbor. I've forgotten how bad it smells.

When people from the Second Ward say they're going to the *sea*, they usually mean they're going north, across the spine of Dragon-back, the headland that bounds one side of Kahnzoka's bay. There's a long stretch of pleasant beach there, bordered by a forest managed by Imperial gamekeepers and dotted with "cabins" (that is, small mansions) owned by various nobles. There the smell of the salt water is bracing when the wind blows strong and cool off the ocean.

Here, it smells of—well, a variety of things, but first and foremost rotting fish. Kahnzoka's fishmongers dump their offal in the harbor, or into the covered streams that drain into it. The rotting heads and guts wash against the shore under the piers and at the bottom of the tide walls. Small children from the Sixteenth Ward go diving in it, hunting for the crabs that live on the decaying meat. That was a job even Isoka never considered, no matter how hungry we got—the offal attracts sharks, too, in packs that will happily tear a child to shreds.

The fish market is still operating, even under the current strained circumstances. Without the daily catch, half the ward would starve. But tension is definitely in the air, and every vendor seems eager to sell what they can and move on. Women with colorful headscarves scurry up and down the rows of wheelbarrows, hardly bothering to haggle when they find what they're looking for.

At the edges of the market, our people patrol in pairs. Hasaka has given them red sashes to mark them out. He's been directing the effort to turn the shapeless mob that has now taken half the city into something resembling a militia, with officers and duty assignments. From his scowls and arguments with Hotara and the others, I gather that it isn't going particularly well.

Two red-sashed women salute him, clumsily, as he and I leave the fish market and thread our way through the Sixteenth Ward's maze. Another pair of guards follow behind us, spears at the ready. Though the Ward Guard have pulled back as far as the Second, everyone is certain the Immortals still have spies and agents in the lower wards. Night patrols have been ambushed, men and women found slaughtered and left in the street. Everyone is on edge.

It's been nearly a week since Garo left for the Royal Ward and his negotiations with Kuon Naga and the Imperial authorities. I've received two letters from him since, both in his handwriting, both urging patience and promising to return soon. In the meantime, Hasaka has taken charge of organizing our defenses, while Hotara works on training and equipment and Jakibsa tries to keep everyone fed, clothed, and sheltered. And for some reason, all three of them insist on reporting to *me*, though I'm not sure what they expect me to offer. Maybe I'm just a proxy for Garo until he returns.

"For the most part, I'm not worried about a direct assault," Hasaka says, as we approach the looming bulk of the outer wall. "It's still too soon for the closest Legion force to arrive, and the Ward Guard doesn't have the equipment for an attack on the wall."

"What about the Immortals?" I ask.

He makes a face, but shakes his head. "If they had the strength, I have to imagine they'd have done it already. Maybe there aren't enough of them left. We don't have a good idea of their numbers."

More information it might be worth extracting from our prisoner, if only she would talk. Unfortunately, she still remains obstinate, naked and chained under the old safe house.

"There are two weak spots I'm worried about," Hasaka goes on. "The first is up in the Third Ward. That's an interior wall, not part of the outer defenses, and it's not as high or as well fortified."

"If they attack there, though, the fighting will be all over the

Third, and maybe into the Second." Where people who *mattered* lived, in other words, and held property that could be damaged.

"Exactly," Hasaka says. "That's why I don't expect an assault there, though we still have to be careful. More than likely, though, when they attack, it'll be right here."

We come out of the last alley, and into the clear space at the foot of the wall, kept free of encroaching shacks by Imperial decree. Kahnzoka's outer fortifications are several times my height, and broad enough at the top for three men to walk abreast. We're at the very end of the line of walls, where the circumference of the city meets the shoreline, and a massive round tower with its footing in the surf guards the boundary. I can see people in red sashes walking on top, and more volunteers carrying bags and boxes up the narrow stairs built into the inside of the wall.

"It looks solid enough," I say.

"It is, as far as it goes," Hasaka says. "The problem is that the walls were never intended to be a complete defense on their own."

He turns, and I follow his gaze, looking out to sea. The shoreline of the Sixteenth Ward is a solid mass of piers and quays. At night, Kahnzoka's fishing fleet crowds against them two or three deep, but now they're deserted, with only a few untended boats riding the surf. Farther out, fishermen work with lines, nets, and traps, oars splashing as they move from spot to spot. Beyond them, larger ships have sails raised, tacking on the morning breeze. There are many fewer of these, now, most of the merchant ships having fled on the news of the revolution.

None of these are where Hasaka is looking, however. Well out in the harbor, cutting through the water with the sleek grace of predators, a squadron of Imperial war galleys flash in the sun, black sails trimmed with gold. I can see a half-dozen ships, and I know there are more, off beyond the horizon.

Halfway along the harborfront is the Navy dockyard. It stands empty now. The entire naval contingent lit out to sea soon after the Sixteenth Ward rose.

"Some of the fishermen told me the Navy has made a new base on the other side of Dragonback," Hasaka says. "Too exposed for a winter mooring, but it'll serve them for now, and we have no way to get at it. They can control the harbor just fine from there."

I imagine war galleys drawn up on the pleasant beaches, the nobles' cabins commandeered by Imperial officers. *At least we'll have cut some vacations short.* Not much of a victory. I shake my head and try to focus.

"What can they do to us?" I ask.

"If they started attacking the fishing fleet, they could starve the city," Hasaka says bluntly. "My guess is they haven't done that because they're worried it'll turn more people against them. I'm sure they're blocking incoming merchant ships, though. And . . ."

"And?" I prompt.

He hesitates, glancing around. Only our two guards are near enough to hear, but he lowers his voice anyway.

"I don't want to lower morale," he says. "But if those ships come up in close support, there's no way we can hold the wall here." He gestures to the open space around us. "Their archers can sweep this whole area, and keep us from bringing food or reinforcements to the wall itself. And a quick landing here by a couple of companies of marines could push all the way to the closest gate." He shakes his head. "Like I said, the walls were designed on the assumption that the defenders would control the harbor, too. Without that . . ."

"What about the small boats?" I say. "Could we use them to attack the fleet?"

"Those are fishing smacks and cargo haulers," Hasaka says. "A proper galley would tear the whole lot to pieces, assuming you could find people suicidal enough to try to attack in the first place."

Boats are not something I have any experience with, outside of books, so I have to concede the point. I wonder how much of this Hasaka really knows, and how much he's pulling out of thin air. He was a Ward Guard, and certainly has more military experience than the rest of us, but I somehow doubt his expertise extends to naval strategy. But he seems determined to project an air of confidence, albeit somewhat gloomy confidence, so I go along with it.

I've been keeping my Kindre senses tightly closed, of late. The fear in the city is building to the breaking point, and trying to see-hear-smell-taste through it has become overwhelming. The rebels, our people, are bad enough, with their worry tempered by excitement, duty, camaraderie. Out in the streets, the vast bulk of the people are simply hunkered down and waiting for the storm to blow over, and from them I get nothing but sickly fear.

"So what *can* we do about it?" I say.

"I'm not sure," Hasaka says. "I'm thinking of trying to establish a secondary line, a block inland, so we have somewhere to fall back to when the time comes."

"What would that involve?"

He grimaces. "Pulling down some houses, essentially, and building a barricade out of the rubble."

There's a sour taste in my mouth. We're supposed to be fighting *for* these people, not tearing their homes apart. "Let's talk to the others about it." Which isn't an answer.

Hasaka nods, no more eager than I to confront the issue. We turn to head back to the safe house when another red sash, this one a young boy, hurries up, gasping for breath.

"Hasaka, sir." No one has formal titles, but Hasaka's people have started saying "sir," mimicking soldiers they'd read about or seen on stage. "Miss Tori."

"What is it?" Hasaka says. "Are we under attack?"

"No, sir." The boy gulps. "Master Garo has returned. He wants to see Miss Tori right away."

The former Immortal safe house—now de facto headquarters of the revolution—is surrounded by a phalanx of excited men and women in red sashes. Beyond these guards, a crowd is starting to gather, thin for now but growing by the minute. People catch sight of me and Hasaka and press closer, and our guards move up to keep them away with the hafts of their spears. A dozen questions are yelled to us at once.

"Has the Emperor given in?"

"Will the Immortals attack?"

"What did Master Garo promise them?"

"*Down* with the draft! *Down* with the Immortals!"

"Will there be an amnesty?"

"When can I go home?"

"Please," I manage to say, shouting over all of them. "I need to speak to Garo. I'm sure he'll tell everyone what's happening soon."

"Out of the way!" Hasaka barks.

A little shoving gets us to the cordon, and it parts to allow us inside. I hurry up the stairs, past the infirmary—emptier now, as more space across the city has been pressed into service to tend the wounded—and into the barracks that we use as a conference room. Hotara is there, one of the early street fighters who has turned out to be a reliable leader, an older woman weathered by years of hard labor. Giniva is waiting by the table as well, and Jakibsa, whose horrifically burned skin and frail form conceal considerable Tartak power, along with several red sashes I recognize as Hasaka's immediate lieutenants.

"Where's Garo?"

Hotara points to one of the bedrooms. "Resting. He said he wanted to talk to you as soon as you arrived."

"Has he said anything?" Hasaka says. Hotara shakes her head.

I push through the curtain, heart suddenly clenched. I'm expecting the worst, but Garo is lying on his stomach on one of the sleeping mats, a little disheveled but otherwise none the worse for wear. He's exchanged his mock-commoner garb for a noble's clothes, a silk robe over a finely cut under-tunic and trousers, and he's snoring furiously. I kneel beside him, hesitate for a moment, then shake his arm.

"Whuzz," he says, or something to that effect, and groans. I smile slightly and poke him again, and he rolls over. "Is that—Tori!"

He sits up so abruptly that I topple backward, laughing. Garo blinks foolishly for a moment.

"Who were you expecting?" I ask.

"Nobody. Sorry. It's just . . ." He shakes his head. "I haven't slept since . . . night before last? Blessed above, it's good to see you."

He grins back at me, and the knot in my chest unclenches. "You too. But—" I glance at the curtain and keep my voice low. "Why haven't you talked to anyone?"

"Wanted to tell you first. I might need your help." His grin widens, and his eyes blaze. "Tori, we *won*."

"What?" I shake my head. "What does that mean?"

"It means the Imperial ministry is ready to make concessions. You have no idea how seriously they're taking this. I had an audience with the Imperial Chamberlain *himself*, and the entire Council of State. They agreed that we had legitimate grievances."

"So what are they going to do?"

"Change on the Council, to start with. My father is going to become a member, and several of his allies, all from the liberal wing of the court."

"Your . . . father?" My excitement, which had been starting to build, feels suddenly shaky, as though its foundation had washed out with the tide.

"I know, I had been dreading meeting with him," Garo says happily. "Honestly I wondered if he wouldn't disown me on the spot. But instead he *congratulated* me, if you can believe that, and said that he was impressed I had the courage to act on my beliefs."

"That's . . . good." I shake my head. "But what else did the government agree to?"

"Amnesty, obviously, for any acts committed during the rebellion. And Kuon Naga agreed to re-examine the draft quotas and keep a sharper eye on enforcement, especially when I told him about the corruption in the Ward Guard." Garo has a thoughtful expression. "He's not as terrible as people say, which I suppose makes sense. In his position, you would want to cultivate a reputation for nastiness."

"And in exchange for all of this?"

"We go home. It's as simple as that." Garo slaps his fist into his palm. "I told you taking the fight to the upper wards would get results."

"I . . ." My throat seems to be swelling shut. I stand up, breathing hard, and move to the tiny waxed-paper window. It's cracked open a bit, and the cooler air from outside tastes good.

I hear Garo moving behind me. After a moment, he puts his hand on my shoulder, tentatively, like a nervous bird.

"I . . . talked to my father about . . . all of this." He takes a deep breath. "About us. I know you worry about . . . your background, but he's a more flexible man than I'd imagined. I really don't think . . . I mean, if you're . . ." He trails off, awkwardly running one hand through his hair.

I shake my head, and turn away from the window. Garo's standing very close, his eyes sharp and intense. He hasn't shaved, and a thin, fuzzy beard is sprouting on his chin. His hand is still on my shoulder.

"What are you talking about?" I say. It comes out as a whisper. My heart is suddenly beating very quickly.

"You asked me once if I wanted to kiss you," he says. "Right now I can say that I do. More than anything." He swallows. "If you haven't changed your mind."

I stare up at him. *Now?* Somewhere in my mind, I'm laughing in despair. *He wants to do this* now? But I'm not saying no, not pushing him away, and he's leaning forward. His lips press against mine, and in spite of everything my mouth opens under his. He pulls me against him, crushing me against his broad chest, one of his hands working into the dense knot of my hair. His silk rasps against my coarser clothing.

I want to stay there forever, his hot breath tickling my cheek. I want him to touch me, so badly it feels like an ache, and I want to let my fingers play across the muscles of his back.

But.

We don't have time for any of that.

Because I think something has gone horribly wrong.

"Garo," I say, when he pulls away to take a breath. "Garo, stop."

It takes him a moment to respond, but finally he lets go of me, steps back a pace. He's breathing hard.

"Right," he says. "Of course. Sorry."

"It's not—" I shake my head. "Garo, this isn't going to work."

"You don't know that," he says. "If it's about a dowry—"

"Not you and me," I say. "Forget about that for a minute. What you agreed to with the Council, it's not going to work."

"What? Why not?"

"Because they're never going to accept it," I hiss, gesturing at the curtain door. "People are *dead*, hundreds of people, and for what? So your father can get a promotion?"

"It's not about him being my father," Garo says, defensively. "He's always been a leader of the liberal faction, ask anyone who watches the court. By putting him on the Council, the Emperor is signaling a major change in policy. It means everything in the long run—"

"In the *long run*? Nobody starts a riot in the street because of the *long run*." I wave at the window. "The people out there were sick of the draft checkpoints, and they didn't like what happened to Grandma Tadeka. Is your father going to do anything about that?"

"I . . ." Garo hesitates. "Eventually. But the draft *does* have to be filled, or else the Jyashtani—"

"Nobody cares if the Jyashtani take some islands we've never heard of." I shake my head. "If this is the best they can offer—"

"It is." He cuts me off, voice low and urgent. "The best they're going to offer. Tori, *please*, this is why you have to help me. We have pushed this as far as we can, do you understand? Right now the government can blame a few bad apples for the draft problems and let us go. If we don't take this chance, the court is going to *have* to crush us, just to save face, and that means everyone is going to *die*."

"We've beaten them so far." My voice sounds weak in my own ears.

"We've beaten the Ward Guard. You saw what happened when the mob attacked the Immortals. If the Invincible Legions march on the city it's going to be so much worse." He swallows. "I can't let that happen. Not to . . . to you. And the others."

There's a long silence, and I hear rising voices from outside, arguments. Garo looks over his shoulder, then back at me.

"It won't work," I whisper.

He smiles. "I have to try."

* * *

The conference room is crowded. Hasaka, Hotara, Jakibsa, and Giniva sit at the table with me and Garo, with the rest of the space packed with whoever managed to fit—red sashes, Grandma's assistants, people from the mage-blood sanctuary, veterans of the street fighting. Garo looks them over, a fixed smile on his face. The muttering in the room has turned sour in the time the two of us have been alone.

"Comrades," he begins, and my heart sinks, because it's going to be his speech in the High Market all over again. Sure enough, he starts to lay out the agreement he's made with Kuon Naga—amnesty, a shuffling of council seats, and all the rest, and it doesn't take a Kindre adept to feel the tide of discontent.

"We're supposed to just go home, after all this?" says a red sash in the front row, a big man with a dockworker's calluses.

"Of course we are," Hasaka shoots back loyally, from his seat beside Garo. "That was the point of negotiating. Would you rather end up on a gibbet?"

"I'd rather keep fighting," the man says.

"Then you're a fool," an old man says. I recognize him as one of the veterans from the sanctuary. "The Legions will roll over us like a cartful of bricks when they get here. We have to make a deal now."

"What do we gain, though?" Hotara says. "We'll still have the draft."

"Kuon Naga promised amnesty for rebels," Jakibsa says. When Garo nods, he says, "That means he *didn't* offer it for mage-bloods. If we stand down, there's nothing to stop him from having us all rounded up."

Hasaka starts at this, staring at his lover, then looking over at Garo, who frowns.

"I'm sure," he says hesitantly, "that we could negotiate something—"

"Not to mention," Hotara says, "the question of whether we can trust that snake. What's to stop him from turning on us when we disarm?"

Several people shout "Nothing!" simultaneously. Someone in back adds, "*Down* with the draft! *Down* with the Immortals!"

"Please!" Garo gets to his feet. "The court is willing to show mercy now—"

"Because we're winning!" someone shouts back, and there are angry murmurs of agreement.

"—but if we take this further, they won't be able to," Garo proceeds, doggedly. "We need to make peace while there's still a peace to be made."

"*How much are they paying you?*" This shriek comes from a woman in the front row, a tall, scarecrow-looking thing in a ragged robe. "How much did you get from selling us out, *coward*?"

"Traitor!"

"We want to fight!"

Garo looks at me, pleadingly.

I open my mind, just for a moment. Even that much is a mistake. The torrent of raw emotion is too much, the carrion stench of bloodlust and scintillating blue of pride. That day in the market comes back to me, and what happened afterward—the street soaked in blood and charred bodies. If I reach out and try to calm them, I have no idea what will happen.

And the shouts are spreading, down the stairs and out into the road. I can hear chanting begin.

I stand up beside Garo. Hasaka does, too, but the crowd is pressing forward. I hear Hotara shouting for calm, a few red sashes trying to maintain order, but it doesn't make a difference. I take Garo's hand and pull him back through the barrack's curtained doorway. Hasaka, understanding, plants himself in front of it, refusing to move.

Garo has the look of someone in a bad dream as I drag him over to the window.

"I have to . . . say something." He looks back at the doorway, blocked by the curtain, the angry chanting rising louder and louder. "I have to make them understand. Tori—"

"You have to go, Garo."

"Go?"

I gesture at the window. His eyes widen. "You're not serious."

"Of course I'm serious!" I grab the collar of his robe. "You're about five minutes from getting torn to *pieces* here. I *rotting* warned you!"

"But—"

"Please. Just get out of here. Go back to your father."

"What about you?"

I knew he was going to ask that, but it doesn't make it any easier. "I'm not leaving."

"They'll kill you."

I don't know which *they* he means, the rebels or the government. Either seems likely. I shrug.

"No," he says. "I won't let that happen—"

"*You* don't get a choice," I tell him. "I have to find Isoka. I'm not going to get a better chance."

"My father can help, if you come with me."

He believes it, I can tell that much without my Kindre senses. But Lord Marka isn't going to have any reason to help me, not if it means going up against Kuon Naga. I shake my head.

"Just go," I tell him. "Before it's too late."

"Tori," he says. "I love you."

I shove him out the window.

An hour later, the safe house is almost empty.

Hasaka was finally pushed aside, and a gang of angry rebels rushed into the barracks, only to find Garo gone. They didn't pay me much attention, just ran back out again to spread the news. I heard the shouting rise to a new pitch.

I hope Garo didn't hurt himself in the fall. I didn't see him on the street outside, at least.

After that, nobody seemed to know what to do next. Some people tried to find Garo. Others fled, assuming the rebellion was finished. The majority, though, looked to the rest of their leaders for guidance, and bit by bit Hasaka, Hotara, and Jakibsa reasserted their authority. The red sashes remembered they were supposed to obey their officers, and went back to preparing for an assault from the Imperial authorities.

Hasaka keeps coming in to ask *me* what he should do. When I finally manage to rouse myself to go back into the common room—filthy now with tracked mud and debris—Hotara gives me a nod, and Giniva asks if I have any messages that need to be delivered.

Is it Kindre? Some side effect, so subtle I don't even notice? Or is it just habit, left over from when I delivered orders in Grandma's name?

I've been fourteen for less than a month. Why in the Blessed's name are they expecting me to know anything?

I want to laugh, or to cry.

If I'd stayed in the Second Ward, like Isoka wanted, none of this would have happened. Or else I'd be cowering there with the other nobles, waiting to see if the rebels are going to kill us all.

Not that there was ever any chance of that. I'm not who my sister thought I was. Not who I pretended to be.

Monster. It's a mocking chant in my ear. *Monster, monster, monster.*

Downstairs, in the basement, the Immortal captain is waiting for me. The two red-sashed guards have stuck nervously to their posts through all the excitement. When I dismiss them, they hurry away eagerly, and I let myself into the cell. No warnings about the danger this time.

The captain looks at me with a strange expression, almost thoughtful. She seems aged, as though her time in captivity has added years to her features. There are angry red welts at her wrists and ankles where the chains have chafed.

"Hello, little sister," she says. Her tone is still defiant. "How is the revolution going?"

"I want to know what happened to Isoka," I say.

"I want to get out of here and see you all hanged," she says. "Tell you what. Come with me back to Kuon Naga, and maybe we can both get what we're looking for. He wants you badly, you know."

"Why?"

She just smiles.

I let my Kindre senses open. *Monster.* I'm past caring.

My mind reaches out for hers. Defiance, bravado, loyalty, duty, cruelty, a potent, noxious mixture. I exert my will, and my power reaches out, crushing it all into nothing. The captain's mind shudders and presses back against my unwelcome intrusion, my forcing myself into her most intimate spaces. Then it gives way, with a feeling like tearing flesh. I note, vaguely, that she's screaming.

Obedience. I give her that, in place of everything else.

After a while, the screaming stops.

"Tell me what you did with Isoka."

"Sacrifice." Her voice is dull, now, her eyes heavy-lidded and empty. "For *Soliton*. A special assignment."

"*Soliton?*" I narrow my eyes, confused. "The ghost ship?"

"Not a ghost ship," the captain says. "Real. Naga . . . wants. Sent Gelmei to bring it back."

"You sent her . . ." I shake my head. "Where is this ship now?"

"Gone. Always gone. Not the first to try, won't be the last." She shakes her head, a rope of drool dangling from her chin. "Dead, for certain. All dead. It eats them. Eats them all."

"She's . . ." I pause, examining her mind for hints of resistance. There's nothing. "Why does Naga want me?"

"Insurance. If Gelmei succeeds. Hostage. Keep her loyal. But she won't."

"I have to get her back," I say. "How?"

"No one comes back. Not from *Soliton*."

"If Naga wants me as a hostage, there has to be a way. He must know it."

"No way . . ." Her mouth gapes stupidly, tongue lolling. "Dead. Dead, dead, dead—"

"Shut *up!*"

She stops. I lean on the cell door, heart slamming against my ribs.

I'd hoped that the Immortals would have Isoka in a prison somewhere. Locked in some noble's basement. Shipped off to the

Legions. I'd been prepared for any of that. I'd been prepared—I thought I'd been prepared—to hear that she'd been killed out of hand and dumped in the harbor. But this—

Sacrificed to Soliton? *To a ghost ship that's not even* real? Except Kuon Naga thinks it was, apparently.

He has to know something else. He has *to.*

I have to get to him.

I look up at the captain. If anyone finds her like this, they'll ask questions I can't answer.

"Die," I tell her.

The muscles in her throat spasm, as though she's swallowed a snake. I wait while she convulses, straining mindlessly against her chains as her face turns first red and then an angry purple. Only when she dangles limp and still in her bonds do I stand up and leave the cell, passing the guards in the stairwell as I ascend back to the common room.

"Tori!" Hasaka says as I come in. "Are you all right?"

I must look awful. I wave a hand, vaguely. "I'm fine. Where are the others?"

"Hotara and Jakibsa went to look at some food stockpiles. I sent Giniva to get a report on the defenses at the northern wall."

"That's good." I stand over the table, looking down at the map of the city, now covered in scrawled pencil notes. "We have a lot of work to do."

22

ISOKA

"Can you show me?" I ask Silvoa.

Her ghost-image looks nervous. "We don't have much time before—"

"I know," I say. "Please. I have to see."

Her expression softens. She reaches out one intangible arm, and passes her fingers in front of my eyes.

In an instant it's as though I'm standing high on Prime's ziggurat, among the rattling strings of bones. I know it must be dark, but I can see, trees and stone outlined in Eddica ghost-light. A stream of walking corpses issues forth from the stronghold's entrance, lurching, dried-out bodies with twiglike limbs and gray, filmy hair. They shuffle down the ramp in a tide, joining the growing swarm at the base.

Beyond them, in a loose line, are the humans of the Harbor.

The three contingents are separate, but side by side. On the right are the Minders, centered on the hulking shape of Harak, with Gragant beside him. With them are a couple of dozen men and women in gray robes, well-muscled from their years of training, now glowing with the colors of their Wells. On the other side of the line, a phalanx of Cresos warriors in wooden armor stand shoulder to shoulder, anonymous behind their carved face masks. I recognize Toranaka's armor, with a bit of surprise, right in the center. Their retainers hold their flanks, with bows and spears or Myrkai fire.

In the center, of course, are the crew. *My* crew. Zarun, spitting-green Melos blade already in his hands, anchors the line. To one side are Jack and Thora—Thora must have overcome Meroe's instructions keeping her in bed. To the other is Aifin, golden light glowing around him, sword in hand. And the others, everyone who was willing. Even the survivors of the first expedition are there, slim, ghostly Bohtal, bald-headed Kotaga, and the others, Blessed knows why. Meroe stands a few paces behind the line, and my throat goes thick at the sight of her. But of course she's here. Just because she can't swing a sword or blast an enemy with fire doesn't mean she's a fragile bloom like Tori. I learned that when we fell into the Deeps. *You'd think I'd remember it better.* Catoria is with her, and Shiara.

The dead move forward, driven by a single will. Among the humans, fire blooms in dozens of hands. As the corpses shamble into a run, bolts of Myrkai energy streak out, blossoming into blasts of flame that send broken bodies tumbling. Blue waves of Tartak force slam into the front ranks, pressing them back as more fire engulfs them. Then, as the swifter monsters close, a handful of Melos blades ignite to match Zarun's.

The vision dissolves, replaced with Silvoa's translucent face. "He's here."

I blink, and realize my hands are clenched tight enough to turn my knuckles white. In my mind's eye, I can see Meroe's face, lit by the flickering glow of multi-colored magic as corpses close in.

This was your idea, Isoka, I tell myself sternly. *She has her job, and you have yours.*

I wonder what Prime is thinking, if he's more worried about the small army outside his gates than he is about me. That's the idea, anyway. Keep his attention divided.

The pair of lizard-birds in here with me certainly don't look distracted. I stand up, stretch, and smile at them.

The doorway explodes.

Rubble showers the room, bits of stone glancing off the bars of my cage, followed by a rolling cloud of dust. An enormous four-legged shape stalks through it, a canine angel, stone-gray mouth open in a silent snarl. The two lizard-birds, shaking grit from their feathers, charge the angel at once, but their long talons only scrape harmlessly across its side. A paw swats one of the things with the force of a falling boulder, and stone jaws close around the other's head, crushing its avian skull.

"Hello, Hagan," I say, as the dust starts to settle.

The angel pads closer, and Hagan's face appears in Eddica ghost-light beside Silvoa's. "So far, so good," he says. "Your way in worked nicely."

"Of course it did." Silvoa smiles immodestly. "Now get her out of there. We haven't got long before Prime tracks us down, even if the battle is taking up most of his attention."

Hagan nods, and his face disappears. The angel throws its weight against the bars of the cage, the same strength the dredwurm used to tunnel through the decks of *Soliton*. With a screech, the ship-metal gives way, and I step out of my cell, brushing dust off my armor.

The dog-angel retreats through the shattered doorway, and I follow. Silvoa mutters directions, too fast for me to hear, but Hagan understands. The angel lopes forward, taking the first right turn, and I follow into the labyrinth of the ziggurat's interior. The corridors, thankfully, are large enough for Hagan's bulky form.

Most of the rooms we pass are as empty as the ziggurat the crew moved into. A few are packed with bodies in various states of decomposition, from skeletons to nearly fresh corpses. Prime must have salted them away over the centuries, saving them for a rainy day. And apparently today counts, because the bodies are starting to rise.

At the next turn, the corridor ahead of us is blocked with them, a solid mass of walking corpses. There are some of the oldest I've encountered, sinewy mummies that are little more than bones and gristle.

In all honesty, I'm glad to see them. Somewhere, the others are fighting, and my palms are starting to itch. I want to *hurt* something.

"You clear a path," I tell Hagan. "I'll clean up behind you."

The dog-angel lowers its head and charges like a bull. I move into its wake, my blades igniting with a *snap-hiss*, and start taking the ancient dead apart.

I really rotting hope Silvoa knows where she's going, because I am utterly lost.

A pair of corpses lever themselves up. The rotting things are getting cannier, throwing themselves flat to avoid getting crushed by Hagan's bulk. I let them come to me, their ancient bodies stumbling into a flailing run. At the last moment, I sidestep the first one, bringing my blade around at neck height and letting its momentum do the work. The other throws itself at my midsection, scrabbling at me as my armor raises crackling sparks. Two quick swipes remove its arms, and I kick the shuddering thing aside and move on.

"Left up ahead!" Silvoa shouts. "Come on, come on. I can feel him looking for me."

The dog-angel reaches the intersection and tears into another pack. I haven't seen any more of the lizard-birds, but Prime appears to have ordinary corpses to spare, and he's happy to throw them away to slow our progress. Or so I assume—I don't know how much attention he's personally paying me, with the battle still continuing.

Continuing not far away, I suddenly realize. I close up with Hagan, dispatching a pair of half-crushed corpses the dog-angel has left in its wake. As he pushes onward, I can hear shouting, and the crackle and blast of magic. Silvoa directs us through another doorway, and I blink in the sudden light as we emerge into a familiar chamber.

It's the room where we fought the lizard-birds, on our ill-fated first expedition to the ziggurat. Silvoa has led us to the balcony from which Prime—one of his puppets, anyway—taunted me before unleashing his ancient monsters. The strobing flashes of magic come from below, mingled with shouts and screams.

Hagan is heading directly to another doorway, at the other end of the balcony. I move to follow, then stop at the sound of a familiar voice.

"On the left!" Meroe's shout of command is more like a scream, so hoarse it barely sounds like her. "Left, now! Rotting stop that thing!" Something explodes with a roar. "More! Keep it down—"

I run to the rail, and spot her at once. Our people are clustered in a loose semicircle at the doorway, a wall of bodies and magic lashing out at a solid mass of walking corpses. Lizard-birds stalk through the crowd, brushing their lesser cousins aside, throwing themselves at the humans in a frenzy of slashing talons and ripping fangs. The monsters fall by the dozens, burning or torn apart or slashed to pieces, but more climb over the blackening corpses before the flames have gone out.

People are dying. A lizard-bird jumps and lands in a cluster of Minders, reducing a man's chest to bloody ruin with its spur-like claws before the others bring it down. One of the Cresos warriors has gotten too far from the line, his Melos armor glowing brighter and brighter as he hacks glowing green lines through a swarm of corpses that latch on and drag him down. I don't envy him his choice—let the armor fall and be torn to pieces, or leave it up and boil inside it. Zarun fights with Melos blade and Tartak force, and beside him Thora's hands move ceaselessly, bands of blue energy gripping the lizard-birds and tearing them asunder one by one. Jack paces at her side, shifting in and out of her own shadow, laughing as she cuts the corpses to ribbons.

Meroe is in the center of it all, surrounded by a rapidly thinning guard, screaming commands even as she kneels to lay her hands on someone torn and bleeding. Her dress is sopping with crimson, hands dripping with gore, and either she's given up caring if people find out about her power or doesn't think anyone is going to notice in the midst of all this. Shiara works next to her, armed with nothing more than conventional bandages and tourniquets.

For the moment, the line is holding, but only for the moment. This is part of a wider fight, stretching back through the complex—I can see shifting shadows in the corridor, and the strobing light of magic back there as well. Humans have limits to their endurance, but Prime's hordes seem to have no end. *They need help, or this is going to be a disaster.*

My mind is already planning. I put one foot on the balcony rail, contemplating the drop—my armor will absorb it, and if I'm quick I can carve a breathing space in the mass of corpses before—

"Isoka!" Silvoa shouts. "No!"

I blink, and look over my shoulder. The dog-angel has half-turned, and Silvoa's ghostly form is beckoning.

I should follow them. I *have* to follow them, or else this is all for nothing.

A lizard-bird gets within a foot of Meroe, shredding a young girl from our crew who's helping Shiara with the bandages. Thora whirls and plucks the monster up with Tartak, mashing it into a paste in midair and letting the pieces fall away. Meroe doesn't even look up until her task is done. Then she sees me, on the balcony. Our eyes meet, and I know I'm not going to be able to turn away.

I take a deep breath and shout. "I'm coming!"

Meroe's answer is practically a shriek. "Don't you dare, you *rotting moron*!"

My princess. Always ready to punch me when I need it.

Rot rot *rot*. I turn and run, and the dog-angel lumbers back into motion as we leave the sound of the battle behind us. The corridor stretches on, then descends a ramp and passes into an arched tunnel lit only by Eddica ghost-glow. A rank of walking corpses stretches across it, and I find my lips curling back in a feral snarl. After everything we've been through, what are another couple of dozen of the rotting things?

Behind them, arms crossed, is the handsome puppet Prime wore to taunt me in my captivity. *I'm going to enjoy tearing that thing to shreds.*

"Clever," he says, as we approach. "One of the angels from *Soliton*, I assume? I didn't realize your control extended so far. I underestimated you."

"People have a tendency to do that," I mutter. Beside me, the dog-angel tenses to pounce.

"Perhaps," Prime says. "But I fear that now you have underestimated *me*. Your friend here is within the matrix of the city-system, which means, now that I know where it is—"

He gives an elegant shrug, and at the same moment the dog-angel freezes in midstep, one paw off the ground. Unbalanced, it tips sideways, toppling with a *crunch.*

"—it is no longer a threat." He turns to Silvoa. "As for *you,* we have had quite enough of your poking your fingers in my affairs. Clearly my torments no longer hold any terror for you, so I'm afraid you'll have to leave us permanently."

"You wouldn't dare," Silvoa says. "You have too much fun ripping me to shreds—"

A torrent of Eddica power, gray and ghostly, slashes across the corridor. Silvoa's shape is outlined in it for a moment, and then she simply evaporates into wisps of fading smoke.

"Poor girl." Prime fixes his gaze on me. "I don't need her anymore."

There is a long pause.

I have no idea what he's done to them, with his mastery of Eddica that's centuries beyond mine. *Killed their ghosts? Is that even possible?* But all I can do for now is raise my blades and step forward.

"Go back to your cell quietly," Prime says, "and I may let your friends downstairs live. Those of them that are left, of course."

I move.

The corpses are strung out in a long line. Visually impressive, but tactically unsound. Especially against a Melos adept. With sufficient numbers, the things could get me off my feet, bury me in decaying flesh until my armor overloads. But they need to catch me first.

I hit the monster in the center of the line with both blades, spearing him through the chest, then bisecting his ragged, ancient body as I rip the weapons free. To his left, a woman with flyaway gray hair reaches for me with fingers weathered enough to show bone beneath the skin. I take her arm at the elbow with the first blow, and her head with the second. Behind her is another corpse, and then another, as I dance down the line. They collapse in my wake, puppets with strings cut.

I reach the wall, bounce off it with both hands to keep my momentum, and face the mob of monsters closing from the other side of the tunnel. Focusing my will, I shift my left-hand blade to a shield of green light, slamming it in the face of the first corpse to close and driving him back into the others. It pushes them off balance, a mass of windmilling limbs and clutching claws, and I spin around the outside, slashing indiscriminately. A few of them work their way free of the group, lunging for me, and I meet them shield-first in an explosion of scintillating green sparks. My blade takes their heads, or cuts their legs from under them and leaves them twitching on the stones.

In a few moments, nothing is left standing except for Prime's mouthpiece. He regards me, still expressionless.

"You haven't won," he says. "You know very well this body isn't me. Destroying it changes nothing."

"I know," I tell him, letting my shield lengthen back into a blade. He makes no move to defend himself as I bring both weapons around at the level of his ears, shearing his skull into several dusty, bloodless chunks. The body falls to the floor. "But you have to take your rotting satisfaction where you can get it."

No sign of Hagan. No sign of Silvoa. Part of me still itches to turn back, return to Meroe's side and help in the battle, but instead I push on into the darkness.

I'm close enough to the access point that I don't need directions anymore. I can feel the flow of Eddica energy, running through the walls and the floor, all the far-flung lines of power converging. My shadow, thrown by the light of my blades, rears huge against the walls.

I hear the scrape of claws on stone. Lizard-birds, a pair of them, trying to flank me before closing. Prime's attention is definitely on me, now, and I hope that means Meroe and the others are having an easier time. I watch the creatures tense as I step between them, and throw myself to one side a moment before they leap.

Four sets of talons hit the ground simultaneously, two man-sized lizard-birds twisting to keep me in view as they land in a spray of dust. I pop back to my feet, not waiting for them to recover. Forming my Melos shield again, I charge. The lizard-bird kicks, as expected, and its talon scrapes along my shield with a crackle. I let the impact throw me into a spin, bringing my blade around with heightened momentum, and the strike takes its other leg out at the knee. It collapses, writhing, even as its fellow bounds over it and comes down on top of me.

I try to roll with the fall, but the impact is still enough to make my armor flare, an uncomfortable wave of heat running over my skin. Wings flapping for balance, the creature rakes me across the stomach with one talon, drawing a wave of coruscating green fire. It's hot enough to hurt, but I ignore it, reconfiguring my blade into the short, sharp spike I used to use hunting crabs. I can't get much leverage pinned under the monster, but I don't need much to punch the weapon into its breast. A moment later, I release the gathered power, like a spring uncoiling, and Melos energy surges through the thing with a vicious crackle. It collapses in a shuddering mess, feathers crisping and burning as energy sparks off of it. I shove it away from me and regain my feet, breathing hard.

The Eddica current is increasing. The access point can't be far ahead, but I don't know how many more monsters Prime has pulled in—

The ground shivers under my feet. A moment later, a faint shower of dust and mortar cascades down all around me.

Of course. *I was wondering where* that *had gotten to.*

The titanic lizard-bird stalks out of the shadows. It's as big as I remember, big enough to swallow me in one bite. *Or*—as I recall Safiya's death and taste bile—*maybe two.* Its talons are longer than my head. Its tail lashes back and forth as it comes on, its footsteps making the stone shudder around me.

"You caught me by surprise the first time," I tell the creature. And Prime, if he's listening. "But it's going to take more than an overgrown chicken to stop me. I've killed uglier things than you."

The monster opens its mouth wide in a soundless roar, then charges.

I let both my blades shift into shields, forming a single wide arc of green in front of me. At the same time, I scramble sideways, out of its direct path. Its jaws snap shut a foot to my side, but this time I don't let my guard down too early. As before, the monster follows up its missed bite with a kick that would have left me impaled on its yard-long claws if not for my magical protection.

As it is, even with the shield between us, the impact picks me up and tosses me casually into the wall. Unlike the first time, though, the shield absorbs most of the blow, leaving me merely winded instead of half-cooked from the surge through my armor. There's a crackle across my back as I hit the stone, another wave of heat. The lizard-bird turns with a predator's grace, lunging forward to snap up its stunned prey.

I let it close, then push away from the wall, rolling forward. Its massive head rushes past above me, and it tries another kick, but I'm moving too fast. I'm underneath it, the huge pale belly bulging above me, gaps in the pebbled skin showing blackened muscles and shattered ribs thick with Prime's Eddica magic. I shape my shields back into blades and bring them up in an X-shaped overhead slash, parting the tattered skin like moth-eaten cloth. A wave of dust and shriveled, decaying flesh cascades down, along with broken bits of bone.

The creature starts to turn, backing up so it can get ahold of me. Before it can, though, I *jump,* arms extended. I catch hold of the splintered end of a rib, and jackknife to swing myself up, feet punching through the opening I cut into the creature's body. The thing is practically *hollow,* Prime's magic preserving its bones and muscles but leaving the guts to slough away over the centuries. I roll over, bracing myself on opposing ribs, pushing through a few stringy bits of rotting flesh.

The monster doesn't know what to make of me. It slams its bulk against the wall of the corridor, nearly tumbling me from my perch, then accelerates into a run and tries it again. I hang on, shifting to a more stable position with my legs wrapped around a rib. Summoning the Melos spike on my free hand, I let the energy flow into it, building up until I feel like my skin is about to catch fire. Then

I swing out and jam the energy blade into the creature's flesh from the inside, beside its spine, and let go.

Green energy lashes out, a wild, shimmering coruscation that crackles in all directions, searing ancient flesh to powder and snapping bones under the strain. The great lizard-bird bucks, then slews drunkenly to one side, its legs going out from under it. I lose my grip as it crashes to the ground, falling against another splintering rib. My armor flares and the world goes dark as broken bones and torn muscle cascade down on top of me. I ignite my blades and start hacking, blindly slashing the stuff, tunneling through the ancient monster's body until I can see the darkness of the corridor ahead of me.

I emerge from somewhere in its midsection, ripping my way free like some horrible glowing parasite. The thing is on its side, legs scrabbling, trying to get up, a huge smoking hole blown in the middle of its back where my strike connected. I stumble along it, feeling the hot lines my armor is drawing under my skin, forcing the energy back into my hand for one more blow. The thing's head stops its thrashing for a moment, and I dart forward.

I barely knew Safiya, in truth, but no one deserves to die like that, and even less so for simply taking their leader at her word. I don't know if the revenge would have meant anything to her, but I mouth her name regardless as I bring my hand down. The spike goes in under the thing's chin, and a moment later the discharge of Melos power blows its head completely apart, spraying bits of bone and desiccated brain against the wall, fangs pinwheeling away.

Bits of black goo drip from my hand as I straighten up, letting my armor dissipate. Cool air washes around me, but I can still feel the bone-deep ache of my exertions.

It's time to finish this.

At the end of the corridor, an arched doorway leads into the access point, the now-familiar jumble of conduits and metal extrusions. The air thrums with Eddica energy. Prime has decorated in his own particular way, fixing a ring of skulls all around the room. I give them a wary glance, but none of them seem inclined to attack me.

I wondered if Prime would confront me in the flesh, but there's no sign of him. Maybe he didn't think I'd get past his lizard-bird. I certainly don't plan on giving him time to correct his mistake. I stride across the room to the dais and lay my hand on the conduits, feeling the tendrils of the Harbor system reach out to examine my essence.

access request received; home//caspar
result:
authorized/accep—cep—cep—

No. Prime's voice—his true voice, the dead rasp—echoes through my mind. *I will* not *allow it. I* will not.

His ghost-image materializes in front of me, hovering over the dais. It looks nothing like his handsome puppet and considerably closer to one of the walking corpses, wrinkled and emaciated, ribs clearly visible in a shrunken chest. Gray hair sticks out in wisps from his mottled skull, and his eyes are black voids, the surrounding flesh cracked and seeping.

I am the Prime Eddicant, he says, his broken voice booming like thunder. *This is my domain.* Mine, *and no other! Who are* you *to threaten me? You mayfly, you transient creature. You have no concept of true power! You know* nothing.

He raises one withered claw.

You think you've won? The processes of this place are mine to command. Here, I can destroy you.

Gray energy surges behind him, lashing out at me from every direction. It feels like a sandstorm, a billion tiny grains abrading my flesh, except it drags its rasping breath across the surface of my mind. I feel myself scream, fall to my knees, desperately invoking my Melos armor, but the green energy doesn't so much as shimmer. It's helpless against this ghostly power.

My power. I bite down on the scream and squeeze my eyes shut, still able to see the maelstrom of gray light through closed eyelids. *I am an Eddicant, just as much as he is.*

You are nothing. I didn't mean to broadcast the thought, but I can feel his mind pressed close around me, a nauseating embrace. *If you had joined me, in a century you might have been worthwhile. Now you will die, and your spirit will amuse me until I tire of it.*

I stand up, extending my hands. For a moment, the Eddica storm pauses, the currents closest to me shimmering uncertainly. Then they press outward, toward Prime's illusory shape, slamming into the energy he throws against me.

You think this is a challenge? I hear his hacking laughter in my mind. *I have studied this art for centuries, girl. What do you have?*

Power bears down on me, a heavier weight than before, and I edge backward a step. He's rotting right, I can *feel* it. I can draw power from the system, but all I can do with it is force it in his direction and hope. Meanwhile, I can feel him slipping around me, worming his tendrils through the conduits. Even as I barely manage to keep his assault from shredding my mind, he's at work shutting down the energy I'm siphoning to protect myself. I try to strike back, tendrils of power fencing one another deep in the conduits, but this truly *is* his domain. He's adept in a way no one else in the world can match.

No. I bear down, scraping for more power, drawing it out of my own flesh. I can feel heat building again, more and more, but it's not *enough. Rot rot rot.* I've come this far, people have died, are *still* dying, and he's going to rotting *win—*

Let me help you, Silvoa says, in my ear.

I feel her pressing against me, her spirit against my mind. I lower my defenses, just for an instant, and she slips inside my skin, my skull. Her hands close over mine, and she takes control of the fight, deep in the conduits. Prime's tendrils pause for a moment, then slash and batter at mine with renewed vigor. But now he's being driven back, step by step.

Impossible, he snarls.

Only for Isoka alone, Silvoa says.

No. Prime's form shimmers, as though in a breeze. *You're dead.*

Of course I am. You killed me, remember?

I destroyed your soul. *I wiped out any remnant of you.*

You tried, Silvoa said. *But it's been five years. You may have studied this place, Prime, but I was* trapped *in it. You don't know its nooks and crannies like I do. Hiding enough of myself away to recover was the least of it.*

I will purge *you,* he snarls. *When I'm finished, there won't be the smallest scrap of your thoughts left.*

You won't, I think, adding my strength to Silvoa's. *Because this is the end.*

I throw my power in Prime's face, raw and unfocused. At the same time, Silvoa works delicately, out in the nearly infinite complexity of the Harbor system, cutting the strands that support Prime's energy one by one. He fights back, slashing and parrying, but her mastery of the system is beyond him. Step by step, Prime weakens, and Silvoa and I come more into sync.

I can feel her, inside my mind. Her thoughts, her memories. Kissing Catoria, the younger girl standing on tiptoe, the warmth of her. And the things Prime did to her, first in the flesh and then in the spirit. Every day a more imaginative, more horrible torment, skin flayed and bones broken, and all with the certain knowledge that there could not even be an escape into death—

I'm not sure which of us is screaming, now. Prime's defending energy falls away, and his ghost-form is engulfed in a torrent of rushing gray power, blasting it apart. The shape glows white for a moment, then dissipates into shimmering motes.

Thank you. I feel the phantom sensation of Silvoa's lips, pressed against my brow. Then she steps away, out from *inside* me, and I can see her again, arms crossed and eyebrow raised. *I have been waiting a* very *long time for that.*

What he did . . . I shake my head, gorge rising, as some of the memories come back to me. *I think I would have gone mad.*

Maybe I did. Silvoa cocks her head. *I knew that someday, something would change. Maybe that brought me back.* She gestures at the dais. *Speaking of which.*

I take a shaky step forward, and grab the conduit.

access error; redo from start

access request received; home//caspar
result:
authorized/accepted
three-step authorization recognized
superuser access granted
And I gasp, as a new world opens in my mind.

23

TORI

In my dream, Garo kisses me.

We're in the back of the closet, in the house in the Second Ward, in the soft nest of old bedrolls that's my private hideaway. We kiss in the warm, dusty dark, and his fingers run up and down my sides and along the small of my back. I take hold of his hand, his fingers thick and calloused next to mine, and pull it to where my belt knots on the side of my robe. He undoes it, haltingly, and unfolds the cloth. I shiver at the breath of air across my bare skin. Then he's touching me again, and I arch underneath him with a sigh.

"You used him."

Isoka's voice. She appears in the darkness behind Garo, one blade glowing. Its green light reflects from a hundred silk-thin strands, running up from every joint on Garo's body and winding together into a thick bundle. I know, without looking, that the other end is wrapped around my finger.

"You used him, and when he wasn't useful anymore, you threw him away," Isoka says. She slashes the strings with her Melos blade, a fat spark of green energy crackling through them. Garo falls on top of me, a dead weight. "I tried to protect you."

"I know." My voice is a whisper.

"I kept you safe." Isoka gathers Garo's strings in one hand, wrapping them round and round her fingers. "And this is what you've become. Whore. Murderer. Monster."

"I know."

In one quick motion, she wraps the puppet strings around my throat and pulls them tight. After a moment, my chest begins to burn. The world is going gray at the edges.

"You deserve this," Isoka says.

My lips move soundlessly.

I know.

"Tori?"

I sit up, gasping for breath. I'm alone, in one of the barrack rooms at the safe house. Golden light slants in through the narrow window, the sun barely above the horizon. The pounding of my heart reverberates in my ears, as though it were a kettledrum. I'm horny as rot.

Someone's watching. The curtain in the doorway is pulled aside, just slightly.

"What?" I say.

"It's starting." Giniva. "You said to wake you."

I did. Hasaka hadn't wanted to. "Give me a moment. I'll be right out."

Giniva lets the curtain fall. I draw in a deep breath, hold it, let it out.

It's true that Isoka wouldn't have wanted any of this. She protected me, kept me safe, tried to keep me innocent.

But she's gone. Maybe dead. But maybe lost and needing help. The only one who knows is Kuon Naga, and the only one who can get him to tell is me. I'll break his mind like an egg, if I have to.

First, though, I have to get to him.

I get up, dress in my sweat-stained clothes, trousers and a tunic and a leather vest. Pulling them on makes me wish for my wardrobe back in the Second Ward, and I wonder if it's still there, if Ofalo, Ridatha, and the others are all right. I wonder what Ofalo thinks happened to me, and what he would think if he knew the truth.

Giniva is waiting outside. Behind her, the common room is filling up with people. Hasaka stands over the big table, looking down at a recently inked map of the Sixteenth Ward. Men and women in red sashes wait behind him, ready to run messages out into the city.

Pointless. We're too far away from the front to exercise any kind of control here. Hasaka's instinctive caution has kept him far from where he can do any good. Hotara, at least, knows better—she's down in the Sixteenth Ward, at the wall, where her expertise as a street fighter might help.

"Tori!" Hasaka says. He doesn't look happy to see me.

"Giniva says it's starting."

"We've got word the Ward Guard are forming up," he says. "Could be a false alarm."

I doubt it. This feels right. They've had more than enough time to prepare.

"I'm going down there," I say.

"I wish you wouldn't," he says. "You know how important you are to this movement."

More important than you know. Without my little pushes, there wouldn't *be* a rebellion, more than likely. *Does that put all of these deaths on my shoulders?* At the time, every step had seemed so obvious.

"Your plan is in place," he continues. "We can oversee things from here."

He's not wrong, at least as far as he knows. I'm no strategist, just a girl who's read a couple of books. I'm not likely to be able to contribute more than symbolic leadership. What he doesn't know, of course, is that my power may be the only hope we have.

"I need to see," I tell him. "I'll be careful, I promise."

Hasaka sighs heavily. "Take Jakibsa with you, then."

I frown, but it makes sense. Jakibsa is one of our only Tartak adepts, and by far the most well-practiced. His powers can protect us from any stray arrows, at the very least. I nod, and Hasaka beckons his lover over from where he was huddled with a pair of messengers. They have a hurried conference, sotto voce, and then Hasaka leans in and kisses the younger man with a fervor he rarely displays in public.

"Bring her back," Hasaka mutters. "And bring yourself back, too."

"Of course." Jakibsa gives me a bright, fake smile, hideous on his burned face. "Shall we?"

Giniva follows us. No one questions if *she* should go along.

Downstairs, wounded men and women are still laid out on the floor, though no longer packed quite so tight. Volunteers move among them, changing bandages and checking wounds, Grandma's old assistants alongside fresh recruits. Kosura is among them, moving with slow, painful steps from still-healing wounds, a vivid contrast to her earlier grace. She looks up at me and smiles as I pass, but says nothing. It's just as well. I don't know what I would tell her.

Apart from red sashes running back and forth, the streets of the Eleventh Ward are as empty as I've ever seen them. The street stalls are empty, the wineshops closed with their shutters down. In every building, windows are covered with curtains or boarded over, and doors are firmly shut. The fighting isn't close to here, not yet, but no one is taking any chances.

Without having to push through a never-ending sea of humanity, it's a surprisingly short walk to the gate. Both sides of the military road are firmly in our control now, and a red-sashed young woman missing most of one arm greets us at the entrance to the Sixteenth District.

"Voliel Breta," she says, saluting me. "Commander Hasaka left me in charge. My squad is ready to go on your command."

She seems keen. I hope her squad are loyal people, because the odds are high some of them aren't going to make it back. At least, not if everything goes according to plan.

There are so many things that could go wrong. I try not to think about it.

"You know your orders," I tell her. "If you haven't heard from me, and the enemy are getting close to the gate, don't wait."

"Understood," Breta says, with another salute.

Jakibsa, Giniva, and I pass on, into the Sixteenth Ward. It's empty here, too, though there are fewer locked doors and more abandoned buildings. People have largely fled—we've been urging them to get out—contributing to the overcrowding in the Eleventh

Ward. Jakibsa and his assistants have been finding them places to live in the upper wards, repurposing elegant townhouses and sprawling mansions to shelter a dozen dockside families.

As we move west, we see more red sashes, in groups with spears and crossbows. Weapons, at least, we have in plenty, having captured most of the Ward Guard's armory. I flag down one squad and get directions to Hotara, who has made her headquarters on top of a warehouse, facing the broad clear space in front of the wall and about a block from the water's edge. We climb a ladder in the alley behind it and find Hotara huddled with a cluster of red sashes.

"Are they coming?" I ask her.

She looks at me, irritated at the interruption, but nods. "They're coming. A couple of thousand of them outside the wall. And . . ." She nods at the water.

I follow her gaze. A full squadron of Imperial war galleys, six ships in all, are loitering just beyond bow-shot of the wall. Their triangular sails are furled, and their long banks of oars barely move to keep station in the calm water of the bay. Chained to those oars, in the depths of the long, sleek vessels, are some of the sons and brothers of the defenders here today—it is the fleet's voracious need for fresh arms to power its ships, more than anything else, that drives the draft.

Along the rails of the ships, marines in fishscale armor and broad, flat helmets wait with crossbows at the ready. Behind them, at the fore and aft of each ship, are the siege engines called *scorpions*, like giant versions of those handheld bows, capable of propelling a bolt the size of a spear.

There are defenders on the shoreline, taking cover behind the crates, coils of rope, and other nautical detritus on the piers. They have their own bows, I know, but few have much experience using them. More red sashes are visible on top of the wall itself, and on the roof of the round tower that anchors it at the waterside. There's a signaler up there, too, with a red flag in one hand and a white flag in the other. As I watch, he holds both flags over his head, then starts to wave them in a complicated pattern.

"Brave rotting bastard," Hotara says. "Signalman from the Navy who came to our side." She turns to a young woman beside her, who's squinting at the shifting flags. "What's he saying?"

"Enemy advancing," the girl says. "Along the whole front."

"Tell them to fire at will when they get into range," Hotara says.

The girl raises her own flags and makes a quick signal. The signaler on the wall wags acknowledgment and disappears. For a few long moments, nothing happens.

A dart of flame rises into the air from the other side of the wall. It blooms into a ball of white fire far overhead, easily visible even at midday. It's too far up to hurt anyone, but that's not the point. It's a signal to the fleet. As one, the ships start to move, gliding diagonally closer to the shore. A bolt skips out from the defenders, then another. The first drops in the water well short of the vessels. The second comes closer, raising a splash only yards away.

Then, at a shout from their officers, the marines raise their weapons, and a moment later the Rot itself breaks loose.

The pair of ships in the lead open fire first, disciplined volleys rising at a sharp angle to scythe down like deadly rain all across the waterfront. The soldiers reload, an operation that requires them to ground their bow on the deck and press down with one foot on a stirrup to re-cock the mechanism. In the meantime, the next pair of ships has come into range, and another volley fills the sky.

Red sashes are shooting back, but piecemeal, and most of the archers have never learned to judge arcing fire at long range. A few shots hit the ships, and I see one marine slump forward into the water, but that's all. The piers and quays of the waterfront are rapidly coming to resemble a porcupine, with quills jutting from every surface. Some defenders are huddled close to their cover, and others are slumped over dead, the difference impossible to tell from here.

One of the scorpions fires, its bolt flashing above the waterfront and into one of the buildings behind it. The huge projectile punches through the wood-and-plaster wall as though it weren't there, leaving a hole the size of a horse and a cloud of fine dust. Answering fire comes from another window of the building, and a second scorpion replies, ripping out an entire corner of the top floor and spilling bodies to the street below.

On the waterfront, there's a flare of light. Myrkai fire zips over the waves, concentrated into tight, brilliant beads. The first one hits the water just behind one of the ships, detonating in a colossal spray of steam. The second impacts one of the Navy vessels at the bow, the blast spilling marines into the sea and sending chunks of wood flying.

I can see the mage-blood now, a short woman with wild hair. She's one of ours, a girl named Enoka from the sanctuary, a few years older than me, excitable and obsessed with boys. Beside her is Sekota, one of the Tartak talents who accompanied us to confront the Immortals. They volunteered to try this gambit, eager to get back at the people who have hurt so many of our friends. Now the defenders on the docks are cheering as she conjures yet another missile to hurl, straining to keep the flame coherent enough to do damage at long range.

Even as she lets the bolt loose, every ship turns its attention to her, volleys filling the air. Sekota stands up, hands spread, and walls of blue force materialize around the pair, deflecting the crossbow fire. Enoka yells excitedly and summons another ball of flame, pressing it between her hands as though squeezing over-tough dough.

Then the scorpions fire again. Sekota snatches the first huge bolt out of the air, sends it hurtling into the water. The second takes him in the chest before he can recover, punching him off his feet and pinning him to the dock like a butterfly in a collector's case. The blue Tartak barrier vanishes in a spray of sparks as he dies, and Enoka barely has time to look up before a cloud of crossbow bolts descends on her. She vanishes underneath them, and a moment later the fireball she was priming goes off, blowing the dock around her into flaming splinters. Out in the bay, the ship she damaged is still underway, the hole in its side smoking but above the waterline.

They volunteered, and I didn't stop them. *It might have worked.*

The detonation takes all the fight out of the red sashes along the water, and they abandon their positions, scrambling up to the street. I hear the shouts of their officers, trying to call them back, but I think not even trained soldiers would stay for such an unequal fight. Crossbow bolts continue to scythe down, sending men and women spinning to the dirt. Some keep moving, hobbling or shuffling toward the buildings across the road from the water, but no one is eager to risk the same fate to go and help them.

"Flags on the wall!" the signalwoman beside us announces. "Exchanging fire with enemy archers. Holding so far."

"It's not the wall I'm worried about," Hotara says. "Grego, go make sure your squad is ready."

Another of her companions, a big man in a long leather coat, gives a wordless nod and leaves the roof by the rear ladder. I glance at Hotara, and she shrugs.

"We can't form a line between the water and wall without getting the rot shot out of us," she says. "If they put marines ashore, our only chance is to try a counterattack."

It quickly becomes clear this is exactly what's in store. Defending fire from the waterfront slackens, as any flicker of movement in the harborside buildings draw a devastating response from the scorpions. A pair of the galleys pull up at a long quay, strewn with bodies and studded with bolts, and at least fifty marines disembark, leaving their ungainly crossbows behind and rushing forward with swords drawn. A few fall to rebel archers, but not enough—they're armored and moving fast, and most of the red sashes on the wall are focused on the Ward Guard infantry outside.

"Go, Grego!" Hotara shouts. "Push them back to the water!"

A hoarse war cry erupts from around the sides of our building, and rebels start pouring out of the alleyway. My guess is that these are the best fighters Hotara has, handpicked men and women, those experienced with violence. They wear mismatched leather armor and carry a variety of weapons—swords, spears, even clubs and knives. There's not much room for tactical niceties on either side. The mass of marines, rushing toward the wall and the gate they hope to capture, turns to meet Grego's squad in a confused mêlée in the strip of clear ground, and the mud is soon churned red with gore.

Here, at least, I can accomplish something. Opening my Kindre senses is a shock, but one I'm prepared for—fear and pain slide over me, a wave of foul-smelling scratches against my skin, but I let them pass and focus. I find the minds of the marines, their training and discipline making them easy to pick out from the wilder rebels. They're confident, and I take that away from them, replacing an easy assurance of superiority with a spreading fear.

For a few moments, discipline holds. Then they break, one man throwing away his sword and sprinting back to the boats, the others following in an unstoppable tide. They're scrambling onto the waiting galleys, heedless of the shouts of the officers on deck. Grego's men go after them, wild with their unexpected victory, stabbing and hacking down their opponents before they can escape.

Hotara turns to one of her assistants. "Go and tell Grego to get back here as fast as he can. They'll start shooting once their own people are clear."

The boy nods and runs off, and Hotara glances at me with a dour smile.

"If that's the best they can do, we may—"

Fire blooms on the wall, directly above the gate. As it fades into a plume of dark smoke, I can see figures in black dropping down onto the battlements, shimmering with multi-colored light.

The Immortals have arrived.

You can't fly with Tartak. Everyone knows that, though I don't pretend to understand why. You can slow a fall—if you're quick enough—but you can't lift yourself.

You can, however, lift someone *else*. The Immortals landing on the wall must have been hurled high into the air by comrades outside, their descent slowed at the last moment by spreading waves of pale blue force. They alight with well-practiced grace, as though stepping down from a carriage, tearing into the surprised defenders with swords and blasts of flame. Crossbow bolts from farther along the wall rain down on them, but more waves of force stop the missiles dead in the air.

I reach for them, desperately, ready to crush their minds as thoroughly as I destroyed their captain in the safe house basement. But, as at the sanctuary, my mental grip slides away, deflected by an invisible bubble. They have their own Kindre users, strong enough to protect themselves from my fumbling efforts.

Which means we are all absolutely rotted. Because the red sashes are no match for these practiced executioners, and they die in droves, bodies piling up at the black-armored soldiers' feet or pinwheeling off the wall in sprays of blood. A man glowing golden with Rhema speed carves a crimson path through men and women who don't even have time to raise their weapons, moving on to his next victim before the first has even fallen. Myrkai fire streams along the battlements like a living thing, reaching outward to claim fresh victims.

At the center of the slaughter, directly over the gate, three dark shapes in chain veils stand motionless for a moment. Then, as I watch, one of the trio raises an arm to point directly at me. At the same time, I feel Kindre power, tendrils of it reaching out to me. I bat them away, terrified. One of the trio speaks to the others, and then all three jump from the wall into the open space, blue energy glowing around them to slow their fall.

Grego's squad, fresh off their victory, is retreating toward us on Hotara's orders. A few of their stragglers spot the Immortals and halt, uncertain about these new opponents. The leader of the three—a woman, I can see now, blank-faced and anonymous in her armor—steps forward, and bright green blades ignite on each of her arms with a *snap–hiss* audible even at this distance.

And all of a sudden, I'm back in my dreams. Isoka stares at me, her blades ignited.

Murderer. Whore. Monster, she says. *Monster, monster, monster.*

Jakibsa, until now a silent presence at my shoulder, steps forward. "We have to stop them. Giniva—"

"No." My throat feels thick. "We run."

Everyone looks at me, even as the fighters below are screaming and dying.

"The battle . . ." Hotara begins.

"The battle is over," I say. "We lost. We knew we probably would. Everyone who can, get back to the Eleventh Ward gate."

She stares at me for a moment, then nods decisively. "Signal the retreat!"

Everyone on the rooftop is suddenly moving at once, a mad stampede for the ladders at the back of the building. The girl with the signal flags stays in place, though, raising them over her head in a frantic motion intended for the soldiers on the walls. It makes her an instant target, and a moment later the flags fall from her fingers and she's slumping forward, riddled by a half-dozen crossbow bolts.

I glance at Jakibsa, and he offers his ruined hands to me and Giniva. We step off the roof, his power gathering around us to slow our fall, bypassing the pileup at the ladders. At the base of the building, an alley leads back into the tangled warren of the Sixteenth Ward's streets. It's crowded by Grego and his men, taking shelter from enemy fire and blocking the way until Hotara and the others descend.

"There!" The shout comes from the alley entrance. "That's her!"

My blood goes cold, and my heart pounds in my chest. I'd hoped they were pointing out the rebel commanders, but—

They felt me use my power. They were waiting for it. Naga wants me in a cage. The Immortal captain's limp features twist in my memory. *"Insurance. Hostage."*

The black-armored woman stalks forward, blades humming. It's not Isoka, it *can't* be her, that makes no sense, but I still feel like my nightmare has escaped into the real world. Whoever this woman is—*it can't be*—she's a Melos adept, and Grego's men fare no better against her than alley thugs ever did against my sister. Her blades rise and fall, carving a path of bloody ruin with casual efficiency, ignoring the terrified return blows. Swords and spears stop an inch from her body, rebounding from crackling, sparking energy. Blue bands of power emanate from one of her companions, following carefully in her wake, batting aside any attempt to surround her. The third Immortal stays close, not visibly assisting, but when I reach out with my mind that same bubble keeps me away.

Melos, Tartak, and Kindre. Three soldiers, split off from the assault on the wall to find a specific target. *Me.*

I feel my own fear welling up, black bile at the back of my throat, and I try to force it down. Hotara has reached the bottom of the ladder, and she stands open-mouthed, watching Grego's men go down against the Melos adept. I have to shout in her ear to get her attention.

"Run!"

"What?" She turns to me, blinks.

"*Run!*"

We start running, what was supposed to be an orderly retreat turning into a rout. I stick close to Jakibsa and Giniva, with Hotara and Grego himself following close behind, along with a few red sashes. The group running alongside us splits as the alley divides, then splits again, individual fighters breaking off to try for safety on their own. The Sixteenth Ward seems horribly empty around us, even the semblance of life now gone.

Our small group pulls up short where the alley empties into a larger street. My chest feels like it's on fire, and Grego is panting hard. Hotara sinks against the wall with a sigh.

"Lost them," she says. "Okay. If we turn left and try for—"

But I'm looking behind us, Kindre senses open, and I can still feel the tendrils reaching out for me.

"They're coming." I sound like a scared little girl. "They're following *me*. The rest of you—"

Blue bands of force shimmer into existence around two of the red sashes at the back of the group, yanking them off their feet and into the nearest wall with bone-cracking force. The three Immortals come around the corner, practically strolling, barely twenty yards away. More Tartak force lashes out at us, but this time Jakibsa responds, and a shifting mêlée of blue light plays out between us in a shimmer of sparks. He grunts, hands raised, and shifts back half a step.

The Melos adept ignites her blades and charges. The closest rebel draws her sword, but takes a sizzling energy blade to the gut before she can swing it. Grego goes at the Immortal with a roar, swinging a heavy club two-handed. It bounces off her shoulder in a coruscating shower of green sparks, and she brings both blades up in a scissorlike motion that separates his head from his body and sends it spinning across the alley.

"Go!" Hotara says, drawing her sword. "Run!"

I'm past arguing. I grab Giniva and Jakibsa and drag them after me, Jakibsa stumbling, still keeping up his fight with the Immortal Tartak adept. I can't help but look over my shoulder, though, and I watch as Hotara and the Melos adept exchange a few blows. The Immortal deigns to parry, her energy blade carving notches in Hotara's sword, until the steel finally loses the unequal contest and snaps in two. Hotara stares at the broken weapon for a moment, which is a moment too long. The adept spears her through the chest, the spitting tip of the energy weapon emerging between Hotara's shoulders.

Hotara mouths something, blood trickling over her lips. Then she slumps against the other woman, hands convulsively clutching at the Immortal's chain veil. She drags the Melos adept's helmet free as she slumps to the ground, and I look on the face of my pursuer, the creature from my nightmares.

It's not Isoka. Of course it isn't. This is an older woman, her hair dead white and cut short, one cheek dark with a bubbling scar from a close encounter with Myrkai fire. She doesn't bother to retrieve her helmet and veil, only waves to her fellows to come after us, as we duck around the corner of an alley and out of sight.

It's not my private demons we're running from. It's Kuon Naga and his minions. I knew that, of course I knew it, but—

Focus, Tori!

We're sprinting down a maze of tiny alleys, the complicated labyrinth that makes up most of the Sixteenth Ward. Somewhere ahead—too far ahead—is the gate leading to the Eleventh Ward, where allies are waiting. But the Kindre user behind us can track me—I can *feel* him—and they're steadily gaining. Jakibsa may be a match for their Tartak adept, but we can't stop their Melos user, and I'm less than useless, a stitch in my side already cutting like a dagger at every step.

For a moment I consider telling the others to go on without me. I have a knife. I can shove it into my breast before Naga's henchmen catch us. Better to die than whatever he has in store, surely—but I know, even as I think this, that I won't be able to do it. I don't *want* to die, however twisted I've become, however much Isoka would hate this new Tori who kills and kisses and twists people's minds.

If you don't want to die, then focus. *Do what you can with what you have. What do you have?*

Jakibsa, Giniva. Not enough. Myself, for whatever I can do. Not rotting *enough.*

We skid around a corner, just as the Immortals come into view behind us. Jakibsa wards off another blue wave of force before we get out of sight. They're getting closer.

Monster, Isoka calls me in my dreams. *Monster, monster, monster. What would a monster do? What would a monster use?*

Whatever she had to.

I open my Kindre senses.

"Over there!" I gasp, as we turn another corner. It leads into a long, narrow alley, with single-story buildings on both sides, flimsy clapboard things with gray, decaying plaster walls. I point to a door, closed and barred. "Jakibsa, open it!"

He doesn't have the breath to question. A battering ram of blue force hits the wood, splintering it inward. I skid to a halt in front of it.

"I have a plan," I manage, straining for breath. "Can stop them. Need you. Buy time. Sixty seconds. *Please.*"

They can't know I'm not simply abandoning them. But they look at one another, and nod agreement. I turn and dash into the house, taking shelter just inside the doorway. There's a single room, empty except for a firepit and kettle, with a single window blocked by a rag curtain. I put my eye to the window, and wait.

I'm gambling that their Kindre user can't track me *that* precisely. I certainly can't track *him* beyond the dead zone he projects. I keep blocking his questing tendrils, hoping I'm not giving myself away.

Outside, the three Immortals come to a halt in the alley, Jakibsa and Giniva facing them from the opposite end, where it splits in a T-junction. No words are exchanged—at this point, there's not much to say. Giniva raises her hand and sends a bolt of fire at the scarred woman, who dodges adroitly, letting the missile impact with a roar on a building behind her. Their Tartak adept reaches out, and Jakibsa blocks him. Soon those two are grappling with twists of blue force, Jakibsa giving ground, retreating around the corner and out of reach. The Tartak adept follows, while the scarred woman charges Giniva, who fires more blasts of flame before fleeing.

The Kindre user stays behind, as I'd hoped, alone in the alley.

But still—a full-grown, well-trained soldier in armor, with a sword at his belt, alert and ready. And me, a fourteen-year-old girl with a knife, already winded. Useless. Unless—

Monster, monster, monster.

I turn to the single doorway leading deeper into the house.

Most of the people of the Sixteenth Ward have evacuated. Those who haven't—*we told them to leave, we* told *them, why wouldn't they listen*—put their own lives at risk. I sensed four minds here, and I find them in the storeroom. A man and a woman. Two children, a boy and a girl, maybe twins, close to my age. A family. The man has a small knife, and he stands in front of the other three. His face twists as I pull the curtain aside. He expected looters, or Ward Guard soldiers. Not me.

A monster—

"W—what do you want?" he says, uncertain.

I swallow hard.

"I need your help," I tell him. And I reach out for their minds. The contents are no surprise. Fear, pride, despair. I crush it all underfoot, careless in my hurry, a giant trampling through a city of ants. I draw new emotions from the depths of their subconscious. Rage. Hatred. And I give it a focus, a figure in black armor and a chain veil, just outside.

A monster uses what she has to.

The girl is the quickest, bursting through the doorway, features twisted beyond recognition with an unnatural fury. The Immortal sees her coming, deflects her clumsy rush with a backhand cuff that sends her sprawling to the dirt. He draws his sword in time to cut her brother down with a diagonal slash that opens his chest in a wash of blood. But the girl is throwing herself at the Immortal's legs, and the mortally wounded boy staggers forward another step and wraps himself around the soldier with a snarl. The parents, close behind, are next, father and mother each grabbing an arm and dragging the Immortal to the ground.

I follow, knife in hand. I can feel the man reaching out with Kindre, but I shut him down. He may be better trained, but I'm stronger, and for a few moments that is all that matters. The mother is on her knees, attacking the soldier's arm with her teeth, and the father shoves his son's corpse aside to get a better grip. I kneel and pull the Immortal's helmet and veil away, revealing a boyish face with a peach-fuzz beard and wide, scared eyes. My knife goes into his throat, under his jaw, and blood bubbles up. His body jerks for a moment, then stills. His frenzied attackers don't notice that the object of their ire is dead, mother and father and daughter tearing at the corpse with teeth and fingernails.

I look up. At the other end of the alley, two figures in black are watching me, the scarred woman and her Tartak-wielding companion. I stare back, defiant, ready to reach for their minds if they come close enough.

They don't. The scarred woman gives me a nod, like an acknowledgement to a worthy foe you might see in some historical drama. Then the two of them take off running, down another alley and out of sight.

I reach for the minds of the poor family, smothering the rage

I granted them as quickly as I summoned it. It leaves their minds blank, featureless slates, their bodies sitting placidly beside the mutilated corpse. I don't know if they'll recover eventually, but I suspect not. Given what comes next, it hardly matters.

Jakibsa jogs back into sight from one alley, Giniva from the other. I walk to meet them, wearily, suddenly feeling a tremendous weight on my shoulders.

"What happened?" Jakibsa says. "Tori, are you all right? Who are those—"

"She'd almost caught me," Giniva mutters. "And then she just stopped."

"I'll explain later." I won't. "Come on, we're not safe yet."

But we make it back to the Eleventh Ward gate, the latest in a stream of stragglers fleeing the disaster on the waterfront. Voliel Breta is waiting for us. She reports Ward Guard troops sweeping through the Sixteenth, defenders dead or in full flight, no resistance left.

When the stream slows to a trickle, I give the order. We close the gate, retreating across the military highway to the Eleventh Ward wall. Giniva sends up a flare, like the one that had triggered the naval assault, a burst of Myrkai fire in the sky visible across half the city.

I know what happens next, because I gave the instructions before the battle began. In basements and back rooms across the Sixteenth Ward, men and women see the signal. They strike matches or use small Myrkai talents. A hundred fuses are lit.

They were each supposed to find themselves a hiding place. Some of them might survive.

A hundred fuses reach a hundred barrels. We didn't have time to arrange any complicated pyrotechnics. There are just piles of things that the harborside has always had in quantity. Kindling—splintered boards and shredded ropes.

And whale oil.

We use a lot of oil in Kahnzoka. It lights lanterns and fires boilers, especially in the upper wards. And it all comes in by ship, transported by traders from the iceling lands, where strange, blond foreigners hunt the great sea-beasts and render them down. At any given time, there are thousands of tons of the stuff on the docks and in the warehouses. It's kept in wax-sealed barrels, fairly safe from accident. But if one were to knock a hole in a few, and let the viscous content puddle on the floor . . .

From the wall, the flames look like blooming flowers.

The buildings where we'd stashed the oil catch immediately. I made sure there was a cache in the Black Flower, and I smile a little at the thought of Thul's pleasure palace going up in smoke. The oil burns fast and hot, and the still-sealed barrels soon start to explode, spraying wood and burning oil across the roofs of neighboring structures.

The lower wards of Kahnzoka are built of dry wood, plaster, and straw. Getting them to burn is no trouble at all. Great sheets of fire are racing across the Sixteenth Ward within minutes, turning it into a set of shrinking islands in a rising crimson sea. The blaze spreads along the docks, leaping to the furled sails of the ships, spreading from pier to quay. The smoke soon blocks our view of everything except for the sullen, leaping glow of the flames.

It all burns. The streets where I grew up, where I watched Isoka suffer to try and feed us, keep us safe. The alleys where she was beaten, the doorsteps where she begged. The basement where we nearly froze to death for want of a few scraps of wood, now burning brighter than a furnace.

The family whose minds I destroyed are burning, now. *See?* I want to tell them. *It wouldn't have mattered. You would have died anyway.*

I know that doesn't mean anything.

And, of course, the Ward Guard are burning. Thousands of them, trapped in the labyrinth of alleys, unable to outrace the leaping flames and get to the sea or the gates. I can't hear the screams above the roar of the fire, but I can imagine them.

Around me, people are cheering. Jakibsa is gone, hurrying back to Hasaka's side. Giniva remains, her face impassive.

"What happens now?" she says.

"Now?" I let out a breath. "Now the Emperor calls in the Invincible Legions to destroy us."

"And what are you going to do?"

Find Kuon Naga. Find Isoka. Or . . .

"What I can," I say, "with what I have."

24

ISOKA

The Harbor system is like the most perfect map ever made, of a city larger than any that ever existed.

It draws itself in my mind's eye, lines of silver-gray ghost-light spreading outward in a branching, intersecting network, thin in some places and drawn tight into knots in others. I can see the angels, like sparkling ghosts, drawing power from the conduits running under the soil as they go about their tasks. In the distance, *Soliton* is its own tree of knots and branches, tied into the Harbor system at the edges, still transferring power in a massive flow into the city's reserves. It's almost done, I can see now, the great ship nearly empty.

Closer to, there are more draws on the system's energy, the simpler, cruder designs of Prime's walking corpses and monsters. I exert my will, and the system responds, closing down these unauthorized taps, and their glowing shapes vanish in an instant.

That's a good start, Silvoa says. She manifests beside me in the strange non-space, looking considerably more solid than I ever saw her in the real world.

I have no idea what I'm doing. I stare at the system, in all its intricate complexity, and fight off despair. I can touch it, change it, I can *feel* that, but I have no idea *how.* Closing off Prime's monsters was simple, but beyond that I feel like I'm walking through a house made of spun glass. *I didn't realize it would be so . . . complicated.*

It's not as bad as it looks, once you figure things out, Silova says.

You'll help me?

As much as I can. She smiles. *Like I told Prime, I've been living—* existing *in here for five years.*

Is Hagan all right?

She nods, and does something I can almost follow, a flurry of Eddica energy that passes between her and the system. A moment later Hagan is standing with us, outlined in gray light.

Worried about me? he says.

A little.

He gives a rueful smile. *Considering you killed me in the first place, I'm not sure how to feel about that.*

Wait, she did? Silvoa says. *I thought you were friends.*

It's . . . complicated, I say. *And I apologized for that. Didn't I?*

This is a story I have to hear, Silvoa says.

Later. I shake my head. *Meroe and the others. Are they all right?*

Most of them, Silvoa says. *They're in no danger now that you've shut down the corpses.*

I need to find them.

There's something we need to take care of first, I think, Silvoa says. She calls my attention to a part of the system that seems to be under attack, some external force bombarding it with Eddica energy in an attempt to gain entry.

It's Prime, isn't it? I say.

I'll show you the way, Silvoa says.

I ask Hagan to help me with *Soliton*, making sure that the ship doesn't leave once it finishes transferring its vast load of energy. Silvoa walks me through the process of giving the two of them authority in the system, below my own but still enough to command the ships and the angels. After Hagan flits away, I open my eyes and follow the ribbons of ghost-light Silvoa strings for me, out of the access chamber and back into the maze of the ziggurat.

This time we're going up, ramp after ramp, and finally a tall, circular staircase, similar to the one in the Cresos stronghold. Near the very top, Silvoa directs me to a doorway. Dozens of corpses lie in front of it, guardians now reduced to empty husks without the

Eddica energy that animated them. I step over the bodies and enter Prime's inner sanctum.

It's surprisingly bare, stone walls and floor devoid of ornament. I'd expected something more like Catoria's throne room, but I suppose this makes more sense. Prime spends hardly any time here, in truth, roaming through the system and his corpse-bodies. All he has is a chair, a heavy, elaborately carved thing that must have come off one of the ships as a sacrifice. In it, almost lost among silken pillows, is the Prime Eddicant.

He looks much like the ghost-image he showed me in the access point. Stick-thin limbs, protruding ribs, skin the color of ash, and a few greasy hanks of white hair. His eyes aren't bottomless voids, but simply gone, the sockets empty and scarred over. He breathes with difficulty, air rattling in his chest.

I can feel his power all around me, trying to get back into the system, trying to tear a hole in its defenses. He's not giving up, even now. Blind as he is, he can sense my presence through Eddica, and he shifts in his cushioned throne as I approach.

"I . . . told you," he says. "Eddicants are driven . . . to rule. We are . . . the same, in this."

"We're not," I say. "You'd like to think that, wouldn't you? That everyone is like you?"

"Not everyone. Only . . . the superior ones." His cracked lips twist into a smile, while his invisible power batters at the walls of a cage. "I can . . . help you, you know."

"I'm sure you could." I shake my head. "But why should I let you?"

"You don't know . . . what I have suffered." He leans forward. "I was born in a gutter, to a dying whore. When I was a boy—"

He stops, because I cut his head off. Only a trickle of thick, black blood escapes his ancient body, sizzling on my blades with a vile stench. His expression, insofar as I can tell, looks surprised.

"You know what?" I tell the corpse. "I don't actually care. We all have sob stories, but not everyone decides they need to destroy the world."

*   *   *

I find the humans of the Harbor in the ziggurat's entrance chamber, tending to the wounded and laying out the dead.

Burned corpses are piled up around the place where they made their stand, five or six layers deep. Tartak users are still busy shoving the dead monsters aside to clear space. Our own dead are laid out in neat rows, covered by blankets or coats. Surprisingly few, all things considered, but every silent body pulls at me.

To command is to sacrifice. In all senses.

"Isoka!"

I have a moment to brace before Meroe hits me like a runaway cart, so I stagger but don't actually fall over. She wraps her arms around me, as tight as a limpet. For a moment she presses her cheek against my chest, as though listening to my heartbeat. Then she's kissing me, over and over, and I finally have the presence of mind to kiss her back.

"You did it," she says, pressed tight against me. "You made it."

"So did you." I smile. "You said you were certain we'd succeed."

"*Obviously* I was lying for your benefit," she says. "You need a lot of reassurance, you know."

"My strange princess."

Someone clears his throat. Meroe, reluctantly, loosens her grip, and we pull apart to find some of the others watching. Zarun is grinning in a knowing way that makes me want to punch him—no changes there—while Thora has one arm around Jack's shoulders and one hand over her mouth, presumably keeping her from making inappropriate remarks. Gragant and Harak look on with monastic calm, but I can't help but notice they're hand in hand themselves. Catoria, standing beside them, looks wistful.

"Um," I say. "Sorry."

"Don't mind us," Jack says, fighting free of Thora's grip for a moment. "If you want to mmmmf—"

Thora raises her eyebrows and sighs.

"I take it Prime is defeated?" Gragant says.

"He's dead," I tell them. "He won't bother us again."

The monk breathes out. "Then the Harbor is going to be a different place."

"Is it?" Catoria says, looking at me.

"I have control of the Harbor system," I say, getting the drift. "But the only thing I plan to do is start up food and supply deliveries to our ziggurat."

"Thank the gods," Zarun says. "I'm not eager to move in *here*."

"Beyond that, we'll have to work out some kind of arrangement to make any decisions that come up," I say. "A council, I suppose. It worked on *Soliton*."

"Hopefully without challenges in the ring, though," Meroe murmurs.

Gragant and Catoria glance at one another. I clear my throat.

"On that note," I say, "there's someone who wants to say hello."

I send a silent message through the system, and Silvoa emerges from the corridor.

Fashioning a new angel turned out to be surprisingly easy. Silvoa did most of the work, of course, spreading Eddica energy through raw stone, animating it and directing it to shape itself according to her wishes. It still needs work, she says, but for the moment it will serve. It looks just like her ghost-image, an iceling girl about my age, barefoot and dressed in a simple robe. She makes her way over to us, hesitantly, and raises a hand.

"You—" Gragant stares, then shakes his head. "Silvoa is dead."

"She is." The angel's voice is rough, not much like Silvoa's own. "I am, I mean. But I'm also . . . not."

Catoria needs no convincing. She runs forward, as Meroe did, and wraps her arms around the stony figure. Silvoa's angel rests her hands on the girl's shoulders, infinitely careful, as Catoria weeps on her carved shoulder.

"I think," Silvoa says, "we have a lot to talk about."

"And I think I speak for the rest of us," Thora booms, "when I say that I need a drink!"

Behind her, the mass of crew—bloodied, wounded, exhausted—raise a raucous cheer.

* * *

Meroe lies in our bed, a tangle of limbs and sheets, sweat slowly drying on her brown skin. Her chest rises and falls in the slow, comfortable rhythm of sleep. I lie beside her, still sweaty myself, my body aching pleasantly from her urgent attentions. My thoughts, though, refuse to still.

The Harbor isn't going to be a return to the grand civilization of the Ancients, like Prime wanted. But it can be something else. A refuge. Most of our crew, like the Cresos and Minders, can't return to the lands they came from. Wouldn't want to, in truth, because what would be left for them? Here there's food and shelter for everyone. Now that I control the angels, the crew can retrieve the goods we left behind on *Soliton*. They can *live* here, cast-offs and exiles.

The original inhabitants, brought here by the first Prime Eddicant, ended up killing each other, of course. There's no guarantee it won't end that way. But they can try.

I look down at Meroe, let out a breath, and get quietly to my feet.

"Going somewhere?" Meroe says, without opening her eyes.

"Just to wash up," I say.

"Liar." She sits up with a yawn. "You're going to take *Soliton* back to Kahnzoka and find Tori."

"I have to."

"I know." She crosses her arms. "And for some idiot reason you think you're going to leave me behind."

"It's safe here now," I say. "Silvoa is running the system. And the crew needs someone to be in charge while I'm gone."

"I don't want to be safe, Isoka. I want to be *with you*. Why is that so hard for you to understand?"

I stare at her, in the semi-darkness, and slowly shake my head. "I don't know."

"Well. I'll punch you as often as needed."

"Please do."

"Besides, you promised to show me Kahnzoka."

"I did." I smile, just a little. "I don't know what will happen when we get there."

"We'll deal with it. We'll get Tori back."

"Are you reassuring me again?"

She shrugs, and I laugh out loud.

A day later, when we're finally ready to go, we find we're not alone.

At my silent command, *Soliton* lowers its colossal ramp. The ship's angels—their shapes twisted and bizarre in comparison to the Harbor's—are lined up at the top, several ranks deep, as though in greeting. At their head is an angel with a dog's shape, which lowers its head to me politely.

"I see you're already getting the place organized, Hagan."

I'm doing my best, he says in my mind. *There's a lot of dust.*

"And you two?"

Meroe, behind me, is grinning. In front of me are Jack and Zarun, eyeing one another awkwardly.

"Clever Jack proclaims that she will accompany her fearless leader wherever the winds may take her," Jack says.

"You don't have to," I say. "Stay here with Thora."

Jack shakes her head. "Jack owes you a debt, Deepwalker and Princess Meroe. She intends to see that it is paid."

"I," Zarun drawls, "just think it's going to get a little boring around here."

"Really." I glare at him. "That's all?"

"That's enough, isn't it? Say this for you, Deepwalker. Being around you is never boring."

"Clever Jack hears that Zarun made an indecent proposition to Lady Catoria," Jack says. "And was rebuffed with some prejudice in the hearing of her retainers."

I roll my eyes. "Boring, eh?"

"Come on," Meroe says, putting her arms around my shoulders. "Show me the Empire."

"I can show you the Sixteenth Ward, at least," I tell her. "It's not pretty, but I know where to get the best noodles."

ACKNOWLEDGMENTS

Once again, I'm here with a list of people to thank! Writing a series can be a long and lonely process, and I'm very lucky to have an excellent group helping me out. Casey Blair got me started in YA and continues to provide me with stacks of recommended reading and gets me out of story jams. Liz Bourke and Iori Kusano once again took on the delicate task of sensitivity reading, and provided invaluable insight. Without Seth Fishman, my agent, this book would never have reached its audience, and the same goes for everyone at The Gernert Company: Jack Gernert, Will Roberts, Rebecca Gardner, and Ellen Goodson.

At Tor Teen, my editor, Ali Fisher, has performed wonders, and generously tolerated my occasionally complex schedule. My thanks also to the rest of the Tor crew: Desirae Friesen, Peter Lutjen, Kevin Sweeney, Ed Chapman, Kathleen Doherty, and of course the legendary Tom Doherty. And, as well, to the Macmillan sales team, the Tor Teen marketing team, and the digital marketing team. Richard Anderson has produced another of his spectacular covers, and I'm thrilled, as always, to get to put my name on it.

Last but not least, of course, my thanks to everyone who followed Isoka and Meroe on their adventure and came back for more. That's why I'm here!